More praise for *82 Desire*

"The reader can't guess where the author is headed. Each scene comes as an intriguing surprise; it's like wandering around an endlessly fascinating but unfamiliar city. The ending is agreeably suspenseful."
—*Los Angeles Times*

"A solid detective yarn with engaging characters and a genuinely baffling mystery . . . [Smith] succeeds admirably. The novel is intricately constructed, and while Smith keeps nothing important unfairly hidden from her readers, she manages to spring some nice little surprises. Readers who enjoy trying to solve the mystery before the writer reveals the solution will have a great time here. The popularity of the Skip Langdon series stands only to be increased with the appearance of this latest installment."
—*Booklist*

"The wealth of crimes and misdemeanors gives the case a Dickensian richness."
—*Kirkus Reviews*

Please turn the page for more reviews. . . .

"EXCELLENT ENTERTAINMENT . . .

82 Desire is fresh and fast paced, gently funny and often touching. In it, Skip Langdon and her creator, Julie Smith, are at their peak. . . . Talba is one of Smith's best creations ever. . . . Smith takes risks in this book, and they pay off. . . . [She] excels at writing across cultures, creating believable black and white characters who live side by side in the sometimes strained environment of contemporary New Orleans. . . . The description of the Quarter in the first couple of pages of *82 Desire* is one of the most immediate and evocative I remember."
—*New Orleans Times-Picayune*

"Smith's strengths are her incredible and sometimes outrageous characters and her snappy dialogue. To read Wallis's poem on how her mother named her Urethra is worth the price of the book. Obviously, she had her name changed. Very funny stuff."
—*San Francisco Examiner*

"Another spirited return to the streets of New Orleans."
—*Library Journal*

By Julie Smith
Published by Ivy Books:

Skip Langdon mysteries:
NEW ORLEANS MOURNING
THE AXEMAN'S JAZZ
JAZZ FUNERAL
NEW ORLEANS BEAT
HOUSE OF BLUES
THE KINDNESS OF STRANGERS
CRESCENT CITY KILL
82 DESIRE

Rebecca Schwartz mysteries:
DEAD IN THE WATER
DEATH TURNS A TRICK
TOURIST TRAP
THE SOURDOUGH WARS
OTHER PEOPLE'S SKELETONS

82 DESIRE

Julie Smith

IVY BOOKS • NEW YORK

An Ivy Book
Published by The Ballantine Publishing Group
Copyright © 1998 by Julie Smith

All rights reserved under International and Pan-American Copyright Conventions. Published in the United States by The Ballantine Publishing Group, a division of Random House, Inc., New York, and simultaneously in Canada by Random House of Canada Limited, Toronto.

Ivy Books and colophon are trademarks of Random House, Inc.

www.randomhouse.com/BB/

Library of Congress Catalog Card Number: 99-94079

ISBN 0-8041-1699-7

Manufactured in the United States of America

First Hardcover Edition: September 1998
First Mass Market Edition: July 1999

10 9 8 7 6

*To Greg Peterson, my mentor and guide
in the baffling world of the silicon chip*

Acknowledgments

Writing a book affords a unique opportunity to see how successful people work. My research makes clear that the secret of success must surely be this: Treat even a request for free advice as if it were a million-dollar job. Each time, I'm astonished anew at the time and effort big-deal experts are willing to put in just to help me write a book.

Skip Langdon simply couldn't function without Captain Linda Buczek of the New Orleans Police Department, and I couldn't without Greg Peterson, who never, ever laughs at my pitiful efforts to master these new-fangled writing machines.

It took a trio of experts to teach me even the most rudimentary facts about oil, and though one must remain a confidential informer, I owe him a huge debt and thank him all the same. The others are Joe Pecot and Ken Bramlett, a geologist whom even I can understand.

Jim Welsh and Walt Philbin brought me up to date on reporting at the end of the millennium, and others gave advice and answered niggling questions: Betsy and Jim Petersen, Chris Wiltz, Debbie Faust, and Ken White.

My heroic assistant, Kathy Perry, once again got through a book without slapping me silly, and my husband, Lee Pryor, helped in so many ways I can't count them.

A thousand thanks to everyone who helped. Anything wrong is my fault, not theirs.

One

NEW ORLEANS CHANGES people, even if they only come for a weekend.

The expected occurs: Teetotalers get sloshed; virgins get laid.

But the consequences are sometimes lasting and large. The story is told, for instance, about the woman who came to JazzFest and faxed her husband good-bye—a long-running husband, too.

The city is a setup.

The very air smells different. You notice it as you step off the plane—there's a hint of mildew, heavy with history. Then, if it's the right season, there's also jasmine, and sweet olive.

Urine and vomit as well, along with plenty of Pine-Sol to take the edge off.

In the bars, a hundred years of cigarette smoke.

In the streets, frying oysters from restaurant vents.

Sweat.

Vodka fumes.

Pheromones.

In the spring, the air is more like velvet than silk—luxuriant, but a little smothery. In summer, it lies on the body like three-inch fur. Tangled fur, at that.

The very name New Orleans conjures up the sins of another century: riverboat gambling, black marketeering, bordello revelry, wicked skulduggery, and relentless scalawaggery.

Today the city's gamblers wear oversized T-shirts instead

of ruffles, its black marketeers are drug dealers, its prostitutes transvestites and underage addicts, its skulduggery institutionalized.

But everyone wants in on the scalawaggery.

The name conjures up Southern graciousness as well. This exists today behind the elegant facades of the French Quarter and the iron fences of the Garden District, yet it is beginning to fade at some of the city's landmark restaurants. Lately, jeans have been seen amid the dark wood and white linen of old-line eateries; on the streets, sartorial standards are a plain disgrace. Men think nothing of taking off their shirts as if it were the beach—and not only young gay men showing their pecs.

Tourists urinate on the nineteenth-century town houses.

Angry residents will stop sometimes to chastise them, but the tourists answer that if the Quarterites don't like it, they should move to the suburbs.

The tourists peek through the iron grilles at the lush courtyards (and who can blame them for that?), but they do not draw the line at mixing drinks on the residents' stoops.

Gutterpunks are drawn to the Quarter as hippies were drawn to the Haight-Ashbury, yet they will move along if asked. They have chosen lives on the fringe, and they know the consequences of crossing the line.

It's the tourists who give lip.

Ladies who'd call the cops if a stranger touched weary butt to their own immaculate steps will argue that in the Quarter, surely everything is public. They are weekend outlaws, and proud of it.

Before they go home, they may shed their denim skirts in merry abandon, or they may not—but they will certainly understand, perhaps for a change or even for the first time, what it's like to want to.

On weekends, living in the French Quarter can be like camping out in the middle of Disneyland.

Yet, around midnight (if nobody's driving by playing rap at full volume), mules clip-clop on the streets and ships whistle on the river. You could swear it's a hundred years earlier, though you know the boats are full of petroleum products and the mules are trudging home after a hard day of hauling tourist buggies.

At about three or four A.M., the drunks commence to shouting, and the paper thuds on the balcony. Sometime after, quiet descends.

Then at eight Monday morning, people open their shutters and greet their neighbors. You hear them up and down the streets: "Good morning, Alice." "Good morning, Donn."

So civilized.

So very nineteenth century.

And for five days—until the tourists arrive for the next weekend—the Quarter is the closest thing to a European village this country has to offer.

Some visitors, usually those who stay more than a weekend, lose not only their reputations and their decent denim skirts, but their hearts—and, ultimately, a good chunk of their cash. They buy property on a whim and repent while they renovate.

For this reason, Skip Langdon worried about her beloved, Steve Steinman, late of Los Angeles—he'd fallen hard for a little Victorian cottage.

"Are you sure," she entreated at first, "that you know what you're getting into? Can you handle pee-ers on the porch?"

"Listen to you," he said. "Don't you remember? You used to want me to move here."

"At the time, I thought you were tougher."

"Thanks a lot."

All that was months ago. Now he was working on the house, getting it ready to move into. The relationship, which had finally evened out after a few rocky years, was starting to wear as a consequence.

"Goddammit," he fumed, "why didn't you tell me this was a third-world country?"

"I tried."

3

"In California, when the plumber says he'll come, he comes."

"You don't smell so hot."

"I've been up on a ladder for twelve hours."

"Want to go get some dinner?"

"I'm so tired I can't move."

For the first time, sharing her garçonnière with him was more work than fun—literally. They spent every spare moment choosing colors, applying them to walls, cleaning kitchen cabinets, hauling debris.

Going to work was like a vacation—and she had one of the world's hardest jobs.

She was a cop in one of the most dangerous cities in the country. Before decentralization, she'd been a homicide detective.

However, New Orleans, following New York's lead, had disbanded its detective bureau and sent everyone out to the districts. Where she'd ended up, someone had bought a huge ledger, marked on it HOMICIDE LOG, and left it empty as a little joke—there had been only seven homicides since the first of the year.

She had moved from the ferment of Headquarters to the Third District, which was housed in a one-story, low-ceilinged brick building right across Moss Street from Bayou St. John. With a really good tailwind, it wasn't inconceivable that a ball from the City Park golf course could come sailing through one of its windows. Which wasn't a bad metaphor for the pace of the Third compared to what she was used to. And that, she supposed, was part of the point of decentralization.

Throughout the department, the load was lighter. More officers were being hired, were graduating from the academy, and were getting on the streets. And they were good, competent police officers, not desperation hires.

More cars and more computers had been bought, and now the cars were being equipped with still more computers.

It wasn't yet a renaissance, but just about everyone thought things were improving.

4

As for Skip, she liked the old system, the way anything could happen in any part of town and she could end up with the case. The Third, compared to some districts, was almost a model of gentility; indeed, it contained the solid middle-class section called Gentilly. It also contained Pontchartrain Park, an upscale black neighborhood built around a golf course, the fancy white districts of Lakeshore (mostly Jewish) and Lake Vista (mostly Catholic), the vast oak forests of City Park, the funky lakeside section called Bucktown, and no fewer than five universities if you counted the Baptist Seminary.

Still, it wasn't any quiet country town. The St. Bernard Project was there, for one thing, and for another, there was the constant pressure to lower the crime statistics and get the city livable again. It was an atmosphere where district captains met once a week with maps, comparing notes on what crimes were committed where, trying to identify patterns and develop military strategies. Though the department denied it publicly, there was no way such a system couldn't lead to rivalry and competition. And so, quiet as the Third might be in some respects, there was still no time for coffee and bull sessions.

Fortunately, Skip had been transferred with her favorite sometime-partner, Adam Abasolo. But she no longer reported to Sergeant Sylvia Cappello, who'd just passed the lieutenant's test. Abasolo was her boss and she wasn't sure she liked it. He had an independent, maverick style that meshed with hers; historically, she'd watched her p's and q's with Cappello and gotten down and dirty with Abasolo. She didn't know if she could do that now.

But what she did know was, she could work with him. If she'd ended up with Frank O'Rourke as her sergeant, she might have considered a new career in banking. The current deal was functional.

Their new lieutenant was newly returned to the department—she'd moved away with her husband, and then they'd moved back—more than that, Skip didn't know. She and Abasolo were reserving judgment. Kelly McGuire, with her by-the-book style, reminded them a bit of Cappello, which was good—but maybe she was a bit too stiff.

On the other hand, perhaps that permanent wrinkle between her eyebrows was about something else entirely.

Skip, six feet tall and twenty pounds overweight, distrusted women who made her feel clunky, and McGuire did, almost. She was average height, average weight—nothing wrong with that—but her light red hair was straight and proper, whereas Skip's was unruly and brown; her blue eyes were pale as ponds, while Skip's were bright green. There was something a little delicate about her, even slightly elegant in a laid-back kind of way. She wore pants, but they were tailored and looked expensive (though they probably weren't); she wore sweaters, but they looked like cashmere—and Skip was damned sure they weren't.

Still, Skip told herself, there was nothing wrong with all that—maybe the problem was that McGuire was scarcely older than she was. Maybe she ought to take the sergeant's test and think about moving up. . . .

It was a Monday in late October when McGuire caught her in the hall. Skip was talking to one of the guys from the Power Watch.

"Look in there," he said. "I got the cat woman."

"Her? That little tiny thing?" The woman's cat had bitten her; she had sentenced it to death by baking—slowly, in a preheated oven.

"She's tiny, but she's sneaky. She got out of the handcuffs—I had to tackle her and wrestle her down."

McGuire joined them. "Handcuffed her in front, didn't you? I know you, Frankie."

The man blushed, staring as if trying to think of a rejoinder.

"You better watch yourself, my man. You're going to get hurt one day." She grabbed Skip by the elbow and steered her a few steps away. Out of the blue, she said, "How do you like working with Adam?"

Skip was taken aback. "We're a real good team."

"I think you're probably dangerous. You know how kindergarten teachers separate the bad kids?"

Skip grinned at her. "You wouldn't do that, would you?"

"I've got a soft spot for bad kids. Just don't screw me, okay?"

McGuire wafted off, not an easy thing to do in a pair of tailored pants. Skip was vaguely pleased, thinking maybe McGuire was really all right—if she liked bad kids, she couldn't be all bad. On the other hand, something was up, and she wondered what.

She got a Coke out of the machine and went back to the tiny windowless, airless office she shared with three other detectives. There were several of these offices off a large room with computers in it—two computers, enough space for a living room; go figure. She was going through the stack of new cases that was waiting in her mailbox, when Abasolo happened by.

Meaning he had taken the trouble to cross the hall, wander through the computer room, and squeeze into her minuscule space. "Beautiful day, isn't it? Too nice to be inside. Come on—take a ride with me."

"What's up?"

"Let's just take a ride."

Skip shrugged into her jacket. Abasolo was wearing a tie and sports coat, which he did only on state occasions.

"I need a VNL," he said.

This was slang the two of them had picked up from a tough-as-nails hostage negotiator—Very Nice Lady, it meant.

"You're barking up the wrong tree."

"You got a good side, Langdon. You just hide it."

When they were in the car, she said, "Okay. Tell me."

"Heater case. Your specialty, right?"

"Not by choice."

"Still. The term 'hot dog' has been used."

"Thank you, I'll stick with VNL."

They were quiet until it dawned on her to ask where they were going.

"Jay Street—how's that grab you?"

"Ah. Lake Vista." If the street was a flower or a bird, it was Lake Vista; if a gemstone, Lakeshore. "What's the deal here? McGuire buttonholed me to mention we shouldn't fuck up."

"Who's famous who lives in Lake Vista?"

"Pete Fountain, I heard. Hey, Pete Fountain? Really?"

"Try again."

"Oh, hell, I'd love to meet Pete Fountain." She wrinkled up her face and thought. "Bebe!"

"Jackpot."

Babette Fortier—Bebe ("B.B.") to her friends and supporters—was a city councilwoman and rather a dull one as local politicos went. Truth be told, she wasn't famous for anything special and she was of more or less good repute.

They turned into the cul-de-sac that was Jay, and Skip was so surprised she gasped before she could stop herself. Trees, gardens, two-story brick houses—very, very nicely done. Not suburban in a boring sense—simply peaceful and well designed.

Abasolo said, "What?"

"Nice. Pretty."

"Yeah, but is it New Orleans?"

Skip had to agree. "You've gotta wonder."

They parked and strolled up a short walk to the Fortiers' house. The councilwoman answered the door in a red suit, dressed for a hard day of complaints and meetings.

Abasolo introduced himself and Skip.

Skip held out her hand.

"You mean you're *the* Skip Langdon? Well, Sergeant— you *have* hauled out the big guns."

Skip hoped she wasn't blushing. She had gotten her name in the paper often and spectacularly in recent months.

"Our best little hot dog," Abasolo said.

8

"I am *not* little." Skip spoke with mock petulance.

Fortier laughed. "You sure aren't. You're as tall as my husband."

"Six feet and growing."

"Come in, won't you?"

Fortier led them into a room that was evidently a family room or den, a room full of books and furniture that was getting shabby, along with the inevitable "entertainment center" containing television and stereo.

She sat across from Skip and Abasolo, glancing around as if to see if she had what she needed. A box of Kleenex sat on the floor near her chair. She plucked a tissue and sat back.

"Can I offer you some coffee?"

The officers declined. Skip noticed for the first time that Fortier looked haggard and drawn, though her makeup seemed newly applied and there were no tear tracks. She was probably in her early forties, Skip thought, with shiny brown hair cut in a neat bob, side-parted and more or less resembling Hillary Clinton's. Her face was round, and her figure was trim. She was a pretty woman, with a fresh vitality, almost an eagerness, that made her more attractive than mere features ever could have. She had lovely, smooth skin and hands that looked cared for, though her nails were short.

"I don't know what to think." Her hands worked the tissue. "I'm just . . . well, embarrassed." She looked the officers in the eye.

"I assure you we'll be as discreet as possible." Abasolo spoke with unaccustomed formality.

"Does Officer Langdon know?"

"Call me Skip, please. And, no; I don't know anything."

Bebe tried on a smile for size, but it didn't work. "I guess you could say it's every woman's nightmare."

Russell's sonofabitch of a father, who had made Russell's life miserable every day Bebe had known him, had finally died two weeks before, and Bebe would have expected her husband to shout, "Hallelujah!"

But Russell was unexpectedly moody on the way to the funeral in North Carolina. She probably should have tried harder to cheer him up, but it came at a bad time; there were so many reports to read, and planes were so good for that.

They stayed at a hotel, as far as they could get from the family madness, scarcely exchanging a word the whole time. And yet, it was a friendly silence; after so many years of marriage it wasn't necessary to talk. Bebe read her reports and made her phone calls; Russell did the family things. It was like a hundred other trips they'd taken.

But on the flight back, Russell turned to her. "Bebe. That was a lot harder than I expected."

"I know it was, darling."

"Let's go away next weekend. Just us. Just for fun."

She stared at him—they never did anything like that.

The idea kind of appealed to her, but it came from so far out in left field. "I have to give a speech Saturday night." She named a big campaign contributor: "I promised Mary Louise six months ago. I can't just disappear on her."

"Oh." He looked as disappointed as a child. "Well, maybe the weekend after."

"Okay." She thought about it. "Sure."

"You sound kind of doubtful."

"No, really, I'd love to. Let's go to Hilton Head."

And so she had cancelled a few little things and they'd taken off in a flurry. Friday night they had a great dinner and made love (though she left that part out when she told the story to the cops).

Saturday, she worked in the hotel room while Russell explored, and they played tennis, had a nap, another great dinner, and watched a movie. Sunday, she made some phone calls, and then they had brunch and drove to Savannah to get their plane.

On the plane ride back, she worked some more while

10

Russell read a Patrick O'Brian novel. That is, she worked for a while, and then she fell asleep. She felt rather wonderfully relaxed after such a nice weekend, and when Russell woke her up as they were landing, thought they really should do this sort of thing more often.

After they'd claimed their luggage, Russell left to get the car while she sat in the terminal, suitcases around her like attentive children. She was still a little zoned-out and quite enjoyed the people-watching, especially the nice warm clinches when family members and lovers found each other and smooched it up.

She was pleasantly tired, thinking at first about toasted cheese sandwiches and television in bed. Then thinking about all the work she still had to get done. And then beginning to fidget.

She glanced at her watch. Oh, well. He'd only been gone ten minutes.

People-watching was starting to pall because nearly everyone from her flight and the one at the next carousel had claimed their luggage and left.

In another ten minutes, she was starting to get mad. How dare he leave her like this? Without even a magazine to read. He'd probably run into some old friend and stopped to chat.

She got up and went to the ladies' room—if he had to wait for her, too bad.

But when she came back, there was still no Russell. She glanced at her watch. Thirty minutes to get a car out of the lot? What was going on?

And then it dawned on her: He'd probably gotten stuck in airport traffic. She got up and stepped to the glass doors. Actually, it looked pretty clear out there.

Only then did she feel the first stab of fear. *Suppose he doesn't come back?* she thought. And then: *Come on. Get rational. He just went to get the car.*

But she didn't get rational. He could have gotten mugged. An airport parking lot would be a perfect place to wait until you saw someone alone.

He could be lying unconscious.

Or maybe he just left—simply walked away, like those husbands who go out for cigarettes and don't come back.

Uh-uh. Not Russell. He was pathetically uxorious—women would kill for a guy like Russell.

But she couldn't make that one fly, no matter how hard she tried. He hadn't been, as they say, himself for a long time.

But still. They'd had a great weekend, which he had suggested.

On the other hand, people went a little nuts when their parents died, particularly the second parent, no matter how poorly they got along.

But Russell just walking out? Not a chance. She'd go with mugging over that one.

What else was there?

Hit by a car, maybe?

Some kind of snafu Bebe couldn't conjure in her mind? *Maybe he just forgot me,* she thought. *Maybe he got the car and drove on home.*

And maybe she was going nuts. That was assuredly it. She was going nuts. She was imagining all this.

She looked at her watch again—fifty minutes, give or take, had now passed since Russell left.

With nothing else to do, she called home. And there being no one home, there was no answer.

Well, she could go look for the car if she had a clue where it was, but Russell had dropped her off and parked it.

What, then?

She couldn't call the airport police and say, "This is Bebe Fortier and I've misplaced my husband." She just couldn't do that.

She thought of calling her brother.

But then she thought how stupid she'd feel if Russell turned up after she made the call.

Hold on, Bebe. Let's try again to be rational.

She sat and tried to think, but her brain simply would

not focus; absolutely refused to. Darted about like minnows in a stream.

In the end, she did call the airport police, who couldn't have been more sympathetic and who located the car in no time, looking as if nobody'd been near it in three days. Then they gave her a nice cup of coffee while they searched for Russell's crumpled and bleeding body. And while she was sipping it, she decided things had progressed far enough to lean on her brother.

She was in full meltdown by the time he came and got her.

Skip said, "Where's the car now?"

"Still there, I guess. I should send someone for it. We called hospitals"—her voice trembled a little—"but nothing. He just disappeared into thin air. I don't know ... what to think." She sat up straighter, pulling herself together. "As you can imagine, I've been on the phone to anyone I dared call. You know how people gossip in this town. I didn't want to call the superintendent—I'm sure you understand."

They understood perfectly. She wasn't an ally of the mayor's, and the superintendent was the mayor's appointee.

"Someone finally gave me the name of Lieutenant Cappello."

Skip put it together: Cappello must have called McGuire and recommended Skip and Abasolo.

"Is your husband in good health?"

"The best. He was in a sailing accident a few years ago and he survived for almost a week with nothing but champagne." She emitted a nervous titter.

"Well, I guess I should ask your opinion before we go any farther. What do you *think* happened?"

"I really have no idea. Could he have been kidnapped? Can you get kidnapped on your way to get your car?"

Skip considered. "Have you had a ransom demand?"

"Oh, no. And we don't have any money, anyway. My

13

husband works for an oil company—neither of us has family money."

"Can you think of any other reason to kidnap him?"

"What other reason could there be?"

"I don't know. Do you?"

"I really can't think of any." Her puzzlement showed in her face—but then she'd forged her acting skills in the public forum.

"Does he have any enemies?"

Fortier thought a minute. "Enemies? I'm the one with enemies—but I don't think you'd kidnap someone's husband because you don't have a stop sign on your block."

Skip and Abasolo exchanged a glance. Stranger things had happened—just that morning, a woman had cooked a cat.

"Can you think of any enemies you have who might kidnap him?"

Again she considered. "No. No, I really can't."

"I'm sorry to ask this, but I'm sure you'll understand. Have you and your husband been getting along?"

Fortier looked surprised. "Yes, of course. We never exchange a cross word."

"I don't know how to say this without seeming cruel . . ."

"Go ahead."

"Could he simply have left you?"

"Out of the clear blue? Without a word? Who would do a thing like that? Why wouldn't he just say, 'Honey, let's hang it up'? Russell's in business, Officer Langdon. He's a pretty direct man."

"Well, but suppose he did? Where would he go?"

"Don't you think you're being a little insulting?"

Abasolo gave her a look that said: *Kid gloves, Langdon.*

Skip said, "I'm sorry I have to ask these questions, but I'm sure you understand it's my job. We want to find him for you as quietly as possible. The more information we can get from you, the easier it's going to be to keep it quiet."

The councilwoman sat up straighter, one professional

dealing with another. She dabbed at her eyes with the tissue, but she said, "I'm the one who should apologize. It's just that this is so upsetting." Her chin trembled.

Skip waited, letting her regain her composure.

Finally, Bebe said, "He works for United Oil Company, where he's a vice president. He hasn't missed a day in years. He's not the sort who'd just take off."

Oh, yeah? Skip thought. But then again, New Orleans was a dangerous city. He could have been mugged or kidnapped. She said, "Was there anything about the car that indicated he'd been there?"

"No, it was still locked. You can go look if you like."

"I will. Do you have a photograph of him?"

Bebe looked momentarily startled. "Sure," she said, and opened a drawer from which she plucked an envelope of snapshots. As she leafed through them, Skip asked for a few essentials—Russell's full name and date of birth, the names of his family in North Carolina, and his Social Security number. Bebe supplied the first three, handed over a photo, and excused herself to look up the Social Security number.

Skip and Abasolo were standing when she returned. "For now," Skip said, "I think the best course is to do some preliminary investigating and get back to you if we need to. How would that be?"

Fortier looked as if she'd gotten a negative biopsy report. "That would be wonderful."

"Okay. Let's stay in touch. Here's my card." She wrote her pager number on the back.

Skip and Abasolo walked to the car without a word.

"See?" he said finally. "You're a great little VNL. I knew you could do it."

"My jaws hurt from clamping them shut."

She spent the next two hours on the phone calling hospitals, the morgue, and the relatives in North Carolina. Then she took a ride to the airport with a crime lab crew and processed the car, though dusting for prints seemed excessive at this point.

Still, this was a heater case.

She drove the car back to the Fortier house herself. Then she called all the airlines that flew out of New Orleans. No one had a record of a Russell Fortier on an outbound flight in the last twenty-four hours.

Bebe called in the late afternoon to see if Skip had any news. No ransom demand had arrived.

Despite all the talk about discretion, it was only the next morning when Skip got her first media call. "Hey, Skip. It's your old friend Jane Storey."

"Janie. How's the wild world of television journalism?"

"Too wild for me. Couldn't stand that superficial shit. I'm back at the *Picayune*."

"You've got to be kidding."

"Good-bye lovely money, hello responsible journalism. I didn't get fired, by the way. It just wasn't for me."

"Well, I admire your integrity. I think."

"Listen, Skippy. I hear Russell Fortier's disappeared."

"Can't comment, Janie."

"Let me put it another way. I got your name from Bebe."

Skip started. That didn't make sense. "She called you?"

"Uh-uh. I called her. She confirmed it."

"Where'd you hear it?"

"Can't say. You know that."

"You going to run a story?"

"Is the pope a cross-dresser?"

"I've got to keep quiet on this one, Janie."

"Well, listen, I'll trade you. I've got a little something you may not know."

"No trades. No way. Not on this one." *Not yet, anyway.*

"So what'll it be? No comment?"

"Police reports are public record unless it's a criminal investigation. You know that."

"That's the best you can do?"

"For now. We've got a public information officer."

"Well, it was worth a try."

Skip had a call waiting for her. She punched the "Hold"

16

button: "Langdon." She couldn't keep the irritation out of her voice.

"Girlfriend. You got PMS or something?" It was her friend Cindy Lou, the police psychologist.

"Lou-Lou. I thought you were another damned reporter."

"Uh-oh. They after you, too?"

"What do you mean, 'too'?"

"Jane Storey's on my ass."

"Jane Storey? What for?"

"It's not nice. You free for lunch?"

"Davis Deluxe. Twenty minutes."

Davis Deluxe had caused Skip to gain five pounds since getting transferred. It was a great neighborhood restaurant—red plaid on the tables, Dr. King on the wall, butter beans on your plate. It was delicious and it was close.

Since it would take her far less than twenty minutes to get there, she called Bebe first. "I hear the press knows."

"Well, it's a little puzzling. I've only had one call, but since they'd found out, I couldn't see the point of lying. Did I do wrong?"

"Up to you." Skip thought a minute. "Probably not. A story might get someone out of the woodwork. I thought you wanted to keep it quiet, that's all."

A sob came over the line. "It's gone beyond that, Skip. I'm scared to death. It's been two days."

"I think you made the right decision. This makes my job easier." A lot easier. Discretion took on a different meaning if the whole city knew.

Something was funny, though. Why Jane Storey and no other reporters? "Has anyone called besides the *Times-Picayune*?"

"No. Jane said she had a tip. And don't worry, I know it wasn't you. She told me it didn't come from the cops. And I've worked with her a lot. I trust her."

So had Skip and she also trusted her—up to a point.

17

Still, she thought, *That's your first mistake. Never trust a reporter.*

She went to meet Cindy Lou.

Two

"I'M IN A heap of shit, girlfriend."

"What's going on?" Skip put down the menu, deciding once again on the fried chicken.

"Well, I was seeing a married man."

Skip sighed. Cindy Lou was African American, beautiful, brilliant, and cursed with abysmal taste in men. She didn't discriminate on account of race, color, or creed—all they had to be was unsuitable. "So what else is new?" Skip asked.

"It was Bebe Fortier's husband."

"Holy shit. Why didn't I see that coming?"

"Why do you say that?"

"You talk first. What did Jane want?"

"She told me she had information I was seeing him and asked me if I knew his whereabouts. I called his office and they said he was out sick. What's going on here?"

"He's disappeared, Lou-Lou. Jane probably thinks you ran away with him. Did you?"

"Hey, back off. What's happening?"

Skip told her the story. "What do you make of it?"

Lou-Lou shrugged. "I don't make anything of it. I barely know the man. It doesn't sound right, though. Uh-uh. It doesn't sound right at all." She was shaking her head. "I don't like it. From the little I knew of him, he was your basic solid family man."

Skip almost dropped her fork. "Oh, right. And you're

part of the family? What do you mean, you barely knew him, by the way?"

"It wasn't a real affair. We saw each other exactly twice. He was at some party without Bebe and we both drank some champagne and flirted. Then he kept calling and hustling and—hell, he's cute. So I went to bed with him. And guess what? He was great. I hadn't had a date for six months. I mean it—I know you don't believe it, but it's the God's truth."

"Lou-Lou, tell me you use condoms."

"What, you think I'm crazy? I keep a whole box on my bedside table."

Skip had to laugh. "Okay, I feel better."

"Then we saw each other a second time and he couldn't get it up. He was feeling so damn guilty about cheating on his wife; you know that one? I swear, married men aren't worth messing with."

"I'm going to type that out and tape it to your refrigerator. You don't get to eat till you repeat it ten times."

"I never eat at home anyway." She turned up her palms. "That was it. The whole thing. And it was two months ago."

"Who knew about it?"

"Nobody. Listen, you're my best friend. Did you know about it? It wasn't worth mentioning, believe me."

"Did people see you at that party?"

"We talked for maybe ten minutes. Yeah, it was intense, but who could have noticed? Nobody, believe me. Everybody was too busy putting the moves on everybody else."

"Did you leave with Fortier?"

"Of course not. I just don't see how this *T-P* babe could know about it."

"Well, she does. But what did you mean when you said you're in deep shit?"

"She's going to run a story about it."

"Come on, she can't do that. It's not news."

Lou-Lou put her palms up. "All I know is what she

told me. Listen, she's your friend. Isn't there anything you can do?"

"I don't know. I just don't know if there is."

But she was sure going to have a talk with Jane Storey.

Jane had become a reporter because she wanted each day to be different, because she liked to hang out with people who told a good story, because she had a lot of questions and needed a license to ask them. She was someone who craved adventure through her work.

She'd become a television reporter for the adventure as much as the money. She'd quit because, to her, TV was about appearances rather than reality—you didn't have to tell a story, you only had to stand before the camera and make mouth noises. What they were signified very little as long as you looked neat and sounded professional.

Stuffy was better still.

And you didn't get to write much.

She'd also become a reporter because she wrote. Not that she enjoyed writing or wanted to write, or even so much had ambitions to write. It was just what she did. She was a lot more comfortable back at the *Picayune*, but she sure missed Walter.

Walter Cottrell had been her best friend at the paper. He was sixty, which made him the second oldest staff member, and he was Jane's idol and role model. This was what a reporter should be—alert but not cynical, smarter than your average Rhodes scholar, and a brilliant writer. He had died in his sleep—of a broken heart, she thought. Because journalism hadn't lived up to his expectations; had become a completely different animal from the one he had tamed as a young man.

Walter loved to talk about matters of ethics and integrity. Nobody else much did anymore. Something else she loved about Walter—he was always a little sloppy, like Skip. Always had spots on his tie, or his shirt hanging out in the back, or hair flying every which way.

Jane's peers in age and experience looked as if they worked in banks. They were hardly the lovable rowdies,

21

the raffish black sheep who'd been drawn to journalism in Walter's day. They were serious young men and women who probably wouldn't give Hildy Johnson the time of day—or even know who he was. They were so politically correct they wouldn't tell Polish jokes on a slow news day.

But the newsroom still had a certain character. A few people who worked there still excelled in the art of raconteurism. A few cared about their work. Some could make her laugh.

Jane clung to that.

The receptionist phoned from the cool marble entrance two floors down: "Skip Langdon to see you."

"Well, well. Send her up. By all means." Jane tidied her desk and waited for Skip to ascend the escalator.

She went to meet her at the entrance to the newsroom. "This has got to be a first. *You're* coming to see *me*?"

"Janie, we have to talk."

"Uh-oh, that's your mean voice. Let's go to the cafeteria."

They went to the second floor. "Buy you a cup of coffee?"

"Make mine water—I just had lunch. With Cindy Lou Wootten."

"Ah. The plot thickens." Jane felt her stomach flutter.

"I came to discuss responsible journalism. Isn't that what you said you were into?"

Jane nodded, trying to keep her cool. "Sure. Tell me what's on your mind."

"Some things just don't jibe. Cindy Lou says you're going to run a story about her and Russell Fortier. I want to hear it from your own mouth."

"I don't mean to be rude—but why?"

"Oh, Cindy Lou's probably one of my three best friends. So I was just kind of wondering what's going on. It doesn't seem like she and Russell are news. So what would the story be?"

Jane felt herself color. She had used a tactic or two to

22

get Cindy Lou talking that might have slightly over-stated the case.

She said, "Well, I'd have to go along with you on that. I'm not going to run anything that's not news. We're not in the business of invading privacy."

Skip snorted.

"Unless it is news. I mean, if Russell had been shacked up with Cindy Lou, it would be."

"Oh, come on, Jane."

"Anyway, it might tell me Russell's disappearance isn't the result of criminal activity. Unless you count crimes of the heart."

"She thinks you're going to smear her. She's a re-spected member of the community and she doesn't de-serve that."

Jane leaned back in her chair. "I'm sorry I spooked her—I'm not going to do anything unprofessional. But she should have thought about the consequences. Bebe doesn't deserve a cheating husband either."

"That's not your business."

Jane took a deep breath; she was having a bad time with men lately. "You're right. I spoke out of turn."

"Can we talk off the record?"

"Sure."

"Cindy Lou wasn't even having an affair with Russell—she did see him a time or two, but she's surprised anyone could know about that. This whole thing makes me ner-vous. I know you don't reveal sources, but there's some-thing nasty about all this."

Jane shrugged. "I hear a lot of stories. Some pan out, some don't. My job is to check 'em out." She looked at Skip. The cop's hair was growing back from an under-cover do—it was no more than an inch long and already curly and wild. She wore a wrinkled rayon jacket, and pants a little too short. Her brow was all furrowed with worry.

You couldn't help but like her.

Jane honestly wanted to be friends with this woman,

23

but Skip was a high-profile news source. Was friendship even possible, given the nature of their two jobs?

"Janie, tell me what you know about Russell. I've got a bad feeling about all this."

"You know I can't do that. You can read it in the paper."

"What if that's too late? Where does journalism leave off and life begin?"

"Well, that's a good question. A damn good question, debated nightly in newspaper grog shops the world over. You and I probably aren't ever going to get to the bottom of it, but I'll make today a little easier. I don't know one damn thing that you don't. All I really know is what Bebe told me. I presume it was less than she told you."

"Did she tip you, Janie?"

"Bebe? Of course not." It just slipped out. The question surprised her so much she forgot to be mysterious.

"Well, that's something, anyway. Look, I'm sorry I barged in on you. I was a little upset."

I'll bet, Jane thought. *I'll just bet Ms. Skip Langdon never does anything without considering mucho carefully.*

She walked Skip to the escalator and returned to the newsroom, thoughts aboil. This was a highly unusual event, a cop with an impeccable reputation for honesty trying to stop a story—if that's what Skip had really come for. On the other hand, if she thought Jane really was going to run a story about some stupid love triangle, and Cindy Lou really was her best friend, it made a kind of crazy sense.

Still, it was strange behavior for Skip.

I wonder, she thought, *if there's something here I don't see. Skip's on the Russell Fortier case and Cindy Lou's her friend—does she have a conflict of interest?*

She tossed that one around in her head. Now that would be a story. But unless there was criminal activity, what did it mean?

Suppose there's criminal activity and Skip doesn't see it because she's too close to Cindy Lou?

She wanted to talk it over with Walter.

24

She wondered if she should run it by her editor. But they didn't have a lot of rapport these days.

He was the philanderer in her life.

He had an eye for the ladies, he was married, and he liked to go out with a woman till she was hooked and then dump her—ask about half the female population of the newsroom.

He made damn sure they got hooked. He sent flowers, made dinners, planned romantic weekends. A seducer, Walter would have called him. Did call him, but had Jane listened?

Yes, for a while. Sure. She'd seen it herself. She couldn't have cared less for the likes of David Bacardi—until one night, with a bottle of champagne, celebrating her return to the *Picayune*.

He had rehired her. Maybe she was just grateful at the time. Now she was supremely pissed off—mostly at herself.

Three

TALBA PLANNED TO spend the day shopping for
exotic scarves to drape over the tattered furniture in the
little cottage she shared with her mother. They lived in
the Ninth Ward between Desire and Piety, a metaphor
she couldn't figure out how to use. It was the house she'd
grown up in. Using the proceeds from the job she'd just
done at United Oil, she was gradually transforming it
into an exotic den.

She was sitting at the old black-painted table in the
kitchen having coffee and toast, letting her mama sleep,
and reading the *Times-Picayune*, when her eye lit on two
words that froze her solid. Russell Fortier.

Russell Fortier had disappeared.

Just fallen off the Earth, if you believed the newspaper
story.

What the hell was this? She knew Russell Fortier, and
she wasn't the kind of person who knew people who
made news (though she expected to make some herself
pretty soon).

The paper said Russell was married to Bebe Fortier,
the city councilwoman. Talba hadn't known that—some
detective she was. It occurred to her that she hadn't
asked enough questions before she took the job.

Maybe she should postpone her shopping trip.

She heard her mama coming down the hall, wearing
those ancient blue slippers of hers, sounding like an old
lady, though she was only forty-seven. It was her day off.

"Mama? You want some coffee?"

"*Ummmm-hmmmm.* I got up 'cause it smell so good."

"You sit down now—let me make you some toast."

Her mother wasn't wearing a wig today. Her hair was cut short, close to her head, so it wouldn't get all dusty when she went to work. She looked better today. She'd been looking so tired lately.

"What you doin' today, girl?"

"I got some business to take care of."

"Bi'ness! Hmmph. You sound like my sister Carrie boy, Jonathan. Spend half his life in jail. Only bi'ness he up to, monkey bi'ness."

"Now, Mama. You know I don't deal drugs, I don't stick up stores, I don't steal cars." Steal *some* things, though. "You don't need to worry about me." Maybe not, anyway.

"You so secretive, Sandra. Can't help but worry. I didn't send you to college so you could lounge aroun' the house, smokin' cigarettes and readin' the paper."

"I'm having a day off just like you. I just got a little somethin' to take care of."

"You ain't in trouble, are you?"

God, I hope not. " 'Course not, Mama. I'm gon' go out, see a man about somethin', then I'm gon' go by Schwegmann's and get a chicken for supper. Then I'm gon' come home and do some work."

"You got a freelance job?"

"My own work."

"Pshaw! Your own work. You better get yourself a steady job, girl. Miz Clara didn't send you to college so you could sit home in that room of yours."

Her mother, who referred to herself grandly as "Miz Clara," had a list a mile long of things she didn't send her daughter to college to do. It included everything Talba did. This, despite the fact that Talba had worked for five years at a good job and saved her money so she could quit it and make her fortune. "Now, Mama, we talked about this."

"That what you always say. I thought you meant a couple of months. Six at the most."

"You know what *you* always say—Rome wasn't built in a day." That was what Miz Clara had told her and her little brother year after year after year when they wanted to know how long it would be before they could move out of their dumpy little house and into something with a swimming pool in back. Her brother had finally done it himself—today he lived in New Orleans East in a nice big house with a pool. But Talba had ambitions to be something more than a computer programmer.

She'd talked it over with her mother; asked if she could move back in with her. Miz Clara had said yes, and Talba felt betrayed every time she started the I-didn't-send-you-to-college routine.

So Talba hadn't told her about this great new way she had of earning money. It was honorable—or almost honorable. And it was certainly fun. Besides, she was learning lots of skills that were going to stand her in good stead. She was going to find the bastard she was looking for and make him pay. *Then* her mama'd be proud of her.

But she had a bad feeling about this Russell Fortier thing. Maybe old Gene Allred had taken advantage of her—gotten her involved in something that was going to come back to haunt her.

Whatever else Talba Wallis was, she was one smart cookie. She knew enough to cover her bootie and she'd better go do that right now; she couldn't call Gene from here, with her mother listening and prying and judging every word.

She went and put on a white blouse and a little navy miniskirt, just like a Catholic schoolgirl. She had seven white blouses and four navy skirts. They looked business-like, they looked humble, they hardly cost anything, and they were almost invisible. They nicely offset the long, gorgeous hair extensions she'd become addicted to—made her just another young black clerical worker who loved to go to the beauty parlor.

By day she was neat Talba Wallis (Sandra to her mother), a young computer whiz or clerical worker—whatever was called for—by night a creature of beauty

28

and glamour and, in a small way, fame, which was soon to spread.

And those were only two of her personalities. She was also a woman with a mission.

The mission was already changing her life. She'd originally gone to Gene Allred about her problem and that had led to a whole new world of adventure and bucks—and sometime criminal activity, which, if truth be told, she quite enjoyed.

I hope that's all it's led to, she thought as she drove to Allred's crummy office out near Elysian Fields and Gentilly. The building it was in looked like a trailer, it was so small and low. Today, his door was slightly ajar.

"Gene?" she called. He had no secretary.

For some reason, she had a sudden outbreak of goose bumps.

She stepped in, and there, in the doorway between the minuscule waiting room and the office proper, stood a man in a ski mask.

She gasped so loud the noise surprised her. She looked wildly around, as if for an exit, and noticed the office was wrecked.

The man came toward her. She backed up; all she had to do was step out on the sidewalk. Someone would see her, or at least hear her if she screamed.

But she opened her mouth too late. A broad ham of a hand smacked against it; the hand was gloved. The man caught her by the elbow and forced her back into the office. He shoved her against an old green sofa that Allred had probably gotten from Goodwill.

"Scream and I'll kill you," he said.

Rage enveloped her like a blanket. She had been the despair of her mother all through Catholic school, always getting in fights and kicking the boys in the shins.

"Fuck you," she shouted, and hurled her body at him headfirst, butting him in the stomach. She heard something crack, probably his head hitting the wall. He started to fall and she righted herself, turned, and split, at more or less warp speed. Sure enough, there was someone there to save her—an elderly white woman was walking toward her.

"Help!" she shouted, and the woman screamed herself, obviously terrified at the sight of a wild-haired black hellion hurtling toward her—probably afraid she was about to be caught in the middle of a shoot-out. Talba couldn't have guaranteed that she wasn't.

The woman froze. "Dial 911," Talba hollered, and kept running. Her car was two blocks away.

She stole a glance behind her and saw that there was indeed a man behind her, though not running. She hadn't noticed anything about the man in the office except his ski mask—though she thought he'd been wearing jeans. This one was also wearing jeans, and he was white. She hadn't a clue if he was the intruder.

About a block further on, when she was nearly to her car, she saw that the man was still walking toward her, and fast, she thought. She still couldn't see his face. She kept running.

She fumbled for her key, glancing around now and then to see if he was close. He was getting into a tan van.

I've got to get calm, she thought. There were lots of cars, plenty of businesses, dozens of people on the streets. Surely she was safe. Surely she could just walk in someplace and ask to use the phone to call the police.

But panic seized her as tightly as the rage of moments ago. *What the fuck am I into?* she thought. *What's the deal with Russell Fortier disappearing?*

The thing was, she had committed a few little illegalities in the course of her work for Allred. Maybe someone was upset about something.

Could she outrun this dude or not? It was worth a try.

Once again, she felt in her purse for the key, and this time her hand closed on it. She saw that the man was already out of his parking spot. She shoved the key in the ignition, but her fingers were so slick with sweat she didn't trust them on the steering wheel.

Still, at this point there was no choice. He could drive up beside her and shoot her through the window.

30

Instead, he drove past her. Could it be that this was a different man? Maybe he wasn't chasing her. He stopped at the stoplight. She was four cars behind him.

As he went through the intersection, she turned right, wondering how this could be so easy.

Yet she drove around a few random blocks, and still the van didn't follow.

Damn, she thought. *Why didn't I get his license number?* But it was obvious why. She was too scared.

Nothing to do but go home. She stopped at Schwegmann's on Elysian Fields, as she'd promised Miz Clara, and was approaching calm as she got back in the car and went home.

But there, in the center of her modest block, smack in the middle between Desire and Piety, was a tan van.

Oh, Jesus Christ, she thought, *what now? My mama's in the house.*

She got out of the car warily, looking around her, wishing she had a gun.

Someone seized her from behind, clamping a hand over her mouth. She felt the roughness of his beard as the man leaned close to her ear.

He whispered, "Open the door," and she realized he meant her own car door.

She worked it.

"No. The back door."

He pushed her in and slid in beside her. She felt something slip over her head, and then she was wearing the ski mask, backward, so that it formed a blindfold.

"Scream and your mother's dead," the man said.

Inside the wool mask was unbearably hot. *Why a ski mask?* she thought. *Why not a stocking mask?* She realized that wouldn't have disguised the man's race. But he'd blown that one. The man was white.

He spoke to her gently, much more nicely than you'd expect from someone who'd just threatened to kill your mother. "You're okay. I'm not going to hurt you and I'm not going to hurt your mother. You're involved in something you don't understand, that's all. Wait till tomorrow and call me at the office." She felt something slide into her hand, something he was pressing into her palm. A business card.

"Now, wait till I'm gone and then go in the house. Your mother's okay." She waited till she heard her car door slam and then ripped off the mask. He had his back to her so she still couldn't see his face, but she damn sure wasn't going to sit there like a dummy when she had a chance to get his plate number.

But it had been splashed with something, probably mud. He drove off while she was still squinting at it. She looked at the card in her hand and let out a little gasp.

It bore the crescent and star of the New Orleans Police Department. DETECTIVE SKIP LANGDON, it said.

She dashed inside. "Mama? Mama, you okay?"

Her mother was watching *Oprah*. "Girl, why ain't you out looking for a job?"

"Did you send me to college to make chicken fricassee? I hope so, 'cause that's what I'm gonna do."

"Hmmph. For ya no-account boyfrien' wit' the horrible hair. Not for ya mama."

Talba had stuffed the damn ski mask into the Schwegmann's bag. She took it out and looked at it. *Fuck!* she thought. *No way a cop would have treated a white person that way—threatenin' to kill my mama! I think I might call Public Integrity.*

That was the office called Internal Affairs elsewhere, but she hesitated, deciding instead to try Allred's office one last time. No one answered. All day she kept calling and getting no answer.

She ran the whole thing by Lamar that night, after they'd eaten the chicken fricassee. Whatever her mama said, Lamar was not no-account, any more than she was. He was a grad student at Xavier, in the art department, and he was a damn good artist, especially, as her mama said, if you listened to him. He had fabulous dreads and looked something like Lenny Kravitz, whom he had once seen in the French Quarter, and whose style he greatly admired.

He was outraged. "Are you kidding? Call Public Integrity! Call 'em *now*! Don't even call the cop back. Just call and report him. Do a thing like that! Damn."

"Well, I just thought—"

"I'm gonna do a painting. You know what, I'm gonna paint what happened. Give me that ski mask. He really put it over your head?"

She didn't have time to answer.

"Maybe I'll actually use the thing itself in the painting—make a collage with it. Yeah, all red and blue. How dare they do that to my baby? Can't imagine a cop doing a thing like that."

"Oh, come on, Lamar."

"I mean, oh sure, I can imagine it. A good cop's harder to find than a good artist in this town. Baby, you just lucky you got one. You want to go to bed?" He nuzzled her.

"Not with my mama—"

"Oh, your mama. You got to grow up, Talba. Fuck this shit. I'm leavin'. Leavin' right now."

He marched out the door, his dreads swinging in the breeze. It was something he did about once a week.

"Pshaw," Miz Clara said. "I come up with that boy's mama. If she was alive, he wouldn't be like that."

"Now, Mama. Lamar's an artist."

"Lamar a sperled brat. That what Lamar is."

Four

IT WAS SATURDAY morning and Skip had been up since seven-thirty. Life was complicated. The whole place was in an uproar, not just her own space.

Skip had the slave quarters—now called the garçonnière—at her best friend Jimmy Dee Scoggin's house. Jimmy Dee shared the Big House, as they'd taken to calling it, with his two adopted children, his late sister's kids, Sheila and Kenny, and a black-and-white dog called Angel.

Steve Steinman, who was staying with Skip, also had a dog—a German shepherd named Napoleon. Skip hated Napoleon and Napoleon hated her. In fact, Napoleon hated just about everybody except Kenny and Steve.

Normally, all this made for a pretty lively household, but with the tension in the garçonnière and one other little detail, it was currently chaos.

The other detail was Jimmy Dee's friend Layne. Jimmy Dee's beloved, if the truth be told. Jimmy Dee was gay, a fact that had turned out to be easier for the kids to accept than anyone thought it would, and Layne was about to be a new addition to the family. Everyone was thrilled about it. The kids loved him. ("His main virture," Dee-Dee said wryly, "is that he isn't Uncle Jimmy.") And Steve was crazy about him, which was a great tension-reliever, since he wasn't entirely insane for Dee-Dee himself.

However, Layne's moving in meant getting a room ready for him, which required more than the normal amount of effort, since Layne was a puzzle designer by trade. This meant any amount of paraphernalia, including games from just about every country in the world.

And that translated to building cabinets and book-shelves, which necessitated a house full of workmen.

That put everybody on edge, just about all the time. Skip was just as happy to be going over to Steve's cottage to help him sand kitchen cabinets. "Can I help?" Kenny asked wistfully. "Anybody can sand."

"Okay, sure. Get Angel and come on."

From where they all stood in the courtyard, they could hear Dee-Dee and Layne arguing in the kitchen. "But I need to have things where I can see them."

"Well, I need to have them where I can't."

Kenny looked forlorn. "They were so nice to each other before all this started."

Skip laughed. "So were we."

And now Steve looked hurt. "I'm still nice to you."

"I'm sorry. I've always been the difficult one. Everyone knows that."

Kenny said, "Oh, never mind, I guess I'll stay here." He went back into the house, elephant-legged shorts flopping about on skinny legs. His feet looked like Nike-clad boards attached to his ankles. His shoulders slumped.

Steve said, "Now see what you've done."

"Damn!" She went after him. "Kenny! Kenny, I was just kidding. Come on—moving's one of the five most stressful things you can ever do. Nobody means anything. We're just discombobulated."

She could have bitten her tongue, knowing he was going to ask about the other stresses. His mother had died a few years ago. He knew firsthand about stress.

But he said nothing, just kept walking, shoulders slumped.

Dee-Dee stared at her. "What'd you do to him?"

"Oh, nothing. He's upset because everybody's snappy."

"Oh, God, is it all worth it? Maybe we all just ought to go for a hike."

Skip shrugged. "Cabinets to sand."

But Kenny turned around. "Yeah. Maybe we ought to." He was the rare kid who didn't mind doing things with adults.

Skip saw he was smiling. "Y'all have fun." She rejoined Steve in the courtyard.

He said, "Listen, I've been thinking. You need a day off. Why don't you stay home and wash your hair or something?"

"You know what? That's not a half-bad idea." She did need a day off.

They drank another cup of coffee and she kissed Steve good-bye. She was puttering about the kitchen thinking about flopping down with a good book when her pager went off, a rare thing for a Saturday morning.

"What the hell?" she said aloud, and looked at it. It registered a number she didn't recognize. "Oh, well." Wearily she dialed it.

A woman answered, and she identified herself. "Detective Skip Langdon."

"Oh." The woman sounded surprised. "I get Sandra."

In a moment, a younger woman came to the phone. "Yes?"

"Someone there paged Detective Skip Langdon."

"I paged Detective Langdon."

Skip said, "Yes?"

"*You're* Detective Langdon? Something's funny here. I'm looking for a man."

"Something's funny all right. 'Cause I'm not one."

"Oh. Okay. Sorry." The woman hung up.

Skip shrugged and went back to loading the dishwasher. In a moment her pager went off again. It was the same number. Impatiently, she dialed again.

The woman said, "I've thought things over. Somebody gave me your card. Said he was you. I think we need to talk about it."

"Okay. Talk."

"Uh-uh. Not on the phone. How do I know you really are Detective Langdon?"

36

"Listen, it's my day off. Why don't you come in first thing Monday morning?"

"The man who gave me your card—I found him rifling a friend's office. He hit me and chased me, and somehow got to my house before I did. He said he'd kill me if I screamed, and he threatened to kill my mother. Then he blindfolded me, gave me your card, and said call him in the morning. I was going to call Public Integrity—maybe it's good I didn't."

"My card doesn't have my pager number on it."

"No. It was written on the back."

"What's your name?"

"I'm not telling you till I can see you."

It didn't matter—Skip had her number. But she didn't like the sound of this. "Okay," she sighed. "Meet me at my office in half an hour. You know where the Third District is?"

"No."

"Seventeen hundred Moss Street."

Skip got there first, carrying yet another coffee. She read the paper while she waited.

And in about ten minutes, an African-American woman arrived, a young, pretty one with gorgeous hair, large of butt and bust, stuffed into black jeans and a white T-shirt.

"I'm the woman who called. Talba Wallis."

"Sit down, Ms. Wallis."

"If the guy wasn't you, who was he? He knows where I live. How the hell could he know that?"

"You better start from the beginning."

"I've been working with a private detective—Gene Allred."

Skip nodded as if it meant something. She had no idea who that was.

"I went to his office yesterday and this guy in a ski mask was there. I told you the rest." She ran through the story again, in slightly more detail. "I thought maybe Gene was in some kind of trouble, maybe in jail—I kept calling him and getting no answer."

"Did you try him at home?"

"I don't know his home number."

"Let me try a couple of things." Skip tried the phone book and she tried Central Lockup; he wasn't listed and he wasn't in jail.

"Can you describe the man?"

"I never saw his face, but he was white and tall. Thin, I'd say."

"What were you working on with Allred?"

"I can't really talk about that."

There'd be time enough to insist, if a crime had been committed. "Could I see the card the man gave you?"

"Sure." She handed it over.

The pager number was there, in Skip's handwriting.

There was nothing to do except get Wallis's address, and Allred's. "Okay," she said finally. "I'll be in touch."

"Wait a minute. Is that all? What do you think happened to me?"

"I think you know more about that than I do. But you don't want to talk about it."

"It wouldn't be ethical."

What the hell. Allred's office was in her district, and practically on the way home. She wasn't going to be happy unless she swung by and took a look.

The door was unlocked. As soon as she opened it she knew by the stink there was a corpse in there.

She stepped in and closed the door behind her, grateful for air-conditioning, yet her nose was still deeply offended. There could be no doubt this was a crime scene, but it would help, she thought, to know how many corpses were in there, and if they were human or rodent.

The place was a wreck—papers and file folders everywhere.

She stepped over and through a sea of strewn paper on the way to the inner office, which was likewise strewn. Glancing around, she saw that the mess came from filing cabinets in both rooms.

Allred, if it were he, was in the second room. He had fallen backward, one hand over his head, a big hole in his chest. He was fortyish, with thinning blond hair, dressed in olive polyester—the fabled cheap suit of private-eye patter. His face was ghost-white, the blood having had plenty of time to sink to the bottom of his body. Curiously, an arm had been thrown over his head, a finger pointing. His mouth was open slightly, almost in an *O*, and his eyes were wide open, staring in perennial amazement. A parade of bugs marched in them.

Rusty-looking stuff—the man's blood—spattered the floor and his clothes.

Okay, fine, one corpse. Human. Male.

She knew enough to call it in, and she couldn't justify contaminating the scene any further. She stepped into the hall, radioed the dispatcher, and waited for a district car to get there.

That done, she was free to find a phone and call her sergeant.

"Skip. It's Saturday—haven't you heard?" Abasolo's voice had an edge—she'd probably caught him in bed with someone.

"AA, I've got a corpse that has my name on it. Young lady paged me at home, told me a wild story, and showed me one of my own cards, with my pager number on it in my handwriting. Said a dude she found at the crime scene in a ski mask chased her, threatened her, then gave her my card and said to call him in the morning. And there's one other thing. I've got a bad feeling the card might be the one I gave Bebe."

"Come on. You must give out cards all the time."

"Let me call Bebe—I called you first. What do you think, by the way?"

"The guy said he was you?"

"Implied it, anyway."

"I think you were right the first time. That's a corpse with your name on it."

Skip found more change and gave Bebe a call. "Ms. Fortier, Skip Langdon."

"Oh, Skip. Call me Bebe." She sounded nervous. "Do you have any news?"

"I'm sorry, I don't. But I need to check something out with you. Remember that business card I gave you?"

"Sure. What about it?"

"Do you still have it?"

"I guess so. I put it in my purse."

"I know this sounds dumb, but do me a favor and check, will you?"

Skip could almost see her shrugging. "Sure," she said, and left the line.

She was back in a moment. "It's funny—I can't find it. What's this about?"

"It may have come back to me in an odd way. Has anyone had access to your purse?"

"Not in the house. The cleaning lady hasn't been here. My daughter's coming in from Wisconsin, but she isn't here yet. Oh, wait. I left it on a counter yesterday—in a drugstore. Only for a moment, though—you know how you do when you're shopping?"

"Was it in your view at all times?"

"No. In fact, I thought I heard someone in the area and I went back to retrieve it. Nothing else is missing, though."

"Okay. Well, it's probably nothing. I just wanted to check it out." She went back to the scene.

Another officer had now arrived, and had had time to put on that disgusted look policemen get at a nasty crime scene. "Can you get over this? Right in his office—somebody probably killed the poor bastard for five bucks."

The coroner's van came, and then the crime lab—Paul Gottschalk walked in full of questions. "Phew-ee, how come no one smelled him before?"

"You couldn't with the door closed. I know—I was first on the scene. The question is, how come nobody heard the shot? If it was a shot."

"Potato, probably. Look—see that spot over there—betcha anything that's potato."

Some months ago, there had been an extremely well-publicized murder in which the perps had stuck a potato on a gun barrel as a silencer. Now everyone was doing it.

Maybe that accounted for the surprised look on the man's face—if you saw a potato, you had to fear the worst.

Skip turned to Denton, the coroner's deputy. "Check his pockets, will you? I want to know if it's Allred—the guy who belongs here."

Denton pulled on gloves, knelt, and turned out the pockets, unearthing a wallet with driver's license and credit cards.

"Yep. Seems to be."

The papers proved nothing, of course, but they were a good indication. "Do you have a home address?"

"Uh-huh. Louisa. Not a great neighborhood."

Gottschalk said, "You want all this paper put in boxes?"

She sighed. "Yeah, I guess so."

She wondered if she was actually going to get through them. "I'd like to look at his Rolodex—could you dust it and pass it over?"

She couldn't leave the crime scene until the body had—she might as well do something to amuse herself.

She looked up Fortier first, just to satisfy her curiosity, but neither Bebe nor Russell was in the file. In fact, there wasn't a single name she recognized except that of Talba Wallis, a young lady she wanted to see almost immediately.

She called her. "I need to see you at my office this afternoon—say at three o'clock."

"Now look. Just because I was nice enough to—"

"Ms. Wallis. Be there." Skip hung up.

When they had taken the body, she canvassed the neighbors.

No one had heard the shot, though two admitted hearing a crazy woman yell for help the morning before.

One of them shrugged. "I couldn't go look. I was on the phone."

The second had the grace to look frightened, if not contrite. "I was alone. I locked the door until it stopped."

"Did you call the police?"

"Yes. I dialed 911 and got a busy signal."

Maybe she had and maybe she hadn't. Today was Saturday and hardly anyone was working. Probably many more people had heard Talba screaming—Skip wondered if any of them had called the police.

Next she headed for Louisa, a block-by-block street, in terms of safety and degree of gentrification. Gene Allred's block wasn't one of the good ones. It was altogether an odd place for a white man to live, but maybe he'd won it in a poker game.

It was a double shotgun, so run-down it surely qualified as blighted property. A black woman stared out one side, through a nearly rusted screen door. "You want Mist' Allred?"

"Does he live here?"

"Yes'm."

"Anybody live with him?"

"Nah. Had a wife. She left."

"Seen anybody around here lately?"

At this, the woman hunched her shoulders, hooded her eyes, even, it seemed, narrowed her nostrils. Someone had most certainly been around. She said: "Nooo. Ain' seen nobody."

"Come on, now. Who'd you see? This is a murder investigation."

The woman's eyes widened. "Mist' Allred dead? Wonder what happen now." She looked frightened.

Skip stared at her, uncomprehending, until it finally came to her. "Did he own the building? Is Allred your landlord?"

"Was. He was my landlord."

She turned and disappeared into the house. Skip tackled the other side. It came as no surprise that it was as thoroughly ransacked as Allred's office. It stank of mildew and dirty dishes left in the sink. The furniture was beyond secondhand—probably picked up at dumps. The place must have been numbingly depressing *before* the ransacking.

What sort of person could Allred have been, to look so

neat and live so pathetically? A drunk, perhaps. Someone who was long past caring. Or a loner, someone unable to connect with people or things, just doing his job and muddling through. Maybe the other tenant could help some.

The woman was older—sixty, perhaps—and rail-thin, with a white handkerchief tied around her hair. Probably she normally wore a wig, but couldn't be bothered on a Saturday morning. Up close, Skip saw that energy crackled from her. She was obviously much sharper than Skip had first thought—she might be quite a good witness if she could be persuaded to talk.

"I'm Detective Skip Langdon." Skip produced her badge and offered to shake hands, but the woman declined. Skip waited, but no introduction was forthcoming. "May I ask who you are?"

"I'm Mist' Allred tenant. Miz Smith."

"Mrs. Smith. If you didn't see anything, you must have heard something—that place looks like a war zone."

"Oh, yes'm. You didn't ax nothin' about that." She cackled. "Didn't ax *nothin'* 'bout that."

"Fine. What did you hear?"

"Oh, just some noise. Car stoppin' and startin' up. Break-in noise, and then throw-things-around noise."

"When was this?"

"Two nights ago. Three, maybe."

"Two or three?"

"Fo'. I don't know." For some reason she wasn't going to say. Skip wondered if she'd done something to rub the woman the wrong way.

"Did you see anybody?"

"Nooooo. I already tol' you that."

"Tell me about Mr. Allred's wife."

"Now, her I know *too* much about. He own this buildin', but he useta rent out the other side to somebody like me—you unnerstan'?"

Somebody poor and black. And probably a little bit desperate.

"Well, the wife musta kicked his white ass right out on

43

the street—'cause he kick out th' other lady and he move in his own sorry self. Two, three years ago. I ain' sure.

"She a fool though. That woman ain' got the sense God gave a earthworm." She chuckled at her own metaphor. "Yes, Lord, some earthworms smarter."

Evidently, she had to be drawn out. "Why do you say that?"

" 'Cause that crazy woman still aroun'! Got rid o' his sorry ass, she still over here all the time, drinkin' beer and runnin' aroun' in her slip. They fight all the time, yellin', keepin' everybody awake. Law, a *baby* earthworm got more sense than that woman."

"What makes you think the woman you've seen is his wife?"

"That what he call her. He say, 'Verna'—tha's my name, Verna—he say, 'Verna, you see my wife aroun' here yesterday? Verna, my wife comes, tell her I lef' without her.' Maybe she ain't his wife, I don' know. I know one thing— nice-lookin' young lady come to see him, day or two ago. Young lady in her thirties. Pretty blond hair, all neat and everything—that wife of his, she always look like she just get out of bed. He treat this one bad, too. She wait nearly a hour for him, he don't show up."

"Did you talk to her?"

"Sho', I talk to her. She come up on the porch and ax me to give him somethin'. I never got the chance, come to think of it—Mist' Allred ain' been home in a couple days.

"Guess he been dead that long. How he die? Somebody shoot him or what?"

Skip was startled. "Why do you ask that?"

Verna shrugged. "So many people gettin' shot these days—I had to ax."

Maybe it had been a lucky guess. "What did the lady leave for Mr. Allred?"

She shrugged again, her face slightly uneasy. "Business card."

"Could I see it, please?"

"I don't see why not—Mist' Allred's not gon' need it." She left and returned with the card, again looking nervous. Skip looked at it and promptly lost her cool. It was Jane Storey's card. "*Jane Storey?* You didn't tell me the lady was a reporter."

Verna seemed to have grown a couple of inches. She spoke with utmost dignity, yet softly, barely above a whisper. "Well, I didn't know."

She doesn't read. Shit. What a dork I am. Skip stopped herself from apologizing, realizing that would make things worse.

She pretended she hadn't heard. "What's the wife's name?"

"Miz Allred, I guess. She never bother to tell me nothin' else."

"When was the last time you saw her?"

"Week ago, maybe. Same ol' thing. She come, she yell, she go."

"Well, thank you, Verna. You've really been a help."

"Did I say you could call me Verna? I'm *Miz* Smith to white police."

"Sorry. I forgot your last name. Thank you, Mrs. Smith."

Skip couldn't help chuckling as she descended the steps from the porch. Mrs. Smith hadn't been all that hostile to white police, fount of information that she was—you never knew what people were going to be touchy about.

She checked out the other neighbors, learning nothing new except that someone had seen a second visitor in the last couple of days—a white man in his thirties or forties, perhaps; maybe medium height. Or maybe older or younger, or taller or shorter. He had knocked, apparently gotten no answer, and then walked to the back. Unfortunately, the informant couldn't remember a thing about him except his race.

Somebody else thought the wife's name was Eloise.

Reluctantly, Skip returned to the wrecked shotgun. She could at least play Allred's messages. Sure enough, there was one from Eloise; also one from Jane Storey, saying that she'd come and waited, and she'd be happy to try again. Eloise just said, "Call me."

That was it. No clients, no other friends. Evidently, Allred wasn't too popular a guy.

Since this place was tied to the other crime scene, she couldn't go through the Rolodex, but she did sneak to the back to see if there was forced entry. It was impossible to tell—there was an open window, but no broken glass.

She radioed Paul Gottschalk to come over when he could, and called for district officers to secure the place. Then she called the station, asked the desk officer to put Eloise Allred through the DMV, and got an address in Metairie.

It was Saturday: Maybe Eloise was home. When the district car came, Skip took off to find out.

Eloise lived in an old apartment complex—maybe thirty years old, late-'60s vintage. It had a pool, but had probably never been luxurious, had probably catered to semitransient semiprofessionals. Now it was pretty run-down.

Skip leaned on Eloise's doorbell and got no answer. She leaned again. Something told her to try a third time, and sure enough, a cranky voice came through the intercom. "What is it?"

"Skip Langdon, NOPD."

"What the hell do you want?"

"I need to talk to you about your husband."

"Gene?" A note of alarm came into her voice. "Has something happened to him?"

"I think you'd better let me in."

The buzzer sounded, and over it, Skip heard a wailing. "Ohhh, no."

The woman was standing at the door, wearing a flower-print housecoat that might have been twenty years old. She was overweight, big in the belly, puffy. Her blond hair looked uncombed, and, futhermore, looked as if that was simply the way she wore it. Skip saw what Verna Smith meant about the contrast to Jane.

This woman was older than Jane, by six or seven years maybe. But instead of healthy skin nourished by plenty of vegetables, she had a pasty, bloated-looking hide already crisscrossed with wrinkles. And bags under her eyes that were probably partly genetic and partly due to cigarettes and drinking and long nights. She looked forty-five going on sixty. She stank of vodka.

"He didn't return my phone call. He didn't call me. I thought it was just because of that little—uh—thing I said to him." Her chin was starting to quiver.

Skip said, "Mrs. Allred, can I get you some water or something?"

Allred shook her head, keeping her eyes lowered so she wouldn't have to see the truth in Skip's.

Skip pushed past her to the kitchen and got her the water anyway. When she got back, Allred was sitting on a reproduction Victorian sofa covered in rose brocade. Skip held out the glass. "Here. Drink this."

Allred shook her head, her eyes staring past Skip to the wall.

Skip pulled up a ladder-back rocker with an orange crocheted pillow in it—a piece absolutely incongruous with the sofa—and waited a few moments.

Finally, she said, "Mrs. Allred, why are you so sure your husband is dead?"

Allred buried her head in her hands and started blubbering.

Skip simply waited.

"He knew this was going to happen. He knew it."

"What was going to happen?"

"He was going to die by violence. He always said it—'I'm gonna smoke as much as I want. Probably be dead before I'm forty anyway.'" She looked at Skip. "He is dead, isn't he?"

"I'm sorry. Yes, he is. At least, we think so. Do you have a picture of him?"

Unspeaking, moving like a robot, Allred got up and fetched a framed photo from the top of the television—herself and the man dead in his office.

47

Skip nodded again. "Yes. Could you make a positive identification?"

Allred held a tissue to her mouth. "What happened? What the hell happened? He was so—he seemed so jaunty last time I saw him."

"I thought you said he expected to die."

"Well, he did." She shrugged. "That was just his nature. He was depressed, I guess. Like, all the time. But last week, he was almost happy."

Skip waited, but Allred said only, "What the hell happened?"

"It looks as if someone shot him, Mrs. Allred."

The woman gasped.

"Who do you think might have done it?"

Slowly, Allred walked the picture back to its accustomed place and sat down again, the tissue once more at her mouth. She seemed to be biting down on her finger, perhaps in an effort to feel something other than pain. She looked alert now, though, as if she were thinking, not simply shocked and numb, staring at the wall.

Finally, she said, "He was into dealing a little."

"Dealing what?"

Her fat shoulders shrugged. "Cocaine, I guess. Whatever. He gave me some blow now and then—and he always had pot, too."

Skip hadn't seen any drugs at his house.

"He was talking about some kind of big score. I didn't really approve of his dealing drugs—I mean, it wasn't immoral or anything, I just thought it was dangerous and"—she stuck a knuckle between her teeth to get a grip—"I guess it was."

Knuckle or no, her face fell in once again, and her big shoulders shook.

Then she wagged her head, as if warding off the grief. "No, no, no. I just don't think it was drugs."

"Why not?"

"Something. Let me think." She drank some of the water and stared at the wall again. "I know! I asked him. And he said no. That's what it was."

48

"And then did you ask what it was if it wasn't drugs?"

"Yes. Yeah, I did. He said, 'You're going to be really surprised, Ellie girl. Really, really surprised. Guess what? It's halfway legitimate. And not only that, it's right. Right and moral.'" Allred laughed, a forced-sounding noise coming out of her throat. "Now how'd I forget somethin' like that?"

Five

_____

SKIP COULDN'T WAIT to get back to her office to interview Talba. She was over an hour late, so the girl would have had time to stew. That was good. She was looking forward to an antsy and worried witness, suffering from so powerful a combination of paranoia and boredom she'd be an easy target.

Instead, she found nothing but a message saying Talba had gone for a walk and would check in from time to time to see if Skip had returned.

Damn. She hated resourcefulness.

In fact, Talba returned in about twenty minutes laden with packages and overcome with enthusiasm. "Whoo—great stuff at the museum store. You ever go over there?"

"Sit down, Ms. Wallis." Skip spoke sharply.

Instantly, the friendly demeanor turned hard. "Hey. Who do you think you're ordering around? I come down here to accommodate you, you're not here, I wait, and now you got nothing but attitude."

"Sit down, Ms. Wallis." This time Skip's voice was slightly kinder, and she thought she might have let a bit of the seriousness of what she had to say creep into her expression.

Wallis looked suddenly frightened. She sat. "Something bad's happened."

"You're damn right something bad's happened. I want you to tell me every single thing you know about Gene Allred and everything there is to tell about your relationship with him."

"Relationship! Listen, Detective, I don't have a relationship with the man. I worked for him some, that's all. I hardly know him. What's this all about?"

"Are you still working for Allred?"

Wallis looked confused, as if she weren't sure what to say. Finally, she said, "From time to time."

"Uh-huh. When was the last time?"

"Last month, I guess."

"You told me you were trying to call him yesterday—why was that?"

"That's private."

"Nothing's private, Ms. Wallis. This is a murder investigation."

Fury contorted Wallis's features. "You . . . white . . . bitch." She bit off each word. "How dare you play games with me? Are you telling me Gene Allred's dead?"

If Skip had been hoping to provoke a reaction, it wasn't this one. She'd never been spoken to quite so rudely by a witness, especially one who might be a suspect. Still, she supposed the woman had registered surprise.

"I hate these damn power games. You treat me like a person or I'm out of here. All day long you've pushed me around. You treat me with a little respect." Her hair extensions were shaking, she was so mad.

"Ms. Wallis, you just insulted a police officer. You want me to make your life difficult, I've certainly got reason. Now, understand the seriousness of this situation. Your employer has been murdered. Calm down and answer my questions."

Skip could not allow herself to be insulted, but in the back of her mind, she thought Wallis had a point—she had probably pushed too far and ended up bullying.

Wallis sulked. She wasn't about to apologize and Skip wasn't about to ask her to. Best to forget the whole thing.

Skip said in a quieter voice: "Were you close to Mr. Allred?"

"No, I wasn't close to Mr. Allred. I worked for him."

Good. Wallis was backing off, too. "Well, then, why did

51

you call him and then go see him when you couldn't get him? It must have been pretty important."

"It was about a client."

"What client?"

Wallis put a hand over her mouth, not as if trying to keep something in, more as if she were thinking. She said, "Oh, God," and held the position for a while. Finally, she said, "I had a bad feeling. I think I better talk about it."

"It's probably best."

"I think I have to call a lawyer."

That was the last thing Skip wanted. "There's no need if you haven't done anything wrong."

Wallis stared at her a minute, possibly relieved, more likely calculating odds. Finally, she said, "Uh-uh. I'd like to help, but I just can't right now. I've got to have legal advice."

Skip suddenly became Ms. Nicecop. "Well, look, do you have a good lawyer? Maybe I could—"

"I'll be in touch." Wallis got up and turned to leave the room.

"It was about Russell Fortier, wasn't it?"

Wallis whirled. "You found the files."

It was all Skip could do not to shout, *What files?* Instead she said, "Ms. Wallis, I need to read you your rights."

"You're arresting me?"

"I really can't let you leave right now. Maybe you could have your lawyer meet us here."

"I don't have a lawyer. I'll have to get one."

Time was pouring away. Skip said, "Allred looked to me like a seedy private eye—seedy PIs do things to get information that aren't completely legal. However, I'm not about to arrest you if you know something that's going to help me solve a murder case—not unless the injured party presses charges. And being a tattletale is not my job. Do you follow?"

Wallis looked interested. Skip poured it on a little more. "Russell Fortier may be in danger."

52

Wallis sat down again. "Look. Are you offering me immunity from prosecution? Something like that?"

"Not exactly. I'm just saying if you didn't kill Gene Allred and you do cooperate in the investigation, I'm not going to go after you for something petty."

"You really think Fortier could be in danger?"

"I sure do." *In fact, he's probably dead.*

"Okay. Okay, I'll talk."

Skip Mirandized her just to get it on the record. And Wallis talked. "To begin with," she said, "I am a poet. Don't ask me why or how. I couldn't tell you. It's just something you do—one does, I mean. That one is born with. Oh, yes, yes, the world is full of MFAs, but did Chaucer have one? Did Shakespeare? Or even Wallace Stevens? Wallace Stevens would have been the world's most prosaic man if he hadn't been a poet."

Skip pointed to her tape recorder. "Ms. Wallis. The tape's almost run out. Were you planning to get started soon?"

"It's all of a piece, Detective."

"I'm not an audience, okay? I'm a police officer investigating a murder case."

Wallis broke into a grin. "Hey, maybe you'd *like* to be an audience. Tomorrow at Reggie and Chaz." She handed Skip a flyer. "I got this poem I just *know* you'd like."

"Ms. Wallis, I'm losing patience."

"I'm gettin' there, okay? The point is, 'poet' isn't a job description—my mama thinks it's a hobby. So I've got to have a day job—you know, the famous 'somethin' to fall back on'? I'm damn good with computers, Detective. Graduated from Xavier, top of my class. But I took some time off to pursue my art. And in the course of it, I got mixed up with Mr. Allred."

Talba had mentioned the poetry mostly as a blind. True, it was the most important thing in her life—in a long-term sense—but it wasn't the engine that drove her, at least right now. Talba hoped to solve her problem

53

and leave it behind, but it had to be handled first. As a small child, she had vowed to do this thing, to find the Pill Man and lay the demons to rest, and now was the time to do it. When it was done, she could move on.

But it had to be done.

She had found Allred's ad in the Yellow Pages. ("Nothing like having a name that starts with *A*," he told her once. "Bet I get half my clients that way.")

She liked his office. It looked seedy enough to make her think she could afford him. And Allred himself, despite his polyester suit and face abloom with gin blossoms, had nice eyes. Eyes like those she'd seen on many an older black man—eyes that said he'd seen suffering and comprehended it. She'd never known her father, and as a consequence was drawn to these suffering men. They looked as if they'd be kind.

She had enough sense to know that Allred, in his job, was no saint, but her intuition told her he wasn't all bad either—that he'd probably treat her honestly—and that was all she needed.

She started at the beginning. "Mr. Allred, you a racist?"

"A racist? You sound like *you're* one. You want a black PI, I'll give you some names."

"Hold your horses now; just hold on. This is relevant. I need you to find somebody for me—and *he's* a racist, whether he knows it or not. If you're a racist, you're just not gonna relate."

Allred rested his chin on one fist and tapped the table with the other. "I'm no racist, Ms. Wallis."

She told him her problem.

When she had finished he said, "Sure, I've heard that story. I've heard about the names. Everybody in New Orleans has."

"Every white person in New Orleans."

"What are you gonna do if you find the guy?"

"Does that matter?"

"I'm curious. That's all."

"I'm gonna make him pay. Some way. Every way I

possibly can. I'm gonna hold him up to public ridicule. An eye for an eye, Mr. Allred."

"And just how do you plan to do that?"

"Through my writing."

"Tell more."

"I'm a poet."

"Well, then." He leaned over, his face so close she could see the twin webs of wrinkles around his eyes. "How do you plan to pay me?"

"I'm also a computer nerd. A really good one."

"And who do you work for?"

"Right now, I'm kind of freelance."

"Oh, really? Well, how would you like to work for me?"

"You got to be kidding."

"Can you search a computer—I mean, just kind of go through its files to find what you want?"

"Sure. Anybody could do that."

"Well, first they'd have to get access to the right computer. And therein lies the rub. See, I could probably find this Pill Man for you—at least I *might* be able to, but it would take me longer than it would take you, because you've got the right demographics."

"You kidding me? I don't have the right demographics for shit. Young, black, and female. Wait a minute; young, black, female, and *fat*—maybe I should run for president."

"Who do you think your typical office worker is in this town?"

Talba got it. She cocked her head and grinned. "A brilliant poet in disguise?"

"Disguise. Now that's the key word, darlin'. That's the key word. Here's my proposition—you work for me on a case I got, and I'll turn you into a private investigator."

"Oh, great." Talba swept open an arm, indicating her humble surroundings. "Then I can be rich like you."

"Then you can find the Pill Man yourself."

She came alert, sitting up straight, as the implications of it hit her. She realized how much she'd love it—

tracking down the slimy bastard all by herself. Oh, yes! She'd adore it.

She said, "Who do I have to kill? And more to the point, how much do I get paid?"

"You're not an assassin, you're a spy. And you don't get paid anything—by me."

"Oh, great, this is like one of those internships where you're supposed to be grateful for the privilege of working for free."

"It's not a bit like those. You got a chip on your shoulder—anybody ever tell you that? Is it because you're black or because you're female?"

She ignored him—she'd often been told she had a chip on her shoulder. "How's this different?"

"Because you do get paid—while undergoin' a veritable graduate seminar in investigative techniques. It's more like those scholarships where they pay *you* for goin' to school. You know—the ones black people get."

"Thought you weren't a racist, Mr. Allred."

"Just seein' if you're awake."

It occurred to her that he had the rudiments of a sense of humor, however crude.

"See, what happens," he continued, "is you get a job over at United Oil and *they* pay you. You think anybody'd believe me as an office worker? No way. But you've not only got the right demographics, you're real bright and real attractive. No way you're not gonna get the job."

"What job?"

"Well, any job they've got, to tell you the truth. All you have to do is get in the building, figure out how to get to a particular person's computer, and rifle it."

"That's all?"

"That's all."

"How's that going to help me find the Pill Man?"

"While you're doing that, I'm going to make a few preliminary inquiries—but I think it's going to come down to the same thing. Getting the right job and getting into a computer."

Talba slapped a hand to her mouth. "Oh, my God."

"What?"

"Sure. Sure, I could do that. I don't know why I didn't see it before." The scenario was suddenly crystal-clear to her—exactly the way to get the information she wanted. She could bypass Allred altogether.

On the other hand, his proposition appealed to her. And there was certainly the possibility of her plan backfiring. She could use his job as a dry run and figure out what obstacles she might run into. She said, "When do I start?"

"Why not now? United uses an agency called Comp-Temps."

"They might as well call it Nerds 'R' Us."

"You got it. Go over to CompTemps and get yourself hired. Just do what they tell you, keep your eyes open, and come by after work."

"Hold it. Hold it, Mr. Allred. I'm missing something here. United Oil can't be their only client. Granted, it's a big company and there might be quite a few openings there—but what if they send me out on some other job? I mean, when you consider the likelihood—"

He patted empty space. "Ms. Wallis. Calm down now. When you're an old beat-up PI with the wrong demographics, you gotta figure out some way to stay in business. I got a mutually beneficial arrangement with a gentleman at CompTemps named L. J. Currie."

He sat back smugly, letting her take it in. When she thought she thoroughly had the hang of it, she wasn't at all sure she wanted to be involved with such a scheme. Or more accurately, she was quite sure she did—she simply understood that she wasn't supposed to want to. She summoned as acid a tone as she could. "How nice for Mr. Currie. Industrial espionage must pay handsomely."

"Well, I don't know about that, but it keeps him out of jail. See, I know a thing or two about Mr. Currie."

"And the minute he helped you the first time, you knew something else about him."

"There's more to the information highway than the Internet."

Talba went over to Gravier Street, where CompTemps had its offices, resisting the urge to brush off the sleaze like so much lint.

Within the hour, she was walking into the air-conditioned chambers of United Oil Company, where she was sent to the seventeenth floor to do a job so easy she could perform it in her sleep—setting up new work-stations. They had staff people installing the network cabling and routers and printers—pretty much a grunt-work job, but one that had to be supervised by someone who knew the whole system. Cheapo temps like herself could install the software.

At the end of the day, she went back to Allred's office, where she found him having a drink and reading the paper, his feet up on his desk.

"You look like something out of an old movie. Real old."

He gave her a half grin. "I try. Drink, Ms. Wallis?"

"No thanks."

Allred took his feet off the desk and sat up in his chair, acting more businesslike. "What department they put you in?"

"Acquisitions and Property."

"Ho!" It was an exclamation almost of disbelief. He struck the table as he said it. "Currie's gone and outdone himself. Who you workin' for?"

"With, Mr. Allred, with. I'm working *with* a brother and a white man who are in exceptionally crabby moods because they're software designers who got pulled off their current fascinating assignments to do stupid tech work."

"A brother. Well, well, well. Better and better. Were you nice to Mr. Brother?"

"Aka Mr. Robert Tyson, no relation to Mike." Talba crossed her fingers. "We're like that." In fact, it had oc-curred to her that, once she found the Pill Man, she might want a cushy job designing software at United Oil, and Mr. Robert Tyson might be just the person to help her. She'd spent a good part of the day buddying up to him. He was nice, he was smart, he was pissed off because he couldn't get no respect, and she was all sympathy. Allred said, "The guy we're interested in is Russell Fortier. I think he might be in your department."

"I'm not sure, but I might have heard the name. He's a muck-a-muck, isn't he?"

"I believe his title is manager of property. Think you can locate his office?"

"Sure."

"Take a look at this." He held up a tiny object. "Hold out your hand."

He dropped the object into her palm.

"Know what it is?"

It didn't look like anything much, but she had a hunch. "It must be a bug."

"Excellent, Ms. Wallis. Go to the head of the class. It's a little receiver. You need to get that in his office somewhere."

"His office? I can get in his computer a lot easier than I can get in his office. How am I going to do that?"

"Well, now. Here's where you learn to be a detective. That's gon' have to be your problem—you're the operative on the scene."

There was nothing to do but bull ahead. "Okay, I'll figure it out."

"Good. Do it tomorrow and report in. How long's the job supposed to last—the installation thing?"

"Till the end of the week."

"Okay. Work out the week. If they extend the job, I want you to keep working."

"Is that all? Just install the bug? I thought I had to get into a computer."

"Be patient, Ms. Wallis. One thing at a time."

She searched out Fortier first thing the next day, finding, in fact, that his office was three or four doors from where she was working. Peeking in, she couldn't see much, but the morning wasn't half over before he was standing in front of her desk. "Hey there." He stuck out his hand. "I'm Russell Fortier."

"Talba Wallis."

He had a firm grip, as well he should. He was tall and broad-shouldered, with short brown hair like half the white men who worked in the building. His hair had golden glints in it, though, as if he spent time in the sun, and his skin was slightly weathered, in a pleasant sort of way. He wore a striped shirt, which was too stuffy for her taste, but otherwise she liked him. He didn't seem the sort to take life too seriously.

He said, "Is Robert Tyson around here? I've got to ask him something."

She was impressed that he had come for Tyson himself instead of sending his secretary.

When he had gone, she asked Tyson, "What's the story on him? He seemed kind of—I don't know—human."

"Fortier?" he said. "Real good guy. One of the best."

She felt a qualm or two about bugging his office, but what the hell, a job was a job. She could do it after work if no one was around.

When the time came, she left her sweater at her desk, took the elevator to another floor, went to the ladies' room just to pass the time, went back, sneaked into Fortier's office, and planted the bug, all in about ten minutes.

She reported in that night from home.

"Well, congratulations, Ms. Dick," said Allred. "Good job."

"What now?"

"Install those systems, baby. That's all you have to do."

At the end of the week, the job was extended. Through no fault of their own, she and Robert Tyson and company weren't done yet—several more departments needed new systems. She was getting to know the United building pretty well.

At the end of the next, she still had a job. She'd been a United Oil employee about ten days—long enough to be joining in the office gossip—when Allred called her. "New assignment."

"Damn. I was just starting to feel at home."

"Good, because it's there. I want you to get into Fortier's computer."

"Piece of cake."

"I've got something for you. Can you come to the office tonight?"

"I was going to paint my toenails."

When she got there, he handed over a list of names, none of which Talba recognized.

"I want you to go into Fortier's computer and see if you can find documents containing any of these names. Can you do that?"

"Probably in about five and a half minutes."

"You're pretty cocky."

"Evidently you don't have Windows 95."

"Are you kidding? I still use a manual typewriter."

"Windows 95 has a 'Find' command. Kind of takes the challenge out of it."

"Okay, okay." Allred sounded grumpy. "Can you copy the documents?"

"Will they fit on a disk or do I need my Zip drive?"

"Needless to say, Ms. Nerd Queen, I haven't the least idea what a Zip drive is."

"Never mind. How long might these documents be?"

"How should I know? I haven't stolen them yet."

"You mean *I* haven't."

"My guess is, they aren't long. We're probably talking about a hundred pages or less."

"No problem. Disk it is." But she made a mental note to take her Zip drive just in case.

"You sound pretty damn confident."

"I told you. I'm good." The only hard part would be getting into Fortier's office, and she'd already done it once. All she really had to do was an instant replay. If most people went home on time, it shouldn't be a problem.

And sure enough, it was the piece of cake she'd predicted. She sneaked back in, brought up the "Find" command, typed in one of the names, clicked the "Find

Now" button, and kept doing it until she had nearly all the names—and all in a single file, called "Skinacat," which she copied onto a disk.

She sneaked a peek before she copied it, but it was about as sexy as a sock drawer—just names and numbers, as far as she could see.

If it was something dishonest, or otherwise secret, it was odd, she thought, that Fortier had done nothing to hide it except give it a funny name. But on the other hand, she half expected that. It didn't occur to the average office worker that his or her drive might be shared. This one wasn't, but she could fix that. Easily.

She knew from having spent a couple of weeks installing software that United's network system was set up with multiple protocols. That meant that, with only a few clicks of the mouse, she could arrange to search Fortier's workstation from her own anytime she wanted.

She went into the control panel, and pretty soon read these kind and generous words: "I want to give others access to my files." Ha! Four more clicks to "Access Type." Triumphantly, she selected "Full."

That was all. Next time Allred wanted something, she could get it by nine-fifteen without leaving her desk.

She caught the PI once again with his feet up and a glass in his hand. He didn't even say hello—just nodded. "Let's see what you got."

Talba popped the disk into her laptop and showed him. Unabashedly, he hollered, "Whoopee!"

Talba made a face. She was about to lecture him on the merits of being cool when he turned to her and beamed. "You done good, girl. You done real good." She didn't have the heart after that.

But she did say, "How's all this going to help me find the Pill Man?"

"You know what to do now, don't you? Just put on your simple temp disguise, get the right job, and rifle the right computer."

To her surprise, she really thought she could do it. It might take a while, but she had forever. As it was, she'd waited twenty-two years, which was how long she'd been alive.

"But come back," Allred said. "Do some more work for me and I'll teach you more secrets."

"When?"

"I'll call you."

Langdon brought her back to the present. "So what was on the disk?"

"I told you. I don't know. I wondered . . . when I saw the office was ransacked, I wondered if that was what the guy in the ski mask was looking for. I mean, with Fortier missing, and Gene dead—there's got to be a connection."

"You don't remember a thing on that disk? Not even one name?"

"No. Nothing meant anything. Look, if I opened the phone book and picked out twenty names, do you think I'd remember a one of them in half an hour? Do you think you would?"

"When was all this?"

"A few days ago. I haven't heard from Gene since."

"Who was the client?"

"I don't know. We never discussed it."

For some reason, that sounded more professional than the truth. Talba had begged to know the client's name—to know what it was all about, this thing she'd worked on for so long.

But Allred couldn't be budged.

Six

RAY BOUDREAUX WASN'T much on poetry, his knowledge beginning and ending somewhere in "Purple Cow" territory, but he was always up for something new. And not only that, he wanted to see The Baroness face-to-face.

So here he was, sitting way the hell in the back at some hole-in-the-wall black-owned restaurant, looking around at a crowd that probably consisted mostly of the poet's friends and family members. But his was by no means the only white face.

The cop was there, for one thing—he knew her from watching Bebe. He hadn't been sure she'd come, but here she was with a couple of teenage kids, and a man. Ray had left her a very simple message: "Sunday night—don't miss the poet called The Baroness. You could learn a lot."

He'd left several of those messages.

To his amazement, all the recipients had taken the bait.

There were three poets on the program, and The Baroness was last. By the time they got to her, he was about ready to walk out. These poets were loud and they were dumb and they didn't make any sense. None of that surprised him except the loud part—he hadn't expected to become a poetry lover at this late date, but he hadn't thought he'd be yelled at.

Yet, almost the minute The Baroness walked to the mike, he was glad he'd stayed. She had fabulous purple robes and that crazy wild hair—how did black people get it like that? A pretty face, of course, but big deal. That wasn't it. Something about her was galvanizing, made him sit up in his chair and feel the bottom of his spine and the top of his head; made his fingers tingle.

It wasn't a sexual thing—there wasn't anything sexual about it, his wife was right there. But it was *like* sex. It was a sense of excitement, a feeling of something big about to happen.

Must be stage presence, he thought. *Star quality, something like that. Well, I knew this was no ordinary chickie-poo. Hoped not, anyway.*

She had a voice like butterscotch sauce, and she sort of singsonged her lines, didn't yell at all, made you feel instead like you were sitting in a warm bath.

At first she just started out talking. "There was a poet named Mr. T. S. Eliot, who you'd expect me to hate on grounds of political correctness, but who speaks to me, not only in the *Four Quartets* and shit like that, but also in a lesser work on which a famous Broadway show is based. Mr. Eliot wrote about cats.

"And Mr. Eliot wrote that every cat has three names—his formal name, like Buckaroo, say; the name the family calls him, like Bucky, maybe; and the secret name he calls himself, like King Ahmat the Nineteenth of Chichunga."

While she talked, a man with dreads for days arranged a series of paintings behind her—one of cats, one that looked vaguely medical, a domestic scene, and the poet reclining, a crown on her head.

The Baroness produced a piece of paper and said, "I am like a cat."

And then she repeated the phrase, reading this time, so you'd be sure it was the title:

I Am Like a Cat

When I was born, I was a little piece of toffee.
Brown toffee.

Soft and sweet and just as innocent as the baby Jesus.
Just as innocent as my mama.
Or maybe I should say my sweet mama was just as
innocent as her own sweet baby.
My sweet mama was so proud.

Here the poet's voice rose. She said the word "proud"
like three words. She repeated the line.

My sweet mama was so proud.
Even though her own sweet baby was born at
Charity Hospital–
(Couldn't have been worse—there ain't really no
St. James Infirmary)
She was lyin' there at Charity like Cleopatra in exile,
and she says to the Pill Man, the one pulled her
baby out of her womb and stopped that relentless
screaming pain.
She says to that nice young man,
"What you think I ought to name my baby?"
My mama so proud of her little piece of toffee,
She wants to name her somethin' fine.
Somethin' fancy.
Somethin' so special ain' no other little girl got the
same name.
And the doctor say, "Name that girl Urethra."
And my mama, she just as pleased, and she so proud,
And she say, "That's a beautiful name. Ain' nobody
in my neighborhood name Urethra.
"We got Sallies and we got Janes and we got
Melissas and Saras—we got LaTonyas, just
startin' to have Keishas—but ain' nobody else
name Urethra.
I'm gon' name my baby Urethra for sure."
And that's my first name—the one they put on my
birth certificate.
I am named Urethra. Now ain't that a beautiful
name?

But somebody knew. *Somebody in our*
neighborhood.
Somebody told my sweet mama she named her little
candy girl after some ol' tube you piss through.
My name is Piss Tube.
My name is Pee Place.
My name is Exit for Excreta.
And my sweet mama so proud.

Every time she said "proud," the poet went all out, so
that it came out like "prowwwwwwwwwwwwd." She delivered the last four lines with her eyes closed, and
started up again, snapping them open.

Now she call me "Sandra."
I never did find out why.
Must be for the sand got in her eyes when she listen
to that white man.
Do I look like a Sandra to you?
My name is Urethra.
My name is Exit for Excreta.

The poet's voice rose again—in fact, Ray had to
admit she did yell, but even so, her voice was still like
butterscotch.

And I am a baroness.
Because a cat has three names,
And I am like a cat.
My sweet mama's broken and weak now,
After what that white man did to her—
She never did trust no one again, black or white.
And I can never say again, "My mama's proud."
But I am a baroness.
And I'm so proud.
I didn't want no African name,
'Cause I am African American, *love it or hate it,*
And I didn't want no LaTonya, I didn't want no

67

LaKeisha Latifah, Tanisha, Marquita,
Shamika—
White asshole steal somethin' from me,
I'm gon' steal somethin' right back—
I AM THE BARONESS DE PONTALBA,
And you can kiss my artistocratic black ass.

Having hollered out the last three words as if the entire state of Louisiana had suddenly gone deaf, the poet bowed her head demurely, a shy light in her eyes. "Thank you," she said, or so Ray surmised. Her lips moved, but he couldn't hear for the applause, his own included. Without even thinking, he rose to his feet, as did the rest of the audience, some of them shouting, "Yeah," and "Brava."

The woman had something. Ray Boudreaux would not have described himself as a flaming liberal, yet tears had sprung to his eyes when she said the word "Urethra." When she hollered, "prowwwwwwd."

His wife touched his elbow. "Do you think it's true?"

He was shocked. It never occurred to him that it wasn't true. The woman's name was Exit for Excreta, he was sure of it. "Don't you?" he said, and she shrugged.

The room spun for a second as he felt a wave of disbelief in himself. Was he as innocent and easily gulled as the poet's mother? Was that what his problem was?

The Baroness called for the man with dreads. "And this is Lamar," she said. "My partner in crime."

More applause, while Lamar set up a new group of canvases, abstract this time, very different from the first, which had been merely a backdrop for the poet. These seemed to come from the heart.

She was starting to read again.

They have little yellow heads and bright green legs
made out of silk
They have tiny little brains and tiny little bones

and zillion-dollar homes
That they won't leave.

They travel in a flock and
They never leave their block
And their husbands have no cocks—
Or then again they might.
The parakeets don't know
Because the parakeets don't care
Because the parakeets don't dare

Have any thoughts,
Feelings
Ideas
Sensations
Fun
Opinions
or
Desires.

But the parakeets do scare.
See a brother comin' down the street,
That little bird's gonna vote with her feet.

They have tiny little bones and tiny little brains
And a whole shitload full of disdains.

Ray's attention wandered. He didn't think this poem was nearly as successful as the first; in fact, wasn't even sure what it was about—a certain kind of woman, evidently.

His wife poked him. "Now, this one I like."

"Why?"

"Oh, you know those girls. Those parakeets."

"What girls?"

"The ones with the tiny little bones. *You* know. They chirp."

Ray guessed it was a woman thing.

The Baroness finished the parakeet poem and sipped

water, giving Lamar time to change the scenery. She continued reading for another twenty minutes, but, for Ray, none of the poems was as powerful as the one about her names. When she had taken her bow and started walking among her devoted fans, trailing yards of purple fabric, he listened to her banter with them.

This was the part of the evening he was looking forward to.

And the thing he was hoping for was happening. A group was forming around the cop.

A gorgeous black woman arrived with her date, who was no less attractive than she. The teenage girl got up and hugged the man. The boy slapped him a high five.

"Hey, Darryl. How's it goin', man?"

"Hey, Kenny. Whereyat? Does anyone say that anymore?"

Darryl. Ray wrote it down.

"Hey, Lou-Lou."

"What are you kids doin' up?"

"Auntie's exposing us to culture."

Lou-Lou. Cindy Lou Wootten, the police shrink.

"Lou-Lou, what are you doing here?" The cop was talking.

The shrink rolled her eyes. "Now that's a story. Later for that."

The girl said, "Are you guys dating?"

"Dating? Naaah, we practically hate each other. We made a deal—I escort her to this and she talks to one of my classes."

"Good, 'cause I might want to marry you."

The Baroness had come up behind him: "You and me both, honey. My name's Your Excellency, what's yours?"

The man bowed nearly to the waist. "Your Humble Servant. Humble for short."

Cindy Lou snorted. "Dear God."

The Baroness bristled. "What's the matter? You didn't like the reading?"

"Oh, I did like it. I liked it very much. I'm Cindy Lou

70

Wootten. And this is Darryl Boucree. You're welcome to him, Baroness." And she leaned over to whisper to the cop.

Next the reporter came over. Ray was nearly beside himself.

"Baroness? I'm Jane Storey. Fine reading! Lovely reading. Is it really true about your name?"

"Oh, Lord, did Chaucer have this problem? Did people come up and say, 'Is the Wife of Bath a real person? And if she is, could you get me a date with her?' "

"No, really. I'm a reporter and—"

"You're a *reporter*? Why didn't you say so? Are you doing a story on me?"

"Actually—uh—that isn't why I'm here, but—"

"You're a fan! Is that why you're here?"

"I think we need to talk."

Jane Storey glanced at the cop and then disappeared with The Baroness.

The man with Langdon, probably Steve Steinman, spoke for the first time. "That name thing didn't ring true for me. I'm sorry, but nobody would name their kid Urethra. Even as metaphor—"

The teenage boy interrupted. "It is true! I know a kid whose dad did his internship at Charity and he tells stories about that."

"What kind of stories?"

"*Revolting* stories. Disgusting stories. About how black women used to come in and they'd have so many children they couldn't think of any new names and so they'd ask the interns. Just like in the poem. And then the interns would always say something like Urethra or Gonorrhea." He pronounced it Go-*nore*-ia. "Or Phyllis and *Syph*ilis for twins."

"Good God!"

But Langdon laughed. "I'll bet everybody in New Orleans has heard at least some version of the story. I've always wondered if it was urban myth or not. It's hard to believe people could be that mean, but they always tell it with pride in their meanness. Like it's the most hilarious thing in the world."

The girl looked down at her lap. "Kind of makes you ashamed to be white."

Darryl Boucree tousled her hair. "Take it easy, kid. White's okay."

Steve Steinman gestured at an empty chair. "Why don't you two sit down? What are you doing here, anyway?"

The man spoke quietly, but Ray could just make out the words: "Lou-Lou got some kind of threat; I'm not sure what it was but when I called her about the speaking thing, she was practically crying. So I offered to bring her." He glanced briefly at the psychologist, who was deep in conversation with Langdon, and then back at Steinman. "You think the dude in dreads is her boyfriend?"

"Cindy Lou's?"

"No, man. The Baroness's."

Steinman laughed. "Now don't you be getting above your station."

"Would a Baroness date a common man?"

"You can't date her, man. I forbid it."

"Why?"

" 'Cause you'd lose your dignity, that's why. Say you got lucky and that magic moment came along. Are you gonna holler, 'Urethra, Urethra!'?"

The shrink turned toward them and spoke with disdain: "Are you two ever going to grow up?"

Ray didn't know what to make of it. He hadn't known they were all friends. He wondered if that would help or hurt him.

The reporter came back with The Baroness. Jane was frowning. "Skip, can I talk to you?"

Darryl Boucree bowed again to the poet. "Your Excellency. May I have an audience?"

"Speak, serf."

"Would you do me the honor of talking to my high-school English class?"

"Are you kidding? Me, a role model?"

Boucree wiped the smile off his face. "Yeah. Yeah, you really are. You don't know how much they need one."

"My story's true, you know."

"About your name? I am truly, truly sorry if it is."

"Don't be. One day I'm gonna get that Pill Man."

Seven

WHAT A SELF-PROMOTER. *But there's something about her. I don't know—maybe it's a story and maybe it's not.* Jane would have given anything to discuss The Baroness with Walter. At the very least he would have had something wry to say about her, and it would probably have been wise as well.

Jane found herself smiling and shaking her head when she thought about the poet—the way you do with a naughty but charming child. The Baroness had gone and done what everyone would like to do—she'd re-created herself.

Maybe I'm envious, Jane thought. *The thing about being a reporter is, it's not living, it's just watching. And sometimes you can't tell what you're seeing.*

She'd been excited when Talba took her aside, but all she got was a pitch to do a story on her. She was starting to get the feeling she was being manipulated in a way that didn't serve her—because, of course, she was being manipulated; she'd known that from the first. The trade-off—information in return for being the tipster's pawn—had seemed fair enough at first. But maybe the thing was spinning out of control.

She snatched up the phone when it rang, ready to hit the tipster with a big piece of her mind. But it was an unexpected announcement from below. "Skip Langdon to see you."

"Not again," she almost said, but her heart beat a little

faster. This ought to be enlightening. "Tell her to meet me on the second floor."

Skip was grinning. She had on a pair of black draw-string pants and a taupe T-shirt: Ms. Non-Fashion as usual. "Hey there, culture vulture."

"Let's get some coffee."

"Let's talk poetry."

The *T-P* cafeteria was really pretty nice—lots of light and the scent of red beans and rice. Jane didn't mind entertaining there.

"So," she said, when they were settled. "How'd you like the reading?"

"Does it occur to you we're bumping into each other an awful lot?"

Jane nodded. "I was pretty surprised to see you last night."

"So was Cindy Lou. She got an anonymous call telling her to attend—the caller said she'd better be ready to defend herself. I got a tip myself. The Baroness claims she doesn't know what we're talking about."

Jane sipped, so she wouldn't have to say anything, but Skip kept staring. Finally she settled on, "Umm."

"Could I ask why you were there?"

"You could, but I probably wouldn't tell you."

"In that case, I'm going to guess. Whoever told you about Cindy Lou and Russell Fortier summoned you to the reading as well. And because Cindy Lou and I received anonymous calls, I'm going to guess that you did, too. Unless you were both acting, The Baroness didn't know who you were. Therefore, it wasn't she. Moving on to another subject—you had all your *i*'s dotted and your *t*'s crossed in your Gene Allred story. You have Saturday off, don't you? How'd you end up covering that story?"

Jane's armpits were clammy. The bad feeling she'd been having when Skip arrived was turning into something like nausea. She held both hands up in front of her chest. "Okay, okay. I got an anonymous tip."

"Ah. Now we're getting somewhere. What did the tip-ster say?"

"Just that there'd been a murder I might be interested in. Because of the other tips, I thought it might have something to do with Russell Fortier. That's why I asked."

"And did you ask Ms. Wallis about that?"

Jane nodded. "She denied all knowledge. Her agenda was to get in the paper. Period."

"Pretty interesting poem about her name."

Jane looked out the window, still undecided. "Yes, I might write something . . . I don't know." She fixed Skip with a glare. "Now I'm asking you—does Allred's death have something to do with Russell Fortier?"

"Off the record?"

Jane wrinkled her nose. "Three little words I love to hate. Okay—off the record."

"Probably. I'm telling you because this thing's nasty. Your tipster could be a murderer, Jane. You watch yourself." Skip pushed back her chair and stood up. "Thanks for the coffee."

Jane was sweating again—and it wasn't the coffee. The tipster knew her phone number. When she got home from the reading last night, there'd been a message on her machine: "Nice story this morning. I'll have something good for you soon."

Mentally, Skip went over the faces of the white men she'd noticed at Talba's reading—or tried to. There were probably ten or twelve and some of them were sitting behind her. Also, it was more dark than light in the restaurant, and a lot of the time she'd been surrounded by people she knew. It had occurred to her last night that the tipster was there, but no one stood out, even seemed worth watching. No one strange approached her or Cindy Lou or the poet.

Of course, the man needn't be white, but she thought he was—mostly because of his accent. It wasn't foolproof, but it was playing the odds.

She was disappointed in her visit with Jane Storey— she was pretty sure the reporter had told her all she

76

knew, which was exactly how much Skip knew. Someone was manipulating both of them.

On the other hand, the informant hadn't lied. Skip had found out something by attending Talba's reading—she'd understood the extent of the tipster's machinations.

She had the feeling of walking in quicksand—she really had no idea where solid ground might be, after a great snowball of a weekend that had led, so far, to nothing.

Immediately after her Saturday afternoon talk with Talba, which had seemed so productive at the time, she'd made a beeline for the offices of United Oil, which, as she'd hoped, were populated mostly with security staff and the random weekend warrior.

A few cover-the-butt calls, a little huffing and puffing on the part of executives reached by phone, and she was in Russell Fortier's computer—and without even mentioning the murder case. She pinned the whole mission on Fortier's disappearance.

The computer, however, proved to harbor neither a file called "Skinacat," nor any file containing either "skin" or "cat" in its name. Someone had undoubtedly been there before her.

Frustrated, she finally called Wilson, the Third's own computer nerd, to see if he had any tips, and nothing would do but he had to come down and join her and rifle through electronic files himself. And still no "Skinacat"—nor, for that matter, anything else of interest.

She and Wilson took a pretty thorough spin, to no avail, through Fortier's computer, finding he didn't even have a calendar program. Then she had a look through his desk drawers and checked out his calendar—the old-fashioned kind that sat on his desk. He had dates for this week, the following week, and the one after. There was nothing at all to indicate he'd been planning a change of scenery.

She began to look carefully at the names, then to thumb backward for repeats. Cindy Lou's was absent, anyway. Almost all names were written out—there were no coy initials and very few women's names.

Finally she left, with his calendar, his Rolodex, and Talba's bug in a plastic bag.

Next had come the odd tip about the poetry reading, and on Sunday, Talba's performance, with its assembled cast of characters.

And then the weekend was over and she was up to her knees in quicksand.

It was time for another talk with Bebe.

She found the councilwoman in neat black slacks and a red silk blouse. Bebe looked as if she'd lost weight; her cheeks were a little sunken, her eyes seemed to turn down at the corners. *The haunted look,* Skip thought.

She said, "How are you holding up?"

Bebe put a hand to her mouth, and Skip could see that the hand held a tissue. Bebe bit her fingers, trying not to cry. "My daughter's here. That helps a little."

"No word from anyone? Not Russell, not anyone with information?"

Bebe shook her head.

"Do you know a man named Gene Allred?"

She looked puzzled. "Allred? I know the name, but I don't know why."

"He was a private detective."

"The murdered man! Of course. I read about him."

"Did you know him?"

"I never heard of him before yesterday. Why?"

"There could be a connection to Russell's disappearance."

"How is that possible?"

"Someone seems to have hired him to investigate your husband." She raised a hand to serve as a wall against the inevitable questions. "Does the phrase 'Skinacat' mean anything to you?"

The other woman was shaking her head, looking as if Skip had lost her mind. "No. Nothing."

"Okay, let's move on to a difficult subject."

Bebe gave Skip a cool, direct glance. "Women."

Skip nodded.

The councilwoman shook her head again. "I don't think so. I've thought long and hard about it. Russell's just too straitlaced. He'd be too guilty."

"He's straitlaced. Okay, there's something I didn't know. Talk to me about him. Help me form a picture of this man I'm looking for."

"Well . . ." She shrugged. "He's a great husband and family man. He's almost dull—goes to work, plays golf, sails. Church on Sunday; Friday lunch at Galatoire's. One martini a night."

Skip raised an eyebrow. "You find him dull?"

"Dull? Why do you ask?"

"I thought you just said so."

"Oh, no. I just meant his stats. He's very interesting to talk to."

"What does he like to talk about?"

"Oh . . . uh . . . city government. What's going on. He gives me advice about my job—we talk about that a lot. And our friends. We gossip."

"Who would you say are his best male friends?"

"Douglas Seaberry and Beau Cavignac, I guess. Beau's probably his best friend. He's going crazy right now—almost crazier than me."

"Where can I find them?"

"Also at United Oil. In the same department as Russell. And Edward's there, too. My cousin, Edward Favret. They all play golf—they even go away on weekends together. Duck hunting and sailing and stuff. I just can't imagine . . ."

Fearing a session of tears and nose-blowing, Skip interrupted. "Okay. I'm sorry I had to probe, but . . . it was necessary."

"Meaning his body hasn't turned up, and he's not in a hospital."

Skip said, "Listen, thanks for your time," and left.

For friends, it looked like one-stop shopping. Except for the Cindy Lou episode, Bebe seemed to have called it—Russell sounded dull. He went to work and played golf with his work buddies. Yikes.

She headed once more for the United Oil building.

Though police officers usually manage to go anywhere they want, Skip found she couldn't control every situation as thoroughly as she'd like. She asked for Cavignac first and was told his line was busy.

Seaberry wasn't in his office. That left Favret, whom she found in conference with his secretary about what refreshments to offer a police officer. There was another man in his office.

Favret rose, the picture of Southern graciousness. Or Southern WASPishness, Skip thought, with slight disdain. Despite efforts to meditate, possibly find religion, and peel off prejudice like a potato skin, she found certain men a little too smooth.

On the face of it, there was nothing wrong with Favret. He was well over six feet tall, and thin, built on elegant lines. His brown hair was streaked with blond, as if he'd graduated from Tulane last month instead of twenty years ago. He had a youthful, open look—even friendly. Skip didn't trust him at all.

The other man rose as well and stuck out his hand. "Douglas Seaberry."

"Bebe called us," Favret explained. "She thought you'd like to see both of us."

Skip raised an eyebrow: Might as well go for broke. "She also mentioned a Beau Cavignac."

The two men exchanged glances. The secretary said, "Would you like some coffee?" and Seaberry said, "He asked us to make his apologies—he's on a conference call."

Seaberry was darker than Favret, with graying hair, at the stage when a man is beginning to make the transition from youthful to distinguished—so easy for men, so difficult for women. He wore glasses, and he was also tall, yet not nearly so lanky as Favret. He probably worked out every day of his life. He smiled, showing teeth so perfect you almost wanted to get bitten. "Would you like to sit down?"

She thought it was odd, his offering when it was Favret's office.

"Thank you, I'd prefer to talk to you one at a time."

Again they looked at each other and seemed to shrug slightly, almost in unison. She had the odd sense they'd just evaluated her and found her wanting, as if they'd agreed tacitly not to let her in their club. Seaberry looked at his watch. "Certainly. Edward, I have a lunch date in ten minutes. Would you mind if I took Detective Langdon back to my office?"

"Of course not. Go right ahead."

Skip followed Seaberry to a large corner office, which told her more about both men and their relationship than half an hour in Favret's office would have. On impulse, she said, "Are you Russell's boss?"

He sat down, lowering his head slightly, possibly meaning to seem modest. He picked up a pencil and tapped his desk with it. "Not for long. He's headed for big things at United—real big things. And sooner rather than later." He frowned. "Or at least he was. We're worried sick about him. The crime in this town . . ."

"Tell me about him, Mr. Seaberry."

"Could we . . . uh—anything we can do to help you guys?"

"I beg your pardon?"

"I mean, can't we offer a reward or something?"

"Sure. You can do that. And you can help me out with information—if you hear from him, for instance, call me right away."

Seaberry nodded, looking slightly relieved, as if he'd seen his duty and he'd done it.

"Now tell me about him."

"Russell? All-around good guy. Terrific sailor. Absolutely terrific. Loves to sail in a way that"—he stared past her for a moment, then pinned her with sharp brown eyes—"well, he loves the sea. He has a sort of spiritual feel for it."

Skip almost said what she thought—that "spiritual" was the last word she expected to hear in the halls of the United Oil Company.

"I have a very bad feeling about this, Detective Langdon. Russell Fortier isn't the kind of man who disappears."

"What do you think happened to him?"

Seaberry lowered both head and voice.

"I think he's dead. I think he's a holdup victim—you just haven't found the body yet."

Skip nodded, pressing her lips together. "I might agree with you but . . ." She paused and let the pause last, looked into space as Seaberry had done.

He bit. "But what, Detective?" She thought he looked slightly anxious.

"The airport. The fact that he was at the airport. It's a little on the pat side."

Seaberry shrugged and spread his arms, palms up, showing he had no weapons, nothing to hide, and not a dangerous bone in his body. "I don't know. Is it?"

The interview went on like that, Seaberry insisting Russell was a good guy with nothing to hide and Skip hovering between boredom and disbelief. Finally, she left him, wondering if it was really possible to know so little about someone with whom you spent long, cold hours crouching in a duck blind—and deciding that if both parties were men, it was.

When she got back to Favret's office, she found only an apology delivered via his secretary—Mr. Favret was so sorry he had to leave for lunch.

Ah, well, she thought. *I'll show him. I'll go see him at home.*

She asked Favret's secretary to direct her to Beau Cavignac's office, something the woman seemed loath to do—corporate discipline appeared downright military in this place.

But in the end, Skip prevailed, finding Beau Cavignac wearing a worried look—a perennial one, she surmised after a bit. He was a shorter, chunkier man than either of his two companions. He probably jogged but didn't lift weights—he looked soft, especially in the middle, as if he never passed up a hunk of pecan pie.

His hair was thick and curly, worn short. His neck was thick as well, along with his waistline and very probably his ankles.

His eyes were brown, matching the curly hair, and also matching a prominent mole on his left cheek.

Skip said, "I hear you're a good friend of Russell Fortier's."

"Real good friend. Very good friend."

"Can you think of any reason he'd suddenly just disappear?"

"You mean, did someone have a contract out on him?"

She couldn't tell if he was kidding or not. She shrugged.

"Well, I'll tell you one thing," he said. "I don't think he's 'the victim of foul play' like everybody's saying around here."

"Why not?"

Doubt flickered across an already creased forehead. This one was clearly a worrier. "I guess I just don't want it to be true. He's my best friend—I can't deal with something like that."

He patted his pockets, looking down. Discreetly, Skip turned slightly away, thinking he was looking for a handkerchief. But apparently he didn't find one—he looked up with too-shiny eyes.

"Can you think of any reason why he'd want to disappear?" Skip asked.

For a split second, she saw something new in his face, something like pleading—or so she thought for a moment.

Apparently unable to compose himself, he only shook his head, again looking down.

The united front presented by Favret and Seaberry was so intimidating, and this such a respite, that she had a sudden thought—if ever there was a time to go for it, it was now. Obviously something was going on here—she wasn't ready to confront it directly, but she could shake a few trees.

She said, "How's business, Mr. Cavignac?"

"Great. Why?"

"Great for Russell? How's he doing in the company?"

He shrugged. "He's a rising star. Practically Alpha Centauri."

"Somehow I don't get that feeling. I think something was wrong."

"Uh-uh. Not with Russell. No way."

She left with the ardent desire to replant Talba's bug in Edward Favret's office. She didn't like his style—and besides, he'd stood her up.

In fact, she didn't like anybody's style at United Oil, even Beau's. That remark about the contract was just a little too flip.

They all mouthed the words, but they didn't seem that worried about their good buddy Russell.

Eight

RUSSELL HAD AT first delighted in all the little things you have to do when you become someone else. He had dyed his hair white-blond and cut it to a length of about a quarter-inch. Then he'd gone to a department store and bought a spray can of fake tanner, so he'd look like he'd been in the sun for the last twenty years. He was so thrilled with the result he completed the look by getting one ear pierced, which to him wasn't a gay look, it meant he'd sailed around the Horn. He hadn't yet, but he meant to, soon.

Next, what to do about clothes? He wore khaki, but the new guy wore white, he thought.

Dean Woolverton. The name signified nothing, he'd picked it out of the phone book before he left—Dean from one page, Woolverton from another. It had a good ring—sort of Italian and sort of something else. Hard to place; he liked that.

The Pearson 38 was a little too modest for the new persona—in fact, a sailboat probably wasn't right at all. Given a choice, Dean would probably prefer a powerboat. But it was what Russell could get for the amount of cash he had (and he had to pay cash), plus it suited him to a T. It was a nice, comfortable live-aboard sailboat. What more could he want? (If he were Russell, that is—if Dean had to have a sailboat, he would probably want a Hatteras.)

Dean had started to take shape only after Russell got the boat. He'd seen other guys around, looking way too

85

blond for their age and way too tan for their health, and he'd suddenly realized he had to change everything. So he went right into the head and started cutting his hair. By evening he was a different person. People looked at him differently. Or, rather, different people looked at him. Flashier women.

He hadn't the slightest attraction to flashy women.

He realized it would probably be difficult for men to take him seriously as well. He looked like a flake, and having no history certainly qualified him for one. Okay, then, he was going to have to be a former lawyer—someone who'd had a tragedy and taken to the sea. A tragedy that hurt him so severely he couldn't bear to talk about it—not a dirty little secret he was deeply ashamed of.

The second night after he left New Orleans, he was sitting in the cockpit sipping Scotch and water, most of his dreams having materialized, when he felt a nasty black hole in the bottom of his stomach.

It was where his life used to be. Having no one to talk to and a loathing for television, he actually wrote down a few things that were troubling him:

What will I do now? Who can I be, really? Should I have stayed?

It was a bold—possibly very bad—thing he'd done. He could still scarcely believe it. And yet, at the moment, the fear was greater than the exhilaration.

It's the damn hair, he thought. *I'll go back to looking normal as soon as everything blows over.*

It was so odd how he came to be here. He could have said it was because of his dad, who had provided both a worthy antagonist and the money. Or because of Bebe— of who she'd become and what their marriage was.

But really it was because of the five days he'd spent upside down in the hull of his offshore racing sailboat. The way he got in that predicament shocked him (as did much about his former life). He was a different person now, and not only because he was Dean Woolverton. Just two years ago, he'd been the kind of sailor—*Oh, say it,*

Dean, he thought, *the kind of adolescent*—who liked to race offshore, risking seventy-knot winds, which indeed he'd caught.

The boat's keel broke off at the hull. He watched it all happen, certain that death was coming in the next few minutes. When the boat started to capsize, the boom got loose and smashed a doghouse window. Water flooded the stern, but miraculously, that much weight in the stern caused the tip of the bow to flip up out of the water. In turn, the air trapped in the bow kept the boat afloat, upside down.

Russell was able to grab some crackers and candy bars; that was all except champagne and water. With the storm still raging, he tied himself with a fishing net to a shelf in the bow. And there he lay for five days in darkness. The dark may have been what made the difference. Because he could see nothing, he had a sense, after the storm was over, of floating not only through water, but also through space. He was nothing and he was nowhere, going nowhere—probably dying.

At first, hearing was the most important thing in his life. Every nuance of sound could mean sudden death— or maybe rescue. But after a while the boat became a habitat like a strange house, each noise at first frightening, but soon familiar, and finally, unnoticed.

There was nothing left then but thought. He thought for a long time only of his situation. Of whether he'd be rescued and how long it would take. He tried to imagine how the search would be organized and who would come for him—a helicopter or a ship?

He thought these thoughts again and again, obsessively going over the details—what the rescuers should do, how they should do it, what equipment they'd need. Finally, he realized, *What's the point? I can't control this.* But he couldn't stop obsessing. He could feel every muscle tight and ready for action, though there was nothing in the world he could do except cling to his shelf. He tried tensing and relaxing, but each fiber jumped

87

back to tense the second he relaxed. He fought sleep as if it were a dragon.

But in the end, it won. He slept for ten minutes or ten hours, he had no idea, awakening when the roiling of the sea finally stopped. The storm was over. Now rescue was possible.

He almost didn't care. That is, he no longer felt it necessary to act out the rescue in his head—he had bored himself silly with it.

For a while, it seemed, he had no thoughts at all. So he consciously cultivated them. He thought of Bebe, of making love to her, something he rarely did these days. Oddly, he couldn't get into it. What had happened to their sex life seemed a much more interesting subject. *I've been too busy,* he thought, *and so has she. How could we have let this happen?*

He vowed to change that if he were rescued. And he realized that he had thought "if"—and that, without realizing it, he'd gotten into that thing he'd heard about, that people in extremis do. He was bargaining with God.

He began consciously to do it, wondering first what he had to negotiate with.

Maybe he could wiggle out of the Skinners; maybe he could even stop the others. But the weight of what he had done engulfed him like a wave.

So much damage had been done. So many lives ruined.

Maybe he deserved to die.

He didn't get far with that one, but it was an easy progression from there to *I'm going to die. Might as well make peace.*

And that was what changed him. He couldn't say how or why, but the minute he thought the word "peace," it came over him. He slept again.

When he awoke, he was a different man. Maybe dead, maybe alive, he was ready for either thing. It was then that he began to float through space, and oddly, he enjoyed the sensation. His previous life at United Oil seemed to tiny, so unimportant. The things he had done were preposterous. He couldn't conceive of why he had done them.

He had passed the bargaining stage now. If he died, he died. If he didn't, things were going to be different, and not because he'd been a former atheist in a foxhole—because it was the way of the world as he understood it now; the only way he could live. If he lived.

When they finally came, he had no idea it had been five days, though that didn't seem unreasonable. It could have been two or ten just as easily—in the dark, in his floating womb, time as he knew it didn't exist.

At first he thought he was hallucinating. But when voices joined the engine noise of the rescue boat, his desire to live came back as strongly as if he were in the peak of condition rather than starving and cramped. He untied himself, eased into the freezing water, took a breath knowing it could be his last, dived, and swam toward the voices. He popped up two feet from the rescuers, startling them so severely that one of them screamed.

He wondered if his metamorphosis would last, and if it would show, and if he could talk about it.

As it happened, it did last in a sort of a way and only showed a little. He tried talking about it only once—to Bebe.

"You don't seem yourself," she had said, after time had passed.

"Something happened out there. I had a kind of revelation."

"Omigod. Don't tell me you found Jesus."

No, he thought. *I found myself.* It was an unbidden and indeed surprising thought that he wouldn't have dreamed of expressing—wasn't even sure he believed.

"I don't know if that's what you'd call it," he said. "I just had a sense of . . . I don't know, exactly. Simplicity, let's say, for lack of a better word."

"*Simplicity?* That was your revelation?"

"A kind of peacefulness." He had read about it—the

oneness, it was usually called, something like that. But nobody talked about it, and anyhow it was hard to remember it. It was a feeling that didn't stick with you; and yet, he didn't think he had to have the feeling every second to know what it meant.

But now, on the Pearson, sipping his Scotch and water, that notion he'd had about finding himself seemed slightly preposterous. He certainly wasn't comfortable in Dean Woolverton's skin.

And yet . . . and yet . . . he wasn't the old Russell Fortier either.

When he came off that boat, he was dazed. He went to work every day and tried not to think about what had happened. He certainly didn't try to interfere with the Skinners. After he came back, he simply found ways to avoid participating in their operations. He no longer had ambition for the things the Skinners could buy him—more power and more money. He had plenty of both.

"You just lie around and look at the ceiling," Bebe hollered one day. "What do you *want*, Russell? Anything?"

"I think," he had said, "a farm in Tuscany."

Bebe had physically drawn back. "What?"

"I don't know why I said that. I don't want anything."

"That's the problem," she said.

He didn't even want her. Or rather, he did want her. He wanted her to himself. He wanted the old Bebe, the romantic Bebe, who had time for him. Bebe the councilwoman had time for everyone *but* him. He didn't want a farm in Tuscany—he wanted two weeks with his wife in Tuscany.

He wanted to be absolved of his sins.

He wanted Eugenie home again (their daughter from boarding school).

There were things he wanted, all right. He just didn't know how to get them—even how to begin to get them, to broach the subject of getting them.

And then he saw Bebe kissing Ernest LaBarre.

Two weeks after that, he met Cindy Lou Wootten, who was two kinds of forbidden fruit, which, given his state of mind, made her irresistible. He proceded to make an ass of himself.

And after that, he couldn't climb out of his depression.

So when crazy Ray Boudreaux came along with all his crazy talk, that was the end of the line. He had actually phoned Bebe to say he wasn't coming home that night and driven out to Veterans Highway, where he had checked into a cheap motel and plopped down on the bed with his fingers laced under his head and stared up at the cottage cheese on the ceiling until morning.

He never again managed the feeling he had on the boat. But it became abundantly clear to him what he wanted, which was out.

He wanted to be off sailing, the wind in his hair, the spray on his face, land nowhere in sight.

His father had made it all possible.

"Mama," Talba said, "what'd you think? What'd you think of your baby?"

Her mama said, "Why you embarrass me like that? Don't nobody need to know about that name thing."

"Mama, it's the central event of my life."

"Yo' life! It ain' my life, too? You think you can just do what you want with ya life?"

Lamar said, "I didn't sell a damn thing. Didn't get but one inquiry."

As usual, Talba's attention went directly to him. "Oh, baby, I'm sorry. They loved it, though. They just didn't have any money. The poetry crowd's not the gallery crowd."

"I don't know why the hell I let you talk me into it."

Talba's mama sniffed. "She didn't talk you into nothin'. It was your idea from the git-go."

Talba saw him start to flare and braced herself. But Miz Clara just got up and flopped into the kitchen, wearing her ancient slippers. Talba absolutely couldn't understand why her mama was so mean to Lamar.

Blessedly, the phone rang.

A voice said, "This is the client."

"What?"

"I'm Gene Allred's client. The one you worked for."

Talba's heart started to pound. "What's your name?"

"Uh-uh. That's not for you to know. You did a damn good job, Ms. Wallis. Mr. Allred was real impressed with you."

His voice was familiar, but she didn't know why.

"He told me so on the phone. He said he had the file I needed, and I could pick it up the next morning."

Talba waited, but he seemed to be at a stopping place. Finally, she said, "Yeah?"

"Friday morning. You remember where you were Friday morning?"

She'd been at Allred's office.

"Meeting me," the man said. "The guy in the ski mask."

"The guy who's not Detective Skip Langdon."

"That's the guy. Listen, you want to work for me again?"

"You gotta be crazy."

"Hey, everybody says that. But I pay well, and the work's real easy."

Not wanting to contribute to her own delinquency, Talba didn't answer. She knew she should hang up, but he'd just said five or six magic words.

The man kept talking. "In fact, I've already paid you half. Why don't you check under your doormat? Go ahead. I'll wait for you."

She put the phone down on the table.

Lamar asked, "What's up?"

"I've got to go see something."

The cashier's check was for $750. She gave it to Lamar and picked up the phone again.

The client said, "Fifteen hundred dollars for one week's work—a day's, really. But you need to finish out the week so they don't get suspicious. Now, I know what Allred paid you: He let you keep your paycheck from United. Where else you gonna make this kind of money?"

He had a point. It wasn't a fortune, but it was sure more than she could get any other way, and it would buy her more time to get her career going.

"What do I have to do?" she said.

"Just what you did before. That's all there is to it. Get that file again."

Talba exhaled. If he wanted the file, he probably wasn't the murderer. "Are you saying you never got the file from Allred?"

"Girlfriend, he was dead when I got there. What does it take to get you to believe that?"

"Don't 'girlfriend' me, asshole. You don't have a real good record of telling the truth where I'm concerned. Besides, you roughed me up."

"I didn't kill Allred, if that's what you're worried about."

"Who did?"

"Frankly, I couldn't care less. I just want the damn file." He hung up.

She turned to Lamar, whose nose was already wrinkled in disapproval. "Who the hell was that?" he asked.

"The guy in the ski mask. He just offered me a job."

When she had outlined it for him, he said, "Uh-uh. No way. You're not doing it."

That irritated her. She said, "Oh, shut up, Lamar. I don't know who you think you are."

"Talba, Allred was killed for the damn file. Did you ever think about that?"

"How dumb do you think I am? Of course I thought about that." She was steaming.

"If the client was supposed to get it and the place was ransacked, and now he doesn't have it, what does that tell you? Whoever killed Allred for it would kill you to keep him from getting it. And that's on the off-chance Ski Mask isn't the murderer. Uh-uh. Too many variables. Uh-uh and no."

"You go fuck yourself, Lamar." Something about his attitude was making her downright evil.

He didn't stalk out, as she'd intended. He enfolded her in his arms. *Perverse bastard,* she thought, and kissed him.

Nine

PUTTING THE CHECK under the mat was a risk, but worth it to Ray. From the looks of the cottage, Talba needed money the worst kind of way, and half of fifteen hundred dollars ought to be damn persuasive.

He needed her to do this job. He knew she could get hired again, he knew she could get the file, and besides, he liked her. She was bright and she was computer-literate and she had the right demographics. How many detectives had those qualifications?

Besides, now that Russell Fortier was high-profile, anybody Ray went to was going to be suspicious. He didn't need that, and he didn't need screwups. He needed to get the damn job done.

He was a good ten years older than these assholes and they'd outwitted him, betrayed him, cheated him, and caused him to lose everything.

His daughter was on scholarship at Vanderbilt, and she was working as a waitress to stay there.

His son was at UNO because there was no money to send him anywhere else.

He and Lucille were living in a stupid little rented house with only one bathroom.

A year ago they'd had a gorgeous, reproduction plantation-style house on the North Shore with four bedrooms, a sunroom, three baths, granite on the kitchen counters, and marble on the bathroom walls.

Not bad for a kid from Shreveport who lucked into a few things, like an education and a wife who more or less fell from heaven and landed at his feet. He'd had some luck; no question about it, he'd been lucky as hell.

He'd also worked his butt off. *And* he was smart. Or so Cille said, and it had to be, considering where he'd come from. He had to admit it might be true—he was the third son of an alcoholic electrician who used to beat him for studying. His dad absolutely could not stand watching him with a book in one hand and a pencil in the other. He had no idea why not, but Cille had theories. She said it had to do with low self-esteem and not wanting his son to do better than he had. *Maybe,* he thought.

Maybe, maybe, maybe.

More likely it was just that he was there. Both his brothers had the sense to stay out of the house, and so did his mother, most of the time—she baby-sat for relatives and volunteered for projects at the church. So Ray was the only one home to hit, until he finally got his license and started going to the library or a friend's house.

Anyway, he got no encouragement.

But he did well and he found Cille and he had a whole shitload of ambition. He not only wanted to be rich, he wanted to be filthy rich.

Texas-rich.

He majored in business and went to work for United Oil for a while. It was just coincidence he got that job—but oil suited him down to a T. He got sent out to Jefferson and Plaquemines Parish, where the whole countryside is crisscrossed with canals built only for convenience of drilling—an ecological travesty. Even he could see it. But it was done fifty years ago or more and not his problem anyhow.

His problem was to figure out what to do with mature oil fields that weren't producing like they used to—that were no longer profitable for a huge company like United, whose interests increasingly lay offshore, where the bucks were so big you couldn't count the zeros.

One thing you could do was find small companies to sell the leases to. Another thing you could do—if you were smart and had endless ambition and absolutely no sense of reality—was start up your own small company and buy one yourself.

Only you couldn't do that without a wife who dropped from heaven. Fortunately Ray had one. And now Cille had gone back to work and was supporting the whole family.

He had met her at a party in New Orleans, when he first started working for United. At that time, to say he was insecure was like saying the ocean was slightly damp. But he was tall and had broad shoulders—attributes Lucille had mentioned a few hundred times since—and he had a seersucker suit and a bow tie.

Cille said he reminded her of Gregory Peck that night—a little hunched over to disguise his height, a little "diffident," as she called it. Terrified, he called it.

He could remember standing on one foot and then the other, holding a glass that had sweated all over his napkin, so that he had a cold, soggy mess in his hand, and trying to talk to somebody's wife, when Cille fell from heaven. Or, more properly, when she floated up to him, actually to the woman he was talking to, but it felt so good to be in her presence, it didn't even matter.

She had one of those distinctly Southern faces that just *look* sympathetic. Her hair was some soft color—blondish-brown, maybe (later, it was quite blond, and later still, when the money ran out, it turned soft-colored again, but a different soft). It was long, parted in the middle, and, even in an age when women ironed their hair to straighten it, it was wavy. Or that was how he remembered it these days.

Everything about her had seemed soft and accepting. Her minidress was soft purple—lilac or lavender or something—but he barely noticed. Mostly, he noticed the sympathy in her face, the way she seemed to want to make him comfortable rather than banter or flirt or argue or try to impress him with long, boring anecdotes in which she was the heroine.

He made *her* talk, though, about her dogs (she had two golden retrievers) and about her job (she was a nurse)

97

and about her ambition—she wanted to establish a foundation to "fight for medical rights for the elderly." He had to laugh when she talked about fighting—her eyes got flashy and intense, her cheeks got red (and presumably hot), and she breathed more quickly. It only made him want to protect her.

He didn't realize until their first date—three days later because that was the soonest she was free—that she was barely five feet tall.

Sometimes these days, at dinner in their hideous breakfast nook, she talked again about her foundation—something she hadn't done for years. Poverty seemed to bring out the kindest, most generous side of her.

And at the moment he had such contempt for himself he could barely stand to look at her. The assholes had outwitted him again.

He knew what they were—he owed his present plight and that of his family to their deception and greed. But if you'd taken him before a grand jury and asked him to swear on the Bible, he'd have said they wouldn't kill anyone. This was a Fortune 500 company, for Christ's sake—these weren't the kind of people who hired assassins.

Hiring Allred was the best thing he'd ever done, and simultaneously the worst. The detective was your basic sleazebag incompetent, but somehow he'd lucked into this Talba Wallis babe. Ray wasn't sure where she came from and what her experience was—Allred never told him how long she'd been with him—but he'd seen her work and the girl was good.

He'd gone to see Allred every single day Talba worked for United Oil, and gotten a detailed report. He didn't want to meet her for obvious reasons—the fewer people who knew who he was, the better. But he'd spied on her going to work and heard tapes of her conversations with Allred, and now he'd heard her read her poetry. He'd run a company a long time, and employees like her didn't come along every day—smart, resourceful, able to think on their feet.

If she were the damn detective, everything would have been fine. But Allred had to mess it up by getting greedy. That last night, the night she came back with the disk, Allred broke his standing date with Ray. Said he was sick or some such bull. And then he called later and changed the terms.

Well, no problem. No fucking problem at all. Ray Boudreaux was as damn resourceful as Ms. Talba Wallis. He could break into a penny-ante dick's office and steal what he had to.

But, Jesus, he nearly threw up when he saw those damn open, staring eyes with bugs trucking across them like they were the I-10 of Bugland. And then, along came Talba Wallis herself. Well, he blew the whole damn thing, but he'd recovered nicely.

Impersonating Langdon was a good touch. Or it had seemed so at the time. Now it appeared that was what was pissing Talba off.

Goddammit, he had to get her. What if the seven-fifty didn't work?

He sat down and he thought about it and, as always, the threads began to come together.

Once more, he dialed her number. "It's me again."

"Hello, asshole."

He hated that. Just *hated* it. How dare she? "How'd you enjoy meeting Jane Storey?"

"You need to get to the point, asshole."

She had courage, he had to give her that. She didn't know if he was a murderer or what, and here she was calling him "asshole."

"Is she going to do a story on you?"

"Why do you want to know?"

"Because, Baroness, Ms. Storey happens to be a good friend of mine. Why do you think she went to your reading in the first place?"

"Something to do with Russell Fortier. Somehow, she thought I knew him or something. You responsible for that, shithead?"

He was going to have to backpedal—he had no idea Storey had showed her hand so fast.

"You want her to do a story or not?"

"Yeah, and I want to win the Pulitzer for poetry. She made it clear that's just about as likely."

"Uh-uh."

"Uh-uh? What you mean, 'uh-uh'? You speak English or not?"

"You help me and Jane Storey'll make you famous. That's a promise."

"Ho and hum."

"And maybe we could get an art critic to take a look at the boyfriend's work."

"What are you talking about? What do you know about Lamar?"

He hung up, thinking maybe he'd overplayed his hand. She might realize he'd seen Lamar at the reading.

But probably she hadn't noticed him. Probably he was just another white potato face.

I'm beginning, Jane Storey thought, *to feel like a windup doll.*

Worse, she was feeling sheepish about it. She was starting to live for the tipster's calls. *It's like dating a married man,* she thought. *And I ought to know. You don't go out because he might call. You don't even want to take a shower because you might not hear the phone ring and he might not leave a message. You spend ninety percent of your time waiting to hear from him and one-tenth of one percent actually with him.*

Only she'd never been with the tipster at all, to her knowledge; she'd gotten a great many more promises than stories; and she still didn't know what any of it was all about. How, for instance, did he know about Russell Fortier's disappearance, and how did he know about Cindy Lou, and *what* did he know about Talba Wallis? And, most worrisome of all, how did he know Gene Allred was dead unless he killed him?

She wasn't at all sure why she'd wasted an evening

going to a poetry reading. True, Talba Wallis was probably a story—not only had Jane heard about the black names for years, she'd been as intrigued as she was horrified by it. But she'd assumed it was an urban myth. And now here was a woman named Urethra. A woman whose art came out of her trouble in such a unique way that Jane could easily shape a story about her for the Living or Book section.

Normally, she'd have jumped at it. Yet she'd rather crossly put Wallis off. She was damned if she was going to write a story about The Baroness just because the tipster wanted her to—if indeed that was what he wanted. Perhaps he just wanted to get her and Langdon and Cindy Lou Wootten all in a room together.

Though why, Jane couldn't have said.

She was fed up with being at his beck and call, yet when he'd called with this new little tidbit about Bebe she couldn't resist. She'd gone out and gotten in her car and driven to Bebe's and parked in front of the councilwoman's house until Bebe had come out at two-thirty, just exactly as the tipster said she would. She was wearing white silk pants and a matching tunic with little gold sandals, a good outfit for a courtyard cocktail party—a destination for which she couldn't possibly be headed at that time of day and at the beginning of the week and with her husband missing. The gold sandals were an odd touch, Jane thought—a bit out of character for a city councilwoman. That intrigued her even further.

She followed Bebe out to Veterans Highway and into the parking lot of one of the many motels that bloomed there like so many weeds.

She saw Bebe disappear into one of the rooms and she waited an hour. In fact, almost exactly an hour—and that part did indeed seem in character, another fact that intrigued Jane. She wondered if Bebe had set the alarm on her watch: *Oops, sorry, darling. Committee meeting in half an hour.*

While she was waiting, she happened to remember she had a camera in her trunk—left over from a recent

101

weekend in Florida. *I wonder,* she thought, *if it has any film in it.*

Just to pass the time, she decided to check it out. There were maybe two exposures left after the Florida photos, but there was also a whole new roll of film. Feeling sheepish, yet unable to resist, she got back in the car with the camera. Again, just to pass the time, she photographed Bebe's car, seedily parked in the motel lot.

After that, she held the camera in front of her and looked at it as if it were a meteorite that had just fallen to Earth. She tried to think of a reason she might need pictures of Bebe emerging from the motel room. There couldn't possibly be any story in this.

And yet . . . and yet . . . one never knew.

Even if this wasn't a story in itself—and how could it possibly be?—it might somehow be part of the emerging story of Russell Fortier's disappearance. How, she didn't know, but she'd gotten a tip to come here, and surely there was some sort of method to the tipster's madness.

There was no doubt this was a tryst—what other explanation was possible? Unless, of course, Bebe, for reasons best known to herself, was meeting at this cheapjack hotel with her own husband.

Jane's heart pounded at the thought. *If Russell's in there,* she thought, *I'll kiss the feet of the damn tipster. I'll propose marriage, maybe.*

If this whole thing were anything other than a wild goose chase, she was going to need proof. In fact, now that she thought about it, she probably should have *planned* to bring the damn camera.

Bebe came out alone, wearing sunglasses, and Jane snapped her picture—several times: coming out of the room, running down the stairs, getting into her car. What there was to get, she got.

Bebe drove off and Jane kept waiting, thinking that if worst came to worst, she could persuade the desk clerk to talk to her. She was inventing various ruses when the door of Bebe's room opened and a man came out, straightening his collar as if he'd just emerged from the shower.

Really, she thought, *men are so transparent.*

The man turned slightly toward her and she found herself bombarded by two emotions at once—disappointment that it wasn't Russell, and shock at who it was—someone Bebe could barely speak to without causing a scandal. It was Ernest LaBarre, a developer who had a huge proposal before the city council.

Not only did LaBarre need Bebe's vote now, he'd needed it in the past and he'd be needing it in the future. This was a man who frequently asked the council's approval on one project or another.

And this was so clearly a story, Jane felt slightly nauseated.

This was not a matter of a public official having an affair, which might or might not be anyone else's business. This was a blatant conflict of interest. Not to write the piece seemed hugely irresponsible. Yet writing it was invasion of privacy. She couldn't see doing it to Bebe.

But she took LaBarre's picture and recorded the time.

She didn't have them together, but that didn't matter—she had enough material to make an editor believe her, and that was all she needed.

She headed back to the office, still feeling queasy, thoughts racing. And by the time she was on the escalator, cooler heads had prevailed. She wasn't going to write the damn story.

What would she write, anyway—OFFICIAL AND DEVELOPER IN LOVE NEST? Hardly.

She had a piece of something, that was all. And she was glad she'd taken the pictures—they were something concrete, to show if she had to, to prove she had some tiny piece of a greater jigsaw puzzle. Bebe and LaBarre might not be a story by themselves, but the affair was a good reason to keep digging. What if, for instance, Russell turned up dead? The fact that Bebe was having an affair called into question everything she'd said about his disappearance. She could have killed him in an argument, say, disposed of the body at leisure, and made up the story about the airport.

In a sort of daze, she dropped off the film in the photo department and then checked the library for clips on Bebe. Browsing through quickly, she could see that, at least once, Bebe had voted for one of LaBarre's projects. Since he had several, Jane wondered if it was a pattern.

She was still scrolling through clips, trying to get a handle on what was happening, when someone touched her shoulder.

"Janie." It was her editor, David Bacardi, her former lover and big, bad mistake.

"I hate it when you call me Janie." She turned to look at him as she said it, and she almost gasped, remembering. He was tall, with a good chest and good shoulders. He had dark hair graying at the temples and curling on his forehead—for which she was a sucker—and wore fashionable round, metal-framed glasses, white oxford-cloth shirts, striped ties. He moved sinuously, like someone who played a lot of squash.

He was absurdly good-looking. Not merely handsome, but darkly handsome—handsome in an intellectual way; handsome in a preppy, take-home-to-Mom kind of way. Sometimes she wondered why she hadn't fallen for him before she did, yet if she thought back, she could remember that, too. He was also handsome in a pat sort of way; a God's-gift sort of way. She'd been contemptuous of him before he decided to make it a point to seduce her.

But since he was also funny, charming, and bright, who could resist, really?

Anyone with a good sense of self-preservation, she thought now.

Walter had hated him. That should have been warning enough.

But it hadn't been, and now she was stuck with her own self-contempt for having fallen for his transparent ploys—having fallen, in a real sense, victim to him. She was stuck with that, and he was her boss, a position that held a bit of the victim in it in the best of circumstances.

She really did hate it when he called her "Janie."

He said, "How's the Fortier thing going?"

"Interesting developments. Can we talk about it in your office?" She didn't want the whole place knowing about Bebe's sex life.

"Hey, Jane, here's your prints." Ozzie Otis, the photographer she'd sweet-talked into doing them, dropped a crisp pile on her desk.

David picked them up. "What's this? You're a photographer now?"

"Ozzie was just doing me a favor."

He looked closer. "Are these what I think they are?"

"Come on. Into your office."

As she told the story, she could see David's eyes begin to glitter. He leaned closer and closer, and finally he blurted, "This is a hell of a story, Janie."

It was absolutely the highest compliment he'd ever paid her.

She leaned back, hoping he'd notice her pointedly drawing away from him, and spoke as frostily as she dared. "Exactly what do you think the story is?"

"Are you kidding? Here's a powerful politico literally in bed with a guy who wants to destroy half the views in the city and make parking some kind of California nightmare. Needless to say, an extremely controversial figure who needs every vote he can get. Have you checked her voting record?"

"That's what I was just doing."

"And?"

"Last time she voted in his favor."

"Big surprise. That alone makes it a story."

"I don't know." She was quiet, trying to think it through.

"What, are you kidding? The woman's husband's missing. Maybe she murdered him."

"Or maybe he left because he noticed the wife was working late a lot."

105

"What's wrong with you, Janie? This is a great story. And you got it—damn! But I don't get it with the amateur pictures. Couldn't you have called the photo desk?"

She couldn't bring herself to reply.

"Go write it, kid."

Reluctantly, she went back to her desk. There were only three bits of reporting left to do: finish checking Bebe's voting record, put together a short profile of LaBarre and his dealings with the city council, and get statements from the principals.

She did the first two, and when there was no more putting it off, she called LaBarre and got no answer. So she had to do what she dreaded most—call Bebe. Her words came out in a rush: "Bebe, I'm really sorry, but we have information you're having an affair with Ernest LaBarre. I tried to keep it out but—"

"You've got to be kidding! That is patently untrue."

"You were seen this afternoon." She named the motel.

"You're mistaken, Janie. That simply wasn't me."

There was nothing to do but call her bluff. "I'm really, really sorry, Bebe. We've got pictures."

Without warning, Bebe started sobbing. "Oh, Janie, you don't understand. It's not what it looks like. Oh, please, please—you've got to keep this out."

Jane was free to use the quote—Bebe hadn't said it was off the record—and she knew a kid fresh out of journalism school probably would. But, of course, she wouldn't.

Suddenly she thought of a reason other than sex for a city councilwoman to hold a secret meeting with a supplicant—to accept a bribe.

"Bebe, tell me. I can't do anything unless I know the truth."

"Can we talk off the record? I just want to tell you—to throw myself on your mercy."

"Sure." Jane was feeling a lot more merciful than usual.

"Russell and I—I don't know, I guess we've been growing apart lately. I don't know why, we just have. And

106

Ernest and I have always been friends. Actually, the four of us have—Ernest and Sharon and Russell and me."

"I notice you've voted for him every time something's come before the council." (By now, Jane had nailed this detail down.)

"I agree with what he's trying to do. That has nothing to do with our friendship."

"Bebe, you're an intelligent woman—"

"I know, I know. But, yes, we've been allies, and things are different now. We started seeing each other—this way—four months ago. And nothing's come up in that time. You see what I'm saying? We were casual friends, I admired him, I voted for him. We became lovers so suddenly—so stupidly, I might add, but omigod, I needed it—and then Russell disappeared and I couldn't go on with it. All we were doing today was saying good-bye. I swear to God that's what was going on."

Jane took a deep breath. "I believe you, Bebe." Because she'd known Bebe a long time and respected her, and also because the whole thing now seemed a sleazy ooze she'd fallen into and couldn't climb out of, Jane did believe her.

"I believe you, but what am I going to say if all that's off the record?"

"You can stop the story. You can be a decent human being and just not write it—it's going to cause a lot of damage, and what good can it possibly do? The whole thing's over." She paused, and said what was in Jane's own mind. "Besides, we've always been friends—Ernest and I. Why is it okay to have dinner with someone and absolutely dead wrong to go to bed with them?"

Philosophically it was unanswerable, yet the practical answer should have been obvious to a four-year-old. "You know why. The appearance of impropriety."

"Jane, I'm begging you—the public good won't be served by this story."

"I'm sorry. It's not my call."

In the end, she had to go with "no comment" for Bebe and "couldn't be reached" for LaBarre.

David had agreed to "the *Times-Picayune* has learned," after Jane threatened to take her byline off if he made her write it as it happened—exposing herself as a love-nest spy. In fact, she might even have quit over it—it was just too cheap and sleazy for words.

The trade-off was, they had to use the pictures to give the story credibility. Jane could have kicked herself for taking them.

After it was all over, she went home, poured herself some wine, and contemplated what she'd become. Only she didn't get far because she really couldn't be sure. On the one hand, Bebe certainly had a whale of a conflict. On the other, if what the councilwoman said was true, running the story was stupid and meaningless and harmful.

But who was qualified to make that decision?

Didn't the public have a right to know?

Surely it wasn't up to a responsible journalist to coddle and protect an irresponsible—and possibly dishonest—public official.

Yet, did that describe Bebe or didn't it?

"Goddammit, Walter, where are you when I need you?" Jane said to the air.

Ten

SKIP ABSOLUTELY COULDN'T believe what she was reading. How could a reporter like Jane take such a cheap shot? And how the hell could Bebe be so stupid? The latter, of course, was none of her business, as she perfectly well knew, but she was so mad at Jane she didn't care.

She breezed into the office with an extra cup of coffee—one for herself and one for Abasolo, to head off any sergeantlike hints about her case. But he raised an eyebrow and tapped the paper on his desk. "Nice pix of our pal." The subject was open.

"You'd think it was the *National Enquirer*."

"I thought Jane Storey was your friend."

"Our relationship's developing a strain." Skip filled him in on the tipster.

"He knows way too much to be up to any good," Abasolo said. "I don't like the way he's orchestrating things—it feels like it could escalate. Have you talked to Cindy Lou about him?"

"No, but that's a great idea."

"The guy gives me the creeps. Anybody that controlling almost reminds me of—" He stopped.

"Who?"

"Your buddy Jacomine."

Skip felt a rush of heat. Errol Jacomine. If ever anyone had a nemesis, Jacomine was hers. A pseudoreligious leader, former mayoral candidate, many times a murderer, one-time kidnapper of Jimmy Dee's niece, Sheila, and avowed enemy of Skip, Jacomine was the one who got away. Got away twice. She would never feel completely safe or comfortable until Jacomine was finally run to ground. He was the sort who would kill someone close to her—Sheila or Kenny, say—rather than Skip herself, just to hurt her.

She spoke involuntarily: "Oh, shit." Drops of perspiration popped out on her forehead. "Let me think about it."

She closed her eyes and put a hand over them, shutting the world out for a few moments. "I don't think so," she said at last. "I could be wrong, God knows he's always changing his m.o., but this isn't a big enough production—so far."

Abasolo opened his mouth, but Skip put up a hand. "Jacomine likes an audience. This doesn't have a public aspect."

"Like you said. So far."

"He couldn't have known I was going to get the Russell Fortier thing—it isn't even a homicide case. He probably doesn't know about decentralization—for all he knows, I'm still in Homicide."

Abasolo's blue eyes bored into her. "Aren't you letting down your guard? Remember how he has spies everywhere?"

She laughed. "How unlike me not to be paranoid."

"I'm glad you can laugh about it."

"Well, I wouldn't rule him out on this one—it just doesn't feel like him, that's all. But I agree with you. Whoever this dude is, he's obsessively controlling. The stuff he's done is pretty boggling when you think about it. He got Cindy Lou, me, Jane Storey, and Talba Wallis all in one place at one time—just to watch us, I presume. He must have spied on Russell long and hard enough to find out about his three-second affair with Cindy Lou; and then on Bebe long enough to find out not only that she was seeing LaBarre, but when and where—assuming that he tipped Jane to the whole thing, which I'd bet my last penny on. Also, he managed to get a bug planted in

Russell Fortier's office and, you have to assume, listened to Fortier's conversations. Plus, he seems to have figured out how to co-opt a perfectly honest reporter."

Abasolo nodded, eyes narrowing. He drummed his fingers. "I see what you mean. Really crazy, creepy stuff. I don't like it, Skip. You watch your back, girl." He paused. "Wait a minute. Maybe Allred's client isn't the tipster. Maybe the tipster is Russell."

"He disappears and then plays puppetmaster? What about the tip about Cindy Lou?"

AA grinned. "Damned ingenious red herring—the guy's so manipulative he might just do it. And this new information lends some credence—Bebe did have a boyfriend. By the way, *is* it new information?"

Skip managed a grin. "I'm afraid so. Jane Storey seems to be eating my lunch."

She gave a little wave as she went off to call Bebe. She'd already picked up the phone when she changed her mind, deciding to pay a visit instead.

Bebe answered the door in shorts and a T-shirt, her eyes red from crying. "Oh, Skip. Come on in."

Once again, Skip was led to the denlike room in the back. She wasted no time. "Bebe, you should have told me about LaBarre."

"Why the hell would that be any of your business?" She spoke petulantly, half like an angry teenager, half like a city official who was used to wielding power.

Perhaps, Skip thought, *there wasn't much difference.* "I'd say a husband in Russell's shoes would have a damn good reason for disappearing."

"But . . . he didn't know."

"Oh, really? What makes you think that?"

Skip watched her wrestle with the question. He could certainly have hired a private detective.

Bebe said, "Russell would have said something."

Perhaps he had, in a loud and angry voice, and one thing had led to another, the whole sorry scene ending with Bebe braining him and disposing of the body.

Skip wasn't about to drag a popular city councilwoman

111

over to the police station to discuss the idea. At least, not yet. Perhaps, she thought, it would be more productive to talk to LaBarre.

He lived out by the lake, in one of the custom-tailored mansions New Orlean's nouveau riche prefer to the stately, elegant, historic, and far less comfortable homes of Uptown and the French Quarter.

Skip had certainly not expected him to answer the door himself, but he did, in shorts, as Bebe had, and he looked equally distraught. But he was holding up the masculine side to the extent that he wasn't crying.

"What can I do for you?" He didn't ask her in.

"I'm investigating the disappearance of Russell Fortier, and I need to talk to you."

He kept his cool, but his lips set in a hard line. "Okay."

"I wonder how long you and Mrs. Fortier have been seeing each other."

"What does that have to do with the price of tea?" A little muscle jumped at the corner of his eye. His jaw looked so tight she'd need a church key to pry it open.

Skip thought she heard something in the distance, some commotion, but she couldn't be sure.

"I know this is hard for you, Mr. LaBarre, but it'll be better for everyone if you'll just be direct and come to the point, so I can go away and leave you alone."

Suddenly there was a keening female scream, followed by, "Oh, God, oh, God, look what she's gone and done."

LaBarre turned and ran, evidently forgetting Skip, who stood on the stoop for a startled moment, feeling like an idiot.

The female voice said, "Oh, God, what am I going to do?" and Skip pounded up the stairs.

LaBarre shouted, "Call 911, goddammit. Get some help."

A child squealed, "Daddy? Daddy, what's wrong?"

Skip heard LaBarre say, "Everything's okay. Everything's fine. Just go to your room."

"What's wrong with Mommy?"

112

"Go to your room!" LaBarre yelled, and the child's sobs joined the general cacophony.

When Skip reached the second floor, the child was gone, apparently having obeyed orders. In a bedroom at the end of a carpeted hall, LaBarre was bending over a woman lying on a bed and covered in blood. "Sharon! Sharon, what did you do?"

The woman was crying, not unconscious, and as Skip stepped closer, she saw that the blood came from her hands, or wrists. Either a botched suicide attempt or a bit of drama, depending on how severe the wounds were.

"Let me help," she said, and as LaBarre turned around, she couldn't mistake the look of gratitude on his face.

The woman on the bed said, "You bastard!" and Skip could see she was in no danger of dying.

"Get some towels," she said to LaBarre, and she said to the woman, "Police. Let me see your hands."

Actually, they were hardly bleeding at all. But a little blood went a long way, and the woman—undoubtedly Mrs. LaBarre—had made a fine mess.

As she held out her wrists to Skip, she stared at them and said, "I don't know what I was doing."

"Did you do this yourself?" It seemed obvious, but she had to ask.

The woman nodded, terror starting in her eyes. What she was afraid of, Skip didn't know. Herself, possibly.

LaBarre returned with the towels, which Skip took from him and folded. She pressed one to each of the woman's wrists. "Here. Hold these in place," she said to LaBarre. "She's going to have to be stitched."

The woman said, "Oh, shit, is this going to get in the paper, too?" and Skip knew what she meant.

Skip said, "I'll go see what's going on with 911."

LaBarre said, "Can you cancel it? I can drive her to the doctor."

Skip shook her head. "I don't think that's a very good idea."

She went to find the woman who'd called 911—the

maid, probably. The woman was moving her lips, evidently praying. She nodded at Skip. "They on the way."

"Mrs. LaBarre's okay. Could you see about the child?"

The black woman looked her in the eye: "No'm. She ain't okay. Gon' be a long time before she okay." She went off shaking her head. "Melissa probably under the bed again."

Skip returned to the bedroom. LaBarre was still sitting there, applying pressure to his wife's wrists. Mrs. LaBarre was sitting up with her eyes closed, tears escaping from beneath the lids.

"They're on the way. Everything all right?"

Mrs. LaBarre said, "Everything will never be all right."

"Do you need someone to stay with you? Are you afraid of your husband?"

The woman pointed her chin toward the ceiling as if she could stop her tears by defying gravity. "No, I'm not afraid of my husband. Go."

LaBarre shot Skip a helpless, pitiful look, as if an animal were dying in his arms. Skip said, "I'm sorry. I can't go yet. I'm going to have to make a report on this."

She would very much have liked to go—to have let LaBarre drive his wife to the hospital and slipped quietly out. But demons had been released and there was no getting them back in their box.

She was so damn mad at Jane Storey she felt like behaving like some cowboy in a 1940s movie—just going over and stomping her for causing trouble on the range. But such an action would have been not only highly unprofessional but quite unladylike, as Dee-Dee might have put it.

Anyway, in some sense Jane was just doing her job— not the way Skip thought it ought to be done, but people criticized the police, too.

The real perp had to be the tipster. How else could Jane have known about Bebe and LaBarre?

Whole worlds were starting to fall apart. And to what end? She couldn't banish the image of Mrs. LaBarre looking up at the ceiling, her husband holding towels to her injured wrists, the shards of their marriage almost visible around them.

If Russell were doing the damage, it might make some sort of twisted sense, but so far, no one had indicated any instability, or even oddity on his part. Perhaps, she thought, she'd try again to talk to Edward Favret.

Later she caught him about to go to lunch, but this time she wasn't about to leave the office till he'd talked. She sat herself down and ignored his frequent glances at his watch, his anxious looks at the door. She didn't like Favret, and this gave her a certain perverse pleasure—a sort of validation of her prejudice against white male privilege.

No, that wasn't it.

Somebody had to be white, male, and privileged. Some men carried it off just fine. It was smug, self-satisfied white male privilege that rubbed her the wrong way.

She said, taking her time, "I understand you're Mrs. Fortier's cousin."

He smiled, trying to look pleasant. "That I am."

"Have you heard from Russell, by any chance?"

"Why, no." He seemed taken aback. "Why do you ask?"

"You must have known him at least as long as he's been married."

"Oh, much longer than that. We went to Holy Name together, and then Jesuit. But then he went off to Harvard and I went to Tulane."

"Not Loyola?" That was often the university of choice after Jesuit.

"We were rebels." He shook his head, smiling in a way that she couldn't quite identify. Perhaps it was the smile of an older and wiser man, at his own youthful indiscretions. "I introduced him and Bebe—in fact, I was their best man."

"And you've remained good friends?"

He looked slightly uncomfortable. "Yes."

"You sound as if you're not sure."

He shrugged. "People grow apart."

115

"Bebe says the two of you go hunting and sailing together. And play golf."

"Yes. Or the four of us do—Russell and I go with Douglas and Beau. Maybe we've known each other so long we just don't have much to say anymore."

She sensed something that might be hostility, or might be hurt feelings. She said, "There's been a change in your relationship."

"We used to be . . . pals." He spoke the last word contemptuously. "Still own a boat together, matter of fact." He paused, bringing himself back to the present. "There's been a change in Russell. Ever since that sailing accident."

"I think Bebe mentioned it. As I recall, it was a few days before he was rescued."

"He spent five days alone in a capsized boat. The guy's a hero."

"How did it change him?"

He opened his hands in the wit's-end gesture. "I don't know; it just did."

She was silent, hoping he'd blather on to fill the void.

"He just got kind of . . . serious."

"Withdrawn?" Skip asked, and was instantly sorry—she was probably feeding him false information.

"I guess so. I don't know, maybe it broke his spirit. He just hasn't been the old Russell lately."

"What do you think has happened to him?"

"How would I know?" He sounded openly hostile.

"He must leave a big hole in the company."

Favret nodded, evidently trying to close the subject.

"You know, you just don't seem worried about him."

What had been smoldering hostility flashed into anger. "What do you know about whether I'm worried about him? You don't see me pacing at night, grabbing Tylenol PMs with one hand and Rolaids with the other—nobody sees that but my wife. You want to talk to her? Sure, I'm worried about him. We're all worried about him."

Skip smiled. "Tell me something—that boat in its slip?"

"Is that a serious question?"

"You bet it is."

"Of course it's there—my wife and I went sailing over the weekend."

"You made Russell sound kind of depressed. I wonder if he might have committed suicide."

"Suicide?" His eyebrows went up. He repeated the question. "Suicide?" He shook his head. "I kind of don't think so."

"But you did consider it. Do you know of anything that's been bothering him?"

"No. Nothing." His chin jerked slightly, and Skip wondered if this was a nervous tic, something he did when he lied.

Eleven

TALBA THOUGHT, I *need to write a poem about this. Whole books have been written about being Jewish and getting a doctor in the family. People like us work for people like them. Does anybody realize exactly how large a pain in the ass it is for one sibling in an African-American family if another goes to medical school?*

She was setting the table with a white tablecloth and her mother's Chantilly pattern silver that someone she worked for had been about to discard and had given to her instead—a woman from Texas, who had also given Miz Clara a worn-out fur coat.

Special ceremony and ritual were required because Talba's brother and his wife were coming to dinner. Never mind that the wife, Michelle, was like one of those Uptown parakeets—such a pretty little tiny thing no one would dream of asking her to work for a living. A kind of woman Miz Clara had absolutely zip use for in either its white or its black form, though, truth to tell, you didn't see it in black form that much, which should have made Miz Clara just that much more contemptuous of her.

But Dr. Corey Wallis, Talba's big brother, could commit infanticide in front of City Hall and his mama wouldn't notice he'd fucked up. Because Corey could not do a damn thing wrong in Miz Clara's eyes, no matter *how* hard he tried.

Becoming a doctor was what Miz Clara did send her children to college for, or at least that was one of the top three options. The others were becoming president or Speaker of the House.

Talba could have killed him for doing it, but she was so damn proud of Corey she couldn't really hold it against him. On the other hand, he *did* have an attitude, for which his butt needed beating, but Talba satisfied that urge by mouthing off at him.

Lamar had said *Noooo-thank-you* to this little family party, so it was just going to be the four of them eating Miz Clara's fried chicken, which she insisted on making despite the fact that she now had a doctor in the family and knew better.

Michelle came in, smelling entirely too much like slightly crushed petals—probably some hip new perfume. If you shopped a lot, you were up on these things.

Corey was right behind her, light glinting off his shaved head and his glasses.

Miz Clara gave Michelle a kiss.

"Baby, you pregnant yet?" She did think if you were going to freeload, you ought to at least drop babies.

Michelle showed pearly teeth in a face several shades lighter than a paper bag (damn Corey for that one!). "Now, Miz Clara."

That was the extent of her wit. Talba didn't exactly loathe her, but she didn't consider her a member of the family. She rolled her eyes at Corey. "Hey, big brother. How do you stand this crap?"

"Now, you shut up, Ms. Sandra Baroness de Pontalba Wallis," said Miz Clara, and Corey kissed her, which left Michelle and Talba to say something to each other.

Michelle smiled. "Sorry we missed the reading. How'd it go?"

"To tell you the truth, it was incredible."

"Really?"

"You sound surprised."

"I guess I didn't think that many people were into poetry. What kind of people were there?"

To Talba's surprise, Miz Clara stepped in. "You wouldn't

119

believe who was there. Black folks, white folks, old, young—*everybody* there to see my baby."

Talba felt a warm, sticky glow. However mean she was when no one was around, her mother stood up for her in front of outsiders, even those who were family.

"There was even a newspaper reporter," she finished.

Corey said, "You gonna be famous, Sandra?"

"*I* am The Baroness de Pontalba." She said it with such exaggerated pomposity that even Michelle laughed, and she was renowned for humor impairment.

Miz Clara said, "Y'all come sit down now."

And things went well for a while. They had some beer and then some wine, and they ate the chicken along with some fresh vegetables Miz Clara had fixed, and then Miz Clara went to get the pie she'd sort of made—though the crust had come from Schwegmann's—and Corey said, "How's that Rastafarian boyfriend of yours?"

"You like his hair, huh?"

"I just hate to see you throwing yourself away on somebody like that."

"Somebody like what? Somebody with dreads? Lamar's a grad student at Xavier."

"You know what I mean."

Their mother came in with the pie. Michelle took care to look at her lap.

"Mama, is this why we're having this party?" Talba asked.

"When I tol' you you could stay here, I didn't mean with that deadbeat."

"Well, why didn't you just ask me to move?"

"I promise you, that's why. I promise you a little time befo' you have to go to work again. But when I see that poetry meetin'—"

"Reading."

"When I see that poetry meetin', I figure it be time to talk to ya brother."

Talba felt as if the top of her head were going to come off. She turned toward Corey and watched him almost visibly withdraw from her—when she got a smokestack of anger up, you could feel it across a room.

"Sandra, we're worried about you. Don't you understand that?"

"I don't get this. I have a nice professional boyfriend. I just had a successful professional performance, and some very nice recognition. I even have an outside chance of getting a story in the paper. I'm doing great. How many poets do you know who're doing so great?"

"I have a good friend who's just done his residency in psychiatry. I was thinking—"

"Psychiatry?" She stood up and hollered, "Psychiatry? You think I'm crazy, big bro'? In case you've forgotten, I worked my butt off to get through school, and I've been nothing but a credit to this family even if I'm *not* a doctor. Mama and I had a *deal* here. What's wrong with y'all?"

Corey patted air like a conductor: *Not so damn loud, please.* "Take it easy, Sandra. This is not about your poetry, and it isn't even about your no-good boyfriend."

"What in God's name is wrong with Lamar?"

All three of the others looked at each other. Finally, Corey said, "You really want to know?"

"Yes, goddammit. Let's get it out, once and for all."

He shrugged and spoke conversationally. "He's an asshole."

He said it so casually, Talba had to laugh. "Oh, is that all?"

And then they were laughing. Finally, she said, "Y'all really have to back off. The thing about it is, he's *my* asshole. Let me just have him awhile, okay?"

"Just don't marry him, you hear me? Otherwise, Mama might disinherit you."

They all had to laugh again. And then Talba said, "Mama, really; why do you hate Lamar so much? It's like you never even give him a chance."

"I don't like the way he treat you, girl. I had my share o' that. You too smart fo' it."

121

Now Talba looked at the table. "I know, Mama," she said, and the phone rang.

Her mother answered and came back, smiling. "It's for you, Sandra. And it ain't Lamar."

Thinking, *It must be the damn client,* Talba hoped they wouldn't decide to eavesdrop.

"Talba? Darryl Boucree."

"Who?" She couldn't quite place the name, yet she felt a vague excitement.

"I met you at your reading. The English teacher."

"Oh, the *English* teacher." The *fine*-looking English teacher. She found she remembered him well, and with so much warmth it surprised her.

"Following up on our conversation."

"Our—oh, your class. You want me to speak to your class."

"You weren't just leading me on, were you?"

"No. No, of course I'll speak to your class. When?"

"Tomorrow?"

She repeated, "Tomorrow?"

"Unless you're all booked up."

Well, she might be soon. "Sure. Tomorrow." She hung up.

"And that," she told her family, "was an English teacher who wants me to speak to his class. I happen to be a role model for young people and I don't want to hear any more of your shit—excuse me, Mama."

"Well, that's wonderful, baby."

Corey said, "Listen, could we talk privately?"

"Don't you ever give up, Doctor Wallis? What you got on your mind you can't say in front of Mama and your wife?"

"You're right. We should all talk together about it. We're worried about this obsession of yours."

"Obsession? You mean Lamar? Lamar's no obsession, he's just a boyfriend."

"Not Lamar. Your name."

"Oh. Urethra."

"That's not your name and you know it."

"It's the name I was born with. It was on my birth cer-

122

tificate till Mama got it legally changed. How would you like to be named Urethra?"

"Sandra, that's not the point. You've got to let it go. You can't go your whole life letting that eat you alive."

"I don't plan to, *Doctor* Wallis. I don't even see how you can stand to be in the same profession with the vermin who did that to your mama."

He threw his napkin on the table. "Well, maybe I'd like to bring a little dignity to the profession. You're not helping with all this."

"Are you worried about your reputation, Corey Wallis? Is that what this is about? Your sister bringing down a member of your oh-so-honored profession?"

"Sandra, you know better than that. It's you we're worried about. What if you get interviewed by that reporter? What if that poem of yours gets famous? Then you really are going to be famous as the girl named Urethra."

"You don't get it. You just don't get it, do you? *I* am The Baroness de Pontalba."

This time no one laughed.

"Y'all don't believe me, but I'm gonna get him."

"Gonna get who?"

"Gonna get the Pill Man. Stay tuned to this channel."

Michelle looked like she'd just gotten a bad oyster.

Until that moment, Talba had thought seriously about returning the client's money, or maybe just keeping it, and not going back to work. But doubling it would buy her some time.

The sooner she got the Pill Man the sooner they'd get off her back. She could go back to CompTemps tomorrow, before Darryl's class.

What the client didn't know, of course, was that Allred had had special ways of getting his operatives hired. But Talba didn't know if his connection would work for her. She called him first thing in the morning. "Mr. Currie? Talba Wallis." She waited, but he gave her no sign of recognition. "Gene Allred sent me over there. To work for United Oil Company."

123

"Yes?" His voice was frosty.

"I need another job. That was a great company—I wonder if they have any more openings."

"Come on in, Miss Wallis. I'll see what I can do." His voice was so tired it sounded like he might take a nap, right on the phone.

Talba came on in, a folded fifty-dollar bill in her right hand for Currie to palm when they greeted each other. She had no earthly idea if that was the right amount, but it was as much as she was willing to pay—if it took more, she could go over to United and apply directly, or call her ex-boss over there and see what he could do. She'd done a good job and probably didn't even need the damn agency.

But Currie didn't even look at the bill, just put it in his pocket as if a dollar would have been enough—and she cordially wished that was what she'd offered. He gave her a name. "Report to this guy first thing in the morning. They liked you last time."

She gave him a smile that was almost flirtatious. "I'm good at what I do."

And then she went off to talk to a high-school class, feeling on top of the world. *The Baroness de Pontalba,* she thought, *poet and detective. What if these kids knew what I do for a day job?*

Sure enough, the first thing they asked her was how much money she made.

And that was after she had hit them with the name poem, which hadn't seemed to affect them at all.

"How much *money* do I make? Is that all y'all care about? Tell me the truth, is there a single person in this room who's interested in anything else?"

No one raised their hand.

"You want to get out of school and just make money, you don't care how? Well, I've got a poem for you. Listen up, now." She gave it full-tilt histrionics.

Money, money, money,
That runs all coppery through your fingers;

Sparkles all silvery
In other people's cash registers.
Crinkles all green and wrinkly in your wallet—
And in your dreams.

What can you do with that shit?
Why, you can buy yourself a house and a maid to clean
it—
You can buy a boat and a man to sail it—
You can buy clothes and cars and fifty-three pairs of
Reebok running shoes.
And then what? You gonna run in fifty-three races all
at the same time?

Now, I love money and I want some so bad
I want it so bad my nose hurts and my teeth hurt and
the bottoms of my feet hurt.
But the best thing I ever did was make this poem—
Well, maybe not this poem—
But any poem at all—any way at all of wiggling two
words and jiggering two sounds,
Any way at all to get that glow-all-over feeling—
That dreamy old warm kind of head-reeling—

It's better than sex—
Y'all know that?

She stopped and bowed deeply, as if they were The Baroness and she were the commoners, and looked at a sea of absolutely befuddled faces.

Finally a fat boy stood up, a boy in a baseball cap and a pair of the maligned Reeboks. "Hey, I want to ax you somethin'—you ever had sex?"

And when they had all stopped laughing some ten minutes later, she spoke to the kid in the cap. "Now *that's* what I mean. What's your name?"

"They call me Two-Ton."

"Okay, Two-Ton, what you just got was a taste of the joy of creation. You made a good joke and everyone

125

enjoyed it, and you felt *fine*, now didn't you? What I'm talking about is work that always makes you feel fine. And good about yourself. And happy. Is anybody here happy?"

Two or three kids raised their hands. Talba pointed to one.

"Okay, what makes you happy?"

The girl shrugged. "I don't know."

She moved on to another. "Okay, you. What makes you happy?"

"My baby boy."

"Okay, love. Love is a *good* thing, and that makes us happy. And money does—we already talked about that. Don't look at me like that—I'm not going to pretend you can be just as happy poor as rich. They tell y'all that in church? Well, this is *school*, and we're supposed to *know* things here. Think I'm not happier writing my poems at my golden desk, sittin' on my ivory chair, wearing my silk and damask robes than at some formica kitchen table, wearing an old, beat-up sweatsuit?"

And miraculously, a kid in the back of the class said, "No, you're not—because when you're writing your poems, you don't care what else is going on. You don't even *care*, 'cause you're happy already."

Talba stared at the girl in utter astonishment. "Now, how on earth do you know that?"

" 'Cause I sing in a choir. I'm just as happy at choir practice as when we have on our robes and all the candles are lit, and you can smell incense, and everywhere you look in the church, everything's real pretty and real . . . expensive."

Talba stuck both thumbs up in the air. "Yes!" she hollered. "That's it! Does anybody else know what she's talking about?"

"I've got a question," Darryl said. "Did you make up that poem just now—in class?"

"It was that raw, huh?"

"No, it just seemed appropriate."

"Well, yeah. I guess I kind of did."

A murmur went up. "You did? You did that right here, now?"

Talba bowed again. "That is why I am a Baroness."

By now, she had them. Somehow, she wasn't sure how, she'd turned them around—probably it wasn't her, probably it was that little girl who sang in the choir, but she didn't care, when she talked with Darryl afterward, when he walked her out, she felt the adrenaline glow she got from a reading.

"I did okay, didn't I?"

He smiled at her, and not for the first time she noticed what perfect teeth he had. "You're a natural-born teacher. If you ever want to come starve to death, maybe you could get a job like mine."

"No, thanks. I already get to starve."

"Listen." He caught her eye. "This really meant a lot to them."

"Oh, sure. They'll think about it while they're knocking over a gas station; or nodding out, maybe."

"They'll think about it," he said, evidently not wanting to get into joking with her. When he shook her hand, he touched it with his left one. "Would you . . . have coffee with me later?"

She could see that he had asked the question on impulse and felt the power once again of her performance— she knew that she could affect people like that, make them want to know her—want to fuck her, maybe, the way a musician on stage affects his fans. And she liked it. The other thing was, she liked Darryl Boucree. There could be no question he was asking her for a date, and she already had Lamar.

She made a little face at him. "I guess so," she said. "Or maybe a beer."

And so, when school was out, after she'd raided Magazine Street for the sorts of things a Baroness in reduced circumstances ought to have, they had not one, but two beers, and she found that smile of his infectious and seductive.

"I was wondering," he said. "How much *does* a Baroness make?"

She laughed. "Well, I didn't want to mention they might have to get a day job to pursue their art."

"Yeah. Let 'em think it's all limos and limelight."

"I know that's *my* life."

"Are you independently wealthy or something? I notice you were free for this little gig."

"I have an extremely interesting little income supplement."

"Legal?"

"Sometimes."

They both laughed.

"Fun?"

"Really fun."

"Can't be robbing banks. That's never legal. Now let me think—*sometimes* legal . . . You're a lawyer."

"Good guess. But no."

"Doctor."

"How's that illegal?"

"Prescriptions."

"Uh-uh. You'd never guess in a million years."

"Mayor."

"Nope."

"Crooked cop."

"Uh-uh."

"Private detective."

"What?" Talba had been in mid-pull on her beer. She actually choked—the game had gone too far.

He hit her on the back. "I was right? You're a private dick? Or do they still say that?"

"Depends on the company. Dickhead's a little more common."

"Really? You mean I got it? How'd you get into, uh, dicking?"

"You've got the wrong idea. I don't dick, I merely dick around. But how about you? Bet you've got a life outside the classroom."

"Well, matter of fact. You ever heard of the Boucree Brothers? I play a little music with them now and then."

She started to say she was impressed (which she was), but he kept talking: "Also, I do a little mixology a few times a week."

"Let me get this straight—schoolteacher, musician, *and* bartender? You're a regular Renaissance man."

He was smiling, showing those gorgeous teeth. She relaxed a little. She had successfully changed the subject, but she wondered. Had he been pumping her? And why on earth would he do a thing like that?

But he was too damned attractive to dwell on it for long. She liked the way he bantered, something Lamar wouldn't do in a thousand years, and the way he really cared about his students, and the way he smiled and touched her hand now and then to make a point.

Still, when she left, when it was either order another beer—which both knew would mean trouble—or get up and go, she had a funny feeling she'd said too much.

Twelve

IT'S ALMOST LIKE *before,* Russell thought. *Just me and the boat.*

This time, of course, I am free to leave the boat. But if I leave it, where would I go?

And I have all my senses, not just hearing. Not only can I see, I am free to see any damn thing I want. The question is, what do I want to see?

It was odd. He had left home to be free and never had he felt so confined, save that one time when he'd been trapped—the time, ironically, that had led to this time.

I'm lonesome, he thought. *That's what's wrong with me. And I happen to be a very eligible bachelor.*

If he went out and had a drink and happened to encounter female companionship, how could that hurt? He wasn't married. Well, actually he hadn't quite thought that out yet. He had simply left. He hadn't thought about whether he was now dead or merely missing for a while. Anyway, he was separated. That called for a babe.

He'd seen a place on the Intracoastal Waterway where there were several extremely popular restaurants all bunched up together. He could just take the sloop there, tie it up, and go get some strange Florida drink like a Fuzzy Navel. He set sail, as they said in the old days.

The establishment with the largest dock bore the unpromising name of Bootlegger, and, something he'd never noticed, most of the boats there were cigarettes— long, skinny, loud, mega-power racing vessels absolutely unsuitable for leisurely jaunts on the ICW unless you were a drug dealer who thought they were phat.

Still, he'd come here and he was going to have his damn drink.

Immediately, he classified it: a T-shirt—not a polo shirt—kind of place. (He himself wore neither, having opted for a slightly fancier blue chambray number—the better, he thought, to entice babes.) Nonetheless, polo shirts were the shirts of sailors, from hired crew on up. These people weren't sailors. From the looks of things, they were football fans—there were at least a dozen TVs in the place, maybe as many as eighteen. And they were undoubtedly beer-drinkers—he should probably forget the Fuzzy Navel.

Dean Woolverton didn't fit in too badly. He was older than most, though not all by any means. There were a few lined, leathery faces scarfing beer above the T-shirts, many fringed by beards. *Aha,* he thought—a beard would be a very good thing instead of the stupid blond hair. Why hadn't he thought of that in the first place? It was much more Russell—more like a sea captain than some asshole beach bum. He made a mental note to reverse his new persona as soon as it seemed safe.

No sooner had he gotten settled—ordered a beer, sipped it, begun a serious TV count—than a woman started talking to him. A young woman, good-looking, with dark hair and white skin—Cuban, maybe. She wore some kind of white shirt with no sleeves—not exactly a tank top, maybe just a sleeveless T-shirt tucked into a pair of very brief blue shorts. As for the T-shirt, it was tighter than a corset, intended to show off her assets, which were worth showing.

He felt old and somewhat dowdy in his crisp shirt and pants.

"Nice boat," she said.

He said, "Uh . . . thanks," hesitating because he couldn't figure out how she knew which boat was his. He realized she must have watched him come in. How about that?

131

She had watched him, and now she was talking to him. This had promise. He said, "Do you sail?"

She turned to her margarita, rather shamefacedly, he thought. "No. I never learned how."

They swapped a few more sentences, during which he got a chance to try out his ex-lawyer routine on her, which at least didn't meet with huge guffaws, and he learned that she had some low-level job at an insurance company. He was searching around for a topic of mutual interest when, out of the blue, another woman joined her, probably fresh from the ladies' room. "Ready?" she said.

"Ready," said Russell's babe, and they departed.

So much, Russell thought, *for babes.*

He looked around and found he could honestly say he didn't find a single woman in the whole place attractive. They were too young, too blond, too busty, too scantily clad, too *Florida.*

Old fart, he thought. *You sound like your father.*

And the thought stabbed him like a needle in the neck. Everything about it hit him at once: that he could be like his father in any respect; that he could even have a father so arrogant, so judgmental, so uncaring. That his father was dead.

The Fortiers had done well in New Orleans. Because of *his* father, Russell's father had had no trouble getting a job with a shipping line that could have taken him as far as he wanted to go. Yet, from the first, at age twenty-six, he had insisted on trying to tell his father's friend, the president, how to run the company. When his suggestions weren't taken, he leaned more heavily on the president, criticizing him personally. Eventually, he was let go, on grounds of "personality conflict."

Russell knew all this from his father, told just about like that, but heavy with judgment—against the company (small-thinking and poorly organized), against his father's friend (stubborn, old-fashioned, closed-minded, and stupid), even against the city (corrupt and backward).

The miracle was, they'd actually kept him for nineteen years before dumping him. He'd found other jobs and eventually retired to North Carolina. He'd even found a second wife after Russell's mother died, though why anyone would want the old goat was unclear to his son.

The self-appointed guardian of righteousness in every respect, Thomas Fortier delighted in getting in the fast lane and driving the speed limit, just to make the other drivers obey the law. When Russell was a child, it had embarrassed him so thoroughly, his shirt was usually soaked with sweat by the time they got where they were going. In retrospect, embarrassment seemed less appropriate than fear; it was a wonder his father hadn't been killed by some outraged citizen.

Now that Russell was a grown man, that story should be amusing. He was aware that it should be amusing. He told it to friends and they laughed. Bebe had laughed. Russell never did. Instead, he always found himself shaking his head and rolling his eyes.

Bebe had said, "Why can't you get over it?"

"When you live with something like that," he replied, "it's just not a laugh riot."

"So, I guess little Russell's report card was never good enough? If you're not valedictorian, it's the same as not graduating? That sort of thing?"

"You can't even imagine."

Not a single thing Russell had ever done had pleased his father, so far as he could tell. And yet his father had given him a check for $300,000 on his deathbed. He didn't approve of probate—it was that simple. The only good thing he'd ever done for Russell, he'd done—as he'd done most things—to show the world how wrong it was.

(Though his father wouldn't view it that way—he would probably say putting Russell through Harvard was a good thing, a paternal thing. But Russell had wanted to go to Tulane.)

Old Thomas had actually sent Russell the check the same day he entered the hospital. If she'd known about it, Bebe might have said it was a guilt thing, to get Russell to go to his bedside, but Russell didn't think so. Thomas

133

had his second wife and wasn't much on mushy family stuff anyway. Besides, guilt wasn't his thing.

Being right was; control was. His wife had also been left a liquid sum, with explicit instructions as to how Thomas wanted to be buried, down to how the headstone should read.

When Russell got the check, this thing with Ray Boudreaux and the Skinners was just starting to break. Ray was just beginning to contact them, trying to get something going, some kind of negotiation. The others were all for ignoring him, but Russell had a feeling things were about to escalate.

A plan formed in the back of his head. Even then, he was thinking about a run for freedom. He deposited the check in a bank he and Bebe didn't use, waited for it to clear, and then withdrew the money in the form of a cashier's check. Bebe never even knew about it.

He turned that into cash once he got to Fort Lauderdale and bought the boat with a big fat chunk of it.

The check thing, so like his father, did make him smile.

He was in a mood to smile. The Cuban girl's drink had looked so festive he'd switched to margaritas after his beer, and by now he'd had two.

I wonder how Mother stood him, he thought, and, as always, the memory of his mother made him feel warm and loved. She was as generous, as kind, as sympathetic and understanding as his father was arrogant and hardnosed, righteous and punishing.

He was starting to go all mushy when another woman talked to him, this one about thirty-five, also dressed like live bait, and for some reason wearing a baseball cap.

Her face was shiny with the heat. She wore pearl stud earrings with her baseball cap and tube top, and she was on the short, chunky side. But pretty.

Undeniably pretty. He supposed they didn't come out to this sort of bar unless they were.

For some reason, she was asking him where he went to college. "Harvard," he said, and that seemed to stop her cold.

Finally, she said, "What was it like?"

"You're asking the wrong person." He gave her what he hoped wasn't too paternal a smile. "I hated its guts. My dad wanted me to go, so I did. Barely scraped through, but did graduate, and then applied myself rather assiduously to becoming a ne'er-do-well."

"Is that what you are now?"

"I'm working on it."

"You're working on getting drunk."

He lifted his glass to her. "I'm Dean Woolverton."

She leaned back, eyes wide, in a kind of self-conscious double take. "That's really your name?"

It was the last reaction he expected. "Why wouldn't it be?"

"It's the weirdest thing. Mine's Dina Wolf."

"Omigod. We're the same person." He heard himself speaking and felt profoundly depressed. Why in hell had he left Bebe? Maybe she was cheating on him, but at least he didn't have to have inane conversations with her.

In fact, he thought, *I don't have to have inane conversations with anybody. I could leave right now and I think I will.*

But Dina Wolf had sat down. "When's your birthday?"

Oh, well. Might as well get with the program. "I'm a Sagittarius," he said, though he didn't really have a clue what he was.

"Good. I was born in the spring, so we can't be the same person. That means I can buy you a drink without seeming selfish."

"I thought the man bought the drinks."

She pointed to their respective glasses. "You're empty. I'm full." She summoned the bartender. "Now. On with your life story."

"You're quite the take-charge lady."

"I used to train dogs. So you hated your father."

"What do you mean by that?"

"People would kill to go to Harvard. You decided not to like it because your dad made you go there."

"Ah. And where did you go?"

135

"Florida State."

Once again he raised his glass, dimly aware that it was a drunk's gesture. "Well, you're a smart cookie."

"Did you like your mother?"

He put the glass down and felt a dopey smile spread across his face. "My mother was an angel."

"Oh, really? Then you'd probably make a good husband."

"I didn't."

She pursed her mouth. "I see. What were your wife's complaints?"

"She didn't complain exactly. She just found someone else."

"And now you're trying to do the same."

There was something unnervingly straightforward about the woman—he would have preferred a softer approach. "What about you?" he asked. "What are you doing?"

"Waiting for my husband—see that big guy over there?"

Russell glanced over his shoulder, and Dina Wolf laughed.

"I'm kidding, I'm a graphic designer, unmarried. Talking to a cute guy, just for fun. No strings, no obligations, just talk."

Actually, he didn't much care at that point who or what she was. In fact, he was extremely confused by her. He'd never met a woman in a baseball cap who talked like this. He said, "You're damn right, Dina Wolf. I didn't like my father much at all. I did a lot of things he wanted me to do—"

"Trying to get his approval."

"You a shrink or a graphic designer? I was going to say, I didn't like the old coot, but he gave me a lot. In a way, I guess I owe him big-time. Everything I became I owe to my father."

"Except," she said, "what you are now."

"Why would you say that?"

She shrugged. "Just being provocative."

136

But nothing could have been more true. He hadn't wanted to go to Harvard, would have been perfectly happy at Tulane. Then maybe law school and an ordinary life in Uptown New Orleans. But once having gone to Harvard, he didn't know what he wanted. He couldn't bring himself to leave New Orleans, yet he couldn't seem to fit in either. He worked for a bank for a while, but it was so deadly boring he finally got fired for taking too many mental health days.

Whereupon his dad about popped a gasket. He was perfectly clear about it, too—Russell's behavior made him look bad.

And so Russell went to work in the oil patch. Being a roustabout suited him. He was young, he was arrogant, and after a couple of months, he looked good with his shirt off. His mom thought the sun rose and set on him, and his dad was pissed as hell. All was right with the world.

Until an accident on the oil rig. He was covered by the company's insurance, money wasn't the problem. It was far more complicated than that—he lost partial use of his leg. Thus he needed someone to drive him to physical therapy, someone to help him with his exercises, someone to cook his meals, someone to shop for him, and someone to do his laundry. And he had such a person. A person temperamentally suited to all these chores, who loved him deeply and wanted more than anything else to take care of him. His mother. He moved back home for a while, which gave his father power over him. Or at least he saw it that way. Russell could hear him now: "As long as you're my son, living under my roof, you'll abide by my rules. When you're well, you'll start acting like a man and get a real job."

One minute you were king of the world, biceps bulging like some latter-day Stanley Kowalski's, and the next you were a little kid, once more dependent on your mother, subject to the whims and temper tantrums of your father. Russell felt the starch go out of him. He felt vulnerable and weak. And not a little desperate.

He read history, which made him feel small and antsy, instilled in him a yearning to be part of something bigger. He read Tolstoy and Dostoyevsky, which made him feel he was. For some reason, he read *Two Years Before the Mast*, and then all the books of Patrick O'Brian. He was desperate, suddenly, to see the world. And he realized with some excitement that he could ꞏ ꞏ easily become a merchant seaman as go back to the oil patch.

He began to plan, to look forward to his recovery.

And then one day his father came home and said, "I pulled a few strings and managed to get you a job at United Oil."

Russell had spoken arrogantly: "Too bad I won't be around to take it."

"What do you mean by that?"

"I've got plans, Dad. And they don't include rotting in New Orleans."

"And what might they include?"

"Lying on the beach in Bali. Playing baccarat at Monte Carlo. Checking out the pyramids."

"Right. They're expecting you next week."

"Dad, I'm serious. I'm going to sign on as a merchant seaman."

His father laughed, leaving him unprepared for what happened next.

"Do you ever plan to grow up?"

"Not if I can help it."

His father had stood and struck him. "Well, goddamn it, act like a man! Are you trying to break your mother's heart?"

Russell felt as if a dark parachute had floated from heaven and closed over his head, the silk getting into his nostrils, cutting off his air, wrapping round his throat. And yet, instead of falling unconscious, or dying, even— or taking the damn thing off—he had simply learned to live half-strangled, encased in darkness.

He had taken the job at United. He had gone to work with a lot of dumb-ass Tulane grads who were barely over playing drinking games on Saturday night—exactly the kind of person he'd once aspired to be. But now that he was someone different, thanks to his dad, he didn't fit into the world the same man had thrust him into. A more philosophical person might simply have seen it as one of life's ironies, but Russell, having the relationship he did with his father, wasn't able to bring to it a philosophical approach. He was miserable in his job and hated his father for it.

It was Edward Favret who saved his life.

He'd known Edward all his life, but by the time he got to United Oil, he had no interest in the man. Edward was too solidly New Orleanian, too routine, too ordinary. But Edward did have a sailboat. Sailing with Edward on weekends was what kept Russell going. He found he loved the water as much as he thought he would and considered Edward's friendship, such as it was, entirely secondary to the sailing, which fast became his obsession. And Edward, when all was said and done, was so damn pushy about being Russell's friend, there wasn't much to be done about it. Russell had few fascinating friends of the sort he felt he deserved.

Exactly who they would be wasn't clear to him, anyway. Dukes and counts, maybe? That wasn't it. He had liked the roughnecks he worked with, but it wasn't really their company he craved. He liked Yankees, actually. Particularly Jews.

But Edward Favret was who happened to be around, and he introduced Russell, in short order, to Douglas Seaberry, who had gone to Yale. Douglas, for reasons Russell couldn't quite put his finger on, was more his type.

He was more Eastern; a little more confident. Edward had always struck Russell as slightly obsequious— someone you couldn't completely trust. He was so damn nice you couldn't possibly know what he was thinking.

And how very precisely subsequent events had borne this out. Edward had as manipulative a mind as anyone Russell had ever met—though he had surprised himself in this area, displaying quite a bit of talent of his own.

But at first they were only sailing buddies—the three

of them, and later, when Beau Cavignac joined the company, the four of them. Beau, utterly preoccupied with sports, was more or less a dolt as far as Russell was concerned. Still, he was an inoffensive dolt.

And over the years he hadn't met any of the fascinating people he meant to, and had come to accept these three as his friends. The whole deal was cemented when Edward introduced Russell to his cousin.

He had resisted. "I don't know, Edward. No offense to your family, but I think I need someone with a real name. Bebe's just a little too adorable."

"Come on, she's a lawyer—she's not even slightly adorable. Call her Babette, if you want to. Call her Queen Elizabeth, I don't care. Just meet her—I promised my mother."

He had imagined someone whose personality more or less resembled cotton candy.

She met him at the door in jeans and a white shirt, though Edward's wife and Douglas's date had on fussier clothes—dressy pantsuits, with lots of jewelry and plenty of makeup. Bebe had lived her whole life in Uptown New Orleans—she had to have known they'd dress that way. He liked the fact that she'd done what she pleased, anyway. She had an honest face, he thought, or maybe an intelligent one. At any rate, she looked different from the women he'd met lately. More serious, perhaps. He liked her instantly.

When, in the course of the evening, they found themselves talking about war and its consequences, World War Two and Vietnam—not just one, but both—it occurred to him that he hadn't had so much fun on a date since Harvard.

Bebe had been a history major; she had opinions about things most women he met had no interest in. She also had values he liked; good politics, which for him meant more or less liberal.

And she had ambition. She wanted a career in politics. Once he met Bebe, he changed. He was so awed by her, by her strength, her ambition, her fineness. He found in himself some shred of self-respect he'd forgotten.

Despite the loathsome fact of his father's interference, his job at United was actually a pretty good gig. In fact, there was a lot about oil to interest him, a lot about business, for that matter, to sink his teeth into.

He married Bebe as quickly as he could arrange to and then set about building a life based around her ambitions, which he admired but didn't have himself. He would make money; he'd be a good husband and, later, father. She would conquer the world.

He settled into a period of contentment, both in his job and in his marriage, a contentment he never expected or even dreamed of. When he looked back on it now, it was undoubtedly the best time of his life.

His father, of course, thoroughly disapproved of Bebe, which made her all the more attractive. The old man mistook her vitality for aggressiveness, her naturalness for a feminist statement—and feminism was something for which he hadn't a moment.

The first time she ran for office, they worked night and day on the campaign, and when she won, the exultance, the sweetness of hard work that paid off, a victory well deserved, was the strongest high he'd ever experienced—more vivid, even, than the birth of their daughter.

Bebe had had a special glow, almost like a garment, that turned her gold and luminous. It was a new confidence, perhaps. He didn't know, he was just overcome with the feeling that he hardly knew his wife and he wanted her like you might want a performer, someone you didn't really know, but found sexy as hell on stage.

She felt it, too. All during the victory party, she kept giving him these looks, and on the way home, leaned far enough over to put her hand on his cock and nibble his ear.

She came out of the bathroom in something he'd never seen before, something white and possibly diaphanous (if he understood the meaning of the word). Her hair was wet and she tossed it over her shoulder with an impertinent turn of her head. "How would you like to fuck a city councilwoman?"

He was already hard.

Their political life had been like that for a long time—a literal turn-on; the glue that held them together. Never, never was he jealous of her—he didn't want to be her, he just wanted to be with her; wanted, possibly, some of the fairy dust to fall on him.

It was a sun-kissed, ever-spiraling high, fed by his own rapidly rising fortunes, which were attributable in large part to his involvement with the Skinners, a drug of another sort. The exhilaration of it was like getting out of a pool after winning a race—tingly not only with victory, but also with the sheer pleasure of using your muscles.

And then came the sailing accident, the five days in darkness; the spiritual dissection of everything in his entire life.

He didn't know it when he was rescued, but Bebe was lost to him at that moment. He had become a different person in less than a week, one she didn't recognize and didn't know what to do with.

In her place, he might have done what she had—tried desperately to understand him, and failing, begun collecting the illicit kisses of Ernest LaBarre or someone like him.

He didn't tell all of it to Dina Wolf, in fact hardly said more than that he'd once had a wife, and now he didn't. But she acted as if she knew everything there was to know about him.

She shook her head, slowly, as if slightly disgusted. "You are one fucked-up dude."

That certainly wasn't the impression he'd meant Dean Woolverton to make. He said, "You mean fucked-up drunk or fucked-up crazy?"

She held two fingers a quarter-inch apart. "You're just about this far from being drunk—and I don't know about fucked-up crazy. You seem like a very nice man. All I meant was, you seem confused."

He said, "Maybe you could bring me some clarity," but he really didn't know what he meant or why he was saying it.

"I think I'd better get you some coffee. Look, where do you live?"

He pointed at the sloop.

"You live aboard?"

He shrugged. "Bachelor's quarters."

"Well, I have a car. I'll take you somewhere and sober you up enough so you can get back to wherever you park that thing."

"I have coffee on board."

"Uh-uh." She shook her head firmly, and he understood that she was saying she wasn't going home with him. She took him to a place with lights so bright that just about did the trick by itself.

Three cups of coffee later, she deemed him okay to drive a boat. Later, when he thought about it, he had no idea what they talked about while he ingested brown liquid.

He hoped he hadn't told her any of his secrets, and made a solemn vow never to get drunk with a strange woman again.

About noon his phone rang, and he was sure it was a wrong number.

But it was she—the weird babe with the baseball cap.

"Hey, Dean—it's Dina. You okay?"

"Fine. Hey, thanks for taking care of me."

"I'm cooking tonight. You eating?"

Well, what the hell? What else did he have to do?

"Bring wine," she said, and gave him an address.

Thirteen

SKIP HATED IT when she stepped into her own courtyard and a German shepherd as big as a pony raced toward her, barking and snarling as if she meant to steal everything in her own house and rape herself as well. It happened these days every single time she came in.

"Napoleon, goddammit," she said, "don't be a chicken-shit. Bite me. Just go ahead and bite me." She held out a forearm for him to gnaw on.

"You're encouraging him," Steve said. "I thought you wanted him to stop."

"Maybe, deep down, I really want to be bitten."

"Oh, God, I better call Cindy Lou."

"Nah. Just give me a beer and let me cry in it."

He went to get the beer. After she had sat down and sipped it, Napoleon having been cowed into lying down, he said, "What's going on?"

"You didn't see the paper this morning?"

"Oh, God. Bebe and Ernest LaBarre. What an embarrassing piece of crap. I had no idea Jane Storey was like that."

"Well, she's not, really. Still, she's a reporter."

"Let's not get off the subject here. Could we go back to 'what's going on?' Possibly expand it to 'what's wrong?' "

"Everything. LaBarre's family's broken up—or damaged, anyway. I walked in this morning to find Mrs. LaBarre's wrists slit and blood all over the sheets."

"My God."

She took a pull of her beer. "Superficial wounds. Making a statement, I guess. It impressed me—don't know about Ernest. And Bebe's a mess. Who needs all this crap, anyway?"

"You think it's somehow your fault? I mean—that remark about being bitten."

"No. Not exactly. But Jane really, really shouldn't have done that."

"What would make her do it, anyway?"

"I don't know. The press these days . . ." She let it trail off, confident he'd know what she meant. "I mean, whose business . . . ?"

He was nodding. "Yeah. Whose? What's this stuff all about? It's the ass-end of the Roman Empire."

She found she didn't really want to talk about it anymore. "How's the house?"

"Great. It's just a wonderful little house. But everybody that works on it seems to think I won't even notice if they're a month late and charge me twice as much as they estimated."

"As I may have mentioned, this is a third-world country."

"I got these guys who were supposed to build a brick wall in the courtyard. They arrived with no bricks."

"They thought you were supplying them?"

"Nah. They just forgot to take the measurements to the brick supplier, so they had to come back and start over."

"Typical," she said, her mind wandering. She was wondering where the hell she was going to go with this damn Russell Fortier thing.

She spent the entire next morning going through Allred's files, bank and credit card records, and phone bills, but finding no trace of his mysterious client. Evidently there was no written record of the transaction.

She called her buddy Eileen Moreland at the *Times-Picayune* for all the clips on Bebe and Russell, thinking, *Talk about a dirty job. There's probably a mountain of them.*

In fact, there was an avalanche of them, mostly having to do with Bebe's runs for office and performance while there. For the moment, Skip put those in a separate pile, concentrating solely on Russell. And saw that there was only one story—or group of stories—that were really about him and not his wife.

They dealt with the sailing accident Bebe had mentioned. Skip found them riveting. She'd had no idea how huge the thing had been—how Russell had survived for days and then been miraculously rescued.

What it meant to the current case she had no idea—but she wondered for the first time if being Mr. Council-woman had grated on him.

She needed to speak with someone who really knew him—someone he confided in. And yet, she'd already talked to his wife, his mistress, and, so far as she knew, his three best friends.

She had asked Bebe for his Rolodex, and she went through it idly. Neither Gene Allred nor Talba Wallis was in it, but that was no surprise. Cindy Lou wasn't either.

Most of the names could have come out of the phone book—none rang bells or waved red flags. Dammit, she might as well go see Bebe again.

She phoned first; the councilwoman was in.

Bebe was looking the worse for wear, having huge circles under eyes that looked permanently red. Skip didn't know whether to ignore it or say something. She settled for, "How're you holding up?"

Bebe shrugged, tears coming to her eyes. She was on the edge.

"I'm really sorry you had to go through that."

"The phone's been ringing off the hook."

"Hate calls?"

"Some of each. A lot of people think I ought to resign."

Skip was silent, thinking that maybe she ought to; also that, this being Louisiana, the whole thing would be quickly forgotten if she didn't. Or it would if Bebe were a man. Skip didn't know if a double standard applied or not—it hadn't been tested that she knew of.

146

Bebe said, "Maybe I ought to."

"Maybe—"

"Do you know what some of them are saying? Some of them think I killed Russell."

And did you? Skip thought.

"Omigod, Ernest LaBarre! What was I thinking of?"

There was so much regret in her voice she couldn't be faking it—but that didn't get her off the hook.

By now, they'd reached the comfortable den in the back of the house. A young woman sat in one of the leather chairs, body curled around a portable phone that she now put in her lap. Skip could see that the girl was nearly as tall as she herself. She was slender and slightly stooped and she had brown hair that hung more or less artlessly. She wore no makeup, but her hair had been highlighted. Her face was set in as obvious a pout as ever was seen on a five-year-old.

Bebe said, "Oh! Eugenie. I didn't know you were there."

"Obviously not, Mother."

"This is Detective Langdon."

A tiny exclamation escaped the girl. She stood up to shake hands, wiping the pout off her face.

Ah, Skip thought. *Respect. I should get it more often.*

"You're here about my father?"

"Yes."

"Any news?"

"I'm afraid not."

The girl seemed crestfallen and Skip couldn't blame her. She said, "You must be close to your father."

Eugenie shook her head. "Not really. But he's my *father.*" She gave Skip a smile that might have been slightly guilty, said, "Nice meeting you," and left the room.

Skip turned back to Bebe, who was staring after the girl, heartbreak so obviously written on her face that Skip had to feel sorry for her.

Bebe said, "Sit down."

Skip didn't remind her of any of their previous conversations. Bebe had had time to think about things and might have a different take on them now. "I was thinking," she said. "Who knew about you and LaBarre?"

Bebe shrugged. "Nobody. Think about it. Who would I tell?"

"Could someone have seen you? Someone who might have mentioned it to Russell?"

"Of course not. We were always very discreet."

"Okay, let's leave that. Would you mind giving this Rolodex a look"—she produced the one Bebe had given her—"and see if any of the names jogs something for you? Is there anyone who had a special relationship with Russell whom he might have confided in?"

"Confided he was dumping me, you mean?"

Skip tried to keep her voice even. "If that's a possibility, yes. But frankly, I think there's something else—something at work, perhaps."

"What do you mean by 'something'?"

"A secret of some sort."

"You mean criminal activity?"

"I really don't know. It could be. He might have known something about someone else."

Bebe drew in her breath, seeing what Skip was getting at. She shuffled through the cards while Skip thumbed through a magazine. Skip thought she heard sobs from another room, but it could have been her imagination.

Finally, Bebe sighed and put the Rolodex aside. "I'm not getting anything."

"Okay. How about a phone bill? Let's see if there's a calling pattern."

Bebe looked at her as if she were speaking a foreign language. And then, having evidently translated, said, "Why not?" And left the room. She walked like someone with very little energy, barely picking her feet up.

She came back with a sheaf of papers. "Here are a couple of months of Russell's bills. He and I have separate phones."

Skip checked them. "There is a number." She showed the other woman. "See? Lots of calls and long talks."

148

Bebe said, "Look at this. Fifty minutes. Seventy-four minutes . . . Russell hates to talk on the phone."

Skip said, "Any idea whose number it is?" She had already memorized it, just in case.

"Sure." Bebe sounded utterly amazed. "It's Beau Cavignac's. Why Beau, I wonder? He's not . . . a confidant. At least, I wouldn't think so."

Skip waited.

"More like a sports buddy."

"Mind if I use your phone?" She wanted to avoid the chance of Bebe's warning him again. "Mr. Cavignac? Skip Langdon."

He said, "Who?" but she couldn't tell if his ignorance was real or feigned.

"Detective Langdon. Can you meet me at the Third District in fifteen minutes?"

"What's going on?"

"I'll tell you when you get there."

"Look, I've really got a lot of work . . ."

"Lunch will have to wait, Beau." *I wonder,* she thought, *if anyone calls him Beauzeau.* He was a man it was hard to take seriously.

She hung up. "Bebe, do me a favor and don't call him this time."

She turned red. "That was a bad thing, before, huh? I'm sorry—I just didn't think."

"It's all right." It was the way New Orleans was, and the way politicians were. This time, though, Bebe might not make a call—not if she was truly surprised Russell was spending so much time on the phone with Beau.

And Skip was inclined to trust that. Bebe hadn't balked at showing her the bill.

As she left, Eugenie stepped into the hall, holding a cat to her face, cradling it against her cheek. She had on very brief denim shorts, and she was barefoot. Her toenails, Skip thought, were probably the only female ones in the whole neighborhood without polish on them.

"Do you think you can find my dad?" she asked.

Skip thought the girl was asking for assurance that her dad was still alive. She didn't feel confident about giving it.

But she smiled and nodded, thinking the nod wasn't really a lie, it could be taken as good-bye. She said, "You take care of that kitty, now," and it sounded so lame she blushed.

Cavignac took half an hour to get to the station, not the fifteen minutes Skip had prescribed. Yet, when he arrived he had the air more of a man who'd been caught in traffic than a manipulator who'd made her wait deliberately.

He was mopping his brow, and his hair was mussed, as if he'd been playing with it.

She decided to be the Good Cop. "Nice to see you, Mr. Cavignac. Let's go sit down, shall we?" He nodded, not speaking, as she turned and led him to an interview room.

She gestured and smiled. "Sorry the accommodations aren't a little more elegant."

He nodded again, looking slightly annoyed. Evidently, he wasn't buying the Ms. Niceguy routine.

She tried again anyhow. "Sit down, won't you?"

He sat and so did she. "I'm missing an appointment, Ms. Langdon."

She looked at her watch. "Ah, twelve-thirty. Due at the Pickwick Club?"

"Ma'am, what can I do for you?" His voice was openly hostile. She thought he meant it to be icy, but he couldn't quite pull it off. He was a bearlike person, a warm person rather than a cool one. Hostility was possible, but not chilliness.

She did a masterful chill herself. "My name isn't ma'am, Beau; nor is it Ms. Langdon. It's Detective Langdon, please." She smiled an arctic smile. "Or Skip if you like." Ha. Got him both ways. She'd pulled rank and still given him permission to ignore it—he couldn't first-name her just to be annoying.

She didn't pause to let him call her anything. "I understand you and Russell are quite close these days."

150

"I told you that, ma'am." His eyes had turned to hard little beads.

Damn him. She felt a quick, electric flash of fury and suppressed it. She didn't think he was the sort who'd blurt things in the heat of anger. Instead, he'd just get stubborn and intractable.

She raised a conciliatory palm. "Beau. Beau." She uttered his name as if patting him. "There's nothing to be upset about. I need your help, that's all. Russell might be in danger."

He might. You never knew. He might also be dead, or living it up in Tahiti. "I know you and Russell have been in touch a lot lately."

She thought she saw a movement somewhere, as if a thumb had jerked in his lap; she couldn't really be sure. "I'll tell you what I think. I think Russell had some real problems and he was talking about them to you. Now that makes me think, why you? Do you have the same problem? If so, you could be in danger yourself."

"What are you getting at, Detective?"

He must be cooling down—at least he was using her title. "If something's happened to Russell, I don't want it to happen to you."

He looked at his watch. "I think I can take care of myself." He got up.

"Sit back down, Mr. Cavignac." (One "Detective" earned him a "Mister.") "I'm just going to ask you, flat out—why have you and Russell been on the phone so much recently? What were you talking about?"

"None of your damn business."

"Mr. Cavignac. You have the right to remain silent. You have the right to an attorney . . ."

"What the hell are you talking about? You can't arrest me."

"Not now, no. I just wanted to remind you where you are, and to whom you're speaking. This is a police investigation. When are you going to start taking it seriously?"

He sat back a little, drawing in his breath. She thought

he looked a little shamefaced. "I'm sorry. We're all under a lot of pressure."

Perspiration broke out on his forehead and once again, pulling a handkerchief from his pocket, he mopped it. "This is hard for me. I feel as if I'm betraying a friend's confidence."

Skip nodded, as reverently, she hoped, as if he'd disclosed the whereabouts of Atlantis.

Beau said, "He knew about Mrs. Fortier. About her . . ." he paused and spat out the distasteful word ". . . affair."

"Yes?"

"He was distraught about it."

Once again she nodded.

"It was . . . well, you can imagine how upsetting it was."

"What did he tell you?"

"Tell me?" He looked bewildered. "That's self-evident, isn't it? That she was having an affair with Ernest LaBarre. What else was there to say?" Once again, he sounded hostile.

She wondered if it were all a big fat squishy lie, or just a little dried-up baby lie, maybe with a grain of truth in it. She shrugged. "You tell me. There sure were a lot of phone calls."

"Who told you that?"

"Nobody. I saw the phone bills."

"Well, you know how people are when they have a problem. 'My wife's having an affair and I'm so unhappy I could just die.' "

"He threatened suicide?"

"No! Of course not."

"I thought you just said . . ."

Beau put up a hand like a traffic cop. "Okay, okay. I see what you're getting at. It was just a figure of speech. I mean, they say they're unhappy and then they say it again. You could die of boredom."

"And when he said he was unhappy, what did you say?"

"Me? I don't know. I just listened, I guess."

"Russell made the calls from home. That puzzles me."

"Why?" Beau was just too innocent for words.

"Bebe could hear him."

Beau looked almost triumphant, as if they were playing tennis and he'd finally scored. "She was always out at some meeting or other. That was part of the problem."

"So you think he left her?"

He looked like a person who'd just found a lost child. He nodded emphatically. "I do. I really do."

"Why didn't you say so before?"

"The LaBarre story hadn't come out yet. I couldn't break a confidence."

Skip smiled. "You've heard from him, haven't you?"

"Of course not." Outrage was written all over his face. But something was off. Had he spoken a little too quickly?

He took a moment to compose himself. "You know, he's a pretty different guy lately—I can't predict what he'll do."

Ha! Maybe we're getting somewhere. She said, "Different how?"

"I don't know. It just seems like he's lost the old killer instinct. He's become less competitive, I guess, less interested in his work."

"And how long has this been going on?"

"A couple of years. Since that sailing thing—you know about that?"

She nodded.

"I think that really took the starch out of him. After that he seemed like—well, 'a broken man' is putting it too strongly, I guess. He's just seemed kind of subdued. Quieter." Beau shrugged. "But then his mother died the week after, and his father died a few weeks ago. So let's see—if your mother died and your wife were having an affair, and your father wasn't doing so well, maybe you *would* be subdued." Beau looked extremely proud of himself.

"Well, speaking theoretically—if your theory is correct, and Russell did decide to disappear, where would he go? You probably know him better than anybody. What do you think?"

Beau did a strange thing. He put both hands over his mouth, separated them slightly, spoke briefly, and then put them back. "Let me think," was what he said. He thought for a full minute.

In the end, he shook his head. "I just don't have any idea." As if as an afterthought, he said, "Your guess is as good as mine." And shrugged again.

Fourteen

RAY WAS SITTING on the levee drinking beer, trying to cheer himself up, convince himself he'd done the right thing, but it was uphill work. He suspected there were lots of bad things he didn't even know about; consequences of his own actions.

The river was itself—big and muddy, like its nickname. Big and muddy and inevitable. It was what it was, it flowed like it flowed, and there wasn't that much could be done about it, unless you were the Corps of Engineers and even then it wasn't easy. He was trying to find a metaphor for life in this. The levee system was a good thing; the Bonnet Carré Spillway was debatable—both were attempts to control the river. Did that do anything for him? He turned it over in his mind a few times.

The part that worked for him was the part about big and muddy. Now, that described life, or anyway, life's problems.

Or anyway, his.

He thought about chucking his beer can into the river because he was already such worthless scum that one more misdemeanor didn't matter, but in the end his better nature won out. He put it on the floor of his car and drove home, where he carefully carried it into the house and threw it in the recycling bin.

The act was like shaving and getting dressed every day even though he had no company to run, and in fact, no job at all. You had to hang on to some vestige of dignity.

He heard Cille's car in the driveway. One day a week

she worked the early shift, but he'd forgotten it was today, had looked forward to an afternoon of wallowing in his misery.

The door banged as she came in. "Hi."

She was wearing white jeans and a white T-shirt, what passed, these days, for a nurse's uniform. She was heavier than she'd been when they met, maybe ten or twenty pounds heavier, but it looked good on her. Her hair was no longer blond, because she couldn't afford to have it colored these days, and remained fairly long because that way she didn't have to pay to have it cut as often. She generally wore it up, in artful disarray. To Ray, she looked like the prototypical Perfect Wife, but he knew in his heart she'd still look that way to him if she weighed three hundred pounds.

"What's wrong?"

"Nothing. Why?"

"Come on." She moved closer. They were so perfectly in sync she always knew when something was wrong.

He was sitting at the dining-room table—his makeshift desk—trying to think of something to do. She took another of the chairs. "What is it?" she said.

"Oh, I don't know. I just had a beer. I guess it got me depressed."

"Tell me."

"It's all this shit." He gestured impatiently at the pile of newspaper clippings that, for some masochistic reason, he was collecting. They were clips about the mini–oil boom out in the Gulf.

"Uh-uh. I don't buy that. It's LaBarre's wife, isn't it?"

He had already agonized about this at length—surely he ought to be over it. But Cille knew; she was uncanny that way. He took her hand. "Cille, what if she'd died?"

His wife shrugged. "If she'd died, it was her time. You didn't cut her wrists, she did. You didn't have an affair with Bebe, Ernest LaBarre did."

"That sounds so cold."

She squeezed the hand she was holding. "I know,

sweetheart. I know. But you want to see cold? Look at United Oil if you want to see cold."

"Mrs. LaBarre isn't United Oil. Even Bebe isn't. Hell, if it comes to that, even United Oil isn't. The very brilliant Baroness de Pontalba proved that—I think."

"Bebe might have known."

"Oh, honey, maybe. Maybe not. The point is, maybe I've gone too far. How do I know I'm not out of control?"

She gave his hand another squeeze, let it go, and got up. "Because your own sweet wife says so."

She really thought he could do no wrong.

It was her money he'd used to start the company. That night when he met her, the night she wore lilac and he fell in love with her, he had no idea she had two nickels to rub together. All that talk about starting a foundation, it turned out, was something more than idle chatter. She could have if she'd wanted to.

Her grandfather had been a doctor and her father had, too, but he had built on it with investments in the sort of places people went to die these days—extended-care facilities for the aged. Lucille's brother was a doctor, and she'd become a nurse, the only one in her family, but it was what she wanted to do, and now she was a nurse-practitioner. To Ray's mind, it seemed her own gentle form of rebellion. She didn't like doctors and didn't mind saying so—didn't get along with her moneygrubbing father and had no use for her arrogant, smug brother. She could have been a schoolteacher and made them all a lot happier, but you had to rebel somehow or other and she was a nurturer by nature.

She was probably the only nurse in New Orleans with several hundred thousand dollars in the bank—courtesy both of Granddad, whom she *had* liked (but who hadn't been around for a while), and her mother, who came from a shipping family and who had died young, despite all the medical men in her life. In Cille's head, the money was earmarked (after college was taken care of) for that foundation of hers, but it ended up going into Ray's dream instead of hers. She knew people and she introduced him to them. She had every confidence, as she said at least once a day over his protests, that he'd make so much money she'd have twice as much for her foundation.

She desperately wanted success for him, not because *she* needed it—she was fine being a nurse, it was her choice—but because he wanted it. She wanted what he did, but not in a clingy way. In that magical, mythical "supportive" way spouses, Ray thought, were supposed to have.

He adored her with every cell of his body.

He had had a beautiful little company—a lovely, profitable, splendid little company—Hyacinth Products, named for the water hyacinth, whose flower was exactly the color of the dress she wore the first time they met.

And then the damn Three-D seismic came in. Actually, that was fine—what had happened certainly wasn't the fault of the technology. He owed his demise unequivocally to Mr. Russell Fortier.

Okay, that did it—changed his mood completely.

Just thinking of Russell Fortier.

Gone too far? How could he have gone too far? Would he ever even have considered messing with people's lives as thoroughly and as utterly ruthlessly as Russell Fucking Fortier?

When it first happened, when he lost his lease, he tried putting himself in the position of the person or persons who'd screwed him out of it. At the time, only one was known, and it was Russell Fortier.

In a way, the thing was like an aikido move, using Ray's own strength against him. It was a thing that twisted and turned upon itself, a thing so devious it was enough to make you shiver in the middle of the night if you happened to wake up in a cold sweat because you could see everything you ever worked for going down the drain like a swatted insect.

When the company fell, he lost everything. Every cent he made had gone back into it. He and Cille had lived well, had even put a decent amount of money in a college fund, but not only was there nothing besides that—*nothing at all*—there were debts. He had put not only his own money into the company but other people's. And then, poof! One day there was no company.

Of course, he had sued. Fat lot of good that did.

At first, he would think about the person who had done this to him and wonder what had driven the man to it—if he had gambling debts, or a disabled child in a hospital too expensive to contemplate, and, assuming he did, if this could even help him. Or did he get some big, fat-cat Big Oil bonus for it?

Or maybe it wasn't any of that. Maybe it was done just for the sheer pleasure of muscle-flexing. Some sort of socially acceptable version of weenie-waggling. Maybe Fortier had done it just because he could.

Maybe he was the Prince of Darkness in a business suit.

That was really how it started—this no-holds-barred, crazy-assed scheme he was involved in now. It had all started with wondering what manner of man would do such a thing. He had researched Fortier and found no gambling debts, no disabled child. He had followed him, spied on him, become more and more obsessed.

Eventually, Lucille, in some mad attempt to help him get the thing out of his system, had suggested hiring Allred, which they had done with the little money they had left in the college fund.

After that, the thing took on a momentum of its own. It was still gaining, the proverbial downhill snowball; maybe it was unstoppable now.

Fuck it, Ray, he said to himself. *Would you really want it to stop?*

No way, José, his psyche answered. *Assuredly not. Negative in the extreme.*

When he thought of the wrong done to him and his family, his investors and their families—even, in some cases, his employees and their families—when he thought of all that, and the senselessness of it, the utter unnecessary-ness of it, the last thing he wanted to do was let it go.

159

He wanted the sons of bitches to pay. He wanted them publicly humiliated, and he wanted to take United Oil down.

United Oil had sold him Hyacinth Oil; had *sold* it to him. And now, out of no further motivation than corporate greed, they'd screwed him back out of it. Not, to be sure, Big Oil as a juggernaut—Russell Fortier had done it.

But had United said, "No thank you, Mr. Fortier. You've obtained this honest man's lease by nefarious means and we will have nothing to do with it"?

They had not.

It made him so mad he wanted to kill.

It made Lucille mad, too. He could see the tension of her muscles, those little ones in her hands, in her neck, her jaw, around her eyes—he could see how truly furious she was, though she wouldn't show it. It would ill behoove a member of the helping professions even to admit to so much anger—but Ray knew it was there. And it was there on his account—because he was her husband and she was an angel. But also because he was the underdog in this situation. Lucille was scrappy that way. She'd bite and scratch and tear flesh to help out an underdog.

Exactly what help Fortier had had, Ray didn't know yet, but with The Baroness on the job, he was sure going to find out.

And there was one other little thing—the murder of Gene Allred. The assholes were going to pay for that. It was just a matter of getting the damned disk, and the world was his.

160

Fifteen

OKAY. ON WITH the white blouse, the navy skirt, and the goddamn pantyhose, and run for the 82 Desire.

Some day she really must write a poem about it—the fume-spewing bus that replaced the streetcar. How poetic could you get?

The Baroness was looking out the window as she rode through the Bywater, thinking that Tennessee Williams had taken license, and he hadn't even been a poet. He had written: "They told me to take a streetcar named Desire and transfer to one called Cemeteries and ride six blocks and get off at . . . Elysian Fields." The streetcar had traveled a slightly different route from the bus, but even in Williams's day, if you were headed toward the cemeteries at the foot of Canal, you were headed to Metairie instead of paradise. In any case, it made a pretty metaphor, though Lamar had the gall to laugh at it. To actually laugh at Tennessee Williams. Well, Williams *was* white, but he was gay—that made him hip by definition. And besides, he was Tennessee Williams; you didn't laugh at Tennessee Williams.

Whoa, girl, she thought. *What's this?*

Usually anything Lamar did was okay with The Baroness. She didn't like thinking bad about him, because her mama and Corey hated him so much. *Somebody* had to defend the man.

Darryl Boucree's getting to me, she thought.

She had gone to bed last night thinking about Darryl.

And then she dreamed she got on a train and took a long trip.

I wonder, she thought, *if they've got trains named Desire? Think I might be on one now. Watch out, girl! He might be cute, but you don't really know him.*

Totally useless caveat, she knew it perfectly well—the guy wasn't cute, he was adorable. And who wouldn't be attracted to somebody who was a teacher just because he wanted to be?

Actually, she'd found out quite a bit about Darryl Boucree in their short but sweet beer date—the fact that he had two moonlighting jobs argued that he had some kind of dependent. But at least it wasn't a wife unless he was a liar, and whoever heard of a liar who liked poetry? (Oh, well, scratch that one—Byron, for instance, had probably had a mendacious streak.) But she didn't think it could be a wife. Probably a mother or something.

The exciting thing about Darryl Boucree, and perhaps the thing that had most drawn her to him, was that he was a musician. Creative people understood each other. Well, actually they didn't, if one were she and the other Lamar, but at least they had a good shot at it. And Darryl was actually one of the Boucree Brothers! (Though he had explained to her that the membership of the band changed nightly and they weren't all brothers—some were uncles and cousins and fathers and sons.)

What must it be like to be from a family like that?

When she asked him that, he laughed—said it was just like any other family, but she didn't believe it. In fact, she knew it wasn't—it was nothing like her family, which thought her crazy and irresponsible because she was a poet.

I hate to think what they'd do if they ever found out about the dicking.

The thought, mundane as it was, set off some little pleasure center in the back of her skull, made her feel warm and chocolatey-sweet for a second. What was that all about?

Ah, she had it. The "dick" locution reminded her of

162

Darryl, because he'd thought it up and they'd had that little exchange.

Something had definitely been set in motion. *Oh, well. Que será.* Which reminded her of something else—in addition to his other sins, Lamar didn't like Alfred Hitchcock movies. He didn't like anything to do with honky culture; it surprised Talba, but she did. Everything was too mixed up together to throw out big chunks without a damn good reason.

She got off at Canal and walked the rest of the way. The name she had, the dude she was supposed to report to, was Edward Favret. She found, to her utter delight, that he was in the same department she'd been in before, Acquisitions and Property. She thought, as they shook hands, *That fifty bucks I slipped ol' Currie must have done the trick.*

But Favret quickly disabused her. "Ms. Wallis, it's a pleasure. I've heard a lot about you."

Oh, shit. She thought she'd kept a low profile.

"Robert Tyson says you're the best temp he's ever worked with, and we ought to hire you permanently— maybe that's a thought, if you're interested." He gave her a look that made her nervous. He didn't even know her. She hoped.

But she smiled and nodded, and a line rang through her head: *All nice like a good little pickaninny.* That was how her poems started sometimes—as lines that she expanded on. *I'm fixin' to write about being a temp for Big Oil,* she thought, and wondered if she could do it on company time.

"Anyway, we're revamping here—we've got a lot more stations that have to go in. I can really use you."

Not good, she thought. *Best not to be noticed at all. But can I help it if I'm a hell of a nerdette?*

He left her alone.

Robert Tyson, hidden by some office module that looked like it belonged in a spacecraft, scooted out, and gave her an amused grin. "My favorite genius. Welcome back to wage slavery."

"Hey, Robert. How's it going?"

"Better now that you're back. You ever think of applying for a permanent job? You ought to consider it. You're good, girl."

"You really think so?" *You don't know the half of it.*

"I really do. We could use you around here. And it's not a bad gig, except when they treat you like a nigger, which in my case is about half the time."

"Been laying a lot of wire, huh?"

He grinned again. "No, actually, I can't complain. I had a few weeks doing what I was hired for—*real* interesting project. Dynamite project."

Normally, she'd have loved to hear more about it. She was starting to miss programming. But at the moment she was anxious just to get him out of the way so she could steal her file—which was going to be a snap, due to the little alteration she'd made last time she was there.

She said, "But if I came here, I wouldn't get to do squat—'cause I'm black *and* female."

He grinned again. "No, that's better—the old double-minority dodge."

She grinned back. "Whatever works," she said, and bent over her computer, waiting for lunch.

She planned to lift the file she needed as soon as he left. Technically she could do it with people around, but the last person who had that file had died. For all she knew, even nice Robert Tyson couldn't be trusted.

After a while, she watched him fetch his brown bag and head off to the coffee room. Okay, good. She connected to the now-shared drive on Fortier's workstation, once more brought up the "Find" command, typed in "Skinacat," clicked the "Find Now" button, and murmured, "Come to Mama."

The status line read, "0 Files Found."

They must have changed the name of it, she thought. *Especially if they know it's been stolen.*

What to do next?

Damn, damn, damn! If only she'd kept the names Allred had given her. It was true what she'd told the cop—once she was done with them, they were out of her head. But if she could just remember one of them, and the renamed "Skinacat" still existed, she could use the "Find" command to sniff out the file.

She closed her eyes and focused.

"Talba! You're back." It was one of the secretaries she'd met when she worked here before.

"Hey, Rochelle—look at you! Your due date must be about yesterday."

The woman stroked her distended belly. "It's got to be a boy—anything this big . . ."

Talba was too impatient to swap wives' tales about carrying high or low. "When *are* you due?"

"Not till the middle of next month. Do you believe that?"

Another voice said, "Rochelle, who're you talking to? Talba! How long you here for?"

Rochelle said, "Come on, Talba—let's have lunch."

Talba gave in. People were prowling about, coming and going from lunch, and she probably wasn't going to have a moment's peace. Meanwhile, she could let her unconscious work on the problem.

And sure enough, the answer came in the coffee room. One of the women had a child who went to a private school named Newman, and she remembered that was one of the names on the disk. Marion Newman— she recalled the first name because it was so unusual.

Back at her desk, she asked the "Find" command to locate Marion Newman and once again found herself looking at "0 Files Found." That could mean only one thing—somebody had removed "Skinacat." *Good-bye, $1,500.*

That was completely unacceptable. Talba's mind turned it over as she did her legitimate nerd work. *Maybe,* she thought, *I spelled it wrong. Maybe it was Marian. Or Neuman, or even Neumann.* She decided to break it down, trying each word individually. She typed in "Newman" and was instantly rewarded—there was a file named that.

She was just about to check it out when she looked up and saw Edward Favret leaning over her cubicle. He had a slightly sloshed look, being apparently just back from lunch. "Brought you a cookie."

She looked at him curiously, wondering. Yes, no doubt about it. He was flirting. She said, "Thanks, Mr. Favret, but I'm on Sugar Busters."

"Oh, Christ. Not you, too." It was the diet of the moment. "You don't need to lose weight."

She smiled, all nice again. "It's not that. I'm already sweet enough."

"Isn't that just the truth?" he said, as if he'd thought of it himself. He wandered off dreamily, the cookie still in its Mrs. Fields bag.

It was too narrow an escape. Talba decided to wait till after work to finish, when Robert Tyson had gone, and Favret had gone, and Rochelle had gone, and she could get a moment's peace.

Tyson was the last to leave. " 'Bye, good-looking. See you in the morning."

" 'Bye, handsome." She spoke absently, not even looking up, to discourage conversation.

He stopped anyway. "Working late?"

"I'm leaving in about five minutes. I'm just at the end of something."

"I'll stay a minute and walk you out."

Shit! she thought. *What if he decides to help me?*

But at that moment, her phone rang.

Lamar, goddamn him. She picked up. "Well, no problem," said a vaguely familiar voice. "I asked for Her Excellency, The Baroness de Pontalba, and they put me right through."

"Darryl? Darryl Boucree, is that you?" She looked up at Robert Tyson and watched a slow smile spread across his features. Evidently grasping the situation, he waved and went on out. "How'd you get my number?" she asked the phone.

"Your mother. Who else?"

"Good thing I don't have any enemies. She'd probably give them my address and everything."

"She said she thought I sound nice."

"Well, you do, darlin'. Can I call you back? I'm just finishing up here."

"Great. That's what I was hoping. Want to grab a bite?"

"I don't know—I'm ... um ... let me call you in a minute?"

"Sure." He gave her his number and hung up.

In fact, she more or less had a date with Lamar. Or anyway, Lamar would expect to see her, as he did every night or so, and if she was suddenly busy, he'd come to the correct conclusion. However, she noticed she hadn't refused. She sat alone in the office, mulling over the situation; trying to figure out a way to have her cake and eat it, too.

Damn it! I like this man.

But if I go out with him, it's good-bye to Lamar. Am I ready for that?

It took her only a moment to come up with the answer: *More or less.*

Now what to do? Call Lamar and come clean? Was she going to do that?

That was easy: *Hell, no.*

Well, then, what? *Say I'm sick. Or better yet, lay the groundwork—say I really need a night off, and if he asks questions, that we can talk about it later.*

She dialed and got his voice mail. "Hey, Lamar," she said. "Listen, I just got a call from Lorene. She's broken up with Herbert again and wants me to come over. I'll call you when I get home."

It popped out, just like that—a full-blown lie that she didn't even have to think about. *Obviously,* she thought, *I'm not ready to deal with this.*

Okay, fine. There was only one problem—the client had said he'd call tonight, and she sure needed to talk to him. He'd called early before—maybe he would again.

She phoned Darryl before she lost her nerve. "Hey, I'd love to go out tonight. Want to pick me up at home?"

"Can't I just get you at work?"

"Sorry, I have to go home first. Or shall we make it another night?"

"Tonight's good," he said. "What time?"

He had a really lovely voice. "Eight," she told him. It was six already; she'd better hustle her butt.

On pins and needles, she opened up the Newman file. It was gibberish.

Talba felt sweat at her hairline. *Shit. It can't be.*

But she knew very well that it could be. Since the last time she worked at United, they'd installed an encryption program. The good news was, "Skinacat" was probably still there—they'd probably just changed its name. Whatever the new file was called would also be encrypted, which was why the "Find" command hadn't worked.

Talba's mind raced. That had to be what Robert Tyson meant when he said he'd just done a dynamite project. If the file was there, there was still a chance of getting it.

She caught the 82 Desire, raced in, and went straight to her room, ignoring Miz Clara's pointed delivery of the message that Darryl had called. She needed to grab a ten-minute nap to clear her head.

She'd just closed her eyes when the phone rang. "Hi, this is your client."

She said, "I'm working on your project."

"What do you mean you're working on it? Why don't you have it?"

"I've hit a snag, to tell you the truth."

"What's that supposed to mean?"

"They've added some security. I haven't been able to get into the file I need."

"What the hell kind of security?"

"Nothing I can't solve. Don't worry, it's happening. Just give me a couple of days."

"I don't have a couple of days."

"I'm doing my best, okay?"

"I guess it'll have to be." He sounded miffed, but fuck him.

Miz Clara came into the room. "You gon' call that young man or aren't you?"

"Mama, he called me at work. He's due here in a few minutes. Does that make you happy?"

"Oh, Lord. I guess I'll have to get my own supper."

But Talba could tell she wasn't that upset about it.

She turned her attention to finding something to wear that wasn't a white blouse and navy skirt.

Sixteen

DINA WOLF WAS the last person he expected to end up in bed with, but there they were in her brass bed with the white-painted finials and floral comforter.

The walls were white in the bedroom, living room, and kitchen, which pretty much comprised her condo, unless you counted the balcony, or whatever they called it in Florida. The place was airy and comfortable, with bright laminated ads on the walls, which at first he didn't get, until he realized they were her own work.

Right, she was a graphic designer. Russell had a hard time with that—it seemed a decent profession and she evidently owned the condo, but there were things about her that seemed so ding-y. Like her clothes, the first night he met her, and the fact that she was in that bar at all (though of course he was, too), and her extraordinary penchant for purple toenails.

Did grown women really go around in baseball caps and purple toenails? She kept saying, "This is Florida, baby. You gotta relax," and no doubt she was right. He really did have to relax.

Underneath the baseball cap, she had brownish, very fine hair cut in a sort of cap with bangs, wispy side ends pushed behind her ears as if she just couldn't be bothered. Her eyes were blue and very big, and her skin tan, but less than perfect—a little mottled from the sun. She favored white sheets (always his favorite), and now, cuddled up in them, she was undeniably cute as a button.

So these were her personalities—cute, kind of bossy

and straightforward, ding-y, and somewhere, somehow, professional, he supposed, but he hadn't seen that one yet.

She was a far cry from Bebe, or from any woman he knew in New Orleans, but maybe that wasn't a bad thing. Maybe he needed to expand his horizons.

He lay on his back and thought, *That's why I left, isn't it?* He looked over at Dina to reassure himself. She was warm and soft and alive and accepting—though way too abrupt for his taste; way too weird for him; in the long run, not his kind of woman at all. But nobody said they were getting married.

He liked her a lot. He just wasn't sure what planet she was from.

He put a hand on the warm, soft skin that covered her rib cage and she stirred a little.

Sex with her had been a pyrotechnical display the likes of which he could more or less remember from somewhere back in adolescence, but which he'd almost forgotten about. It had never been that way with Bebe; it was always just sort of companionable and sweet. It had been downright scary with the too-beautiful Cindy Lou— not that Cindy Lou wasn't what Douglas Seaberry called "technically perfect," but he just couldn't believe he was in bed with her, and that really put a damper on the process of enjoying it.

This girl Dina was like some prerational protohuman, all tongue and legs and slippery, sliding surfaces, twisty moves, odd little noises. She was so aggressively sexual, he wondered if she'd had a sex change—women, in his experience, just weren't this wildly, wonderfully demanding. It confused the hell out of him.

He'd kill to do that again—what they'd done the night before, which was everything. But this girl was a wild animal. Weren't they supposed to be dangerous?

She woke up and smiled. "Hi," she said, and touched his cheek, more like a little kid than an animal.

"Hi." He reached for her and she snuggled against him, closing her eyes as happily as a puppy.

She's so trusting, he thought. *She doesn't know me any*

better than I know her, and I'm the one who could be dangerous. In fact, if she happened to get a gander at my driver's license, she'd probably wonder why someone named Edward Favret claims to be Dean Woolverton.

Before he changed his appearance, he had looked quite a bit like Edward. What could be easier than lifting the wallet of someone whose coat was constantly hanging up a few doors away from Russell's? Voilà—license, cards, the whole nine yards. Of course, he couldn't charge anything on the cards—and wouldn't want to anyway. All he wanted was a picture ID to get on a plane, backup cards for it, and a Social Security number. That would be enough paper to open a bank account and buy a boat. The boat thing was a little sticky, because of taxes, but too bad; for that purpose he could just continue being Edward.

Soon enough, though, he'd have to tackle the problem of getting a fake set of papers.

The tangled-web cliché flitted briefly across his psyche, and he thought that in his case, it was more or less backward. The line went, "when *first* we practice to deceive." For years, he and his pals had woven a magnificent mesh of deceit, not so much as a kink in the silk, much less a tangle. If not for one madman, Ray Boudreaux, they might have gone on doing it until they took over United Oil Company, which in time they might have, they were so successful at what they did.

Which was screw people out of what was rightfully theirs.

Of course, the company didn't know that; they thought the Skinners (a name they'd never hear) got results just because they were brilliant strategists. Which was true. Oh, it was certainly true. Over the years, they had come up with some unbelievably brilliant schemes, many of them crookeder than a mountain trail. The one they'd pulled on Ray Boudreaux was about the best.

In fact, that was the one that haunted Russell the most, the one he'd thought about most in the darkness of those five days. It was so relentlessly, revoltingly mean it

172

made him wonder if there was any possible redemption for those who'd participated.

But the Skinners hadn't started out to be mean at all, or even to be dishonest. They were four perfectly ordinary young balls of fire (well, Favret and Seaberry were balls of fire—Fortier and Cavignac were just guys doing their jobs), who happened to get a nearly impossible assignment.

That is, Seaberry got the assignment, and recruited his buddies to help him with it.

Somebody at the top didn't like Seaberry, or else (no doubt correctly) perceived that Seaberry posed a threat to him. While everybody else was out doing exciting stuff in the Gulf, Seaberry had been charged with the job of finding lucrative reservoirs in Jefferson and Plaquemines Parish. They were there, all right, and because of the new Three-D seismic equipment, they were being found. The problem was, they were often on land already leased to someone else—someone who wouldn't be interested in selling.

It was a stupid, thankless, frustrating assignment, and they were having fairly poor results. All of them were feeling tense, and one weekend they'd gone duck hunting.

Russell hadn't thought about it in so long he'd forgotten that part. They were in this camp, this male-bonding kind of place that belonged to a friend of Favret's, where they'd just made some robust firehouse meal like spaghetti ("pasta" was far too effete) and garlic bread. They'd tossed back quite a few brews and probably some Scotches as well, and they were probably telling some sort of macho lies—about past football prowess or something—when somehow the talk took a swing toward the thing that was getting them down.

They'd been tense with each other at the time—tense in general—and they were feeling relaxed for the first time in weeks or even months. How it happened, Russell would never know—maybe the stars were right for it.

But the general atmosphere of guy-type exaggeration had somehow spawned it.

One minute they were sitting there cursing the assholes who'd gotten them into this and the next they were joking about outrageous ways out of it—kill the guys who were doing the glamorous stuff, or maybe kill the guys with the leases.

Russell could remember the exact moment it had started. He could see Beau Cavignac waving a beer, wearing some stupid flannel shirt that belonged on a lumberjack, and saying, "Listen, there's more than one way to skin a cat—let's just kill 'em all."

"Blood!" someone shouted.

And then Seaberry said, "Why don't we just screw 'em out of their damn leases?"

There were all sorts of legal tricks possible with leases. The jokes that went on that night were of a somewhat technical nature, but nonetheless jocular in the extreme.

"Hey, here's one," Seaberry had said, with regard to some dude who wouldn't sell—call him Smith. "We get him for discrimination. We find some person of color who used to work for him and we just pay him to start a lawsuit that'll wipe Smith out."

"How about this one?" Cavignac added. "You know how nobody's very careful about paying their royalties? Well, we just stir up the landowners. Simple as that—a bug in the right ear, and voilà, an audit—followed by a lost lease."

"Beautiful," Russell said. "Magnificent in its simplicity. But why go simple when you can be devious? We hire our own accountant, see. And his job is to sign on with Smith."

"Hey, wait," Favret objected. "Maybe Smith doesn't need an accountant."

"Well, we kill his or something. And then we say to our guy, all you have to do is cook this dude's books, and United's business is yours till the end of your days."

"What does that do?" Cavignac asked.

But Seaberry had already put it together: "Leases

have to produce in 'paying quantities,' or they terminate. Suddenly the books show losses."

"Goddamn, let's do it! Let's just goddamn do it."

Well, they had. It had started out as absurdity, and then they'd simply done it—done all the things they thought of that night and more. Everything they could think of, in fact, over the next few years—except for the murders, that is. Even the Skinners had drawn the line at that.

They'd given themselves the name after Cavignac's cat-skinning remark. At the time, it had some resonance involving wildcatting, but all that had been lost in the mists of time.

They had a system. Whenever they had a problem, they'd get drunk and get loose, and let their criminal sides take over. It never failed to amaze them all how inventive they could be. And if it were outrageous enough, they did it.

For Russell, at any rate, it was like that giddy time when he was first learning to sail. What a high! What a sense of exhilaration!

He hadn't given a thought to the people they were hurting, or to their families—he had seen them only as the enemy, had seen each problem as a challenge.

And it paid off. Oh, did it pay off—in raises and bonuses and promotions.

They were high rollers who couldn't lose, and the other three were still doing it right now, unless Boudreaux had succeeded with his plan to expose them all and right their wrongs—if in fact, that was what he wanted to do. Russell wasn't all that sure. They'd offered Boudreaux money to go away, but apparently it wasn't enough. Maybe they *would* kill him.

Russell had already started to come apart when Boudreaux surfaced. By that time, he was just getting through, having lost the heart to be a corporate criminal.

But if he didn't continue, if he joined Ray in his whistle-blowing, he'd end up in jail. Worse, though, where did it leave Bebe? She couldn't help but be tainted by it.

He'd done enough, and hurt enough people without

dragging Bebe down. Sure, he wanted to be Dean Woolverton—start a new life, take the sloop cruising, all that glamorous stuff. Sure he did.

But also, he had no choice.

Dina Wolf stirred. "I'm hungry."

Russell said, "I've got a nice sausage for you."

"Oh, please. It's first thing in the morning." She stretched. "I'd kill for a bagel."

"Okay. Let's go out and find one."

"I've got plenty in the freezer. All you have to do is somehow cut them and heat them. I can wait. I've got some eggs in there, too."

"Hey, how'd this get to be my responsibility?"

"I thought you volunteered." She looked at him with those huge blue eyes, her bangs covering her eyebrows, her nose a bit sharp for his taste, and she reminded him of his daughter—so cute and innocent, he couldn't imagine her manipulating him into making breakfast.

Ray could remember it like it was yesterday—the first time he ever met Russell Fortier. He and Lucille and Margaret Ann had been on one of those scouting weekends families go on to scope out colleges. They had had two days away from Ronnie, who was in what Cille called a "bad stage of development," meaning he stayed holed up in his room all the time, probably masturbating, coming out only to heap scorn on everyone and everything in his immediate vicinity.

Margaret Ann tended to get sulky around him, but in fact that wasn't her nature at all, a delightful fact Ray had almost forgotten. The three of them had had meals together, had gone shopping, even sandwiched a movie in between appointments, and his daughter hadn't once tried to duck out of sight, embarrassed to be seen with her parents. At Vanderbilt, she'd acquitted herself splendidly, chatting and asking intelligent questions as if there was something she cared about besides *The X-Files*. Ray had for the first time a sense of who she really was, the nearly formed adult they'd be shipping off next fall.

They got back late Sunday night, and even after the flight and the seemingly endless drive across the causeway, he had felt exhilarated. Margaret Ann went off to her room, Ronnie didn't come out of his, and he and Cille had an unaccustomed nightcap, drinking to the excellent job they'd done, bringing up this child to be a credit to her age and sex and social position. In fact, they were feeling so warm and fuzzy about it all, they went upstairs and made love.

Ray was feeling on top of the world when he went in to work the next day. It wasn't ten o'clock before the phone rang and an unfamiliar voice spoke to him: "Mr. Boudreaux. This is Russell Fortier over at United Oil. I wonder if I could talk you into having lunch with me?"

Just like that. Lunch, for no reason. These Big Oil bozos behaved this way—as if anyone in the world would be thrilled to pieces just to spend a couple of hours in their boozy presence.

Ray decided to jolly him along. "United? Really? I used to work there myself."

"Oh, yeah, we all know you—bought a lease from us and built yourself a nice little company. Must be nice being your own boss."

"Can't beat it."

"How about Galatoire's on Friday?"

Ray didn't know what this guy wanted, but he evidently thought he was going to get it—Russell Fortier had the confidence of some high school football captain who didn't know any better. Ray said, "I'd rather eat my gun."

"I beg your pardon?"

"Last thing I want to do is get into that kind of trouble." Galatoire's on Friday was more like Mardi Gras than lunch. People went at noon and didn't come out till six P.M. It was a place for a power lunch in the networking sense only, unless of course you were the object of the power play—in which case, it was a great place to get you drunk and friendly toward your host. Serious business was sure to be interrupted by table-hopping friends, single women on a flirting mission, even, sometimes, too-friendly waiters with a snootful.

Fortier laughed to show he wasn't put off. "How about Thursday?"

"I think maybe you ought to give me some idea what this is all about."

"I've got a little business proposition I thought you might be interested in."

"You? Or United?"

"Why, United, of course. I'm in Acquisitions over here. We're interested in Jefferson Parish."

"You mean Hyacinth? Hold it, I bought it from you."

"Now isn't that an ironic note?" Fortier laughed long and hard, but to Ray the humor sounded forced.

"Sure," Ray said. "I'm free Thursday. How about the Rib Room?" Just because Fortier had picked Gala-toire's. He believed in keeping his opponent slightly off-balance. And, till he found out what was going on here, he decided to consider Fortier an opponent.

The guy wasn't a bad sort—Ray liked him on sight, found him less slippery, maybe a little smarter than your average urban corporate robot. He did notice that they had barely ordered their Caesar salads when Fortier got it on the table that he was married to Councilwoman Bebe Fortier.

Well, Ray didn't blame him. He was proud of his own wife and he could certainly understand the impulse. As it happened, he and Cille both were great fans of Bebe Fortier, though they lived in St. Tammany Parish, and couldn't vote for her. "We admire from a distance," Ray told Fortier, spearing a crouton and jumping right to the point. "Now, what was it you wanted to talk to me about?"

His lunch companion was staring out the window at some ragtag redneck street band. "You know, I love those guys. They've been playing on Royal Street for years." He had a dreamy look on his face.

Ray resigned himself. "I like the woman who plays the clarinet in front of the A&P."

He was going to have to go at United Oil's pace—they were paying for lunch, they could have it their way.

He was stirring his coffee when Fortier said, "I want to plant a thought in your head—just a tiny little thought, maybe nothing you and I want to act on right away. But here's the idea—United might be willing to buy your company and let you keep running it."

"Now, why would they do a thing like that?"

Fortier looked him in the eye. "Money. Why does United Oil do anything?"

They got a good laugh out of that one.

Ray said, "Obviously you know something we don't."

"Tell me—if a new reservoir were detected, could you afford to drill?"

Ray shrugged, forbearing to say, *None of your damn business.*

Fortier named a number in seven figures, leaned back in his chair, and said, "Think about that. You'd get the bucks, plus a generous salary for doing the same job you do now. But it would be about half the work—think how many headaches we could relieve you of."

The offer was insulting—less than half what the company was currently worth, even without a new reservoir. Ray wiped his mouth to cover his anger and then forced himself to smile. Sometime during lunch, they had achieved a first-name basis, but Ray said, to make a point, "No, thank you, Mr. Fortier."

"We're flexible, of course. That's certainly not our final offer—it's just a starting place. Call it a number to think about if you should want to get together some figures of your own."

Ray had taken Fortier for a smarter cookie than this. He was disappointed, not only in the wasted two hours, but also in the man. He'd liked him. Now he didn't know what to think.

He said, "I'm really not interested in selling the company at any price," and with that, he sealed his doom. That was what the damn lunch had been all about—eliciting a secret so open Ray would have told the press if

179

they'd asked him. But of course that didn't dawn on him till after he'd lost his lease.

It was another month before Fortier called again. Once again, he didn't sound right on the phone: "Ray! How you been, boy?"

Just a trifle too hearty. "I've got some real interesting news for you. Real interesting. How about we have another of our famous lunches?" Like they were best buddies.

Ray said, "My schedule's pretty full these days. Maybe we could talk about it on the phone."

"Oh, no. This is much too good for that. Come on—break away for a while."

"I'd love to, but I really can't manage these days."

"Listen, I'm gonna tell you what this is about. We've acquired some very exciting seismic data that might affect you. You haven't acquired your own yet, have you?"

Ray didn't answer, and Russell jumped in to fill the void.

"Look," he said, "I'm out front in my car. Why don't I just come in?"

It would have been churlish to say no, and Ray was feeling churlish—but in spite of himself, he was interested. He sighed mightily, a man much put upon but just this once making a concession: "All right." If he'd said no, he'd still have his nice house on the North Shore and Ronnie would probably be in MIT instead of UNO.

When Fortier had come in and sat down, Ray glowering at him all the while, he said, "How much do you know about Three-D seismic?"

Ray shrugged. He had known before, during their lunch at the Rib Room, that all that talk of a new reservoir was dependent on what was then new technology—"profiling" done with Three-D seismic equipment.

Fortier said, "Look, it's very simple. It's a way to predict oil reservoirs. Nothing to it, really—you put earphones on the surface that can record sound waves. Then you shoot off dynamite, and the sound waves are reflected off the layers of the earth in different ways. If you've got gas or oil-bearing reservoirs, you can tell by the way the sound hits and returns to the surface."

"Sounds like magic," Ray said, though he well knew it wasn't.

"Well, it takes some of the guesswork out." Fortier reached into his briefcase and started unfolding things. "Look at this. This is exciting, boy."

He handed Ray a document, poster-sized, completely unintelligible. "Ever seen a seismic profile?"

"Are you going to get to the point, Mr. Fortier?"

"Sure. Sure. I just thought you'd like to see it, that's all." He brought out a map of the northernmost part of Ray's land, superimposed over a subsurface map, a "structure map" presumably made from the data in the profile. "See what we got here? The beginnings of a great big oil field. It starts on our land—but it looks like you got most of it. See, the equipment doesn't have to be above oil-bearing sand to predict that it's there. By shooting on one tract, you can extrapolate what's under another."

Ray was cool as a pool. "Well, it's mighty good-hearted of my alma mater to let me know about all this."

Fortier grinned. Sometimes he did seem to have the sense God gave a bunny rabbit. "Oh, not at all. Not a bit. We still want to buy your company."

"I told you—it's not for sale."

"Now, Ray, be sensible. Why don't you think about it awhile and then we'll talk about it?"

"There's nothing to talk about."

Ray could just see him grin and lean back in his chair. "Oh, I bet I could get you interested. I just bet I could. We're prepared to double our offer. Double it—did you hear that? And keep you on to run the company at three-fifty a year. Does that do anything for you?"

Ray wasn't at the time making anything like three-fifty a year and Fortier must have known it.

Ray asked, "Why don't I just drill it myself?"

"You know how risky drilling is. It usually takes

several tries to find a profitable well. Can you really afford that?"

"Well, I really appreciate your willingness to help out an old employee. I think that's mighty generous of you. But why do I get the feeling it's not going to work to my advantage?"

"Ray, be reasonable. How could three-fifty a year, plus a healthy profit on the company, *fail* to work to your advantage?"

Because you people are not stupid, you are merely ruthless. If you're willing to pay that much, it means there's a lot more money to be made.

That was his first thought, but it wasn't that that destroyed him. It was his pride. "Russell, I appreciate it, but I've built this company. I've got a lot at stake here."

"Look, Ray. Don't be too hasty. Just think on it. Will you promise me that? Just that one little thing." Ray could hear the desperation in his voice. He must be due a hefty bonus if he landed this one.

There was no reason Ray couldn't drill the well—or wells—himself. Actually, Fortier was right—it was exciting news.

Think of the expense, Fortier had said. Ray was thinking of it. He would have to borrow the money, but he could. He could get it from Cille.

In truth, the company wasn't doing as well as it should have been—had been producing less and less in the last couple of years. It would cease to be profitable soon, and United had to know that. Ray knew it, too—he just hadn't faced it.

Eventually, he would have had to borrow money from Cille to acquire his own seismic data, hoping against hope for results good enough to get new investors. But as it turned out, he didn't have to.

Russell said again, "Look, I really need you to think about it." He stood. "It's a ways back to New Orleans. Do you mind—"

"Bathroom's down the hall and to your right."

182

"I—uh—well, is there any place I could make a phone call?"

Ray showed him an empty office and went back to his own. The map and the seismic data were still on his desk, just waiting to be photocopied. Ray had qualms about it, sure, but he thought if Fortier was that careless, he must be pretty confident Ray couldn't afford to drill on his own. And other rationalizations; at the time, he lay awake thinking of them. Never once did it occur to him that the whole thing was a setup.

One of the many things he realized when it all shook down was that Fortier had called him from his car—if he had his cell phone, why did he need to make a call from the Hyacinth offices? He thought of that years later—literally years.

He took the photocopied profile and structure map to a geologist, who seemed mightily impressed. "Put it this way," the scientist said, "if it were me, I'd drill."

Ray drilled. Repeatedly. And failed to find oil.

He could still have gone on as he was, but for the law. Since he'd found no new production and his producing wells were running out, in a few years' time his lease was no longer producing in paying quantities—which meant that it terminated.

And none other than United Oil held the top lease on the property, the one that now became effective. Within four years of meeting Russell Fortier, Ray had lost his lease, his company, his livelihood, and his balls.

As soon as United took over the lease, Ray knew there had to be oil.

And there *was* oil—just a few hundred yards from the area where Ray had drilled. Once more Ray ran the map and the profile by the geologist, who came to the same conclusion he had. If the shot points—the sites of the dynamite blasts—were five hundred yards to the west of those shown on the map, oil would very likely be found where United had found it. In other words, Fortier had planted skewed data and a skewed map right where Ray couldn't resist stealing it.

183

Ray had reflected on the entire years-long sequence of events almost continually since it happened. The loss was enormous, the humiliation well-nigh unbearable. With perfect hindsight, he could see that if Fortier had never come calling, he would eventually have done what he had to do. He would have acquired his own data and found the new production himself, before his producing wells played out and his resources were exhausted.

There was no question in his mind he'd been defrauded, yet so cleverly that he'd executed part of the fraud himself. The scheme was a little like a pigeon drop, and he was the perfect pigeon—stupid enough and greedy enough to fall for it. His ears rang with anger whenever he thought of it.

He needed with all his being to get Russell Fortier and United Oil and make them pay. He was going to do it if it took him the rest of his life.

Ray knew just how, too; didn't even think it ought to be difficult. There had to be others like himself. All he had to do was find them, and he had a class action suit.

But he'd pored to no avail over records of leases that had changed hands, interviewing leaseholders who held bottom leases when United held the top ones. So far he hadn't been able to find a single similar case. And United held literally thousands of leases—there was absolutely no way to check them all out.

There was nothing left to do but get the data from United itself.

He'd almost had it when he made his fatal mistake. He shouldn't have threatened Fortier before he actually held it in his hand.

What he'd said was that he'd been talking to some of his neighbors, and it wouldn't be long before he blew United out of the water. He might have saved Allred's life if he'd kept his mouth shut.

And now he wondered if Fortier were in it alone. His wife's account of his disappearance just about squared with the time of the murder.

At any rate, there was nothing to do but proceed

calmly and heed Cille's advice—*he* didn't kill Allred and he didn't bed Bebe and he didn't cut Mrs. LaBarre's wrists. He had no control over any of that, and could only do what was in his power. That was where The Baroness came in.

"Grab a bite," Darryl had said.

Either that was a euphemism for an actual date, or the thing had taken on unexpected proportions.

Talba had dressed in a flowing outfit made of African cloth, cheaply procured in Krauss's last days and run up for her by a neighborhood seamstress. When she wore The Baroness's clothes, heads turned.

Miz Clara appeared mysteriously in her room, something she never did. Evidently she was checking up. She said, "Girl, where you goin' in that? That's not clothes, that's a costume."

"What should I wear, Mama? Crummy old jeans like I do when I go out with Lamar?"

"How 'bout just a ordinary dress?"

"I don't have any."

Well, that was true. There were three choices—the navy and white uniforms, the crummy old jeans, or the royal finery.

Miz Clara went off harrumphing, putting Talba in mind of Mammy in *Gone With the Wind*: "Young ladies who wear strange clothes most generally don't catch husbands."

When she was ready, Miz Clara was in the living room reading the paper, something else she almost never did.

Talba said, "Mama, if you insist on inspecting him, you could at least put on real shoes."

Her mama loved her slippers so much Talba didn't expect her to budge, but she looked down at the floor and laughed. "Guess you right."

Talba smiled at her. It had been a long time since she and her mama had laughed together. Maybe it had as much to do with Lamar as Miz Clara's rigid expectations of her.

The doorbell rang while her mama was getting shod. Darryl was on the other side, in jeans and a sports shirt with a button-down collar. He wasn't Talba's usual type at all, but his handsome face made up for it.

As if reading her mind, he said, "Sorry, I forgot my dreads."

Talba said, "Come on in. I want you to meet my mama—I may never have another opportunity like this."

When Miz Clara came out, she'd not only put on shoes but a clean blouse and an ear-to-ear smile—or maybe the smile came after she got a gander at Darryl. She came right over and stuck out her hand. "Hello. I'm Clara Wallis."

She just could not stop beaming.

Talba was surprised at how deeply embarrassed she was. "Mama, we've got to go."

Her mother slipped back into neutral. She said automatically, "Y'all have fun now," but her gaze followed them all the way down the walk.

Darryl said, "That poor lady! I wanted to tell her how sorry I am about that doctor."

Talba said, "What doctor?"

"Your Pill Man. The one who named you."

"Omigod."

"What?"

"I forgot for a minute. Usually, I'm obsessed with it. I almost never meet anyone new that I don't think about it. 'What would he think if he knew my real name?' It makes you feel shitty to have a name like that. Like you don't deserve any better."

Darryl looked over at her. "Well, I'm not new. We've seen each other twice before."

Talba couldn't think of what to say in reply. Was he setting her up to get in her pants? (Third date, almost.)

Or just making conversation? She was aware of a fluttery, ill-at-ease feeling.

Darryl said, "What's the matter?"

"I don't know. I'm nervous, I guess."

186

"Yeah, well. Girl named Urethra ought to be."

She said, "Where are we going?"

"To tell you the truth, your outfit's given me a real craving. How about the African place on Carrollton?"

"Benachin! Great idea."

It was a modest place, but atmospheric, and in some ways not unlike the place they'd met—a perfect place for a first real date. Not contrived, but a little romantic.

Darryl seemed almost simplistically happy. "This is great, you know that? This is really great. I was supposed to play a gig tonight, but it got cancelled. This is so rare—mmm mmm."

"What's rare?"

"Getting a night off in the middle of the week. Usually I'm bartending or playing a gig."

"Must play hell with your social life."

"Social life? I have no social life."

Was he telling her something? Talba assumed he didn't have a girlfriend, or what was he doing with her? But then, she did have a boyfriend. It took guts to ask out someone who did.

"Well, I was kind of wondering," she said, "why you wanted to see me tonight."

"Don't you know?"

"No." *Don't say you want to get in my pants.*

"You're an interesting woman—and I *really* like interesting women."

"You must meet lots of them. They say there are a lot more single black women than men."

"I think that's more *eligible* black men—there's a difference."

"What makes you so eligible?"

He took a sip of beer. "Well, I'm not sure I am. I have a child to support, three jobs, no free time, no money—"

"Hey, I hope you're planning to pay for dinner."

He laughed. "I figure even *I* make more than a poet. But then again, *you* have some mysterious other gig—maybe you're a cat burglar."

She shook her head. "Uh-uh. Remember, I said it's mostly legal. Right now, though"—she raised her palms, as if in apology—"right now I'm just doing some computer tech work." She made a face. "Seriously boring."

"I thought you were taking a break from all that."

"I am—from programming and software designing. This is just temp work."

He looked puzzled. "What's the firm?"

"Oh, just an oil company." Almost immediately, she saw her mistake. An odd, startled expression flickered briefly on his face, the kind people get when they run into an old acquaintance with a new spouse. Quickly, lest her silence seem suspicious, she said, "United. They're putting in a bunch of new workstations."

"I don't understand why you're doing it—it can't pay as much as what you usually do."

"Yeah, but it's easy work to get and good for pocket money."

"Isn't United where Russell Fortier worked?"

"Oh, law. As my Aunt Larcenia used to say. That's all they talk about over there."

"Larcenia! You've got to be kidding."

"Weird names run in my family. Seriously, I've often wondered if there was a Pill Man in her past, too—it's spelled with a *c*, just like 'larceny.' "

Darryl hooted, just once. And because of the momentary tension, Talba started to giggle. That got Darryl going, and next thing you knew, they were deep into a laughing fit that had people staring.

When she got control, Talba had to wipe her eyes. "Whoo. What was that?"

"I don't know. Do you always have that effect on men?"

"No. Usually they get down on their knees and call me 'Your Excellency.' "

"We might get to that. Your Excellency."

The mini-crisis evidently had been averted—if it was that. Talba wasn't sure what harm it would do to let this man know what she was up to, but Allred had always stressed the importance of utter secrecy. He was paranoid, of course, but maybe he knew something she didn't.

Seventeen

SINCE THE DAY before yesterday, it had occurred variously to Jane Storey to quit her job, to disappear in the night, to swallow Dranó, and to get unattractively drunk.

She had settled on the last, which was, after all, the time-honored working journalist's solution to immediate problems. Her good friend Jeffrey—gay, currently unattached, and always sympathetic—had been happy to join her at Vaquero's for six or eight margaritas.

She could remember Jeffrey grabbing her forearm and squeezing it tight. "Don't let that asshole do it to you, sweetheart. I hate to see you like this."

"I've got a bad feeling we should have had this little talk a few days ago. He's already done it to me. Or, more accurately, I've done it to myself."

"You get so precise when you're drunk."

"Jeffrey, I went against every instinct I had. I broke all my own rules."

"Maybe it's not too late for a life of prostitution."

"That's what the problem is—I've already got one."

"Well, for heaven's sake, you could at least make it pay—go back to television. You could probably name your price if you call tonight."

"Oooh. First the knife, and then the twist."

As a matter of fact, the local stations had broken the story of Mrs. LaBarre's sudden, mysterious hospitalization the night before. David Bacardi saw it and called

Jane at home. "Janie, are you watching the news? Why didn't we have the attempted suicide?"

"You don't know that's what it was."

"Well, why don't I? Why didn't you tell me and our thousands of loyal readers?"

Jane felt so humiliated she couldn't answer.

"Janie, are you there?"

She summoned all her resources, thought of what she wanted to say, and the gentlest way to say it. "David. Does it occur to you we're causing a lot of pain here?"

"Janie, for Christ's sake!" He sounded furious. "Toughen up. This is your job—if you don't like it, maybe you should consider a career in public relations."

That was supposed to be his biggest insult. It was an article of faith among certain newspaper folk that if you couldn't cut it as a reporter, you became a flack.

When she tried to explain it to Jeffrey, he said, "Let me get this straight. Am I buying the drinks tonight?"

"If you insist—why?"

"Do I always buy the drinks?"

"Oh, you sweet thing. Are you offering?"

"And why do I always buy the drinks? Because I make more money than you. Which brings up the question, Who doesn't? Hold it, I'm getting at something here— you bust your butt at that crummy little job for pennies instead of getting some cushy, good-paying job in the highly respected public relations field, and this is supposed to make you *better* somehow?"

"You don't get it, Jeffrey. It's like a fraternity or something. You know, a macho thing."

"Well, did it ever occur to you that that is garbahge?"

She had to laugh. "Yeah. Yeah, about a million times. But it's what I do."

"Personally, darling, I'd wish you a more lucrative life that would make you happier. And take you away from that Bacardi faggot."

"Jeffrey! Who're you calling a faggot?"

"Well, it's what he'd call me, isn't it? Tit for tat, dearie."

She laughed again. "Jeffrey, you're a sketch."

"Listen, when you call people, are they happy to hear from you?"

"Are you kidding? They get out their garlic and crucifixes."

"I know. And how do I know? You complain about it all the time. You don't make money, you don't get respect, nobody likes you, and you have bags under your eyes."

Jane felt her eyes moisten.

"Oh, honey, don't get mad. I didn't mean *nobody* likes you—I mean, it's an adversarial job. Nobody you call likes you; nobody you write about likes you."

"Some of them do," she said sulkily.

"And you never meet any decent men."

"Amen to that."

She wanted to blame the whole debacle on David Bacardi, but she simply couldn't shake the notion that she didn't have to do it—that she should have refused even if it cost her her job; that at the very least she could have taken her byline off the story.

The byline trick theoretically wouldn't have cost her a thing; but she hadn't wanted to antagonize David. She could kill herself for ever having gotten involved with him, either professionally or personally.

Jeffrey said, "You miss Walter, don't you?"

And the waiting tears finally spilled.

Jeffrey was cool, though. "Hey, hey, hey! Don't get mad, get even."

She smiled through her tears and said, "Yeah!" or something fake like that, and let him first buy her another drink, then skillfully turn the teary mood around with stories about his neighbor, Sharleen, the queen-sized drag queen. ("She's too fat!" Jane insisted. "It's ridiculous." "Oh, honey," Jeffrey said. "I've seen her without her makeup. Trust me, this way is best for everybody.")

She floated home on a cloud of tequila, but she awoke in the night, sweaty and panting from nightmares. What was chasing her she couldn't quite remember, but for some reason, Jeffrey's words echoed in her head like "The Tell-Tale Heart": *Get even.*

She woke up mad, which made her oddly energetic for a woman with a hangover. The first thing she did was call in sick. The second was make strong coffee, and the third was use the high from that to get to the Camellia Grill, where she ordered a hamburger. Jane believed devoutly that hamburgers could cure hangovers.

If it didn't work, at least it made a dent.

She couldn't do a damn thing about David Bacardi being her boss, or her ex-lover, or a perfect prick, but he wasn't the only one she was pissed at. In her shame at what she'd done, she'd almost lost sight of the fact that she'd been a prize marionette for too long.

The time had definitely come to turn the tables on the tipster.

I'm an investigative reporter, she thought. *Why not put my skills to good use for a change?*

The mission was: find the tipster or bust.

She went home and drank three more cups of coffee, turning the whole thing over in her mind and making lists. She approached it like a crime, which didn't seem to her a bad way to think about it.

First, she listed the tips themselves:

1. *Russell Fortier's disappearance*
2. *Fortier and Cindy Lou Wootten an item*
3. *Gene Allred's murder*
4. *Baroness's reading*
5. *Bebe and LaBarre*

Okay, good. Obviously 1, 2, and 5 were connected—the players were the same. All five must be part of a whole, but how?

Gene Allred was a private eye, so he must either have been working for the Fortier family or investigating them. (So far, Bebe had claimed to know nothing.)

The Baroness was a tougher row to hoe. The fact that the tipster had invited Langdon to the reading bolstered the idea of a connection. Jane sat and chewed her pencil. She was guessing Langdon knew what it was. Also, for that matter, that she knew what Allred's was—but she hadn't solved the case, so she sure didn't know everything.

Her second list was entitled "Things I Need to Know." It had seven entries:

1. *Russell's whereabouts*
2. *Tipster's identity*
3. *What this is all about*
4. *Tipster's motive*
5. *Baroness's connection*
6. *Allred's connection*
7. *Identity of Allred's murderer*

The last she underlined three times. She had almost forgotten Langdon's warning to be careful. It was very possible the tipster was the murderer, but why was Allred murdered? She added to her list:

8. *Murder motive*

Well, hell, for that matter:

9. *Reason for Fortier's disappearance*

It was a little on the overwhelming side, especially since none of the entries were simple little things like addresses or dates, arrest records . . . wait a minute, arrest records were a possibility. She made a third list, "Sheets On:"

1. *Sandra Wallis*
2. *Russell Fortier*
3. *Eugene Allred*

Because it was easy, she made that the first chore. She knew a friendly cop (not Langdon) who'd get them for her. She called him and went back to studying the second list. Everything was so huge, so cosmic . . . except for one thing. One glaring thing, now that she thought of it: "Baroness's connection."

How hard could it be to figure that out? The tipster obviously wanted her to—he'd brought the poet to her attention.

Well, Langdon wasn't going to tell her, and neither was The Baroness—Jane knew that because she'd asked her already. However, the poet was unabashedly courting publicity—maybe they could deal, Jane and The Baroness. Wait a minute! Maybe The Baroness herself had asked her there, through the tipster. Maybe the five items on the first list weren't related at all. Say the tipster was hatching some plot or other that involved the Fortier family, and in the course of it decided to take advantage of the fact that he now had a trained reporter in his kennel.

Sure enough, The Baroness had an unscrupulous-looking boyfriend—or, at least, assistant. Wait another minute—she'd introduced him as her "partner in crime." Jane felt the exhilaration of an adrenaline rush. "Lamar" something; she could find out by calling the restaurant where the reading was held. His art—such as it was—was for sale there.

She dialed Reggie and Chaz. "Hi, this is Irene Adler. I was in the other night for a poetry reading . . ."

A male, slightly accented voice answered her: "Oh, yes. The Baroness de Pontalba. Very good, yes?"

"Excellent, I thought. A really enjoyable evening. I liked the paintings, too, by the man who helped her—her boyfriend, I guess." She made the sentence faintly interrogative.

"Oh, yes. Mr. Lamar Foret. Her boyfriend."

"Is the show still up?"

"No, I'm so sorry. It was only for that one night. We felt so bad he didn't sell anything."

"Hey, it's not over till it's over. I'm calling because I can't get one of them out of my head. I was going to ask the price."

"Ohhhh. Ohh." He seemed to be mulling things over.

195

Finally he came to the perfect solution: "I could give you Mr. Foret's phone number."

"Oh, could you? Fabulous."

She got it and dialed. A machine answered: "This is the robot of Lamar Foret. Leave a number or he'll send me to kill you."

Damn! It wasn't the tipster's voice. She was about to hang up when someone answered: "Why is a famous *Times-Picayune* reporter calling a simple graduate student?"

She was glad they weren't face-to-face—she was sure she must look utterly taken aback and stupid. But she said smoothly, "Ah. Caller ID Deluxe—number *and* name."

"You must be an *investigative* reporter."

She couldn't think what to ask him except her original question. "I was wondering if you were the person who invited me to the reading the other night."

"What are you talking about?"

"I got a tip about it."

"What, a hot poetry-reading tip? Yeah, it's Talba's cheap way to get a publicist—you get a guy to call up all the reporters and tell 'em she's Page One material."

His voice was nasty with sarcasm. Even over the phone, Jane disliked him. She needed to get off in a hurry. "Well, just thought I'd check it out."

"You want a tip? I'll give you a tip."

"Oh, yeah? About what?"

"About that story you're working on."

"What story?"

"You know what story. How much will you pay me for it?"

"Sorry. We don't pay for information."

"Bullshit."

Despite universal journalistic policy, Jane privately considered paying for information unethical only in cases where the seller could feed you lies that could end up in the paper. Paying for tips, she felt, was merely bad—and very expensive—policy.

She said, "What the hell. Twenty dollars."

He hung up.

Her head hurt.

A hangover, she thought, *is like a cold. You have to feed it. In fact, you have to feed it gross stuff.*

She was on her way out to the kitchen to fix a peanut butter sandwich when Lamar called back. "Fifty," he said.

She'd already forgotten the conversation. "Fifty what?"

"Hey, reporter. Wake up. I've got something you need to know."

"I told you, we don't pay for information."

"Then you told me you do."

"Well, I had a weak moment. I can't do it."

"It concerns Mr. Russell Fortier's place of employment."

"United Oil. What about it?"

"Ms. Sandra Wallis, aka The Baroness de Pontalba, has a day gig."

"What? Are you telling me she works for United Oil?"

"Fifty bucks."

"It's pretty easy to check out."

"Yeah, but you got to admit it's a damn good tip. If you're an honest woman, you'll pay."

That kind of got to her. She had halfway promised him. She made a mental note to go against all advice and send cash through the mail. It wasn't a damn good tip, it couldn't have been better. It was the tip of tips: United Oil was the link. But why the hell had he told her?

Lovers' quarrel, maybe. She shrugged, though there was no one there to interpret the gesture. And then she set about interpreting the data.

She was starting to wish she hadn't called in sick. But wait, they wouldn't know that in the library, and Jane knew a trick—she could get in via modem and download the United Oil file.

In half an hour she was inundated. But there wasn't a blemish anywhere that she could see. There was a great deal of activity, though. United Oil was expanding like crazy, both in the Gulf and elsewhere. You'd think they planned to take over the world.

Suspicious indeed, in Jane's opinion—you had to wonder where big bucks came from.

She called the company, and, having endured endless voice mail choices, she finally scored a human being, whom she asked for Sandra Wallis. The human was silent for a few minutes. Finally, she said, "Sorry. We have no Sandra Wallis here."

Jane refused to believe it. Absolutely wouldn't accept it. This was the first break in this ridiculous thing, and she wasn't about to give it up just because it wasn't true. She was considering asking for The Baroness de Pontalba when the human said, "Could she be a temp?"

Jane didn't think so, but you never knew. "Yes," she said. "I'm really not sure."

"Well, if she is, she could be here. We don't have all the temps' names."

"Can you just ring them all? How many are there?"

"No, I really can't. There are twenty or so, it looks like."

"Okay, thanks." She thought, *There's more than one way to skin a cat,* and picked up the phone book. There were only a few Wallises; no big deal.

She called the first three and asked for Sandra, or would have if she'd once more gotten a human. But robots, to quote Lamar, were guarding the phones of the Wallises. She kept trying, and on the fifth got one that said she worked for "Sandra and Clara Wallis," though not in the butterscotch tones of The Baroness. *Must be Clara,* Jane thought, and wondered if she could be the mama who got duped. "In case of emergency," the message said, "you can call me at work."

Jane scribbled down the number. She didn't bother making up an emergency, figuring Clara was used to anyone who got the machine just going ahead and calling.

The same voice answered the phone: "Landry residence."

"Ms. Wallis? Is that you?"

"Yes, it is."

"I'm a friend of Sandra's from her old job—I've been trying to get her at United, but I don't have her extension."

"Well, they move her around so much I don't recollect it, exactly. She work in Property, though; Property and something else. Acquisitions! I'm pretty sure it's Acquisitions."

"Okay, Ms. Wallis. I sure thank you." *Sounds like a nice lady,* Jane thought. *Last thing she needed was that asshole at Charity.*

She called back, got Acquisitions and Property, asked for Sandra Wallis, and once again ran up against a blank wall. She was about to find some nails to chew when the receptionist said, "We have a *Talba* Wallis."

"Ah. That's her."

There were clicks and then The Baroness's butterscotch voice. Jane said, "I didn't know Baronesses had nicknames."

"Who's this?"

"Jane Storey from the *Picayune*."

"I know which Jane Storey you are. How many Jane Storeys do you think I know? You want to do that story?"

"That's not why I'm calling."

"Oh." The voice deflated. "I had a real bad feeling it wasn't."

"Yeah, I finally figured out the Russell Fortier connection."

If butterscotch can be haughty, the voice was. "I really can't talk about that now."

"I'm coming right over."

"No!" The Baroness was practically shouting. Definitely losing her cool.

"Okay, then talk."

"I don't know anything."

"Still want me to do a story about you?"

"After work? Please?"

She sounded so pathetic Jane took pity on her. "Okay. I'll meet you in the lobby."

"Definitely not here. If someone saw us . . . uh-uh. No way."

"Okay, what's near there? How about the Fairmont? Say, the Sazerac Bar."

"Not the bar. I haven't got long."

"The lobby, then."

Jane spent the rest of the day going over and over the clips on United Oil. She got a yellow legal pad and her lists and rethought things:

Let's postulate that this is about United Oil. Either Russell disappeared voluntarily for some reason having to do with the company or he was banished or he was killed for some reason having to do with the company. Once you bring United into it, all this stuff about cheating spouses looks like so much smoke.

No. Not smoke—a nasty, mean, manipulative way to keep the Fortier disappearance before the public eye.

So suppose it's that. Any way you slice it, it looks like corporate chicanery.

She looked at the clips some more, but all they really told her was that United was buying up a lot of oil leases. Well, suppose it had to do with that?

She kind of liked it.

When The Baroness arrived somewhat out of breath and dressed like a Catholic schoolgirl, Jane barely recognized her.

"Baroness. You're not yourself."

"Oh, honey, you don't know the half of it. You got to promise you won't tell my adoring public about this." She indicated her outfit.

"We've got to have 'before and after' photos."

"It's my disguise." She glanced over her shoulder. "I don't even want to be seen with you, much less overheard." When she was satisfied they were alone, she said, "Okay, ask."

Jane thought, *Oh, well. Might as well start at the top.* She said, "What happened to Russell Fortier?"

The Baroness laughed aloud. "You're asking me? A lowly temp?"

"There's a reason I was at your poetry reading—along with Skip Langdon and Cindy Lou Wootten."

"I thought you were my fans." Once more, The Baroness glanced around. Finally she said, "Look. I don't want to blow my story, but this is, like, a pretty serious thing. I don't really think I should talk about it."

"I'm damn sure you should talk to Langdon about it."

"Oh, I have. You know how the cops are—they never want you to talk to reporters."

"Okay, let's start slow. How long have you worked for United?"

"Off and on for a couple of months."

"Were you working there when Russell Fortier disappeared?"

"No. I was there for a while and now I'm back."

"What departments have you worked in?"

"Only one. Acquisitions and Property."

"Do you happen to know what department Fortier was in?"

"Uh-huh. That one."

At last, Jane thought. *We're getting somewhere.*

"Who else is in that department?"

"You mean everybody?"

"Oh, name a few." Jane was fishing.

The Baroness shrugged. "Well, the big cheese is someone called Douglas Seaberry. Guy I report to's Edward Favret." She shrugged again. "That's about it for executives. Secretaries, though. I've got plenty of those. What am I bid for secretaries?"

"Hit me with a few names."

"Well, there's Sharon and Mary Louise, Susan (there's always one of those), Rochelle, Keisha (and always one of these), Melissa, Wanda . . ."

She was starting to sound like one of her poems. "Hold it," Jane said. "Last names?"

"Haven't got 'em." She looked at her watch and stood up. "Listen, I've got a date."

"Five minutes." Jane didn't give her time to answer. "What's the office gossip about Russell Fortier?"

"You won't believe this, but I haven't heard a peep."

"Come on."

201

"Hey, I'm a temp and a computer nerd. I only hang around with the other nerds, and they talk about hardware and software."

"You sure don't look like a nerd."

The Baroness flared. "Well, maybe that isn't such a big compliment. Women don't get taken seriously because we don't look the way people expect in some role or other."

Jane certainly wasn't going to rise to that one. "We're getting off the subject here. Have you seen anything suspicious or unusual at United?"

Jane held her breath. If Langdon had really told The Baroness not to talk about something, it was probably this.

But The Baroness only looked thoughtful. She said, "No. I can honestly say I never have." She looked at her watch again. "I've really got to go. When do you want to do the story?"

"I'll call you."

"Forget that shit. I'll call you." And she left.

Jane felt let down. She sat there in the lobby for a few minutes, more or less gazing into space. She felt more than let down—she was depressed.

Get a grip, she told herself. *Come on. What do you want here?*

The answer came fast and brought with it a rush of energy:

To get out of that asshole's control.

She found the phone booths and looked up Douglas Seaberry and Edward Favret. They were both listed, addresses and all. A little flush of delight warmed her: *Come to Mama, little chickens.*

She'd spoken to Seaberry before, in connection with Russell's disappearance. She tried him first, and was rewarded with a male voice on the line.

"May I speak to Danny Seaberry, please?"

"This is Douglas Seaberry. You must have the wrong number."

"Oh, gosh. Sorry." *Nothing should be that easy. Let's try Favret.*

But this time a woman answered and said her husband wasn't in.

Douglas Seaberry lived on Walnut, a gorgeous street near Audubon Park. *A lovely place to visit. But on what pretext?*

A diabolical plan began to form in her mind. *The tipster would be proud,* she thought, *to know what he inspired.*

The man came to the door himself, with all the commanding air of a big cheese, though at the moment he was dressed not for success but speed. He wore a white T-shirt and tiny, tiny royal blue running shorts, and he was all but running in place. Jane had a sense of contained energy, somewhat like that of a cat in a cage.

"Douglas Seaberry?" she said, and took him in. The man was a miracle of engineering.

"Yes," he said. She almost mentioned how happy she was not to have caught him at the office, thus missing the spectacle of legs that would make a lesbian weep.

But she caught herself, and said she was Jane Storey, *on* a story.

He raised one eyebrow, giving an irresistibly asymmetrical look to a face that, under other conditions, might have caused her to hyperventilate.

"It's about Russell Fortier."

His demeanor was instantly grave, as if he expected the worst. "They've found him?" he said, and it was clear from his tone that he was really asking if they'd found his body.

In spite of herself, she felt guilty. "No, I'm sorry to give you a start. So far as I know, they haven't." She decided to keep going. "I know you really care about him; that's why I'm here."

(For all she knew, Fortier and Seaberry were bitter enemies, but what was he going to do—deny it?)

He nodded, as if a reporter on the porch were a perfectly normal occurrence right before a nice jog, but she thought she saw his jaw work slightly before he said, "Won't you come in?"

"Thanks. I won't take much of your time."

He led her into a living room of period perfection. Even Jane, on a reporter's salary, knew that serious bucks had been spent here, on heavy draperies, eighteenth-century everything, magnificent antique rugs. She could see the dining room as well, with its gleaming table, silver candelabra, and more silver on the buffet. Seaberry caught her looking. "My wife and I collect silver."

"Lovely."

"What can I do for you, Ms. Storey?" He put his right foot on his left knee, in casual fashion, but it was also, to Jane's way of thinking, incredibly sexy.

As if on cue, any incipient fantasies were quickly nipped in the bud by a female voice: "Doug? Who is it?"

She was already at the door, barefoot and wearing a bathing suit, wet hair dripping, though unmistakably colored a luscious and expensive blond. Her limbs were tan and toned, her body impossibly perfect. "Oh," she said, in a hushed little voice, as if she'd caught Jane and her husband in bed.

Seaberry said, "This is Jane Storey from the *Times-Picayune*. My wife, Megan."

Megan might look like a movie star, but she was never going to win an Academy Award. She was clearly a woman whose home had been invaded. "I just got out of the pool," she said, in lieu of hello.

Jane was at a bit of a loss. She thought of apologizing for her presence, but caught herself, thinking of The Baroness's parakeet poem: *I'm not going to be pushed around by this little bird.*

She smiled: "Nice swim?"

Megan looked utterly amazed, as if she'd ordered Jane off the premises and she'd failed to obey.

"Ms. Storey's here about Russell," Seaberry said.

"Oh. What does she want to know?"

Jane was starting to loathe this woman. She smiled again, putting so much effort into it she'd probably have to go lie down in a minute. "We haven't talked yet." She glanced over at Seaberry, who was adjusting his glasses.

Megan said, "Oh," and continued to stand there.

Finally, Seaberry said, "She says it'll just take a few minutes. Why don't you get dressed and join us?"

Megan only nodded, evidently not wanting to waste precious words on so lowly a creature as Jane Storey, and padded off on feet that looked so pampered they probably felt like little silk pillows. Jane wondered, and not for the first time, how smart men with pouty little pets for wives made it through the day. You couldn't screw for twenty-four hours. Okay, you had to work eight and sleep eight; that still left eight to get through. You could play tennis, you could work out, you had to get dressed—that took care of another three. And you *could* have sex for one, say. So four hours a day of making conversation with a ninny. She personally would rather live on Rikers Island. Or was she just being snotty because she was attracted to the parakeet's feeder?

He said, "Megan's a little out of it—hard day in court."

"I beg your pardon?"

"She's a civil rights lawyer. Plus, the kid's sick—we've got a seven-year-old."

Jane took a moment to feel slightly silly and then got to the business at hand. She didn't mind apologizing in aid of her own agenda. "I'm sorry to invade your home," she said. "I wanted to see you here to protect your privacy." Once again, she thought she saw a little jaw action—some almost indefinable sign of discomfort.

But you had to be fast to catch it. He smiled like he showed teeth for a living, and nodded.

She said, "I'm trying to get some background. Everything we say will be off the record."

"Yes?"

"Well, it's difficult to know how to say this. Let me ask you first—have you any idea what happened to Russell Fortier?"

He shrugged and waved his hands a bit, perfectly friendly. "Are you kidding? The guy's one of my best friends. I've been worried out of my mind."

"Was he in some sort of trouble at United?"

205

"No."

"Embezzling, maybe? Something like that?" She didn't expect an honest answer; she was just hoping for a reaction.

She got one. Seaberry did a virtual double take. "Embezzling—Russell? That's the last thing I can imagine."

"I was thinking that if he did something criminal that was about to come to light, he might simply have found it a good time to disappear."

Seaberry's face clouded up. "Ms. Storey, do you want me to confirm something? I can't understand what's going on here."

"We're developing a story on United that isn't going to thrill you over there." She told herself it wasn't exactly a lie—the Money section was always writing about United; surely some stories didn't thrill them.

"May I ask what it's about?"

"We think Russell Fortier's involved."

"Yes?" he said.

Jane said nothing, just kept staring at him—partly because he was such an eyeful. Ever the gentleman, he didn't get mad—he just seemed to make a decision that she was wasting his time. "I wish I could help you, but I really can't if you don't ask me any questions."

Jane was deeply embarrassed. What she was doing was unprofessional as hell, and she couldn't imagine what had ever made her think it would be productive. "We have information that Fortier was involved in some problems with the company. I was wondering if you'd like to tell me about them."

"I don't know what you're talking about." For the first time, his voice sounded irritated.

Jane remembered what department he ran. "Were there any problems with acquisitions?"

"I'm really at quite a loss here." His voice came out of a soon-to-be-active volcano, and Jane had to admit she'd given him provocation. The thing to do was get out fast.

She produced a card, stood, and handed it to him.

"Well, as I said, the investigation is at a very delicate stage. If you should need a sympathetic ear, I'm here."

"Thanks for coming by." He tried a smile, but he hadn't quite recovered his composure.

Driving home, she chastised herself. *Brilliant, Jane, brilliant. Sure, some oil exec is going to spill the beans just because you asked him. Say, Mr. Executive, know of any recent criminal activity at your company? I need a story for my high school paper.*

She hoped he wouldn't report this visit to David Bacardi, and gasped as David's face came up on her mental movie screen. He and Douglas Seaberry were cut from the same cloth.

They were both superior specimens; in fact they looked rather alike. They were smooth as K-Y jelly, confident as Marlboro men; and there was something else. What was that quality she hated so much in David?

She let her mind go blank. Oh, yes—an unhesitating willingness to swat any fly that landed on his lunch. How had she escaped Seaberry's wrath? Probably she hadn't—he might very well call David, and they'd probably hit it off so well they'd go to lunch and think up whole new ways to torture her. Maybe these corporate guys were all like that.

Maybe she should go out with her neighbor, the unemployed actor.

Eighteen

TALBA TOOK THE bus to work on the days her mama worked. She never boarded the 82 Desire without going into some flight of the imagination. Just the sight of the name on the front got her revved up. It had to be the most poetic damn bus in the world. Sometimes she reflected on how lucky she was actually to live on the Desire line; sometimes she thought about the poem she was going to write about it one day, trying out phrases and half-formed ideas. One day it occurred to her that it would make a round, resonant name for her first volume of poetry. *Eighty-two Desire.* Now that had a ring to it.

And some days, when real life overwhelmed poetry, it still kicked off a tangent—usually an obsessive, angry focus on her own desires. Today was like that.

She had awakened in a cold sweat, dogged by guilt. She really should have solved this disk thing yesterday. She shouldn't have agreed to go out with Darryl when she didn't yet have the files. She shouldn't have gone out with Darryl at all, no matter how happy it made her mama. She certainly shouldn't have lied to Lamar.

She went and splashed cold water on her face, but that only worked for a minute. The same obsessive thoughts kept circling in her head, wouldn't leave even when Miz Clara came in and asked about her date, something she'd never done before in her life. Talba felt like crying and she didn't really know why.

Riding the 82 Desire was clarifying. *What I want,* she thought, *is never to have heard of Gene Allred and his*

*stupid client. What I want is out of this. I just want to go
home and pull the covers over my head.*

What I don't want is the damn fifteen hundred dollars.

And yet she did.

But that wasn't the worst of it—she was in it now,
whether she wanted the money or not.

The passenger across the aisle was having a coughing
fit that shouldn't have been allowed outside a hospital.
She got up and moved toward the back. She was feeling
too vulnerable to do battle with germs today. She had to
save her energy for her own psyche.

The truth was, she was a little afraid. Life had become
uncertain. She was afraid she couldn't handle all the effort and hassle and—frankly—the fear that came with a
new man. She was afraid to break up with Lamar. She
was afraid Darryl wouldn't call again.

Then, too, she was afraid for her life.

She hadn't the least idea who this mystery client was.
And her first meeting with him—wearing a ski mask in a
room with a dead body—truly failed to inspire confidence. She must have dreamed last night. The reality of
what she'd gotten into suddenly came home to her.

If she failed to deliver, who knew what this man might
do. On the other hand, if she did come through, maybe he'd
give her a bullet in the heart instead of seven hundred and
fifty dollars. Furthermore, he was almost certainly doing
something illegal even if it wasn't murder—stealing
corporate secrets, for instance. Or rather, getting her to
do it. *I think I'm in love,* she thought. *Why the hell am I so
pessimistic?*

And then: *Is that the beginning of a poem?*

Quickly, she wrote it in the notebook of first lines she
kept in her backpack.

When she discovered the encryption, she'd quickly
developed a plan—in fact, recognized instantly that
there was only one course of action. She had to get Robert Tyson to reveal the unscrambler key, which would
probably be pretty easy. She could just ask him about the
fascinating project he'd been working on before they put

him on tech duty, and he'd talk, and eventually, he wouldn't be able to resist demonstrating just a few little things. He would probably draw the line at actually showing her the key, but she could watch his fingers when he typed it in. It wasn't foolproof, but it was all she had.

That depressed her so much she thought of getting off the bus, crossing the street, and taking another one headed for home.

But, as she was still ambivalent, she kept going.

Everyone was cheerful at United Oil. Evidently not having guilty consciences, they had slept better than she had. Rochelle was still pregnant, Favret still flirtatious, everything normal. Except that Robert Tyson had called in sick.

Damn, damn, damn. Why the hell hadn't she dealt with this yesterday?

Well, it wasn't a big deal. She had time. Back when she was working for Allred, most of the time she'd been at United, all she'd done was install software. She had to work out the week anyway, in order not to draw attention to herself.

She just wouldn't think about it for a while. That ought to be easy enough.

"So how're you doin', kid?" Abasolo put a hand on Skip's shoulder and paused only a second before sitting down on her desk.

"Your management style is sure different from Cappello's."

"Oh? How so?"

"You're kind of hands-on."

"Oh, God. You're not gonna scream sexual harassment, are you?"

She chuckled. The remark would have been half-serious coming from some of the bozos around here, but she and Abasolo had been through far too much together. He was just messing around. "How about plain, no-frills harassment?"

210

He looked hurt. "I thought you liked going over cases. We used to do it all the time."

"Oh, hell, A.A. I guess I'm being defensive because I'm not used to having you as my sergeant yet. Yeah, let's talk about the case. If you've got a minute."

A smile of such genuine pleasure spread across his features that she made an inner vow to try to get back to the old relationship—clearly, he was willing. "I'm trying to get into Russell's head—I mean, he might be dead, but the events leading up to his murder still might be relevant, right? It didn't happen in a vacuum."

He was lanky as a cowboy, draped on that desk like he was, handcuffs hanging from his belt, reminding her inanely of balls. Far from judgmental, he looked eager. He nodded. "Let's hear what you've got."

"Random thoughts, that's about all. You have time for this?"

"Sure."

"Okay, he was in this amazing sailing accident about two years ago—it was five days before he was rescued. Shortly after that, his mother died. Matter of fact, you know where Cindy Lou met him? At a workshop she was teaching—on dealing with grief."

"What! That doesn't sound right."

"Why not? Think he picked her up in a bar?"

"Oh, the part about Cindy Lou's perfectly plausible. Anybody would go for her." (Skip had always suspected he had a soft spot for Lou-Lou.) "I just don't see a hot-shot executive going to some touchy-feely thing."

"Kind of a discordant note, isn't it? Well, a few people say he was different after the sailing ordeal. Maybe—I don't know—maybe he questioned the meaning of life or something. Oooh, now that's good. He has some sort of religious experience on the boat, his mother dies and he feels hopeless, his father dies, and he decides to cash it all in."

"You mean suicide?"

She considered. "Could be. But that wasn't really what

I was thinking of. I mean, what if he was just fed up with his life and decided to get a new one?"

"There's no body. It's not a bad bet. But for the sake of argument, what about Bebe and the daughter—what's-her-name?"

"Eugenie. Well, we already know about Bebe—maybe he knew about her affair with LaBarre."

"Plausible."

"So he tries that little thing with Cindy Lou, it doesn't work—"

"What do you mean, it doesn't work?"

"Girl-talk. Evidently, *it* didn't work."

An odd expression crossed Abasolo's movie-star features—something like a wince. "I don't really need the details."

Skip shrugged. "Well, you asked." She was keeping it casual to save his feelings, but she could tell he had it bad for the psychologist. She and Lou-Lou had talked about him—Lou-Lou said he was way too decent a fellow for her. With her fabled bad taste in men, it was undoubtedly true, but Skip wondered if there wasn't more than that at work here—Abasolo was an Italian, macho, Southern cop. Guys like that just didn't date black women. Period.

His loss, she thought, and had the uncomfortable feeling he felt that way as well.

"Anyway," she said, "Bebe's otherwise engaged, Eugenie's away at school, Cindy Lou doesn't pan out, he's depressed because he's lost his parents—"

"What about the job?"

"Well, therein lies the interesting part. We just don't know what it is. First of all, Allred was investigating Fortier for some mystery client, using an operative posing as a computer technician. As you may recall, the file she copied has since disappeared."

Abasolo nodded. That had been in Skip's original report on the Allred murder.

Skip continued, "Beyond asking his boss—dude named Douglas Seaberry—if he knew whether Fortier was up to anything, there wasn't much I could do. Naturally Seaberry said he didn't know. Fortier had a couple of other friends there, but I don't really want to tip them to All-red's connection with Fortier.

"However, they're all way too nonchalant about this thing—even uncooperative. One of them ducked out for lunch when he knew I was waiting to interview him."

"You think if something funny's going on, they're in it with Russell?"

"I sure wouldn't rule it out."

"You want to try to subpoena their phone bills—see if they have any unusual long-distance calls?"

"I don't think so. I have a feeling we wouldn't find anything." She gave him the half smile that let him know she'd already checked through the confidential phone company source most good cops manage somehow to have.

He said, "Did you go through Fortier's computer? Maybe there's something in there."

"I took a look, but to really do it justice, I'd have to download every single file and read it—and he's got years of work in there. I'd say it would probably be a full-time job for the next six months, and since I don't know what I'm looking for, I'd probably miss it. Not only that, if someone killed Allred to keep it from coming to light—Russell, say—you've got to figure he'd have deleted it."

"So where are you going with all this?"

"You put your finger on it—not only was all that other stuff true, but, as we just mentioned, work was getting pretty hot. He could have stood Bebe up at the airport so he could get some time alone to kill Allred—but why do that if he wasn't trying to protect his own little universe? I mean, if you were willing to give up your life, all you'd have to do is disappear—you wouldn't have to kill someone, *then* disappear."

"Point well taken."

"So, maybe he just went sailing."

"What?"

"Well, sailing's what he did. If he was going to disappear somewhere for good, he'd probably do it on a boat."

"Did he have one?"

"Oh, yes. It's still in its slip—or so says the co-owner."

"Maybe he bought another one."

"His bank records don't show any large withdrawals—he could have sold stock or something, I guess. Or maybe he had a stash somewhere. Or maybe he borrowed or stole it."

"Okay. So maybe he's off sailing. Where does that get us?"

"I've already checked with every clerk in the airport who was working that day. No one remembers him."

"And anyway, how could he fly? You have to have a picture ID."

"Well, needless to say, no Russell Fortier flew that day—"

He opened his mouth, but she held up a hand "—or the next couple of days; we checked that out, too. If he flew anywhere, he had to have a fake ID."

"Well, where would an oil company executive get something like that?"

She tapped her mouth with her open hand—it was a mannerism she had when she was thinking. "Very good question, AA. Provocative in the extreme."

He stood up and gave her a macho grin. "You lose me when you start with the four-syllable words."

As he walked away, she pressed her hand against her mouth and started to rock a little bit, completing the thought that had started coming to her: What if he had stolen an ID?

She liked this idea. She was just getting into it when the phone rang. "Hey, good-lookin'."

It was a sexy male voice and she recognized it. "Darryl Boucree. To what do I owe this honor?"

"Hey, I've got to talk fast. I'm between periods here. But something's bothering me. There's something funny about The Baroness."

"I'm glad to hear you say that. I thought you were smitten."

"Uh-oh. You know something about her." He sounded so crestfallen she knew she had it right the first time.

"No, I don't—that's what's known as a flirtatious remark. What do you know?"

"Well, I just think it's kind of strange she works the same place Russell Fortier did."

"What?" She heard the electricity in her own voice, and hoped she hadn't spooked him.

"I guess you didn't know, huh?" He sounded so glum she hated to give him the bad news.

"She *used* to work there."

"She's working there now. I take it this isn't good."

"For romance? I don't know, I think she likes you. She's obviously been a lot more candid with you than she has with me."

"Oh, terrific—got to go. The bell just rang."

"Wait a minute. You wouldn't have her phone number, would you?"

But the other end clicked gently. Either he hadn't heard, or he didn't want to rat The Baroness out any more thoroughly than he already had.

Phoning didn't seem like the best plan anyway. It would warn Talba—give her time to destroy evidence. On the other hand, assuming The Baroness was innocent of murder, marching into the office could alert the wrong people. And waiting till after work just wasn't going to cut it.

On third thought, phoning was the best—she borrowed Abasolo's cell phone so she could call from the lobby at United. After a little back-and-forth about temps and who supplied them, then a call to Comp-Temps, she located her quarry. Without a hello, she said, "You should have told me you were working here again."

A frightened voice said, "Who is this?"

"Skip Langdon. I'm in the lobby—be here in two minutes or I'm coming up."

"I can't, I'm—"

"Say you're going to the ladies' room and duck out—I'm timing you."

The Baroness, so quick to lose her temper, even at the law, stepped out of the elevator with something like fear on her face. She looked over her shoulder and said, "Let's get out of here."

"Fine." Skip opened the door for her. "My car's right here."

"I've only got a minute."

"This is a murder investigation, Ms. Wallis. Don't keep telling me how valuable your time is." She wasn't eager to arouse suspicion herself—this would have to be short, but she wanted this woman's full attention, and she couldn't get it in a car. Besides, Talba had a bad temper. Skip had to get her in a controlled situation. She drove to the nearest police station, which was the Eighth District (in the French Quarter), and secured the loan of a room.

Talba brushed her hair back with an angry swipe. "What the hell's this about?"

"That attitude's not going to get you anywhere."

The Baroness sat down, and Skip said, "What are you doing at United?"

The other woman shrugged. "I'm a good temp. They asked me back."

"Don't lie to me. You're scared to death of something."

Talba breathed deeply a few times, chest heaving. Finally, she seemed to come to a decision. "I can't believe I'm so stupid. No way do I need money this bad! Look, I'm working for Allred's client."

Skip's heart started to pick up speed, but Talba interrupted her fantasies of a coming revelation: "But I still don't know who he is."

"Don't bullshit me, Talba."

"I'm not!" She yelled it so loud Skip put her hands to her ears.

"Sorry. I just hate being called a liar when I'm not lying."

Skip gave her the "come on" sign.

"He called me," Talba said. "I guess he got my number

216

from Allred. He knew everything I'd been doing at United, and he wanted me to go back."

"If you don't even know the man, why do you think he'll pay you?"

"He said I'd find seven hundred fifty dollars under the mat and I did. I'd call that earnest money."

"Okay. Tell me what he wants you to do."

"Get the same file as before."

"Dammit! *Why* didn't you call me when this guy called?"

Talba shrugged, looking a little ashamed.

"Well? Did you do it?"

"Not yet."

"Why not?"

"I haven't had the right opportunity."

Skip could have chewed nails. "Talba, come *on*."

"Look. It's encrypted—it wasn't before; they've done it since I was there last."

"And you didn't think this was important enough to tell the police? Have you forgotten a man was murdered? Is this some sort of game to you?"

The poet's face told Skip she more or less *had* forgotten; Talba looked a bit like a child caught stealing. "I'm sorry—I didn't think."

Think. Skip tried to think. If they'd encrypted the system, it probably meant the information she needed was still inside it. She said, "How does encryption work?"

Talba said, "First of all, you'd only encrypt certain files."

Skip nodded. "The ones you were trying to hide."

"Yes. The encrypted files look like gobbledygook until you run them through a decryption program—talk about a rude awakening."

"Are you telling me you found 'Skinacat'—you just couldn't read it?"

"No. Either someone's removed it or changed its name. I remembered one of the names in it, and it turned out the guy had his own file. *That* one I couldn't read."

217

"Wait a minute. Just hold it a minute while I try to figure you out. When we talked Saturday, you couldn't remember any of the names. You knew damn well they were important in a murder case, and yet you just couldn't remember. And then, all of a sudden, you miraculously recovered your memory. And you *didn't tell me*! What the hell's wrong with you, Ms. Baroness Sandra Urethra?" Skip was so mad she wanted to pound her. It really bothered her how irresponsible people could be.

Talba looked as if she had been pounded. Tears popped into her eyes and spilled. "Oh, God. Oh, God, I don't know. Oh, shit, how could I be so stupid? I was just all caught up with all my little petty things. I never thought . . ."

"Okay, okay, okay." Skip was cooling down. "What was the name?"

"Marion Newman. I remembered it because of the school."

"Is it a man or a woman?"

"A man, because, on the original list, it was actually, 'Mr. and Mrs. Marion Newman.' Somehow I suspect he's the main guy in this, though."

"The main guy in what, Talba?"

"In whatever he was screwed out of. That's what this is about, isn't it?"

Skip would have liked to ignore the remark, but it might mean something. She said, "What makes you think that?"

"Isn't it always?"

She was back to her arrogant self. Skip said, "Look, I'm delighted you've decided to cooperate, belated though it may be. Think carefully—is there anything else you can remember that might be helpful—anything at all?"

"No."

"Thanks for thinking so carefully."

"I *have* been thinking about this. Think I'm sitting here with my mind in neutral?"

"Where's Mr. Newman from? Can you remember that?"

"Mr. Newman. Let me see." She closed her eyes. "Belle Chasse. You know what? It might be Belle Chasse."

"Well, that was so good, maybe you should try for his street address."

She waved a hand. "That was random. Can I go back to work now?"

"I wouldn't if I were you. Somebody in there might be dangerous."

The poet stood up, smiling. "Oh, girlfriend. They're all dangerous."

Having a vested interest in Talba's not being missed, Skip dropped her off before heading back to the office, taking care to conceal her excitement. Marion Newman was a name she knew.

Nineteen

THE PLACE SHE'D seen it was in some record involving this case. She got out the cardboard box where she'd stored certain of Russell's things she'd borrowed, and there on top was an address book. She pounced on it, perfectly remembering the name "Marion Newman" written in neat script on a blue line.

But it wasn't there.

Okay, then, one of the Rolodexes. She plucked out the larger one first, the one from work. And there it was— black ink on a pristine white card. Go figure.

She cross-checked it against the home Rolodex, but it wasn't there. So Marion Newman was strictly a business acquaintance. That made sense.

Probably no one was home now, or at best only his wife was, but Skip phoned anyway. A woman with a black accent answered.

Skip could hear her holler, "Mr. Newman? Mr. Newman. Ya girlfriend's on the phone?"

Good time to hang up, Skip thought, *and drive out to Belle Chasse.* This was a bedroom community in Plaquemines Parish, reached by taking the Mississippi River Bridge (aka the Crescent City Connection) and driving through quite a few miles of McDonald's and Dairy Queens, and finally coming to, of all things, the same river you have just crossed.

Because of an exceptionally kinky meander, you actually run into the Mississippi again. Having gone due east on the bridge, you've fetched up on its west bank; if you were to cross it again (which you could, by ferry), you could drive back to New Orleans without crossing it a third time.

But you don't have to cross it again to get to Belle Chasse—if you've reached that second bend, you're there.

To the right is a development of nice-looking, though aggressively neat houses. Skip drove through, looking for the Newmans' address and marveling at what she saw. Nothing could have been farther from the French Quarter. About every second house had a wreath of dried flowers on the door, making her think of pagan customs involving harvests. Somehow, she didn't think that was what this was about. It was probably part of the same non-pagan deal that caused each of the houses to have a leaded glass door. These were new houses and the doors, by the look of them, weren't antiques—had obviously been made to order, to lend a look of modest grandeur. Then there were the mailboxes, sitting out on the road a good distance from the houses. Most of these were encased in little brick housings, like birds in cages. It was a phenomenon Skip hadn't seen before.

I wonder, she thought, *who lives in Belle Chasse?* There was no one outside.

The single exception was an old man in a straw hat riding a tractor lawn mower at the Newmans' address.

Skip got out of her car and hailed him. "Can I talk to you a minute?"

He eyed her as if she came from Mars.

"Mr. Newman?" she said, and he nodded briefly. "Skip Langdon. Police." She held up her badge.

"Police," he repeated. He looked as if she'd told him someone was dead, and she wondered if that was what he thought.

"It's nothing to worry about," she said. "Just a long shot in a case I'm working on. Over in New Orleans."

He pulled a bandanna from a pair of khaki shorts, took off his straw hat, and wiped his forehead. He grinned at her. "My grandson just got a car for his birthday. I thought you were here to tell me the worst."

With the hat off, she saw that he was a handsome man, with a bit of a belly, maybe, but otherwise fit, and an inch or two taller than she was. He spoke with one of those very soft Southern accents designed to be pleasing, never to give offense, and to sneak up on you in the dark—the sort a Southern senator has, one with half his colleagues eating out of his hand and the other half running for cover at the sight of him. In a suit, he'd be the type to get the best table in every restaurant he set foot in, whether or not the maître d' knew him. He didn't seem to go with the neighborhood.

She said, "My case involves a company named United Oil, and your name came up."

"United Oil." He said the words as if they were the name of an old girlfriend, one he remembered none too fondly. "In what context?" he said.

"I'm wondering if you ever knew a Russell Fortier."

"Fella who disappeared? Don't b'lieve I did." He looked at her warily. This man was not only no fool, he was used to getting his way, and probably more manipulative than she was. She was going to have to tread lightly.

She smiled. "Well, that's the context. You're in his Rolodex."

He gave a mock shake of the head, as if completely befuddled. "That so? Well, I called him once—called a lot of people over there, but none of 'em ever called back. Surprised he kept my number."

Skip waited for more, but he seemed to be waiting as well.

Finally, she said, "Mr. Newman, it would be a great help to me if you'd simply describe your dealings with United Oil."

"Now why should I do that?" He gave her a practiced, crinkly eyed grin, the sort that had probably won over many an unsuspecting business associate—or female target.

She gave him one just as practiced. "To be a good citizen?"

He laughed. "That. And 'cause I got nothin' else to do. Thanks to United Oil." He paused. "Come on in and have a lemonade with me." He turned his back on her, one finger gesturing at his waist for her to follow, as if she were a grandchild. He padded toward the house, evidently quite confident that she would.

The house had one of those enormous kitchens with a counter separating it from a family room. Newman led her in there and rooted around in an overstocked refrigerator for a pitcher of lemonade. There was no sign either of the maid who'd answered the phone or of anyone else.

Newman poured and held up his glass. "Cheers."

Skip nodded and sipped.

"Shall we?" Gallantly, her host pulled out a light-colored chair at a round kitchen table. She sat down at a place marked with a plastic placemat in the shape of a green and white frog, its mouth open, red tongue cocked for a plastic mosquito. The thing looked so hungry she was afraid to put her hand on it.

"Do you know anything about me, Detective?"

Skip shook her head, more or less mesmerized already; mesmerization was probably this one's stock-in-trade.

"Shall I start at the beginning?"

"By all means."

"I inherited a little company from my father—little oil company in Jefferson Parish named after our family." He spoke softly and seriously, and a sadness came into his voice. When he said "our," he made it two syllables, a pronunciation that somehow fit the word, giving it a proprietary, almost familial feel that managed to express what it meant to him. Skip found she was feeling moved and sympathetic, though the story hadn't even begun.

"I grew up a child of privilege, taking everything for granted, never expecting to do anything but run my daddy's little company and marry some nice woman and have fine sons who'd one day run the company. Well, I found the woman—Mary Alice Gingrich, God rest her soul. My wife died six months ago."

"I'm sorry," Skip said, and indeed she was near tears, so complete was this man's dejection.

"Oh, so am I," he said. "And would that she knew how much I loved her." He lifted his eyes, which had been staring at his own plastic frog, the tongue of which seemed to have captured a stray cornflake. "Forgive me," he said, and forced a smile, but it wasn't the practiced, crinkly eyed variety. This was a tired, apologetic one. "I have a lot of regrets these days and few people who'll listen to me talk about them."

He took a sip and continued. "We had daughters instead of sons—two of them. And I was so disappointed—though not in my girls, never for a minute—just that, for the first time in my selfish, narrow life I didn't get what I thought it was my God-given right to have. I was so disappointed I made poor Mary Alice keep on trying until we had a boy, which we didn't until nine years after our daughter Sarah was born."

He looked at Skip, narrowing his eyes, perhaps, she thought, to keep her from seeing tears. "You know how they say a boy has the devil in him? Well, our boy *was* the devil." He flailed a hand about. "Oh, I know all about hyperactivity and attention deficit and all the things they've attributed to children through the years. Sarah says that if Baxley were coming up today, he'd be diagnosed with ADD. That may be; that may be. All I know is, first he made his mother miserable, and then his sisters, and—in the end—his father as well. When he was a baby, he cried, and when he was a toddler, he tore things up, and when he was ten or eleven, he drank, and when he was twelve, he shoplifted, and after that, he took drugs. Today, I could not honestly tell you where the boy is. He used to ask for money, but that has now become futile."

He waved a hand in front of his face, as if swatting a particularly lazy fly. "But I wanted a son and I got a son, at the cost of the whole family's happiness. Yes, that's

224

true, Detective. Everything was sacrificed at that altar. And I was angry because the boy was not what I expected. *Angry!* My father had never spared the rod—and, in my arrogance, believing that was why I had turned out so almighty well, neither did I. The more I punished, the more he rebelled."

Skip glanced nervously at her watch—when she'd said start from the beginning, she hadn't meant from the beginning of time. She moved her head only slightly, wondering if she should say something, but Newman caught the gesture. "Bear with me, Detective, bear with me. I'll tell my story in its entirety, or not at all." He was definitely a man used to getting his way.

"Because my attention was on that evil boy—on turning him into a perfect little replica of Marion Newman, who in turn, is a near-perfect replica of my father, J. W. Newman—I neglected my wife and abused my two lovely daughters. By abused, Ms., ah, Detective, by abused, I mean I barely noticed them. Everything they did to please me—and it was considerable for a while; in Sarah's case, it still is—was nothing to me because I was simply incapable of noticing.

"Francine, my older daughter, took the path of overachieving and is now a psychiatrist in Atlanta, a path I believe she followed because of her own unhappiness in this family. She is also an activist in the lesbian community, and I have to wonder if this is a path she chose for the lack of good male models."

This guy, Skip thought, *gives new meaning to the term "self-flagellation."* But if what he was saying was right, he no doubt deserved as much punishment as he'd meted out to poor Baxley and the girls. The fact that he had thought it out so well gave it a revolting fascination.

"You're thinking of *The Ancient Mariner*, aren't you?"

"The wedding guest, actually," Skip said, and Newman was suddenly seized by great, shaking fits of laughter.

"I like you, girl. You're a breath of fresh air."

"Actually, Mr. Newman, I'm a police officer . . ."

"How come a cop knows her Coleridge?"

This line of inquiry always infuriated her. She didn't let it go. "You sure are a man who divides people into roles you think they should fit."

To her surprise he had another laughing fit. "Touché, Ms. Detective. I deserved that. But your point is well taken. You are a police officer, however overeducated. Let us get back to making good use of the taxpayers' money." He looked around him, as if hoping to get his bearings. "Where was I?"

"Francine."

"Ah, yes." He shook his head. "Francine. I am not her favorite person. As I say, she took the path of over-achievement, and Sarah . . ." He swept an arm around him, indicating his surroundings. ". . . Sarah settled. She married the first boy who was nice to her, and to our surprise, the marriage worked. Or works, I should say. Sarah and Larry Neville are still married today, but I never expected to see my daughter the wife of an HVAC man." He paused. "Living in Belle Chasse. Are you familiar with that term—HVAC? Neither was I till I had occasion to learn it. Heating, Ventilation, and Air-Conditioning. Quite a good business. I don't know if you see what I'm getting at. If I had raised either of my girls to take over the business—to care about it at all—things might have been different. Maybe somebody—*somebody*—could have talked some sense into me.

"As it happened, we were doing all right, while all around us, many wells were playing out, becoming less and less profitable. It was bound to happen to me sometime, but this was our family business and perhaps I still had some absurd notion that Baxley would turn around and I would pass the business to my son. This is where United Oil comes in—they made me an offer and I refused it. I had no one to advise me, no one else who had a stake in the business . . ."

His head moved from side to side in unconscious regret, and Skip forbore to ask the obvious: *What about your wife?* This was a man to whom a professional woman was an "overachiever," a cop who knew a poem was "overeducated"; not a man who ran decisions past his wife.

In the hope of speeding things up, Skip said, "You lost the company?"

He laughed. "Bide your time, young woman. Just bide your time."

What a control freak, she thought. *He must run Sarah a merry chase.*

"I ran that company for fifteen years, exactly the way my daddy ran it before me, and we ran it just like everyone else in the parish runs their company. Now, I'm not making excuses, I'm just telling you. We were as honest as anybody else, but maybe we weren't all that careful about the royalties we paid to the landlord—the people we leased the oil field from. Maybe we were a little late, maybe we were a little inaccurate—but we did the best we could."

Oh, sure.

"And one day, out of the clear blue, we got word that we were about to be audited by the State Mineral Board. Now why didn't this happen to everybody else in the parish? Why didn't it happen to United Oil? I don't know why it didn't, but my company ended up having to make a huge settlement with the fellow to avoid a suit and a scandal and criminal charges and everything else, and the upshot was, we went bankrupt. And now I live in Belle Chasse with Sarah and Larry and Jimmy. Mary Alice did, too, until she died. You know how hard this was on that woman? We used to live in a great big house out by the lake. She had the most beautiful garden you ever saw—loved her roses. And of course, she had her bridge group and her church . . . and then she had a bankrupt husband who was known to be 'in some kind of trouble.' "

Skip shook her head and said, "Mmmph," to show her sympathy.

He leaned toward her, tapping his forefinger on her frog mat. "Now, here's where it gets good. United Oil bought up our lease and drilled a great big, bodacious new well. Brand-new well. I should have known there was something funny about their offer—big oil companies can't afford to operate mature fields. It just doesn't pay 'em. So they already had information there was oil there."

"How could they possibly know that?"

"Something called Three-D seismic profiling. You know about that? The offer came about the time the equipment was just becoming available—the rest of us were hardly even aware of it." He leaned back, his wad shot. "So, what do you think of that, young lady? You're a detective. Are those two things connected?"

Skip hated it when people asked her things like that. She settled for a shrug, with palms turned up. "Do you remember who you dealt with at United?"

"Sure. Man named Beau Cavignac. Nice little fellow. I liked him a lot."

Bingo, she thought. *Wonder what's in Beau's computer?*

"Anyone else?" she said.

"No. Just Beau."

"I'm going to ask you once more—did you have any connection with Russell Fortier?"

"Well, maybe you could say I did. He refused to take about seventeen of my calls."

She smiled and stood. "I'll get out of your hair, Mr. Newman. That was a very interesting story."

"Anything useful in it?"

"Well, you never know."

As she drove back to the city, digesting the interview, it occurred to her that the old tyrant had been right to tell her everything. Though the one name was the key she needed to proceed, having the whole family's life laid bare like that gave an outline of what United might have been up to. Cavignac evidently had something to hide. Maybe Russell Fortier did, too—the same thing.

All she needed was an expert. And Wilson was always a pleasure to work with.

He was a man evidently sent to Earth to improve the image of nerds. He was young, buff, tall, with neat brown hair and green eyes—frankly, more or less a hunk. Didn't wear glasses, didn't even have a goatee.

Skip told him the problem. "Uh-uh," he said. "No way, no how. If it's encrypted, you gotta have cooperation—the days of codebreaker software are pretty much over. People use gibberish phrases for encryption keys. Unless it's really amateurish, I couldn't break it, not that I'm that great, but I wouldn't even know who to send you to."

"So when you say cooperation, you mean within the company?"

"Yeah, probably. From somebody who knows the code—and that could be an outside consultant, but if you ask who it is . . ." he shrugged ". . . you've already alerted them. They could just erase anything incriminating."

Skip said, "Damn. So I better go over there with a court order."

"Looks kind of that way."

She glanced at her watch—four o'clock. She could just make it. She had to get the order (for Russell's computer)—plus a search warrant for Beau's—and make a United-assisted sweep before she could properly question Beau.

If she found what she thought was there, she was very close to a motive for Allred's murder. A lot was riding on this.

And yet nothing came of it. Absolutely nothing. She got both the order and the warrant, secured the cooperation of United Oil through its agent, Douglas Seaberry, and with Wilson's help, searched both Russell's and Beau's workstations, and failed to find a thing.

No Marion Newman. No "Skinacat." Nothing at all incriminating, enlightening, or interesting in any way. Either she was barking up the wrong tree or they were onto her. Whoever "they" were.

Twenty

SKIP WAS A wreck when she got home, in the mood to put up her feet and watch a movie, if she could get Steve to go down to Tower Video and get one. She was utterly unprepared for a courtyard confrontation. But as she was coming up the walkway from the street to her slave quarters, she heard Sheila shouting, "*You* are going to get fried!"

Napoleon barked from inside the house, and Kenny answered, "Oh, come on. Everybody's cool. They worship on the *altar* of cool. Nobody's going to give me any shit."

Skip had to smile. Kenny was a perfect child in front of adults. She didn't even know he knew the word "shit." She rounded the corner to see Sheila in amazed contemplation of a kid about her brother's age and size, wearing clown-legged shorts, a black T-shirt with the name of God knew what devil-rock band on it, and a shaved head—evidently a friend of Kenny's.

Sheila turned to her in horror, as if she'd been caught shoplifting. "Aunt Skip!"

The boy turned, too, and grinned. "Hi, Auntie."

She liked being called "Auntie"; they never did it unless something was up. "Kenny Ritter," she said.

"You recognized me."

She was fighting for words, any words. She had heard him say they were cool around here, and cool she must try to be. Because she'd be the only one.

Whoever had thought up the term "ear-to-ear" must

have at some point come into contact with a fourteen-year-old bald kid. Kenny's small white face was nearly split in two by metal-banded teeth, teeth that alone would have wrecked the image had not Kenny's whole persona got to that first. Instead of his usual ankh, he wore a jaunty rhinestone in his ear, which glinted merrily in the light as if it were going to a party, instead of the domestic free-for-all that was about to follow.

He was a skinny kid, slight and sweet-faced. He looked ridiculous in the outfit, even with hair. Bald, he looked preposterous. Grinning, he looked like a newborn with braces. But he was evidently so damn pleased with himself, the last thing Skip could bear to do was burst his balloon. Anyhow, there'd be plenty of time for that.

She finally said, "Quite the fashion statement, sir," and leaned down to pet Angel, who'd been trying, without success, to get her attention.

His grin got wider, as he noticed she didn't start shouting or anything. "You like it?"

The question she'd been dreading. She settled on, "I'm trying to decide."

"At least you don't *hate* it. Do you?"

"Well . . . I kind of have to think this through."

The grin finally faded. "You don't like it."

Napoleon began barking again, and Angel's tail started to wag. The gate clanged and footsteps sounded on the walkway. They all waited for someone else to fill the void. Steve's voice came round the corner. "Hey, there. I must be in heaven. It's the Archangel Angel. Hey, Angel. Hey, girl." He was still looking down at the dog as he came into the courtyard. When his head came up, he did a double take. "Whoa. Everybody's here."

And then, Kenny's cueball finally registering, he said, "Heyyyy. Mr. Clean," and moved forward to give the boy a manly scalp brushing.

Kenny grabbed both of Steve's forearms. "No fair. No noogies. No fair."

"Noogie! Hey, you want a noogie, I'll give you a noogie."

Skip breathed a sigh of relief. Roughhousing was good—it postponed things.

Sheila took advantage of the moment to close in on Skip. She wasn't exactly older than her sixteen and a half years, but she was certainly at the height of her teenage powers. Though they weren't related by blood, in some ways, she and Skip were built alike. Skip was six feet tall, Sheila was five-ten; Skip had a tendency to overweight, Sheila to overripeness. But despite her height, Skip had never been spectacular in the boob department, while Sheila sported a pair of Aqua-Lungs.

The girl's hair and eyes were dark, but her skin was a veritable sunrise of color, tawny and pink and glowing. Her mouth was huge. And unlike many girls her age, she seemed perfectly aware of the power of her sexuality. She was also, by nature, more aggressive than otherwise, while Kenny tended toward passivity—or at least an uncommon, and to Skip, quite winning, gentleness.

If Kenny wasn't awed enough by Sheila in the way any younger boy would be by an older, taller, more sexually advanced sister, he should have been terrified by the way she pushed the older-sibling routine. She said to Skip, "Have you ever seen anything so utterly stupid and childish in your whole life?"

Skip thought, *It's remarks like this that put the challenge in being a near-parent.* "Fashion's fickle," she said.

"That's not fashion, that's *retarded.*"

Skip said, "Where's Uncle Jimmy?" hoping against hope that he'd flown off to see the pyramids.

"He and Layne went to Langenstein's. They're *shopping* together now." Sheila rolled her eyes.

"What's wrong with that?"

"And then they cook together. Pretty soon they're going to be wearing matching ruffly aprons."

Skip bristled. Jimmy Dee had gone through nine or ten different kinds of hell for these kids, inherited when his sister died a few years ago. Kenny had always been a pleaser, but Sheila was like the little girl with the curl—she'd quite often been horrid. Not lately, though, and Skip wasn't up for any more acting out. But she held herself in check. "Do I detect a tiny bit of homophobia on the home front?"

Sheila looked horrified. "Homophobia! What's that got to do with anything?"

" 'Ruffly aprons'? What's that about?"

"They're just so damn cute, that's all." She turned and flounced into the house, as well as one can flounce in a denim miniskirt. As she opened the door, Skip heard the domestic clatter of Dee-Dee and Layne putting away groceries.

"Hey, gorgeous," one of them said.

"Oh, hey, Layne." Skip could imagine Sheila giving him a half-contemptuous glance as she passed.

Dee-Dee said, "What's wrong with her?"

"Hormones, I guess. Where's Angel, I wonder?" Layne stepped out to the courtyard.

Kenny turned instantly from Steve. "Hey, Layne—like my hairdo?" He put one hand on his hip and the other on the side of his face, primping.

Layne stood riveted, eyes round and naked as checkers. He opened his mouth and closed it again, doubtless trying to think of a way to protect Dee-Dee from the spectacle.

Dee-Dee chose that moment to follow him outside. His comment was unequivocal and loud. "Aaaaaaaagggggghhhh." But seeing Kenny's sweet face crumple in misery, he tried to inject some humor: "Help! The Martians have landed!"

Kenny smiled again, a little uncertainly, but clinging to the desperate hope that approval would after all be forthcoming.

Sheila chose that moment to rejoin the group, a malicious little smile on her face. "Don't you just *love* it, Uncle Jimmy?"

Skip saw Dee-Dee marshalling his resources. "I'm getting there. I'm getting there."

Kenny was starting to catch on that his sartorial experiment wasn't a success. "Everybody *hates* it!" He started to go in the house, about to go through the whole teenage door-slamming routine, but Layne caught him. "Hey, sport. Hold it. It's cool. I'm not kidding, it's really . . . um . . . cool. Really. It just kind of takes you by surprise, that's all."

Kenny wriggled away. "You're lyin'," and he pushed past him into the house.

Sheila slunk away behind him, chastened a bit.

Steve said, "I need a beer."

"We were, uh, going to barbecue in the courtyard," Dee-Dee began. "Layne's making his famous potato salad and we *were* going to have this jolly old time . . ."

"Are you asking us to join you?" Steve asked. "We accept. Looks like Sheila and Kenny won't be around—somebody has to eat that chicken."

"Oh, dinner's an hour away. They'll have time to cool down."

Steve went to shower off after a hard day of home improvement, and Layne went to construct the famous salad. Dee-Dee sat dejectedly in one of the green-painted chairs. "Why, Minerva? Why, why, why did he feel the need to do that?"

Skip said, "Are you speaking to me or invoking the goddess of wisdom?"

"Both, my tiny trifle. As you are the living embodiment of wisdom—or at least the closest thing in this courtyard—*please* tell me what's wrong with that boy."

"Same as ever, Dee-Dee. He's insecure."

"Oh, God—I mean Goddess—when will it ever end? What does it take to get a kid secure?"

"Well, I think Sheila's coming into her own. Speaking of goddesses."

"Oh, shit. Forget it in that case.'"

Steve came out in fresh shorts and T-shirt, sipping the aforementioned beer. He spoke thoughtfully. "First the earring and now this. Something's going on with that kid."

Dee-Dee said, "Wonder if he's gay."

Sheila came out with a plate of chicken, which she began forking onto the grill. "He's not gay. Gay people always think everyone else is gay."

"Is that so, Missy-Wissy? Tell you who's not gay—all those hunks that hang around *your* young patootie. I don't think for a millisecond *they're* gay."

"Oh, Uncle Jimmy, you're so protective." Her voice was whiny and irritated.

"Oh, Niece Sheila, I can't do anything right. What is the problem around here?"

All of a sudden she was crying. "You just don't know what it's like to live with two randy old coots!" Once again she did her mini-flounce.

Layne came out. "Old? Who's she calling old?" He was fifteen years younger than Dee-Dee.

"And randy! After we've been so discreet. Separate bedrooms and everything."

"Hold it. Hold it a minute," said Steve. "I've got an idea. I'm going to spend some time with Kenny and see what I can find out." He stood up. "Kenny? Hey, Kenny! I'm going to take Napoleon for a walk—want to bring Angel?"

Talba was pissed as hell at the damn cop, and pissed at Darryl Boucree, who had to be the one who dropped the dime on her. Fuck him and fuck her, in that order.

She called Lamar, intending to ask him over for dinner.

"Hey, Lamar. What are you doing?"

"Baronessa. Gettin' ready for a date. Why?"

Was she hearing right? Ahh . . . she realized what must have happened. So this was his cute way of confronting her. "No reason," she said, and hung up. "Mama?" she called. "Mama, did Lamar call here last night?"

"Sho' did. I tol' him you was out on a date."

Well, that was that, then—she and Lamar were a former item. Lamar was a petty bastard—she'd be lucky if he didn't come over and cut up her underwear or something.

Damn. She'd been hoping to bounce her current dilemma off someone. Couldn't be Lamar. Couldn't be Darryl. Even if he called, he couldn't be trusted. And it certainly wasn't going to be her mama.

Damn, she thought again. *What am I going to do? Go back to work? Guess I have to, to keep them from getting suspicious. And anyway, I might want a job there sometime. I've got to keep in good with Robert Tyson. Maybe I could still get him to show me the back door to that encryption program.*

But, no. The damn cop would probably have been in the computer by now. No way that file was going to be there. *But it might.* She just couldn't shake that thought.

But so what? Even if I got it, I'd still have to turn it over to the cops, and I could hardly justify selling it to the client as well.

The client who might also be the murderer.

Damn, she was mad at that cop. She did feel bad about failing to give up Newman's name—she should have, no two ways about it—but the damn cop didn't have to be so nasty about it. Who was the bitch, anyway? Well, easy enough—Talba had about a dozen ways to access the *Times-Picayune*'s database.

Idly, her hands began playing over the keys. About a million references came spewing out at her.

Well, look at this. The bitch is somebody—and somebody I know, too.

Everybody knew about the crazy policewoman who'd twice had the misfortune to mess with Errol Jacomine—just about the most dangerous man in the country right now.

I'd better be a little more careful, Talba thought. *This bitch is tough.*

Hey, hey, hey, look at this! The girl's father's a pill man. Dr. Richard Langdon—hey, she was a debutante. Queen of a carnival ball? You've got to be kidding. How's that possible?

236

When she had read it all, Talba found she had a new respect for the complicated creature who'd so unceremoniously jerked her around this afternoon. There'd probably been hell to pay when she became a cop. Miz Clara was probably nothing compared to Miz Lizzie (if that were Elizabeth Langdon's nickname).

Just for fun, Talba checked out the parents. Uh-huh, there it was. Lizzie was a volunteer queen—if it was a museum, she worked for it; if a disease, against it.

Omigod. Look at this. Not only was Dick a pill man, he was a gynecologist. What if he were her pill man? The doctor who named her? Their ages were about right.

She riffled through the clips, but couldn't find a thing about his residency or internship. She tapped into another database, a local doctors' directory. Aha, there it was. Charity Hospital. It didn't give a specific date, but the time had to be about right. Had to be.

She started fantasizing about it—about the moment when she could get into Charity's computer. What would she do? Look up her mother's records? There was a doctor on her birth certificate, but her mother said he wasn't the one. It was another one, a young, cute one who came around in the mornings, and seemed so nice.

Morning rounds, Corey had told her—a resident or intern. To complicate matters, he could have been either at LSU or Tulane—it would have to be hospital, not med school, records. And who knew, these many years later, if they even had records of who did which rotation when? She began to get dizzy, the way she always did when she felt overwhelmed.

Okay, stop now. Stop, Talba, just stop. Just breathe for a minute.

But no one was going to let her breathe. She just wasn't going to get to do that. Her damn phone was screaming at her.

"Hello," she said, in the tone of someone expecting a bill collector.

"This is the man who's going to give you seven hundred and fifty dollars. Can't you be a little nicer?"

Hmmph. Hell you are. She almost said that—but this was a kid-gloves situation.

"I hit another snag. Maybe another couple of snags."

"What the hell do you mean you've hit a snag?"

She had to hold the phone away from her ear. "You're yelling."

"Goddammit, what's the problem? I paid you good money to do what a child should be able to do. I thought you were a professional."

"Hey, I'm doing what I can."

"Well, it's not good enough, Talba. You must be the most overpaid little computer nerd in Louisiana, and day after day you keep coming up with nothing."

"Wait a minute . . ."

"No, *you* wait a minute. Tell me one goddamn thing you've done to earn your damn money."

"That's it. I quit. Find yourself another nerd, Mr. Asshole." She broke the connection.

The asshole called right back, of course. She picked up and said, "Not interested."

"What about my seven-fifty?" He sounded slightly chastened, which gave Talba an idea.

"Look, I'll make a deal with you. I took a peek at that file when I got it for Allred . . ."

"You did? Well, what the hell was in it?"

"A bunch of names and numbers that didn't mean a damn thing to me. So naturally I forgot 'em. But yesterday, I remembered a name."

The client didn't speak for a moment. She heard him draw in his breath. He said, "You remembered a name," all quiet and reasonable, as if the fact alone might be important.

She went for it. "Here's my proposition. I give you the name, I get to keep the seven-fifty, we call off the rest of the deal, and we're square."

He didn't speak for a while, just breathed heavily into the phone.

* * *

One name? Was it worth seven-fifty?

It could be. It might be all he needed. On the other hand, it might be worthless.

Ray closed his eyes. "All right."

"What? Why are you whispering?"

"Give it to me."

"Okay, you got a pencil? It's Marion Newman. That's . . . M-a-r . . ."

"I know, I know."

"Are we done now? I'm okay, you're okay?"

"I'll be in touch." He hung up.

Marion Newman. He might have just hit the jackpot. "Cille! Cille, I've got a name."

Cille came flying in, grabbed him around the neck, pressing his head into her abdomen. "Wheeeeeeee!" It felt good there.

"We're going to get the rest of those bastards."

"Yes, Lord!" She threw up her hands and wiggled them.

"Thank you, Jesus!" He did the same. It was a ritual they had, more profane than sacred, as neither of them was particularly religious.

Usually they both did it, didn't even notice it, but everything seemed so fragile these days, Ray had begun seeing the details of his life in high relief. *Where had that thing come from?* he wondered. *A movie? Something they'd actually seen?* He literally couldn't remember the first time they'd done it. It was one of the tiny tiles that fit together in their marriage mosaic, that made it a rare and satisfying artwork; the most precious thing in his life. It made them laugh.

"Git 'em," she said. "Git 'em. Go git 'em, big boy." That was another of their private . . . well, not jokes, more like little habits that made them feel part of each other. He felt like they shared a skin sometimes.

He pulled up his Rolodex on the computer and dialed Marion Newman. The number had been disconnected.

That could be a good sign, he thought. *I don't have my old number, either.*

Let's see now. He had a son. Bad actor, though. Always in trouble. Ah, yes. Son-in-law in the air-conditioning business. But what was his name?

A little conference with the Yellow Pages, and he had it: "Neville. Like the brothers." He could hear the guy saying it now. It was too late for business hours, but there was an emergency number. Ray dialed it and waited for a callback, which came within the half hour—maybe the longest half hour of his life. Larry Neville himself called, and seemed all too happy to put his father-in-law on the line. ("Are you kidding? No trouble at all. It's got the hell beat out of going out to fix an air conditioner.")

Ray could hear Marion Newman in the background. "Who? Do I know a Ray Boudreaux? Who the hell's that? Don't want to talk to anybody." He sounded like a crotchety old fart—the Newman Ray remembered was a perfectly turned out, perfectly polished gentleman.

His hello was even nastier than Talba's.

Ray said, "You remember me, Mr. Newman. Hyacinth Oil."

"Why, Mr. Boudreaux." The old fart was suddenly re-formed. "It's a pleasure to hear from you."

"How're you doing, Mr. Newman?"

"What can I do for you, sir?" Definitely didn't want to get into the story of his life.

"I think we might have something in common, Mr. Newman. If you can just give me a few minutes of your time, I think we might be able to help each other."

"Very well, sir. You have my full and complete attention."

"I'm wondering if you know a man named Russell Fortier."

"Russell Fortier, you say? Why no, but that name's been comin' up lately. Why do you ask?"

"I'm going to put it in a nutshell, Mr. Newman. I don't want to waste your time or mine. I've lost my company, thanks to some very dirty tricks played on me by United Oil. I have . . . information that something similar might have happened to you."

240

"You do, do you? I guess you can't trust anybody these days."

"Meaning large and powerful corporations? I'd say it's a risky business at best."

"Meaning the police. I thought they were supposed to be like priests."

"I beg your pardon?"

"Two in one day is just a little coincidental for subtlety."

"I'm afraid you've lost me, sir."

"No sooner do I get through pouring out the whole sordid story to that diesel dyke of a cop than the phone rings, and it's you."

"Diesel dyke . . . ?" What on earth could the man be talking about? "Oh. Do you mean Skip Langdon?"

"You know damn well I do, and what kind of name is that for a girl?"

"Mr. Newman, I assure you I'm not in touch with Detective Langdon or any other police officer. I got your name from another source entirely."

"Is that right?" Newman sounded utterly unconvinced.

"Look, I'm calling because I hoped we might work together." He was about to elaborate, but Newman interrupted.

"Tell me something, Mr. Boudreaux. Did you always pay your royalties on time?"

"We tried; we certainly tried. But you know how it is. I can't say that we did, no."

"Is that how they got you?"

"What? On delinquent royalties? Oh, no, they were much trickier than that."

"But you were guilty of it and so is everybody else in the industry. Am I right about that?"

"Well, sir, I wouldn't argue that."

"Well, I'm the one they dragged down with it. They not only got my company, they made sure I turned up tarnished in front of God and everybody. Including my late wife, rest her soul."

The last thing on Ray's agenda was stopping the conversation to make his manners. But there was no help for it. He offered his condolences in as abbreviated form as he dared, and as soon as he decently could, he said again, "Listen, Mr. Newman, I'm calling because I'm hoping we can work together on this."

"That would depend, sir, on what we'd be working on."

"I'm hoping for a class action suit. But first I'm trying to find out if there's a class. We both just found there are at least two of us, and I think that's exciting." Exciting was hardly the word for it. Ray's heart was about to pound out of his chest.

"What do you want from me?"

Those words, Ray thought, *for openers. Yes, Lord! Thank you, Jesus.* "I just thought we might put our heads together and trade information."

Newman went irascible again, having evidently had a moment to let his brain catch up with his mouth. "Two in one day! That's just a little much, don't you think?"

"This Russell Fortier thing's about to bust open, Mr. Newman. That's what the whole thing's spinning around right now. The cops are trying to find him before we do." His heart in his mouth, he asked, "You don't have any ideas, do you?"

"Ideas? I'd barely heard of the man before I read about him in the paper—I didn't even know he was married to Bebe Fortier."

"Wait a minute—United must have made you an offer."

"Oh, yes, certainly they did. But Russell Fortier was never involved."

"Oh. Well, then, who did the offer come from?" Ray tried to keep his voice as level as possible.

"Man named Beau Cavignac." For the first time, Newman chuckled. "Sounds like somethin' out of *Gone With the Wind*, doesn't it? He wasn't nearly as dashing as he sounds. Little roly-poly fellow. You'd swear he was just barely competent." He paused and chuckled again. "Some kind of Peter Falk–Columbo act. The man's a great actor, I'll tell you that."

Ray chuckled along with him, thinking that at last he

might be getting somewhere. "Mr. Newman, could we get together and talk about this?"

"I don't know what there is to talk about. I don't *know* anything else."

"Okay. Let's leave it like it is for now. I know it's a lot to assimilate—the fact that they did this as policy. But I believe they did and I believe we can prove they did. And I believe we have recourse. Let me just give you time to think it over, and then I'll call you back."

"Fair enough, Mr. Boudreaux. Fair enough." His voice told Ray he'd already started processing it.

Ray disconnected, feeling triumphant, almost ready to holler out at Cille that things were finally starting to break, when he heard the little stutter tone of his voice mail. He decided to check it before hollering, to see if anything else good had happened. It was Ronnie, his son.

"Dad, I need a little help. I'm in . . . uh . . . Central Lockup . . . uh . . . there's been a little trouble. If you could do anything to get me out of here, I'd really appreciate it."

Central Lockup. How was Ray supposed to take that in?

But he grasped in a millisecond the fear and misery in his son's voice. It was heartbreaking to hear the boy trying so hard to be cool, yet unable to hide his desperation.

Ray hung up the phone and walked very quietly out of the house, trying not to attract Cille's attention. Now if he could just get away . . .

He backed his car out of the driveway at about sixty, swung around, and laid rubber like some high school gangster. But at the end of the block he slowed to a normal pace—Cille wasn't going to run down the street chasing him.

He drove over to South Broad Street—the thing was somewhere near police headquarters, he knew that much—trying to picture his baby son, towheaded Ronnie, in Central Lockup. Thank God, Cille hadn't picked up the phone—maybe he could solve this thing, whatever it was, without her even having to know about it.

Central Lockup (officially the Intake and Processing

Center), which sounds like something out of prerevolutionary Russia, in fact looks more like an airport waiting room than a jail. Ray exhaled as he walked in, realizing that he'd pictured an environment where everything was metal, a good deal of it rusty, all of it clanking. On the drive over, he could almost feel a coldness that permeated first the air and then the brain of anyone who breathed it, detaching it from the skull, spinning it around like some mad, squishy top.

When he saw the reality, his spinning brain had only one thought: *This isn't so bad.*

Yet reason told him it could hardly be worse.

He let himself be led docilely through the steps in getting his son out of jail—he had to find a lawyer who could get a bond set, then find some cash, a near impossibility, and then a bail bondsman. Then he had to post bond, and then he had to get his son in the car and take him somewhere other than home—he couldn't really be around him right now—and listen to how he had been stupid enough to get busted for a joint or something.

It turned out it was theft—or that's what the cops called it.

He had yet to hear Ronnie's version.

He already knew a lawyer from his troubles over his lease, and the lawyer was home and so, in time, was a judge. Ray used his ATM card to get the cash.

His normally red-cheeked son was as pasty as cinder blocks. The boy's hazel eyes—neither brown nor really green—were huge with remorse and pleading. *I'll do anything. I'll go back to first grade and start over. I'll be a Cub Scout again, I'll clean my room every day, I'll scrub the toilets, for Christ's sake. Just take me out of here now!*

And after Ray had, when Ronnie was safely in the car, he said, "What if your mother had had to see that?"

"Dad, I'm sorry. I'm so sorry I could kill myself. I swear to God I could." And at nineteen years of age, he burst into tears.

Ray drove round and round till the tears dried up and Ronnie could tell his story. "It was just a big misunderstanding," he said. "You know? I picked up two shirts instead of one. I was at The Gap, shopping, and I bought this blue polo shirt, but then when I walked out, this guy stopped me—this guard or something. He searched my bag, and sure enough, there were two in there. I don't know how the other one got there—I swear I don't."

"Son, don't lie to me."

"I'm not lying."

He was, though. Ray felt as if a Toyota had been lowered onto his chest.

Much as Ray wanted him out of his life right now, Ronnie lived at home and it would probably be best for him to be there until things cooled a little. So, against his own wishes, Ray took the boy home.

He had called Cille from the processing center, to say Ronnie'd had a little trouble and they'd be home soon. She was waiting up, and when she saw her son, she asked no questions, simply enfolded him in her arms. And when she had hugged him enough, she said simply, "Go to bed now."

Ronnie certainly didn't wait to be told a second time. He disappeared around a corner, not even detouring by the kitchen—and he had to be starving.

When they heard the door to his room close, Cille came close and hugged her husband this time. "What'd they do to him?" She was wearing only a T-shirt and a robe, which was now gapped open to reveal a pair of black bikini panties. To him, she looked like a high school girl.

Ray nodded to himself, not even realizing he had done it. She had a right to know, and he knew she could take it. He told her.

She said, "Oh, honey! Oh, honey, we can't even say, 'You don't have to steal. If you need shirts, just ask us,' like normal parents would." She started to cry.

"Yeah." That was the part that got him, too.

"Those bastards have done this to us, Ray."

He only nodded.

245

"They don't know who they're fooling with. They really have no idea what's coming at them."

It was scary how much alike they thought.

Twenty-one

RUSSELL HAD NEVER been all that fond of Fort Lauderdale, and now he was growing to hate it. The good things were the beach and the old marina, straight out of John D. MacDonald. But the bad things were myriad. There were the wall-to-wall condos, the acres of low-ceilinged '50s houses, the dumb bars where they had hot-bod contests and wet T-shirt contests and raw oyster-eating contests and, unwittingly, dumb-joke, dumb-line, dumb-talk contests. And there were the horrible restaurants. He'd found a good place for sushi, and one where they had nice Asian dishes, but mostly it was suburb cuisine—plenty of salt, not much style. This might not mean much to most people, but it was the kind of thing a person from New Orleans noticed.

He'd only gone there to get the Pearson, and make plans for what to do next, but so far he had only one plan—lose Dean Woolverton. Dean was like an albatross around his neck—he wished he'd never heard of the man—but he owed him. He owed him because it was his stupid name that had caught Dina Wolf's attention.

Dina Wolf was certainly the most interesting thing about Fort Lauderdale, by far its most unique property. Plenty of towns had beaches, but few had wild, wriggling aliens with animal names.

He was established here as Dean Woolverton (meaning he had a phone, a leased car, a boat, and a slip for it), which made it tempting to stay a little bit, except that he was so restless. What he really needed were some papers—a driver's license, passport, maybe even a credit card, though how an imaginary person got credit, he wasn't sure. But he figured with the amount of dope traffic in Miami, South Florida was the counterfeit-papers capital of the universe. It was just a matter of getting to know the right people. And figuring out who he wanted to be.

Dean Woolverton was three things and three things only, it seemed to him: blond hair, an earring, and a name. He'd already dumped the earring and started growing a beard. Now all he had to do was figure out how to change his hair color and name without arousing the suspicion of the only person he knew. He could, of course, simply set sail for somewhere else—even somewhere close, Delray, say—and that would be that. But, aside from the Pearson, Dina Wolf was all he had. Literally all he had—the only person he had to talk to, the only distraction from a life of solitary afternoon movies. He was desperate to buy golf clubs, but he had no idea how much the fake papers were going to cost, or how much he'd need for other expenses. He *had* treated himself to a tennis racket, and occasionally took out his aggressions on yellow balls.

He still had hopes for the vagabond life, once he started actually living it. He could just sail to the Bahamas and gunkhole around, living on the boat and buying groceries now and then, occasionally consuming a beer at a bar in some lonely port, so as to keep in touch with the human race. That was all he really needed.

But in the meantime, he was uncomfortably dependent on Dina Wolf. She was just so damn fascinating to try and figure out. Plus great in bed.

He'd taken to calling her so much, she had said, "Don't you think we're moving too fast?"

It stopped him cold. It really hadn't occurred to him they were moving anywhere at all. He was so taken aback, he could only stammer. "I didn't ... I mean I don't ..."

She nodded. "Right. And that's how men and women are different. Look, you're recently out of a marriage, or maybe still in one, I can't tell, and you're not used to being alone. I, on the other hand, have a life, such as it is. I don't want you messing it up."

"Messing it up. You mean it's messy having me phoning when maybe you're entertaining someone else? Or . . . you mean you're spending too much time with me and not getting enough sleep?"

He was trying to think of other explanations when she said, "Are you being deliberately obtuse, or are you really that innocent?"

Russell felt like some bumbling professor in a Jimmy Stewart movie. What was it with this girl?

She said, "Listen, let's understand each other. You're just looking to pass the time, but you're taking all my time. This is usually considered a sign of serious intentions."

Though they were only talking on the phone, he was blushing. "Dina, listen, I'm sorry. I never for a minute meant to give you that impression."

"I *know* that, Dean, and you didn't." She sounded angry. "What I'm saying is, you're breaking the rules—you can't have your cake and eat it, too."

He was hugely embarrassed. His mother had taught him better than this—or at least he knew that was how one behaved when dealing with women like Bebe. He had somehow thought that women one met in places like the Bootlegger played by different rules. He simply did *not* know how to deal with this woman. What the hell was he supposed to say now?

But she saved him. "Look. Think about it and call me back when you feel like it, okay?"

She hung up, leaving him exhausted.

What the hell to do? He put his hands behind his head and lay back on his bunk, feeling about as depressed as he'd ever been in his life.

And then slowly, a plan began to form, a plan born out of the outrageousness that had spawned the Skinners—a plan that made him laugh.

He called her back, held his nose, and pitched his voice a couple of octaves higher than normal: "This is Western Union, we have a telegram for Miss Dina Wolf, please do not interrupt—our time is of the utmost essence. Is Miss Wolf available, please?"

"This is . . ."

"Please *do not interrupt*. Mr. Dean Woolverton requests the pleasure of Miss Wolf's company at dinner Wednesday night and dancing afterward. If such an arrangement meets with Miss Wolf's approval, Mr. Woolverton will call for Miss Wolf at seven-thirty o'clock. Dress is, of course, optional. It will not be necessary for Miss Wolf to bring her own bottle."

She chuckled. "A for effort, Dean. But not A-plus, since Wednesday's tomorrow night. And by the way, it's Mrs. Wolf. As it happens, I'm free."

A dial tone buzzed in his ear, and he felt suddenly bereft. He hadn't realized how much he enjoyed their time together, or how callously he'd seen her merely as a way to pass the time. That "Mrs. Wolf" bit hurt—she evidently meant he'd never even asked her if she'd been married, but surely he must have. He wasn't that self-involved.

He wondered what she did on nights home alone by herself. He hadn't heard a television. Maybe she read. What? he wondered. Romances? The classics? Self-help books, maybe—*Women Who Love Men Who Are Truly Buttholes*. Maybe that was what the lecture was all about.

He grabbed the copy of *Sailing* magazine he'd picked up at Eckerd, and then thought twice about stereotypes. But there was nothing else on the boat except a Travis McGee novel he'd bought for the local color. He fell asleep reading it.

In the morning he awoke feeling excited for the first time since buying the sloop. He had preparations to make.

First, he went to a hairdresser—an actual salon instead of a barber shop—and said, "Do something. I hate this hair."

"What's the matter? Blonds don't have more fun?" The guy obviously took him for gay.

"My wife won't sleep with me anymore."

"Well, honey, maybe you should try Viagra."

Russell got up and flung off his smock, but the guy smoothed him down. "Take it easy, take it easy. Teeny little joke, that's all." And then he was all business. "Okay, what shall we do? How about something sandy—like mine—with a few highlights to make the transition?" He cocked his head, assessing. "And maybe a little more contemporary cut."

When he left there, Russell felt human again. Of course, he now looked a little like a straight man trying to pass for gay, but that was better than looking like himself or Dean. In fact, the effect took ten years off his age, in his own humble opinion. Even the three-day beard wasn't that scruffy.

Next he went and bought a pair of khakis (God, it felt good to wear them again!) and some kind of unconstructed linen jacket. After that, a dozen red roses, and he was Mr. Smooth Swain.

Dina had gone to trouble as well. She had on a black dress with halter top and little swing skirt, the old Marilyn Monroe style, and her short hair had somehow been persuaded into curls and waves and things. She held out her hands for the roses. "Why, Mr. Woolverton," she said. "How very kind of you."

He bowed. "My pleasure, Mrs. Wolf."

After that, things got a little more informal. In fact, they went so well he had to congratulate himself on combining his makeover with his lady friend's tiny request. And indeed it did seem tiny when you considered how genuinely pleased she seemed to be. After dinner, she said, "Let's don't go dancing. Let's find a motorcycle to ride."

He certainly wasn't stealing one, if that was what she meant. But apparently she didn't mean anything. "Or maybe a horse," she said.

"No, let's just walk." He pulled into a beachfront parking lot. "And you tell me about Mr. Wolf."

She kicked off her shoes, slithered out of her pantyhose, and slid out of the car, chattering like a little girl. "Well, his name's Akela and he hangs with Kaa, the snake, and Bagheera, the panther. They don't like tigers much."

"You want to go over that again?"

"You never read Kipling when you were a kid? 'Now this is the Law of the Jungle—as old and true as the sky. And the Wolf that shall keep it may prosper, and the Wolf that shall break it must die.'" She sighed. "It's the hardest thing in the world to find someone with the same frame of reference. Don't you think? Bet you read *Sailing* magazine, and that's about it, right?"

He was speechless. "Why are you looking so surprised? Caught you, didn't I?"

You don't know the half of it, he thought. He said, "You are one surprising babe."

"You know what? Just 'cause you brought me roses, I'm going to let you call me babe. You know, I really like your hair that way—the blond thing just wasn't you."

"Are you going to tell me about your ex-husband or aren't you? I'm really sorry I never asked you about him."

"Well . . ." She seemed to get shy all of a sudden. "He was my high school boyfriend, and then he was a rep for a printer—I got him the job. And then he was pretty much of nothing." She gave Russell a strained smile, the sort he thought of as "brave." "Mr. Wolf liked his toddy," she said. "Hey, want to go swimming? You know what? It's a gorgeous night. We could skinny-dip." But she didn't. She simply waded into the surf, fancy dress and all, holding the skirt up so that the wind caught it and came under it, and made it a black mushroom floating on the water. "Come on in," she shouted.

But he hadn't left his old life so far behind that he could just wade in. He first removed his jacket, shoes, and pants, and then he ran in, feeling the water like a healing spring around him. He caught her and held her, thinking they could make love right there, right in the water, but in the end he didn't want to, only wanted to hold her and be comforted by her. As he held her in the softness of the night, and the gentleness of the water, a tenderness came over him, part of it simple joy in her presence, and part of it a great longing, something tinged with sadness.

He thought, *My God, I feel something for this woman,* and the thought so surprised him that he lost his balance, tipping toward her and nearly knocking her over. He managed to right himself before they were both underwater, and she said, "Whoops. Time to go in."

He dressed quickly while she scampered to the car. When he got in, she moved over to kiss his cheek. He smiled and touched hers with the backs of his fingers, and all the way home, she rubbed his thigh. He parked in front of her building and reached for her, the feeling nagging at him that he shouldn't be doing this. They necked like teenagers, her perfume—Opium, he was pretty sure—living up to its name. The more he held her and kissed her, the more he felt his judgment slipping. He was aware of behaving like a robot, yet unable to find the "off" button, until she spoke.

"Let's go in," she whispered, her breath a feather on his neck.

He pulled away and looked at her. Her eyes were wide and soft, and he thought, *I can't hurt this woman.*

He was trying to think what to do when she said, "You okay?"

"That's a good question." At times like this, he wished he smoked.

"Uh-oh." She turned from him, staring straight ahead. "Here comes the let's-be-friends speech."

He had to chuckle. "Uh, no. That's the last thing on my mind. I'm just a little . . ."

"Confused? It's the I'm-a-little-confused speech." He could swear there was a wet track on her face.

This was a woman who was obviously a veteran of a lot of things Russell was not. He wanted to protect her from the assholes who'd dumped her with stock phrases, and at the same time, it made him mad that she lumped him with them. (Though, in fact, he *had* been about to say he was a little confused.)

He said, "You know what your problem is, Ms. Wolf?"

She whirled toward him, fire in her eyes. "I'm a castrating bitch?"

"Your problem is that you have obviously come in contact with some pathetic specimens of masculinity. I, Dean Woolverton, have taken a special vow to restore your faith in the existence of that elusive species known as the 'gentleman.' "

"Oh, yeah? How? By sleeping with me a few times and then saying you don't want to hurt me? That makes you a real terrific guy, Dean." She slammed out of the car and clicked into the building.

Dean Woolverton, you asshole! Russell Fortier just wouldn't be in this situation. He bought a fifth of Scotch on the way back to the boat and poured himself a double. He took the bottle and went up to the cockpit, downing his drink by the time he sat down.

The night was as beautiful as it had been when he and Dina were wading, and yet the vastness of the water, the softness of the air, failed to work their invariable calming magic. A deep, thick, mucky sadness had descended on him, or perhaps had burrowed out of him, chewing and biting its way to the surface like some trapped parasite.

He had an almost overwhelming urge to talk to his wife.

But that couldn't be. He didn't even want to think of the consequences of that one.

But someone from his old life. Surely there was someone he could talk to, someone who knew him as Russell Fortier, husband and family man, well-known business figure, solid citizen (except for a few unfortunate lapses), loyal friend. . . .

Who am I kidding? I just ran out on my wife and friends. And my kid, goddammit, my kid. Russell Fortier doesn't exist anymore.

Eugenie's face floated into his consciousness, so trusting, so utterly undeserving of what had happened to her.

It was better this way, he had thought. This way she wouldn't have to suffer the public indignity of a disgraced daddy. But he saw, through mists of Scotch, that he was wrong. She would go through that no matter where he was. And this way, he wasn't even there to say he loved her, low-down scum though he was.

He had to tell her at least that he was okay, he wasn't dead, that he'd acted in the way he thought best for everybody.

And yet that wasn't true.

The alcohol couldn't blunt the facts, which were simply that he had acted first stupidly, and then selfishly. It was not a nice thing to face.

He poured himself another Scotch.

He thought, *I have to talk to her,* a thought he'd had plenty of time to think in the last few days, but which in the sober state had never occurred to him.

The thing built and built until he had to pace the deck to keep from calling her. And in the end, he did. He called her at school, but was told she'd gone home.

Because of him, he was sure of that. She was probably missing half the damn semester, and all because of him. He had to tell her to go back to school, to quit worrying about him, to quit hating him, to love him anyway, no matter that he was pond scum.

He definitely could not call her at home. Bebe might pick up the phone and if he heard Bebe's voice, he'd probably bay like a hound.

Maybe he could somehow get a message to Eugenie. He could call someone else.

He liked that idea a lot.

Okay, there were three choices—Doug, Edward, and Beau.

Three choices and no contest.

Of the three, only one would be unequivocally and genuinely glad to hear from him. Only one would be likely to keep his secret and not try to use it for his own gain. Only one was a real human being and not the shell of one. Beau. Lumbering, blundering, slightly stupid Beau. Big old tears filled Russell's eyes as he remembered all the snotty things he'd ever thought about Beau—thought and said, most of them.

Russell was truly aghast at the life he'd led, and starting to fear this new life was just more of the same. He didn't want to think about what the alternative might be. Certainly didn't want to undergo another moment of truth like that time on the boat two years ago. If he had yet *another*, where the hell could it possibly lead?

He looked at his watch—eleven-thirty. That made it a mere ten-thirty in New Orleans, the shank of the evening for a man who never missed Jay Leno. Which Beau was.

Russell didn't even hesitate. He dialed from memory, and in about fifteen seconds he was listening to that old-shoe voice. He said, "Beau, if Deb's with you, go to another room." Surely his old pal would recognize his voice.

Good old Beau—he didn't miss a beat. "Wait a minute, the TV's on in here. Let me get to a different phone."

Russell drummed his fingers. But in just a moment, Beau was saying, "Russell! God *damn*, it's good to hear your voice. God *damn*. I mean it."

Now that Russell had him, he didn't know what to say: *Sorry I left y'all in the lurch?* Somehow, that didn't seem to cut it.

But Beau was taking the lead. "You okay, fella? Anything I can do for you?"

"I'm fine, Beau. I just wanted to hear your voice."

"Man, you just don't know. Lots of people think you're dead." A beat passed, and then Beau apparently remem-

256

bered something. "Oh, God, you don't know, do you? Listen, there's a lot to cover. Let me talk a few minutes, okay? There's some stuff you've really got to know."

"Oh, Jesus." Whatever was coming couldn't be good.

"After you left, somebody tried to blackmail us. Guy named Gene Allred. Two-bit private eye who'd been hired by crazy Ray Boudreaux to get some dirt on us. Well, he did get it, God knows how—out of the 'Skina-cat' file you left in your computer."

"Oh, Jesus," Russell said again. He remembered the file all too well. "I didn't think anyone could get to it." Actually, he hadn't thought about it at all.

"So, as near as we can figure out, he decided to double-cross Boudreaux and blackmail us instead. But here's the bad part—here's the really, really bad part. The guy ends up dead."

"What?"

"Murdered. Shot in his office."

"Jesus, Beau." Russell was having a pretty profane night. "Who did it?"

"I don't know."

Russell couldn't miss the absence of the plural pronoun. "Are you saying what I think you're saying?"

"All I'm saying is, the police haven't caught the guy." His voice got louder, and carried a note of pleading in it. "Hey, Russell, this is murder. That other stuff was bad, yeah, but it probably wasn't even illegal—or at least most of it wasn't. It was just mean, stupid shit. But this is *murder*. You follow me?"

"No. No, I don't." Right now, he probably couldn't follow a map of his own backyard.

"I think we ought to come clean, buddy. I don't think we can hide this shit anymore."

"What do the others think?"

"I don't know. I just don't know. We're going to meet tomorrow to talk about it." He sounded troubled. "Listen, buddy, I could sure use any support you could give me."

257

Russell was trying to think of an answer when Beau spoke again. "Uh . . . there's one other thing you need to know. There's a school of thought says you did it."

Twenty-two

THURSDAY MORNING SKIP woke up with a new lease on life—or at least on the case. She had a headful of new ideas, most of them, curiously enough, out of the mouths of babes.

Things had been up and down on St. Philip after Steve and Kenny came back from their walk. (Naturally, Kenny had agreed to go—no way was he going to turn down an opportunity to be with Steve and Napoleon. In fact, Napoleon had once been his dog until Skip and Dee-Dee laid down the law—and now they were stuck with the big lug anyway.)

The chicken was just getting done, Skip had had a shower, and Kenny and Steve were in terrific spirits when they returned. Dee-Dee and Layne were up for fun, but clearly on edge. And Sheila was sulking all the way through the meal, putting a damper on the whole event. At first they tried ignoring her, just nattering on about anything at all.

But the girl was like a storm cloud, emitting black energy and random lightning bolts. So Skip did something she rarely did, except in extreme circumstances—turned the conversation to her work. Sometimes she told stories about past cases, a guaranteed icebreaker; but by now Kenny and Sheila had heard all the good ones. Sometimes—and she usually did this only with Steve—she'd postulate a problem. As it happened, she had one on her mind, a little thing that had niggled at her ever since Abasolo brought up the notion that Russell might have used a false ID to get out of the airport.

The thing had merit, but she hadn't yet had a chance to put her mind to it. "Listen," she said, "can I run a police problem by y'all?"

Five avid pairs of eyes turned to her, Sheila's no less alert than anyone else's. Kenny said, "Yeah! Yeah!" and Sheila gave him the requisite withering big-sis look, but it was only a glance, really. This stuff never failed.

"Okay, yesterday I robbed a bank with a security camera trained right on me . . ."

Sheila said, "Nobody would be that dumb."

"You'd be surprised. Say I'm a first offender—how're they going to ID me?" Mouths popped open, but she put up both hands. "Wait a minute, wait a minute. That has nothing to do with reality, it's just how criminals think—in the event they do think, which most of them don't. And I'm no exception. But say I've smeared my license plate with mud, thinking that's real professional, but then it rains—so there I am with naked plates. I'm making a getaway and I hear sirens. I get home and my house is surrounded by police cars."

"Oh, sure. They're really going to send a whole fleet of cars . . ."

Once more, she held up an open hand. "Oh, wait, I forgot to mention, I killed somebody in the course of the robbery. Let's make it worst-case scenario.

"So I can't go home. All of a sudden I realize I've got to start thinking. I abandon my car because it's no longer safe, quickly get some new clothes and a backpack for all my new money, some sunglasses, maybe—I do the best I can to look different. But I know what I really need to do is get out of town. So what do I do next?"

Jimmy Dee said, "Take a taxi to the airport and get on the next flight to anywhere."

But Sheila objected. "The cops would be watching the airport."

"You'd have to get there before they got around to it," Jimmy Dee said.

Kenny said, "Hey, I've got it. Just keep going. Take the taxi all the way to Baton Rouge and fly from there."

"Or," said Sheila, "you could rent a car in Baton Rouge." It was a thought. Skip hadn't considered it.

Dee-Dee said, "How about a boat? You take a taxi to some little fishing town and hire a fisherman to take you somewhere—maybe somewhere with an airport."

"Hey, wait a minute," said Steve. "Why don't you just steal a car?"

" 'Cause the cops would put out a bulletin on it—right, Auntie?"

Sheila said, "Hang on. You could also steal a license plate and switch it with the one on the car you stole." Her cheeks were pink and her eyes were bright as pennies.

"That would work," said Skip. Anything to keep the good mood going.

Layne, the puzzle-maker, finally spoke. "Greyhound bus is always good. I think you can buy an anonymous ticket—not like if you rent a car or fly." He paused and thought a minute. "But what you really need's a fake ID. Because you've changed your appearance, all they've got is your name. You've got to get rid of it."

This was going nicely, Skip thought. She'd successfully thrown them off the track of what she was getting at, and they were getting there anyway.

She said, "I forgot to mention—I was so dumb I left my gun at the scene. I can't hold anybody up to get an ID—and even if I could, I'm thinking now. My adrenaline's kicked in, and I'm trying to be smart."

Dee-Dee said, "Couldn't you just get a brick and knock someone in the head?"

"Or you could grab them from behind, stick a finger in their back, and pretend to have a gun."

"Trouble is, how do you find someone who looks like you?"

"Maybe you could just borrow an ID from a friend." The ideas were coming thick and furious now.

"But then you'd leave a witness."

Sheila shrugged. "So steal one from a friend. Ask him

out to dinner and then when he goes to the men's room, take his wallet out of his jacket."

" 'Course, you'd have to pay for dinner," Dee-Dee said.

Layne said, "They're always warning office workers not to leave their wallets in their pockets. You know how you hang your jacket in your office? Anybody could come along."

"Not if they looked like they didn't belong," said Sheila.

"Hey! I got it." Kenny was shouting. "You get a belt like Steve's."

Everyone stared at him, mystified.

He turned to Steve. "You know. That belt you wear when you're working on your house."

"My tool belt?"

"Yeah. You get one of those so you look like a repairman. Then you walk into any building you want and no one notices. You've got your choice of wallets."

Dee-Dee tousled the boy's imaginary hair. "Hey. Pretty smart, kiddo."

Skip nodded. "Very elegant."

But Sheila evidently felt her little brother was getting attention that was rightfully hers. "So how *did* Russell get out of town?"

Skip said, "Who?"

"Russell Fortier. That's what this is about, isn't it?"

"Of course not. You know I never discuss my cases." She hadn't meant it as a joke, but for some reason it provoked merriment.

It may have been unconventional, but it was a damned good brainstorming session. She'd gotten at least one good idea and a bunch of backups from it. She eliminated car-stealing and mugging on grounds they just weren't Russell's style. The Greyhound bus was a possibility, but she put it in the backup category for several reasons—first of all, the inconvenience. If you were at the airport, why take a bus? An easy answer might be simply that you wouldn't need ID to do it, but if you'd planned this thing in advance—unlike her postulated bank robber—why not plan a smooth, clean, easy getaway? Second, the taxi dispatcher and dozens of cab drivers had been shown Russell's picture and no one remembered him (though that certainly wasn't conclusive). The taxi ride to Baton Rouge or a nearby fishing village wasn't likely either, for the same reason. (Though she would check car rentals in Baton Rouge and maybe some other places, like Biloxi, maybe.)

The fake ID stolen from a friend was the plan she liked best. And best of the best was the office idea—only Russell wouldn't need a tool belt to get in. He already had the run of the United Oil building.

She dropped by there on her way to the office, surprising Douglas Seaberry sipping his morning mug. He had on a crisp striped shirt with the sleeves rolled up, and his face was all pink and healthy, like he'd jogged before work. He gave her a million-dollar smile—the man was nothing if not attractive—and then banished it almost immediately, as if he expected the worst. "Detective Langdon—do you have news?"

She was so wrapped up in her ID fantasies, she was momentarily taken aback. "News? Oh, about Russell. No, I'm sorry to say I don't. I just came by to ask you a question."

"Sit down. Can I get you some coffee?"

She accepted the seat, but declined the coffee. "I was wondering if you've had any problems with thieves lately."

Seaberry looked truly mystified, as well he might. "What I mean is, is this the kind of place where you can go to the ladies' room with your purse on your desk, and know it'll be there when you return?"

He seemed to be thinking. She was trying not to ask the question too directly. "Small robberies. Purses, wallets—any problems like that?"

"Can you tell me why you're asking? I guess I could call Security and ask them." Uncertainty blinked like a sign on his features.

Skip nodded. "Good idea."

He made the call, and as they waited for the man from

Security, Seaberry suddenly snapped his fingers. "Yes. Here on this floor."

Skip raised an eyebrow.

"Edward got his wallet stolen." He picked up his phone and punched in an extension number.

Skip said, "Edward Favret?"

He nodded and spoke into the phone. "Edward? Detective Langdon's here. Can you come in for a minute?"

Favret was there in thirty seconds, Bill, the security man, in forty-five.

Skip explained what she wanted. Bill shook his head, though what he said was, "Sure. There's usually one or two a month. You tell people, but they just don't listen."

"Can you get me a list of the people it's happened to in the last couple of months?"

"Sure." He pointed to Favret. "There's one of them right there." He left to check his records.

"So I hear. What happened, Mr. Favret?"

Favret looked sheepish. "Well, you heard the man. Some people don't listen. I left my wallet in my coat and hung it on a rack in my office—as usual, I might add. I've been doing it for years. I guess by the law of averages, it had to happen."

"How long ago was this?"

He made a face, thinking. "I don't know. Sometime in the last month."

"Did you file a police report?"

"No. What for?"

There were reasons, but Skip didn't think it was a serious question. She shrugged. "What did you lose?"

"Oh, nothing much. I had to go to the bank anyhow."

"Driver's license? Credit cards?"

He nodded. "And one check. That's the last time I leave a check in my wallet."

"Why? Did someone try to use it?"

"No. Not yet."

"The credit cards?"

"No."

She stood. "Okay, thank you. You, too, Mr. Seaberry."

Seaberry seemed out of sorts. "Do you mind telling us what that was about?"

"I'm not sure yet."

He smiled grimly. "You sound like Joe Friday."

She left to get the list of victims from Bill. As it turned out, there were only two names on it besides Favret's, one a woman's, one a man's. She asked about the man: "Who's Percy Vickery?"

"He's one of the mail room guys."

"What does he look like?"

"Fiftyish. Stocky build. Black as midnight." His eyes narrowed, awaiting her reaction.

She only nodded. "Okay, thanks."

She left, feeling exhilarated. She looked at her watch. *A good day's work, and I'm not even there yet.*

There was plenty of grunt work to do, but for once she couldn't wait. Superficially, Edward Favret matched the description of Russell Fortier. A picture of one might well pass for a picture of the other.

She had it nailed by ten A.M.—an Edward Favret had taken a Southwest flight from New Orleans to Fort Lauderdale the afternoon Russell disappeared, approximately twenty minutes after he and Bebe claimed their luggage.

Why Fort Lauderdale? she wondered. *Probably because the flight was convenient. He could be anywhere.*

Without much hope, she dialed Fort Lauderdale information, and got nothing. Well, okay, that she expected.

What was in Fort Lauderdale, anyway? It was near Miami—that could mean drugs.

Or maybe his Aunt Sara Sue lives there. It could mean anything.

She called Bebe. "Does Russell have any connection with Fort Lauderdale?"

"Fort Lauderdale? Why do you ask?" That question again. Why did everyone have to ask it?

"Would he have any reason for going there?"

"Skip! You know something. You've found something out."

"Well, not really. Let's just say I'm following up a lead. From the sound of your voice, it seems like he does have a connection."

"It's just that we used to go there a lot to charter boats."

"Oh, really?"

"It's a jumping-off place to the Bahamas, and it's— you know—kind of a sailing center. I guess, *the* sailing center in the South. The Bahamas?" she said, as if to herself. "Could he have gone there?"

Skip's palms began to sweat. She was close. She could feel it. But the department wasn't about to spring for a trip to Florida to run down a missing person who was probably just having a midlife crisis. If she could work up a little enthusiasm for him as a murder suspect, that might improve matters; but she couldn't see it.

She went back to the office and reviewed the case and thought about what to do next. It seemed to her there was only one option. She wondered if Steve had his cell phone turned on. She tried it and it rang about fifteen times before he got to it.

She said, "Hi. Were you up on a ladder?"

"How'd you know?"

"Good guesser. Listen, I've got a great idea. Why don't we get out of town this weekend?"

"You mean, like, declare a moratorium on remodeling? Am I that bad?"

"It's not that. I think my favorite case leads to Florida, and that seems like a good place to spend a weekend with your sweetie."

"Oh, it does, does it? What do I do while you're working?"

"Swim, maybe? I hear the beaches are beautiful. Besides, I won't work that much. I promise. We could go down to Miami and check out South Beach."

"Tell you what—I'll do *that* while you're working."

She took that for a yes.

She was so grateful to Steve for being such a good sport that she dropped by the Five Happiness and got a

266

carload of Chinese takeout to have for dinner. She was met, as usual, by a barking, threatening Napoleon.

Steve was home, already showered, dressed in clean shorts and T-shirt, and drinking a beer in the courtyard. This was getting to be a regular homecoming sight, and she liked it. *If it weren't for Napoleon going for my throat, I could be pretty happy,* she thought. *There's always some damn thing. . . .*

Steve stood to greet her, drawn by the fragrances emanating from the Five Happiness bags. She said, "This is a lot prettier sight than the courtyard last night."

Steve pointed with his beer. "All quiet in the Big House. We could have those goodies out here if you like."

"Maybe Napoleon could go in for a while."

Steve frowned. "I used to think you two were going to end up finding common ground."

"Only if we're both buried in it."

He sighed. "If you'd just *try* a little . . ."

"Me! He goes for my throat every time he sees me."

"He just smelled the food, that's all. Why don't you go take a shower, and I'll set the table."

"Let's put the food in the oven for a while. I feel like a drink."

By the time she got out of the shower, the damn dog had settled down and so had she. It was a soft, summery evening, with a light breeze and hardly any mosquitoes. She and Steve sat in the courtyard and sipped, thinking that on nights like this, New Orleans was a good place to be.

Steve said, "Kenny and I had a little talk while we walked the dogs last night."

"I figured you did."

"Well, I need your advice. I don't exactly know what to say to the parents. All this acting out's about them."

"Oh, big surprise."

"It's a really weird thing. You know how Dee-Dee says they like Layne better? Well, they do, sort of. But they've got a problem with him."

"What? I'm dying to know."

"Well, Kenny didn't exactly put it like this, but I guess the bottom line is, they're jealous."

"How exactly did he put it?"

"Oh, about the way Sheila did. It was the context that made it clear what it was all about. I just said, 'How are things going since Layne moved in?' and he went through that whole business about how terminally cute the guys are. And you *know* that's not like Kenny. That's probably about it for Sheila, but I think Kenny's got something else going on as well."

"What?"

"Masculinity issues."

Skip got that punched-in-the-stomach feeling she sometimes felt when she'd heard a truth. "Oho. The tough-guy thing. Is that what you mean?"

"Yeah, a real need to prove he's not gay, now that he's surrounded by people who are."

"The only thing is, that doesn't exactly explain the earring."

"Oh, yeah, I think that was a mistake. He got it because it was weird, and then he was afraid it made the wrong statement. So he shaved his head."

"What could be simpler?"

"Are you being sarcastic?"

"No. It's just that it's anything but simple."

"Well, Kenny's a complicated little person. I feel sorry for him. If I were in his situation, I'd probably have tattoos all over my body."

"I'd go ahead and tell them."

"Tell them what?"

"Wasn't that what you asked? What to tell the parents? I wouldn't hold back—just be straightforward. They can handle it—you know how they are. They like to get in there and *parent*."

"That's what I'm worried about. Maybe they should just leave the kids alone and let them work it out."

"Okay, so don't tell them."

For some reason, both Skip and Steve loved to go on like this, discussing the relative merits of some tiny point of human behavior. Skip particularly liked this subject, because Steve hadn't always gotten along with Jimmy Dee, and when the kids first arrived had been utterly indifferent. These days he seemed to consider them as much family as she did.

The two of them continued minding other people's business for a while and eventually got around to their Chinese delicacies, which they polished off with gusto, still sitting out in the courtyard. It was getting on toward ten o'clock, and the mosquitoes were starting to come out when Skip said suddenly, "My pager. Damn."

"Double damn."

She went in to call, though it was a number she didn't know. "Skip Langdon," she said. "Did someone page me?"

"Oh, Detective Langdon. Thanks so much for calling back, I—uh . . . didn't know who else to call." It was a woman's voice, and the woman was frantic.

"Who is this, please?"

"This is Deborah Cavignac. Bebe gave me your number. I'm calling because my husband hasn't come home."

Skip felt a sudden flush of alarm. "You're Beau Cavignac's wife?"

"Yes."

"What time does he normally get home?"

"Oh, between five and six. Six-thirty if he has a drink first. This has never happened before—and we've been married seventeen years. Bebe said you'd know what to do."

"Have you heard from him today?"

"Yes. He called before he left work and said he was going to stop for a drink at the Marlin Bar. And that he'd be home by six-thirty. Come to think of it, he actually said that." She started to sob. "Oh, my God. I'm so worried."

Under the circumstances, Skip couldn't really blame her.

"Have you called the hospitals?"

"Why, no."

"Well, why don't you start there, and then I'll see what I can do."

"I don't know . . ." Cavignac's voice was uncertain, as if she really couldn't be expected to make the calls herself, but Skip hung up before she had time to argue.

She called the coroner's office, which, happily, had nothing to report. She could hear, somewhere in the distance, that Steve had turned on the television.

She joined him for fifteen minutes of mindlessness, and then the phone rang again. "Nobody's got him," said Mrs. Cavignac.

"That's good news, isn't it? He must not have been in an accident."

"Well, where is he now?"

A very good question. One which she, in good conscience, had to try to answer. She said, "Let me make a couple of inquiries for you." Having already checked the morgue, she called the jail. Beau wasn't in it.

This had a déjà vu kind of quality about it, but Skip had a bad feeling Beau wasn't in Fort Lauderdale. She made her apologies to Steve, then slipped out of her shorts and into a pair of rayon work pants.

The Marlin Bar was more or less hopping—some say the weekend begins Thursday in New Orleans—but eventually Skip caught the bartender's eye. She said simply, "Has Beau Cavignac been in tonight?"

"Beau?" The man's head swiveled, made a quick survey of the place. "He left an hour or two ago."

Skip had no desire to flash her badge, but it looked as if the time had come. She palmed it, hoping no one would see but the bartender, and said, "One or two?"

"Something wrong, Officer?"

She smiled. "Not that I know of. How about you?"

A hush had fallen among the nearby customers, the ones who'd seen the badge. One of them heaved his body around on the barstool to get a better look at her. "More like two," he said. "Beau left two hours ago."

The bartender shrugged and went back to work. Skip held out her hand to the man. "Skip Langdon. Are you a friend of Beau's?"

"Bill Tyler. I just see him in here—we talk about sports and the weather."

"Did you talk to him tonight?"

"Yeah, a little bit. He had a beer or two and then said he was going home to dinner."

"Did he come in with anyone?"

"Came in alone. Left alone."

"Talk to anyone else?"

"Just Joe." He pointed with his chin to the bartender.

Knowing it was too much to hope for, she asked if Tyler knew where Beau parked.

"In a parking lot, I guess—he works for United Oil."

"That sounds right. You know what kind of car he drives?"

"Afraid not."

"Okay, thanks." She tried to give him a grin of gratitude, but she couldn't get her face to move properly. Her heart was picking up speed.

She retrieved her flashlight from the car and walked back toward the United building, trying to cover the same ground Beau would have covered, shining the light in every doorway, playing it over every sleeping body. Most of the bodies stirred, and those that didn't weren't Beau either.

She was glad to see a guard in the lobby of the building, and he was glad to help out a police officer, but unfortunately he didn't know Beau's car. He let her use the phone to call Deb Cavignac. "His car?" Cavignac was getting steadily more hysterical. "Why, do you know something?"

"I'm trying to find him."

Finally someone else snatched the phone, a daughter presumably. "It's a white Lexus, last year's."

He probably hadn't parked it on the street then. She said, "Does your mother know where he usually parks it?"

The girl conferred with her mother and came back on the line. "In a parking lot. Fairly near." She gave directions.

Skip was on her way to the lot, still searching doorways for bodies, when one of the bodies spoke to her. "You lookin' for the dead man?"

The speaker was a white male, maybe thirty, maybe sixty, his body thin and stringy with alcohol abuse. His eyes remained closed.

"What did you say?"

"Dead man over there." The body didn't move.

Skip said, "Open your eyes and look at me."

"Don't have no interest in women."

"Get up. Now. I'm a police officer."

He opened a pair of eyes decorated with red nets. She almost wished he'd kept them closed.

But something about her must have impressed him. Laboriously, he sat up. "Knew you wanted the dead man." This time he got up the energy to turn toward downtown and point. "Over there. Behind the garbage."

The street he indicated was little more than an alley. Someone had left a lot of trash on the narrow sidewalk in front of one of the buildings. From where Skip stood, you couldn't see what was on the other side.

"Okay, show me."

"I just showed you."

"Come on. Let's go." If this guy knew something, she sure wasn't going to run the risk of losing him.

"Shit. You try to be a good citizen and this is the shit you get. Can you beat that, man? This is the shit you get. What kind of shit is this, man?"

He unfolded himself very slowly and carefully. She herded him over to the place he meant, disregarding his mumbled complaints, which didn't cease for a second. As soon as they got close to the first of a number of discarded boxes, she saw the foot, a well-shod one obviously not belonging to a street person. She edged forward a little more.

Her informant was nodding vigorously. "They hit him and stabbed him both. Killed him two different ways." He nearly collapsed laughing, seemingly so incapacitated that she risked getting closer to the man on the ground. He was lying on his side and wearing a suit.

"Beau?" she said. He didn't answer and didn't move.

She said to the witness, "What's your name?"

"George Trulock."

"George, do you have some ID?"

"You kiddin'?" George fell into another of his laughing fits.

"George, come with me." She walked him to the nearest car and handcuffed him to the door. "Hang out here a minute, will you?"

"You can't pull this shit on me. For Christ's sake, I ain't done nothin' . . ."

She tuned him out, bent over the body, and turned it far enough over to see the face. It was Beau.

Dead. Dead with a hole in his jacket and blood all over his chest.

George might well have been right—he could have been hit and stabbed.

Skip called for backup.

After an eternity, a district car arrived, its young, eager driver ready to kick butt. They waited for more help, the coroner, and the crime lab. This was the Eighth District, whose homicides would normally be investigated not by its own detectives but by Cold Cases, which was all that was left of Homicide. She'd worked with these guys, and anyway, they had no reason to be territorial—she'd have no trouble getting assigned to the case.

She turned back to George. "What happened here?"

"I told ya. They killed him twice."

"Who did?"

"Black kids. Who else?"

"What'd they look like?"

"How would I know? I didn't see it."

Damn. She should have known. "You must have some reason for thinking that black kids killed him." *Sure he must. He's stoned out of his gourd and probably a racist. That's two reasons.*

But he said, "Henry saw it."

273

"Who's Henry?"

"Ol' black dude. Shoppin' basket."

"Where's Henry now?"

"I don't know, man. Am I s'posed to keep track of every wino on the street?"

She got as many details as she could for a bulletin on Henry, but she didn't hold out much hope for it. Unless there was physical evidence like hair or fibers, this case needed a reliable eyewitness. If Henry did turn up, he probably couldn't convince a jury it had twelve members. George was bad enough, and he didn't even have a shopping basket. If Henry had dreads, that was it—the killer walked.

When the formalities were complete, she let the bright-eyed kid take George in to sober up and wait for questions later. Quickly, she canvassed the neighborhood, a chore which took very little time, as no one lived there; and then she went back to question the men in the bar a little more carefully.

Finally, since there was no way to put it off any longer, she went to break the news to Deb Cavignac. Deb said what Skip had heard before, maybe every third time she had to inform someone: "Why? Why *my* husband?"

For once, Skip thought she knew—though a lot of good it did her.

Twenty-three

WHEN HE HAD drunk as much of the Scotch as he could get into his body without an IV, Russell dragged himself to bed and flung himself on it. At some point, he woke up, registered briefly that he found himself disgusting, pulled off his clothes while remaining supine, and dozed all night in the fitful fashion of drunks who haven't quite managed to pass out.

He woke up early and often, finally deciding at about seven-thirty to get up and take a walk, maybe get some coffee. He felt like a sack of manure.

After brushing his teeth for about twenty minutes, he gave up on making progress in that area and drove to the beach.

This truly was the most beautiful thing about Fort Lauderdale—maybe the only beautiful thing—and this morning the play of clouds and sun and green, green water was so stunning he simply sat on the sea wall and watched the show for a while. He got some coffee and came back and did it some more. The caffeine gave him such a lift he actually did start out on that walk he'd promised himself. He worked up a sweat in about ten minutes, but he was so weak it took all he had to continue for another ten.

Okay, twenty minutes. Some experts say it's plenty, he told himself.

He moseyed across the street and found a hotel restaurant serving breakfasts of eggs and bacon and hash browns with sour cream on top. Plenty of butter on the toast. And a whole lot more coffee.

He tried not to think of Dina while he wolfed it. Not to obsess about whether he had truly blown it once and for all. Surely not, he thought. She was just in a mood, momentarily pissed off and confusing him with the T-shirt–wearing cads and bounders she met in bars with too many television sets. If such was the case, though, a peace offering was required, and it should probably be some nice flowers.

Florists weren't open yet. Or maybe they were, but he wasn't up to picking up the phone. He headed for home and a nap, first stopping at a 7-Eleven for *The New York Times*—as long as World War Three hadn't broken out, it should make a nice soporific.

Days like this, he thought, *you kind of wish you watched the soaps.*

He made himself yet more coffee and sat in the cockpit with the paper. He was starting to carve out a sense of comfort and well-being, full of grease and flying on caffeine, when he saw a story about New Orleans: The city was having one of its record crime weeks. Once there had been fourteen murders in a week—or was it nineteen in three days? Actually, Russell had forgotten the numbers, just that crime had run rampant. And here we were again—a dozen in four days. Maybe the piece was premature, he thought—why not go for fifteen in five?

He started to skim the story, but got no farther than the second sentence before he felt his body go rigid: "The latest victim was identified as oil company executive Beau Cavignac."

No, he thought, *not Beau. Not sweet Beau who was my only link with home. This can't be—I just talked to him.*

And then it occurred to him that the two events might be connected. He shivered in the light breeze. This could *not* be happening. They had killed Beau—or more likely, had him killed. His two best friends, Douglas and Edward. They had killed their buddy to save their own sorry asses.

276

Or one of them had.

And whoever it had been was probably going to kill the other soon. He'd killed Beau because Beau wanted to come clean. Now he'd have to kill his other buddy because he was the only one who knew he was a murderer.

Not my problem, Russell thought. *Those two can duke it out any way they want.*

Still, surely he owed Douglas something. He had some feeling for Douglas—less as the years went by, but something. They'd done a lot together.

So had he and Edward, but the trouble with Edward was, he was a pompous ass.

Fuck it, he thought. *Just fuck it. I wouldn't cross the road to save either one of them. What goes around comes around.*

Of course, if that were the case, Russell Fortier, aka Dean Woolverton, wasn't exactly safe either. But then again, he was. No one had the slightest idea how to find him.

He went to make himself some more coffee and found himself staring out the windows of the galley—just staring, trying to put this thing out of his mind.

Poor Beau—so unremarkable in life, finally getting his fifteen minutes of fame. As a murder victim.

What was he thinking of? His best friend had just been killed by his other best friend (or friends). Surely he had to go talk to the police.

And yet, what for? The Skinners were parasites. If they wiped themselves out, so what?

There was definitely room for argument. Unless they killed each other in a duel, there was going to be only one left standing—and that one was going to be not only a parasite but an assassin.

Russell was struck with a choice of matching clichés, as Ms. Smart Dart Dina would probably say: To go back and face the music, or to get the hell out of Dodge. *This,* he thought, *must be what's meant by the fight-or-flight instinct.*

He had an almost uncontrollable urge to talk to Dina. He got up and paced the deck, looking out at the horizon, staring at water and sky, at the things that always calmed him, and failing to be calmed. Today, they only made him feel small and alone. He felt the muscles of his throat constrict as he took in his situation, looked for the first time at what he'd really done to himself.

I'm alone in the world, he thought. *By dumping everyone I ever knew or who ever cared about me, I've cut myself off completely.*

He realized with shame that he had been so stunned by the revelation of Allred's murder that he hadn't remembered to ask Beau to get a message to Eugenie. He didn't even deserve to have a daughter, and he couldn't call her, anyway—his current situation was nothing a child could deal with. Bebe was out of the question, and his parents were dead. He'd always regretted having no siblings, and never did he regret it more.

It would be comforting, he thought, *if someone cared whether I lived or died.*

And he found he absolutely could not resist the urge to make someone care, to grab the only line he saw and see if it would hold. Against every ounce of judgment he had, he called Dina, thinking that if she hated him, at least they could get that squared away and he could start thinking about suicide.

"Dina? Don't hang up . . . I'm really sorry about last night."

"Dean. I was about to call you. Listen, I acted like a jackass. I'm the one who should apologize."

He felt his throat constrict again. "I need to see you."

"Uh . . . okay. I'll cook dinner."

"No, I mean now."

"Now?" He could see her in his mind's eye, looking at her watch, calculating. "It's almost noon. I'd cancel my lunch date, but . . ."

He didn't let her finish, simply pretended he'd heard something different. "Great. I'll pick you up in ten."

Then he waited for her to call back and set him straight, and when the phone didn't ring, found himself grinning. He got in the car, thinking, *What in hell am I going to tell her?*

He took her to Indigo, where they could sit outside and not be overheard. And when he had talked her into having a glass of wine and while they were waiting for it to come, she said, "You look like shit."

"I didn't sleep. I felt really bad about the way I've treated you . . ."

"Oh, come on, it's not like you hit me or lied to me or something."

"Uh . . . you're making it worse."

"It *is* like one of those things? I think I know which one."

"I'm sorry. My name isn't really Dean Woolverton. I'm not even a lawyer."

The waiter set down two glasses of wine and almost before his hand was out of the way, she picked hers up. "Oh, really?" She sounded utterly unfazed. "What are you?"

"I'm just an asshole who left his wife and job. And former life."

"Just picked up and left? No note, no nothing?"

"It's not a pretty story. I did some pretty bad stuff."

"Involving your wife?"

"Involving business."

She nodded. "Oh. The export/import business."

It took him a minute to catch on to what she meant. "No, no. Not drugs. This was about a kind of fundamental dishonesty—of a corporate kind, say. And then a couple of years ago, I had a sort of revelation about the way I'd lived and how stupid and immoral it was. And how much I wanted to leave it behind."

Her eyes flooded with sudden sympathy, and she grasped his hand, which was nervously demolishing a shrimp chip. "But my wife didn't . . . get it." Somehow, he couldn't bring himself to mention that Bebe knew nothing about either the Skinners or the revelation. "We grew apart, she started seeing someone . . ."

At least, that part was true. Dina squeezed his hand. ". . . and I left at the first opportunity."

"Whew," she said. "I was afraid it was going to be a lot worse than that."

"Well, it is. I've left out a few details."

They had drunk their wine by now, and could manage a laugh. He told her about the Skinners, just the bare outlines, disguising the company and even the town. And then he detonated the bomb: "Two people have been killed."

"You lied. It is drugs."

"No, I didn't. It's what I said it was. But understand—I know enough to . . ."

"No! No, don't go back. That's what you're thinking, isn't it? That you could go back and tell the police what you know? What would that accomplish?"

"Well, there are more people involved. Two of them could get killed."

"How about you? You could get killed, too." Her steamed vegetables had arrived and she tucked into them with relish, not speaking for a minute. Then she said, "Wait a minute. I've got a great idea. Remember that wonderful old movie, *Three Days of the Condor*? Why not just go to the press and tell them everything— then nobody'll have a reason to kill you or anybody else."

Russell shook his head vigorously. "Can't do that. Uh-uh."

"What's the big deal? Why not?"

"My wife's a very high-profile woman—it would do her irreparable harm."

Dina's voice got kvetchy. "Oh, come on. How high-profile can she be? Is she the mayor or something?"

He nodded. "She's in politics. She might be mayor one day—if this stuff about me doesn't come out."

"You still love her, don't you?"

He searched for her hand. "Things between us didn't work out. I've been trying to face that for a long time—I

280

wouldn't have left if I thought we had a ghost of a chance as a couple."

"Ah, 'it is a far, far better thing that I do, than I have ever done.' " She gave him an ironic look, but he drew a blank. "It's from a book," she said. "Oh, never mind. The point is, you're a liability to her right now. But, on the other hand, people might die if you *don't* speak up. Is that it in a nutshell?"

He nodded. "That's about it."

"May I make a suggestion?"

"Please. That's why I'm telling you."

"How about an anonymous tip?"

"Hey." He chewed on it a bit, along with some seaweed that came with the seared tuna. "You might have something there. Why couldn't I just write a letter detailing the whole thing and FedEx it to the police? And not sign it?"

"Not bad. Not bad at all. But even if you don't sign it, they might figure out who sent it. Who are you, by the way?"

He took her hand and kissed it. "Russell Fortier, my dear Ms. Wolf. Late of Louisiana."

"*Enchanté.* If they figure out Russell Fortier sent it, they'll know where he is."

"Yeah. Damn. I wish I could get out of the country. But I have no papers—either as Russell or Dean."

"You need some forgeries."

"Well, I've been meaning to do that. The problem is, I'm the new kid in town. I suppose you wouldn't know where the bad guys hang?"

She was silent for a moment. "Let me make a phone call."

"Huh?" He was staggered.

"My brother's a probation officer."

She borrowed some change and left. It was a good ten minutes before she came back. "You have to call him."

"What? I don't get it."

"Well, first I had to swear on a stack of Bibles I wouldn't go with you to get the papers. Then in the end he refused to give me the address. You have to call him to get it." She gave him a number on a scrap of paper. "Go do it now."

There was no name on the paper. He dialed and said simply, "I'm Dina's friend."

"What's your name?"

Not knowing what she'd told him, he said, "I have two names."

"Yeah. Russell Fortier's the real one. Russell, you're a dead man if I find out Dina's been to Miami with you."

Russell was unaware that probation officers talked so tough.

He said, "Don't worry. Nothing's going to happen to your sister."

"My sister? Is that what she told you?" He got a huge laugh out of that one. "Look, here's what you do. You got a boat? Dina says you got a boat."

"Pearson thirty-eight."

"Save it. I don't know from boats. Sail it on down there and tie up at Dinner Key. Be there at four o'clock today and somebody'll meet you. You got twenty-five thousand dollars?"

"Are you kidding? You've got to be kidding."

"You got it or not?"

"I can get it."

"Cash only—half up front. The guy's name's Lou." He hung up, and when Russell returned, Dina wasn't there.

She'd left a note: "Sorry to say I've got a secret or two myself. Hope things work out for you."

Damn, the woman was mercurial. He went to get $25,000 out of the bank before setting sail, mentally composing the anonymous letter he was going to write.

She might be weird, she might be strange, she might even be a Mob princess—but she sure was smart. This was a solution that would protect Bebe and might even give Russell a choice or two.

Skip's lieutenant called her in the morning after Beau's murder. "How're you doing on the Fortier thing?"

"Great. Fortier's alive and living in Fort Lauderdale—or, at least, he passed through there. Frankly, I don't think he killed Beau or Allred, because why go to Fort Lauderdale and then come back?"

"Who did kill them?" Kelly McGuire was wearing an emerald green blouse perhaps a tad too bright for her paleness. But other than that, she was, like Cappello, the very personification of crispness—pink-red hair pulled back on the top and left long in back, tube-shaped silver earrings that made her long face longer, the merest touch of pinky-coral lipstick. You wanted to call her Madam Chairman, just for the way she looked. And she could stare you straight in the face and say, "Who did kill them?" like she might say, "What time is it?" Like she expected a serious answer. Something about the woman was scary.

Skip wasn't quite sure how to answer. Finally, she shrugged. "Still working on it."

McGuire smiled, which made her look almost friendly. "You need some manpower. Let's give Beau to somebody else."

That was the last thing Skip expected her to say. At first she was deeply offended: She could handle the damn case herself. But then it occurred to her that, frankly, she did need some manpower—as long as it was a help, not a hindrance.

Holding her breath, she said only one word: "Abasolo?"

McGuire nodded. "Let's see how he feels about it."

They called him in and asked him. "Fine," he said, giving Skip a what-the-hell-is-this look and, afterward, they compared notes.

"Her idea," Skip said. "She thought I needed help. I didn't want to get stuck with O'Rourke, so I said you might do."

Abasolo stared after the lieutenant. "She's—uh—different."

"Yeah, but in a good way or a bad way?"

He chewed his lip. "Might be good," he said, staring at her some more. "Might be just fine."

Skip thought he was speaking beyond the professional level. "She's married," she said.

"Her husband cheats on her."

"What on earth makes you think that?"

He shook his head. "She's just got that look."

"Want to go get coffee?" Skip wanted to talk with him outside the building.

"You got something on your mind, don't you? Sure, let's do."

Abasolo and Skip were happily ensconced at the Plantation Coffeehouse, well into a latte and a cappuccino, respectively, when Skip said, "Look, let's just partner up on the whole thing. It's all of a piece, and I think that's what McGuire had in mind. It's almost like—" She didn't want to say what she thought.

"What?" Abasolo said. "It's almost like what?"

"Like she's a mind reader. Look, I wouldn't want to get into it with her, because the truth is, I don't know anything right now. But Russell sure as hell does—and I think he's the quickest way out for us. These dudes were screwing people out of oil leases. What if one of the screwees is exacting revenge? Russell splits, but his partner gets killed. Russell's got to know who did it."

"Well, great. Let's just ask him."

"Here's the thing. I think I know where he is. With you working the routine stuff on Beau, I can duck out and run him down."

Abasolo leaned his lanky frame against the back of his chair. "Langdon, you never cease to amaze me."

"He's probably in Fort Lauderdale."

"You're just such a hot dog."

She was slightly taken aback. *This must be a guy thing,* she thought. *Something to do with ego.*

She shrank back. "Oh, God, AA. I never know when I'm going to offend someone. I may talk Southern, but I'm not a true Southerner. If I were, I'd never make these mistakes. Listen, you want Russell? You got him. I'll take Beau—I'm sure McGuire could care less who does what."

Abasolo laughed. "I don't want Russell. I just enjoy watching you hustle your butt, that's all."

"You're so damn superior."

"Come on, run it down for me."

"I've traced him to Fort Lauderdale. I think he went there to get a boat."

"Ah. Which he no doubt sailed away, days ago."

"Maybe not, though. Maybe it's taking him a while to get things together. A loan to buy a boat, maybe."

"He probably chartered it."

"Well, anyway, I want to go down there and poke around."

Abasolo nearly spilled his latte. "How're you planning to break the news to the lovely lieutenant?"

"I'm going on my own time, AA."

"Own money, too, I suppose?"

"That's the idea."

"Okay, I'm finally getting your drift—you want me to cover for you while you're gone."

She nodded.

"Well, I have to. The lieutenant gave me Beau, remember?"

"That's what I meant by the way she read my mind."

"It's possible, Langdon. It's possible. That woman's probably as big a hot dog as you are. So naturally she'd figure out how you wanted to play it."

"Feeling used, AA?"

Abasolo ignored her. He had a worried look on his face.

"What is it?" she asked.

"I don't think she's going to make it here. She's too straightforward. Too independent."

"Oh, come on. I do okay."

"Yeah, you're their poster girl—they don't need two. Besides, you know your place. You could take the sergeant's exam, move up, everything's cool. But once you got to be a lieutenant, if you still acted like you do now, they'd bust your ass just to show they could do it."

"Who would?"

"You know who. The old boys."

She had a sudden surge of affection for the lieutenant, suddenly saw her in a new light—as someone like herself. Someone not given to suffering fools or obeying other people's rules. Abasolo was right—she probably wouldn't last long.

But for the moment, she'd given Skip her freedom. She fooled around the rest of the day, trying to help Abasolo with some of the routine stuff regarding Beau, but chafing to get out of town.

Which she did early the next morning, Steve Steinman more or less good-naturedly in tow. "You know what this is costing me? Three days' work on the house."

"Yes, but you know what you're trading for it? Three days of sanity."

In the end, of course, he didn't go to the beach while she worked. He tagged along as she took Russell's picture to every charter place in the phone book—it was an absurd long shot, she knew, because she had to find the one person who'd waited on him. He'd disappeared on a Sunday. She figured he'd probably chartered the boat— or bought it—the next day.

Fort Lauderdale being huge in area, they spent almost all day crisscrossing Broward County, showing the picture and asking for the guy who worked Mondays—who was almost invariably off Saturdays.

By the end of the day, Skip was sure she was on a fool's errand, and slipping into a depression. Steve, on the other hand, was poring over a restaurant guide. "Hey, Asian food. You know how much you miss that if you're from California? Along with fresh fruits and vegetables. What do you think about sushi?"

Skip feigned gagging.

"Good. You can have tempura."

Skip didn't answer. She was too busy phoning guys who worked Mondays.

But in the end they did have sushi, and after that, they walked on the beach near their hotel.

The next day they hit the yacht brokers.

It was after lunch when they found the guy who sold

him the boat—Gilbert Angus at Angus Yachts, sole proprietor, and from the looks of things, sole staff member. Angus was in his mid-fifties, perhaps, fit and tan, with slightly bowed legs sticking out of khaki shorts. He took one look at the picture of Russell, nodded, and said, *"On Y Va."*

Skip was buffaloed. Angus was the last guy she could imagine saying a mantra, which was what it sounded like to her.

But Steve said, "Let's go where?"

Angus laughed. "The name of the boat. 'Let's go' in French. A Pearson thirty-eight; eighty-four."

Gradually, they sorted it out: the boat was thirty-eight feet long, and used—an '84, in car terms. The man in the picture paid cash.

"Cash?" That was a shocker.

"Fifty-six thousand."

"May we see the papers, please?"

It turned out an Edward Favret had bought the boat, giving the same Uptown New Orleans address as the real Edward Favret and using his driver's license as identification.

"Nice guy," Angus said. "What's he wanted for?"

"Routine questioning."

"All the way from New Orleans and it's routine?" He snapped his fingers. "Hey, wait a minute. Hold it here." He turned his back on them and started picking through a pile of newspapers on a table. "Here." He tapped one. "This is what it's about, isn't it?"

It was a story on the mini–crime wave in which Beau was featured as the star victim. "It's all here. United Oil, United Oil." He was looking back and forth between Edward Favret's stats and the story on Beau. "This guy killed his partner, didn't he? I should have known. He didn't seem like a druggie, but he had all that cash. Goddamn, I just should have known."

After that, he was so helpful Skip couldn't get a word in to ask a question. "You know, the guy just didn't seem right. 'Course, nobody who pays cash seems right.

Edward Favret his real name? 'Cause, you know, that picture on his driver's license—I remember thinking it didn't look much like him." He gestured so wildly Skip was afraid she'd be hit. "But, you know, nine out of ten people—that's the way it is—I just didn't think."

"Did he give a local address?"

"No, just that one. He said he didn't have a slip yet."

"In a marina, you mean?"

"I guess." He thought a minute. "You can rent a mooring from someone who lives on the river or one of the canals, but that's dicey. Must have meant a marina."

"Wait a minute. See if you can remember the conversation exactly."

"I just told you what it was." Angus was suddenly testy.

"How did he happen to mention he didn't have a slip?"

"I told you. I asked for a local address and that's what he said."

"Tell me about this sailboat he bought—is it something you could live on?"

"That's what I just told you."

"Uh-huh. And could you take it cruising?"

"Of course. That's what it's for."

"But was it your impression that he intended to live on it?"

"That's what I'm trying to tell you."

"Are there special marinas for that?"

He shrugged. "Some might be better than others. Why don't you call around? There's lots of them." He swung an arm wildly. "All up and down the coast. Unless he had a friend—and it sounds like he didn't—he probably did what I'd do." He stopped and licked his lips, evidently thinking he had a hot tip.

"What's that?"

"Just turn to the *M's* in the Yellow Pages and call till he found a slip."

Steve rolled his eyes.

Skip punched him gently. "Thanks. Say, I'm wondering

something. Did you happen to notice what kind of car he was driving?"

Angus looked chagrined. "Nope. He walked in—don't know where he parked."

"Well, thanks again. We really appreciate your help."

When they were outside, she said to Steve, "He had to have parked somewhere. I mean, he could have taken a taxi, but renting a car's cheaper."

"He bought the damn boat—maybe he bought a car. Naah. Probably not. He probably fired up the boat and headed for Timbuktu."

"I don't know. I've got a feeling that slip thing was— you know—a slip. You just wouldn't think about mentioning a slip as an address unless it was."

After that it was a piece of cake. She did exactly what Gilbert Angus suggested—looked in the Yellow Pages— and pretty quickly found the *On Y Va* at the Bahia Mar Marina. "Got it!"

Steve was napping on the other of the two queen beds in their small beachside hotel. His eyes snapped open. "Got what?"

"Found him. Be back in a while." She checked her gun.

"You're going over there alone?" He lifted his head, looking alarmed.

"Haven't you heard? I'm a police officer."

"I don't know. I don't feel great about this."

She chuckled, giving him a wave as she left. "You're so cute when you're worried."

"Just be careful." He lay down again and waved back. He'd long since given up putting up much resistance.

The marina was bustling—it was a gorgeous Sunday, boats coming and going on innocent errands, no one, seemingly, with a thought in his head beyond a picnic or a pickup. And there was the Pearson 38, a blue sailboat floating merrily, like anyone's weekend toy. She saw no sign it was occupied.

She didn't quite know what to do next—how did you knock on a boat? She ended up hollering: "Mr. Favret! Mr. Favret, are you there?"

Evidently he wasn't.

Or maybe he was. Maybe he just hadn't heard. She climbed aboard, still shouting. There was still no answer.

She wondered if she was trespassing, concluded that she probably was, and decided not to go below. Not yet, anyway. She settled for looking in the windows of the low structure built on deck. At first she wasn't sure what she was seeing. It looked as if Russell hadn't been taught the word *shipshape*—cabinets were open and things were on the floor that she thought shouldn't be, almost as if someone had gotten drunk and clumsy, knocked over one thing reaching for another.

Slowly it dawned on her that the place had been rather gently tossed. It wasn't the kind of thorough going-over in which pillows are pulled off and slashed, but someone had very definitely been looking for something. Perhaps for Russell.

She went below, thinking he could be injured in there. . . .

In fact, nobody was aboard, and since she was already far, far over the line, she hadn't the first qualm about looking around. There was a fascinating item in plain sight. Attached to the bathroom mirror was a Post-it that read, "Passport!"

It was the sort of note she wrote to herself when she didn't want to forget something. "P.U. cleaning" meant "pick up cleaning." But "Cleaning!" meant "No margin for error here. Pick up cleaning or go naked."

A passport would be a very fine thing for the pseudo–Edward Favret to have—or for someone else now in the process of being invented.

As she climbed back onto the dock, it occurred to her that this was an excellent place to disappear. She stared out to sea, out to where she knew the Caribbean was, with its hundreds of tiny cays and coves. It would be so easy to drop off the face of the earth . . . if you had papers. And something told her they wouldn't be that hard to get down here.

Maybe, she thought, it would be a good idea to go introduce herself to the Fort Lauderdale police. For one thing, she might need backup later. For another, they probably knew a few forgers.

Twenty-four

OFFICER MARTINA RUDOLFO was a dark woman with pitted skin and long curly hair that didn't quite go with her crisp shirt and creased trousers. She probably thought the hair was her best feature. And a little shorter, it would have been, Skip thought.

She looked at Skip with evident curiosity. "I've heard of you, Langdon."

"You've *heard* of me?"

Rudolfo nodded. "My sister lives in Louisiana—married a man who works on oil rigs. They're always sending me clips from the New Orleans paper—about the police department. They've sent me two about you, with little notes saying, 'Why can't you do stuff like this?' "

"They're kidding, of course. No one in their right mind . . ."

Rudolfo cut her off with a laugh. "You're right. You're sure right about that. Now, what can I do for you?"

"Well, I've only got today to find this guy—the one I mentioned on the phone. And I'm wondering if he's got a new name. Could he get papers in Fort Lauderdale?"

"Oh, sure. But my guess is, he'd go to Miami. Has he got any money?"

"He must. He paid cash for a sailboat."

Rudolfo nodded. "There's a couple of first-rate forgers down there, but I doubt they'll reveal the names of their clientele."

Skip gave her a grin. "You never know till you ask."

Rudolfo was tapping on her desk. "Let me make a phone call."

She called someone and spoke in Spanish. Skip was encouraged by much nodding and repetition of *"sí."*

Rudolfo wrote something down before she hung up. "I called a guy I know in Miami. One of these clowns isn't too active right now. My friend thinks he left the country for some reason." She passed the paper over. "This one's your best bet. Real popular with high rollers. And there's something else—my friend in Miami says she's got a kid."

"She?"

Rudolfo nodded. "Eleanor's a pioneer in her field—real poster girl for equal opportunity crime. But Stefan, the kid's been in a lot of trouble a lot of times."

"Drugs?"

"Yeah. And here's the good news—they've got him in custody right now. His mom may not know about it yet. Maybe you can use that for some kind of leverage." She shrugged. "It's about an hour's drive down there. Plenty of time to dream something up."

Skip frowned. "How do I find her?"

Rudolfo gave her directions and wished her luck.

It wasn't far to Miami but Skip had a panicky sense of time racing by too fast. The note must have meant an appointment with the forger—today, probably. But suppose Eleanor Holser wasn't the right forger? *I wonder,* she thought, *if I should call in sick tomorrow?*

She phoned Steve but got no answer—he must have been at the beach. She left a message and started driving. It was that difficult time of day when the sun is sinking and manages to shine in your eyes no matter what you do with your visor. It occurred to Skip that it was going to be dark soon. But traffic was light and she made good time.

Holser lived in what seemed to Skip a fairly upscale, if, to her mind, decidedly tacky, part of town. Her house was some sort of split-level A-frame that managed to look like a cross between a barn and a beach house. It appeared to be built of driftwood, and if Skip had to guess, she'd have put it at late-seventies' vintage. By now, the evening was only a hair from pitch-dark, and the forger apparently hadn't turned on her porch lights.

There were also no lights in the front of the house, but the curtains hadn't been drawn and from somewhere, maybe a den in back, came an orangy glow. Probably someone was watching television. Skip approached gingerly, listening a moment before planning to ring the bell.

Instead of the expected drone of television news, she heard a thump followed quickly by a kind of truncated scream—a short, staccato sound that meant sudden pain, a woman's pain. She thought later that it was a yelp.

Quickly, she dropped to a crouch and listened more closely. It could, after all, have been the television.

The woman yelled, "Goddamn you!" and there was another thump, far too close, too immediate to be electronic. Grateful there wasn't much light, Skip dug her gun from her handbag and crab-walked to the corner of the building. Here she straightened and ran to the back, which was glass nearly all the way across, the room, thus enclosed, perfectly illuminated by a single table lamp.

It was quite astonishing. The place was like a ruin lit for a son et lumière—so magnificently displayed a mouse couldn't have hidden in it. As she had surmised, it was a den, low-ceilinged and lined with bookshelves that held as many tchotchkes as books. The furniture was Naugahyde, all placed for optimum viewing of a television screen so large it destroyed any pretense of proportion. On the sofa sat—or rather huddled—a woman with her hands behind her, as if tied, and in front of the woman, obscuring her partially, was a man in jeans and a black T-shirt. He held a gun loosely, by its barrel.

He's pistol-whipping her, Skip thought, and the woman gasped, coming to attention. She had seen Skip. The man couldn't miss the fact that there was something outside. Skip dropped to the ground as he whirled, shooting through the glass, wildly. The glass made a horrible noise, but the shot didn't. *Silencer,* she realized—and it had already been on the gun.

She couldn't return fire for fear of hitting the woman, but the gunman evidently saw she had a gun. He disappeared into the other room.

Skip struggled to her feet, looking wildly around her in a moment of indecision, and then ran back around the side of the house. Gaining the front, she saw a car pulling out across the street, its lights off, no way to see its plates, or even its make. But she was pretty sure at least two people were in it.

She looked back toward the house and saw that the door was open. Thankfully, no curious neighbors lined the sidewalk.

She wished she could call for backup, but she was on her own here. Gingerly, she peeked in the house, and then, cautiously, she entered. It was quite dark, except in the back of the house.

She saw movement, low, toward the back. It was the woman who'd been on the sofa, wriggling like a snake. Her feet were tied as well as her hands. "Who the fuck are you?" she said.

"Police. Who else is here?"

"Nobody. The asshole's gone." She sighed, and Skip had the impression she was keeping back tears. Skip came in, shut the door behind her, and searched the house quickly. It had an odd smell to it, like new wood, though it was probably at least twenty years old.

The woman was crying when she came back. "Eleanor Holser?"

"Yes."

Skip untied her. "I'm Skip Langdon. New Orleans Police."

"New Orleans! Shithead Favret's from New Orleans. I hope the fuck the river floods the Superdome."

She rubbed her ankles and stood up. Skip saw that she was very short, scarcely over five feet, with an hourglass figure poured into a tight red dress. An odd outfit for a forger, but this was Florida.

Skip said, "Can you walk?"

"Yeah, maybe."

"Let me help you."

But Holser pulled away. "What the fuck do you want?"

Skip took a step away from her. "Did you see the silencer on that man's gun? He was going to kill you, are you aware of that?"

Holser only gaped.

"I just saved your life, Ms. Holser. You mean, what do I want as a reward? Five minutes of your time—would that be too much to ask?"

Holser stared at her. "I've got things to do."

Skip was getting angry. "Eleanor, you've got problems you don't even know about, and I don't mean your little cottage industry here."

"What you talking about?"

"What you think—your kid."

For the first time, Holser showed an emotion other than anger. Her face turned a whole-wheat color. "What you mean, my kid?"

"Get nice and I'll tell you."

"I don't got to—"

"Stop being stupid, Eleanor. Make your life easier."

Holser looked at her out of eyes like quarters—big, but glittery and hard as metal. Finally, she said, "My kid okay?"

"Why should I tell you?"

The forger let some of the belligerence go out of her stance. "Okay, all right. Tell me what you want."

Uninvited, Skip sat on the sofa, and Holser followed suit. "For openers, who was that man and what did he want?"

"A hired thug. I don' know who hired him." She shrugged.

"Why do you say that?"

"He had a silencer, he wasn't bright, and he was looking for a client of mine. Looking for Edward Favret." She gave Skip a shrewd look. "Popular guy, Edward Favret. You want him, too?"

"You got it. Where is he?"

"I did a little job for him, he didn't pick it up."

"When was he supposed to?"

"Today."

"What do you mean, today? When today?"

"Just today, okay? He said he'd come; he didn't."

"Don't give me that shit. All the hired gun had to do was wait for him."

"I told him Favret'd already been here."

"Why'd you do that? It just about cost you your life."

"Well, I didn't know that, did I? I didn't want the creep hanging around."

"And you wanted the money—in case Favret did show up."

"He's not gonna show." She looked at her watch. "I told him I was going out at seven. It's seven-thirty now."

"Okay, here's what you do. You give me the papers you made for him, and when you see him, you tell him I need him."

"Fuck, no. How'm I gonna get paid?"

"You just told me he's not gonna show. Which is it?"

She sighed. "You got it. He ain't gonna show. I don't care—take the fuckin' papers. Just tell me where my goddamn kid is." A note of desperation had crept into her voice.

Skip had what she wanted, she gave something back. "Look, your kid's okay. He's in custody in Miami. I've got to call an officer in Fort Lauderdale—she'll give you the particulars."

She called Rudolfo and outlined what had happened, leaning heavily on the gun with the silencer.

"I think," said Rudolfo, "I'd better send somebody to check on the boat."

"I'd appreciate it." Skip turned the officer over to the forger, and when she had collected the tools of Edward Favret's new identity, headed back north. She stopped at a gas station, and while she was there, she gave Steve a call. "Hey. Good," he said. "An Officer Rudolfo just called. Hung up no more than ten seconds ago."

Wings fluttered in Skip's stomach.

"She said to tell you the boat's gone."

The forger had said seven sharp, no earlier, no later, and Russell had arrived on the minute, this time having been allowed to drive himself to her house.

Some friends Dina had. *Life with Bebe was never like this,* he thought, on the way down the coast. Thought it uneasily.

He still hadn't the least idea how Dina came to know someone who wasn't her brother and knew where to find a forger—someone who probably wasn't a probation officer, either. But then when he thought about it, the bar where Russell met her didn't seem out of the question. Ex-boyfriend, maybe. But the curious part was how protective the man had been—Dina was unquestionably a very unusual, very special person, one he had truly come to cherish.

He'd called her right away after her mysterious departure, to make sure they were still on track, whatever that might mean. They were, but he still didn't know what it meant.

He thought it would be relaxing to be with a nice, if extremely busy woman who didn't know any forgers. On the other hand, Dina was so intoxicating he didn't know if he could live without the excitement. Not that it mattered—he was going to have to get out of the country, and he'd probably never see either Dina or Bebe again.

It was a thought that had the potential to depress him deeply, but at the moment, driving to Eleanor Holser's, he was in a great mood, about to make the second payment on his ticket to a new life and a new world.

And that night, he and Dina were going to cook on the boat and go for a midnight sail, maybe anchor somewhere peaceful, where the water would rock them to sleep. It was Dina's idea, and Russell couldn't imagine Bebe agreeing to such a thing, much less suggesting it.

He had told her there might be a lot of wind, making

the sail the wet, vigorous sort, and she had said, "All *right*." It was over the phone, but in his mind's eye he could see the playfulness in her face, the way her eyes would brighten as she thought about it.

Were women that way before you got married, even got close to them, and then they changed? It wasn't a question the Gallup Poll was likely to tackle. Too bad, because lots of men needed to know.

He got off the expressway and threaded his way through quiet streets where every lawn was mowed, American-dream streets, the yards of which were planted with hedges of ficus, beds of hibiscus and crotons and cycads, poinciana trees and palms and fragrant ginger. Criminals had to live somewhere, he mused as he turned the corner onto Eleanor Holser's block.

A woman as big as a biker was standing at the front door. The woman had a gun.

What the fuck was this?

He nearly drove up on the curb trying to double-check his first glance, but it was the same information the second time around. Nothing to do, he concluded, but drive on by.

It must be some kind of setup, he thought—the two women were going to kill him for his twelve-and-a-half grand.

But he couldn't make that make sense. Holser was a forger, not a shanghai-er of sailors. Then there was the deeper problem of why the biker woman had her gun drawn *outside* the house. All his corporate and Uptown instincts told him to get the hell out without a backward glance, but he wasn't about to, not without his papers. He had a lot of money invested and little time to lose.

When he had circled the block, the woman was gone. He parked down the street, as a neighbor might, or a neighbor's guest, perhaps, got out of the car, and walked toward the forger's house, thinking to mount a discreet investigation.

He heard the gentle clicking of a car door, and then

the authoritative voice: "Freeze or I'll blow your head off."

Fuck. The law. The woman must be a cop and this guy was her partner—he hadn't even noticed another occupied vehicle.

Russell froze, his hands a foot from his body, as non-threatening as possible.

"Turn around." The cop was burly and dark, vaguely Latin-looking.

Russell obeyed.

"Get in the car, Russell." The cop seemed infinitely world-weary. Russell walked toward him, noticing that he had a hand stuck in his pocket, but no gun showing. Probably his way of trying not to alarm the neighborhood.

Russell sighed as he walked. The jig, apparently, was up—there would be no midnight sail, no escape to the Bahamas, no new life. Just scandal and degradation.

Oh, well, he thought, *I always knew this might happen. It's better than that lie I was living. Anything is.*

He'd gambled and lost. He could be a good sport about it.

The cop put him in the backseat of the car, got in the front, and did draw a gun, which he trained on him, a gesture Russell found quite a bit more threatening than anything life had held up to that point.

He said, "Aren't you going to handcuff me?"

A shadow crossed the cop's face. Under other circumstances, Russell might have said his captor was taken aback, but surely that couldn't be the case.

He heard footsteps, a man running, and turned to look. The new man got in the car and said, "Holy shit!"

The first cop said, "Cover him, will you?"

The second cop took the gun, said, "Freeze or I'll blow your head off," and the first cop drove. Fast and furiously.

No one followed.

When they were a good distance from Holser's house, the burly one said, "Manny. What the fuck's going on, man?"

"Why the fuck didn't you cover me? Didn't you see that fuckin' broad?"

"If I'd've covered you, we'd have lost Prep-boy here. They got there at the same time—don't ask."

"Fuck. Let's ask him. Hey, Russell, who's the lesbo?"

"I, uh—I thought she was with you."

"Fuck."

Manny stayed turned toward the back, keeping the gun on Russell, but neither of the cops spoke again.

Because he hated the silence, and because in New Orleans, everyone talks to everyone, he said, "Where are y'all from?"

"This ain't no time for small talk," Manny answered.

"I meant, uh, which police department," and the same shadow crossed Manny's face that had crossed his partner's.

Before his head had time to work on it, Russell's body broke out in a sweat. Noticing a piece of paper in the backseat, he reached for it. Manny nudged him with the gun. But he had it already.

Turning it over, he saw that it was a faxed photo of himself.

"Where are you taking me?" he said, and there was a tremor in his voice.

No one answered.

When they were well out of Holser's neighborhood, they stopped and put Russell in the front seat and Manny in the back so that he could keep the gun at Russell's temple without having to strain his neck.

Eventually, they got on the expressway and drove north for nearly an hour, no one speaking except Russell, who tried periodically to get some kind of response. No matter what he asked them, no matter how provocative, the other two were sphinxes.

During the long drive, Russell tried to clear his head, to focus on his breathing, to give his mind a rest until he had more information. He succeeded so well he fell into a kind of waking nap, a numbness that might have been shock. He barely noticed when they arrived at Fort Lauderdale, and they were nearly at the marina before he realized they were taking him to his own boat.

It was about the time he'd have been getting back if everything had gone smoothly.

Dina would be there soon. He found he was sweating again. He had deliberately tried not to entertain the question of whether these dudes were thugs or just exceptionally nasty cops, but his body was telling him now. He knew who they were.

"Shit!" the driver said.

"What?" asked Manny.

The driver pointed. "Lights."

Lights on the Pearson. In the galley and the main salon. Dina was aboard.

The driver said, "I'll go." He parked the car and got out. Russell tried without success to think of something to do. Then, almost without realizing he was going to, he reached over and leaned on the horn. Manny grabbed him by the hair, tugged him back, and stuck the barrel of the gun in his temple. Again without thinking, Russell called her name, hollered, "Dinaaaaa!" so loud it hurt his vocal cords.

"Fuck," was the last thing he heard.

Next, someone was slapping his face, trying to revive him to get him on the boat. "Dina," he said. "Dina . . ."

"Shut up, asshole. She can't hear you and neither can anyone else."

His head was killing him. He thought he could remember being hit, but he honestly wasn't sure. Perhaps he just thought so because that had to be what happened.

"Walk."

He did what they said because Dina was on the boat and there was no way to help her unless he could get to her. Or so he believed at the time. He thought later that another attempt at loud noise might have been a better idea.

They gagged him, tied him up, and threw him in the berth beside Dina. She had already been trussed. They stared at each other, working their eyebrows as if they were mouths, letting each other know they understood the gravity of the pickle they were in, and that each was sorry the other was involved.

Russell could smell garlic and olive oil and something salty and pungent—capers, maybe. She had been making pasta when they arrived.

"Fuck, yeah, I know what to do," said one of the men. "I used to drive a boat for the big guy."

"What big guy?" the other one said, but there was no answer Russell could hear.

He could hear and see movement as the one who knew what to do cast off and started the engine. *They must be going to drown us,* he thought, cartoon images of talking rabbits walking the plank firing inanely in his brain.

The boat chugged for a while, and then Manny came into the room. He was pointing his gun and wearing latex gloves, two extremely ominous signs. Russell broke out in a sweat again.

"We need you to help us."

Manny untied him first, and then took the gag out.

"Come on."

Russell didn't speak. Silently, he helped them drop anchor, and then, amazingly, the driver, the one who wasn't Manny—and who was also wearing gloves—said, "Hey, let's get the girlfriend up. I'm hungry."

How did those two things fit together? Russell couldn't make it work.

They took Russell into the stateroom and had him untie her while they watched, holding the gun. It occurred to him that maybe they planned to rape her, but he didn't protest. The two of them had a better chance if they were both free.

While Dina was still rubbing her wrists, Manny said, "Russell, ya hungry?"

Russell was too stunned to say a word.

"Hey, uh—what's your name, baby?"

"Beulah."

Russell winced, remembering that he'd bellowed her

303

name, but they didn't seem to care. "Hey, Beulah, rustle us up some grub, will you?" Manny elbowed his companion. "Hey, 'rustle.' That's a pun, get it? Under the circumstances."

Russell said, "Who are you guys?"

"I'm Manny, and this is . . ."

"Jack," said the other one.

"Yeah. Jack."

"That's not what I meant."

They ignored him. "Beulah, what you makin'?"

"I was making pasta putanesca. For two."

"Great, great. Go to it. Russell, why don't you whip us up a little salad?"

Jack said, "Y'all want a drink? What can I make you?"

What was this—a party? Puzzled, Russell shook his head.

"Come on. Let me fix you something."

Dina said, "Gin and tonic."

Jack nodded like the perfect host. "Good choice." He had on a white polo shirt with blue slacks. If it hadn't been for the gold chain, he'd have been almost dapper. "Russell, you, too?"

Russell didn't answer. Instead, he found lettuce, cucumbers, things like that in one of the bags Dina had evidently brought over, and began making a salad. Jack tried to thrust a drink into his hand.

"No, thank you."

"Ah, come on."

"I said no." The last thing he needed was alcohol.

Manny said, "Hey, Russell. You don't talk to my buddy like that." He grabbed Russell by the scruff of the neck and held the drink up to his lips. "Now drink."

Russell spat.

"Oh, not nice. Not nice at all."

This time he grabbed Dina, throwing one hand across her breasts and squeezing, the other pulling her hair till tears came to her eyes. Over her shoulder, Manny stared at Russell. "Drink."

Russell shrugged. "Oh, well. Just to be sociable." He

took a sip and could have sworn Dina smiled at his feeble joke.

"That's more like it."

By the time he and Dina had finished making the pasta and the salad and heating some French bread, they had consumed their drinks.

Manny and Jack watched them like nannies at a park. Manny said, "Beautiful, Beulah. My Italian mother couldn'ta done better."

Jack said, "Don't let him kid you—he's Cuban."

"Shut up, goddammit. Set the table, Beulah—that's short for Beautiful, right? Russell, open us up some wine, why don't you?"

Dina had brought a nice Rioja, one of Russell's favorites. Obediently, he opened it while Dina set the table. "For two or four?" she asked.

"Just two."

He filled the glasses she set.

Manny said, "Now y'all sit down and have yourselves a little feast."

Russell couldn't believe what he was hearing. Despite the episode with the drinks, which he took for some macho show of power, he'd assumed they were cooking for Manny and Jack.

"What?"

"Go on, do it."

Manny gestured with the gun.

The captives sat across from each other. Fear showed in Dina's eyes, and Russell hoped it didn't in his.

"Drink a little toast, why don't you?"

Russell lifted his glass. "To you," he said to Dina.

She did the same. "To life. I liked it a lot." And she began to cry.

Manny roared, "Come on. Eat."

"Leave us alone, goddammit." Russell tried to stand, but Manny pushed him back down and held him.

Jack came up behind Dina, pried her mouth open, picked up a wad of noodles in his gloved hand, forced it

305

between her teeth, and clamped her mouth shut. "Chew, goddammit."

Manny said, "Russell? You gonna eat? Or is Jack gonna do that again?"

Somehow, both he and Dina forced down a few bites.

Manny said, "Drink. Come on . . . have some wine."

Dina gave up and did it, and eventually Russell did, too.

"Have another." Manny poured, Dina drank. And then he dropped something into Russell's wine and stirred it up. "Drink."

Unable to help himself, Russell stared at Dina, willing her to forgive him, but mostly not even trying to communicate, wanting only a glimpse of the person fully occupying his thoughts now, the woman whose life he would give anything to save; he wanted one last link with humanity as he remembered it, before the two animals had entered his life.

Jack jerked her head back again, and held a knife underneath her eye, nudging the delicate tissue, nodding at Russell, who drained his glass without further prodding.

The drug didn't put him out. It only made him feel muzzy and relaxed, and silly, so that he giggled as they made Dina drink her wine, which also had something in it. And he gladly drank more of whatever they wanted, some single malt scotch, some brandy—it was all the same to him. He knew he was already dead.

Twenty-five

THE MORE SKIP talked, the more frustrated she became. Rudolfo's superiors took the view that a person who had not committed a crime had a right to disappear in his own sailboat if he so desired. Therefore they declined to involve the Coast Guard.

Since Russell wasn't officially a suspect in Beau's murder, they weren't buying him as an unofficial suspect. Eleanor Holser told a vastly different story from the one Skip told—one in which Skip had completely misread a little fight with her boyfriend—and that didn't help either. Skip felt Russell was in grave danger if not already dead—that there was no time to be lost. The Fort Lauderdale police, despite every argument she could muster, simply could not be talked out of a wait-and-see view.

It was nearly ten o'clock when Skip left in frustration. She stormed into the hotel room, ranting, gesturing, yelling out the story, so wrapped up in letting off steam that Steve finally resorted to the time-out sign to get her attention, which only made her madder.

"You know I hate that."

"I've got an idea. It doesn't happen every day."

She acknowledged him only with an impatient look, not about to be cheered up.

"Let's charter a boat," he said.

"What? It's the middle of the night. Anyway, the *On Y Va* could be anywhere. And I can't sail. And who can afford it?"

"Well, let's put it this way. I happen to be a successful

307

film editor with quite a few bucks, which qualifies me to be eccentric. I have a yen to take my girlfriend on a mid-night sail—scratch that—we have a friend who's a little eccentric . . ."

"Hold it. I'm getting the idea. You're saying if we pay well enough, we can probably find a charter, no matter what kind of cockamamie story we tell."

Steve had already gone on to the next part of the problem. "We need someone who knows where to look—maybe someone with a little experience in the import business. And a fast power boat—one of those cigarette things."

"Oh, hell—we really need a helicopter."

"I went out for a drink a little earlier. As luck would have it, I found this bar on the ICW where people come in their boats. There was a whole pack of cigarettes there. A carton, maybe."

"So?"

"So, you know the kind of guys who have those things? Macho, gold chains. I bet we could talk one of them into a midnight search."

"Oh, come on."

"I mean it. Why go through the Yellow Pages when it's the middle of the night and there'll be paperwork and deposits and God knows what, in the event we actually find someone sitting by their phone? Why don't we just go find some half-drunk dickhead with a penis boat and offer him a grand?"

"I beg your pardon? Who the hell's got a grand?"

"Me. And if we save Russell's ass, no doubt he'll reimburse us."

"Oh, sure."

She was sitting on the bed, staring out at the ocean. He sat next to her and covered her hand with his. "Skip. Let's do it."

She looked up into his face, so sincere, so boyishly ex-cited. He was like any man trying to give a gift to the woman he loved—only she was a police officer and the thing she wanted was to do her job. It was a little weird, yet she couldn't help being touched.

She thought the chances of finding the *On Y Va* were practically nonexistent without the Coast Guard, but Steve was giving her a chance to look. Gallant, but there was a lot working against it—it might be dangerous to him, and to the owner of the boat, and to the boat itself.

Reluctantly, she said, "I can't."

"Look. Let's just go for a boat ride, okay? If we find the *On Y Va*, then we'll figure out what to do. What's the harm in a boat ride?"

"What do we do—go back to that bar and ask around?"

He looked so happy she wanted to hug him. She hadn't really meant the remark as a "yes," but what he said made sense—until they found the boat, there was no need to worry. And there wasn't a snowball's chance they would.

"Sure," he said. "Let's just go find us a captain."

In fact, it wasn't hard at all. Most of the cigarette pack—if that wasn't an exaggeration—had left by the time they got there, but there were three long, sleek, nasty-looking boats moored at the bar, and inquiries promptly turned up three owners.

Steve got straight to business. "We need to charter a boat for—oh, about three hours, four at the most—" He was making it up as he went along. "We can pay a thousand dollars."

One of the owners said, "What do we do? Flip for it?"

Another said, "Count me out. I gotta work tomorrow."

The third said, "Is this legal or what?"

"Wait a minute. We need a really fast boat. Whose boat's fastest?"

The third guy, the cautious one, said, "Keith, baby, this one's yours."

They had a boat. Now how to explain what they wanted?

Finally, Skip said, "Look, I'm an off-duty cop. This isn't official, but we're looking for a sailboat."

Keith shrugged. He had dirty-brown hair and wore a T-shirt with khaki shorts. His face was ferrety—triangular, no jaw to speak of—but he looked quite a bit more intelligent than someone Skip expected to find in a Florida bar in the middle of the night.

"I need to know why," he said.

"I think the owner's in danger."

"From someone chasing him or someone on the boat?"

"I sure hope it's from someone chasing him."

"Well, I do know some pretty good hiding places—where you could drop anchor and stay for a while."

Steve said, "Look. Why don't we just cruise around awhile?"

"Sure." Keith gave them a sly smile, and in a few minutes Skip saw why. She'd really had no idea how fast these boats could go.

They'd been out no more than half an hour when they saw two boats close together, a dinghy between them. Keith pointed. "Some kind of deal going down. We'll just pretend we never saw a thing."

They whizzed by at a safe distance, Skip unable to resist watching with Keith's binoculars. Two men got out of the dinghy and boarded the farther of the two boats, and it took off. She trained her binoculars on the second. "*On Y Va*! That's it."

There it was. Right there, not far from shore at all; out in the open, not hidden—as if Russell wanted to be found.

But the two guys leaving wasn't a good sign.

Steve said, "What now?"

"I hate to say it, but I've got to try the damn police again."

"Thought you were the police," said Keith.

She hoped he wasn't going to go paranoid on her. "I'm not local. Have you got a phone?"

He shrugged. "Sure."

This time the police listened, evidently sobered by the tale of two men in a dinghy. Keith gave them his location, and they were assured the Coast Guard was on its way.

Steve said, "Let's get closer."

Skip said, "No."

Keith paid no attention. Through some mysterious process, the two guys had bonded and decided to defy her. He pulled the cigarette close to the sailboat, and they saw the lights were on.

Keith said, "Let's talk to them." He picked up his radio, and Skip ardently wished she hadn't involved civilians. Predictably, there was no response. *So much,* she thought, *for the element of surprise.*

Keith said, "They could have the radio turned off." He took a breath and hollered, "*On Y Va!* Anyone aboard?"

There was no answer.

"Let's go aboard."

"No! We wait for the Coast Guard."

The two guys looked at each other and shrugged. Keith said, "I'm going. You going?"

Steve said, "I'm going."

There was no choice. Skip said, "Wait a minute! Hold it, I'm armed, I'm going first."

She clambered down the companionway, saw no one in the salon, and went through to the stateroom. A man and a woman were on the berth, fully dressed.

"Hello!" she said, and got no response. "Russell. Russell Fortier!"

Nothing. She went closer, noticing no movement of chests and feeling suddenly sleepy.

A voice behind her said, "Shit! Carbon monoxide." And Keith flung open a window. "Let's get them out of here."

Behind her, Steve had started to open more windows. Skip gulped air and then grabbed the woman. She didn't seem to be breathing at all.

Keith helped her, while Steve got the man. They were starting CPR when the Coast Guard arrived.

Beau Cavignac. Dead. Ray couldn't wrap his mind around it. Russell Fortier's disappearance was one thing, but this!

First Allred, now Beau. And Russell was gone—the murderer or the also-murdered?

For the first time, it occurred to Ray to go to the police. These things had to be connected, and they had to be about the Skinners. Maybe he could bust the whole thing open that way. But *what* way would that be?

Uh-uh. No, he thought. *Cille and I have come this far by ourselves. We've got to keep going.*

What he wanted was proof that the Skinners existed and that United Oil had systematically defrauded him— something he could take to court. He didn't trust the police to get it—and if they did get it, he didn't trust them not to lose it.

Anyway, their agenda was different. They were trying to solve a couple of murders, not personally avenge Ray Boudreaux. Only two people in the world had that goal, and thank God Cille was in it with him.

The thing he needed was the Skinners' disk, and, so far as he knew, Beau Cavignac was the only Skinner besides Russell Fortier—certainly the only one whose name he knew. So maybe Beau had it. Maybe he'd been killed for it.

With infinite attention to detail, Ray read Beau's obituary, carefully noting the time of the funeral. He'd always heard funerals were excellent times for break-ins.

He cased the house ahead of time, finding, to his surprise, that it wasn't the requisite Uptown double-gallery mansion. Instead, it was a brand-new replica of a gorgeous old house on the North Shore. Clear across Lake Pontchartrain, where he'd probably fled to be safe from crime.

Lots of people were coming and going, as you might expect after a death. *Maybe I should send them some food,* he thought, wondering if a delivery could get him into the house. But he couldn't think of anything big and bulky enough to preclude whoever answered the door from simply taking it with a "thank-you."

Trays of things, maybe. Finger sandwiches or something. He and Cille together, balancing a bunch of trays.

But he didn't want to involve her in this—in fact, didn't even want her to know about it.

Ronnie? No. With luck, the boy's life of crime was over.

Maybe not trays. Liquor was good—a case of something heavy. That would have to be carried in. He wasn't sure people sent liquor after a death, but then it was coming from an imaginary person—propriety hardly mattered.

He found himself a pair of overalls at a thrift store, jammed a cap down over his eyes, and procured a case of Chardonnay from a place where he still had a charge account.

When he rang the Cavignacs' bell, the maid asked him to bring the goodies around to the back, just as he'd hoped she would.

"You can just put it on the counter," she said, obviously trying to make it easy on him.

"Oh, no," he said, "this stuff's *heavy*. Be glad to put it wherever you want."

For a moment, she looked a little confused. "Well, let's see. The pantry, I guess."

He was bent over the goods when high heels clicked into the kitchen. "Marka? Someone's spilled iced tea on the sofa."

Aha. Dream come true, he thought, as Marka sped to the rescue. Quickly, he checked the kitchen windows. They were out of view, unencumbered by alarm sensors, and equipped only with standard closings. A twelve-year-old could open them—but it might be noisy. Still, it was a start.

He didn't dare go up the stairs, and guests prowled everywhere on this floor. He checked the door itself. It had one of those standard push-button locks set in the locked position. He imagined it was probably kept that way, so the door couldn't be opened with a casual turn when the dead bolt was off.

He punched the button, moving it to the unlocked position. And then he put away the wine. He was just coming out of the pantry when Marka returned.

"Beautiful house," he said, and the maid teared up.

"It's a sad house now," she said. "It's a real sad house."

She'd evidently been fond of Beau. "I'm real sorry," Ray said, and found that a part of him was. No doubt Beau had been a rotten little bastard—a rotten little criminal, actually, who'd made other people suffer and had gone scot-free. But Ray *was* sorry for Mrs. Cavignac. He could no more imagine losing Cille than losing the sun.

That night he made love to her like they were newlyweds.

And the next day found him outside the Cavignac house an hour before the funeral. He made sure he saw the widow and children leave—along with a knot of black-clothed relatives—and then gave them ten minutes to come back if they'd forgotten something. Nobody did.

He stepped to the back of the house and listened. There was a clatter of kitchenware—Marka loading the dishwasher, probably. And then a mechanical roar. Yes, the dishwasher. He stepped closer, actually sticking his face up to the window, just in time to see Marka disappearing. He waited a minute to see if she'd come back. When she didn't, he pulled on latex gloves and his ski mask, and tried the door.

It opened. Miraculously, it opened. Whoever had locked up the night before had probably just put the dead bolt on without trying the lock.

He ducked into the pantry to get his breath and let Marka come back, in case she'd heard him enter. He waited ten minutes, trying to figure out a plan. Actually, if she did come back, he could step out and explore the rest of the house while she was in the kitchen.

On the other hand, he had to be out of here before they got back from the funeral. He waited another five minutes, and shrugged. Five more, then full speed ahead— if he ran into her, he'd deal with it. He was wearing shorts, a polo shirt, and sneakers. Except for the ski mask, he could be anybody at all—no reason to connect him with yesterday's delivery.

She didn't come.

He was halfway to the second floor when he ran into her. Because the stairs were carpeted, neither had heard the other till it was too late.

314

Without uttering a sound, she turned to run. Good. She'd be upstairs, which would make the whole thing easier to deal with.

He caught her in about five strides, holding her from behind, one hand over her mouth. "I'm not here for you," he whispered. "I'm not going to hurt you." She was a black woman, about fifty-five and very dignified. He thought she must be scared to death, but he didn't know what to do about it, except whisper to her while she breathed hard and whimpered. He stuffed a handkerchief in her mouth (brought specially for the purpose) and pulled a roll of duct tape out of his pocket, along with a Swiss Army knife. He taped her hands behind her back before she could get the gag out, and then taped her mouth, meanwhile whispering, "Sorry I have to do this to you, but nothing bad's going to happen. I'm just here to steal something. You're going to be fine."

There was a sofa with a lamp table in a landing at the top of the stairs. He led her over there. "I want you to be nice and comfortable. You just sit down and I'll tape your ankles real gently, and then I'll leave you alone. You okay now?"

Her eyes told him she wasn't, but she sat down obediently, pressing her legs firmly together while he taped her ankles—no doubt to reassure herself he wasn't going to rape her. "I'm real sorry about this, but they'll find you when they come home. I'm going to leave you alone now."

He could hear her release her breath, maybe for the first time in the encounter, as he strode away. *Nice lady,* he thought. *I hope she doesn't have nightmares.*

The upstairs was such an odd warren of rooms he felt uneasy—he wasn't sure he'd hear if anyone came in. And as luck would have it, the room equipped with computer, humidor, television, and hunting-lodge photos was way in the back.

Nervously, he sat down, turned on the computer, took off his ski mask, and wiped the sweat off his face. Ray

315

looked in the index for "Skinacat," but of course it wasn't there.

He used the "Find" command to locate his own name, and sure enough, there it was, in a file called "Xmas List."

He opened it up and . . . yes! A veritable Xmas present. A list of names, including his. Descriptions of properties, with stats—leases, seismic findings; in some cases, dates. In his case, it was the date of sale. The next-to-last word in the entry, just before the date, was the name Fortier.

Marion Newman's name was on the list, too, and his also had a date by it, preceded by the name Cavignac.

Ray's heart speeded up. It must be a target list; a wish list. And in cases where they got the leases they wanted, they added the date. The name must be the person assigned to get the lease. He skimmed the list for more names and came up with two: Favret and Seaberry.

He pulled a disk from his pocket and copied the file. Then he copied it several times more onto Beau's hard disk and gave each copy a different name. So if anyone deleted "Xmas List," there were plenty of backups.

On his way out, he dropped by the landing where Marka sat. "I'm going now, baby. I'll undo your ankles, okay? At least you'll be a little more comfortable."

She made a deep sound in her throat as he slit the tape. It could have been fear, or a grunt of gratitude for not killing her.

Twenty-six

"JANE, IT'S ME."

Calling her at home again. She didn't need to be told who. She knew the voice perfectly well. "Mr. Tipster," she said. "How are we today?"

"We are tip-top this fine Sunday, Ms. Storey—funny you should use that particular pronoun, 'cause this is *our* day."

Her heart fluttered briefly. Maybe he was just some kind of stalker. She kept quiet.

"I'm bringing the goods."

Oh, sure. They all say that, she was thinking, when it dawned on her whom she was talking to. "Did you say *bringing,* or did I misunderstand?"

"I'm coming right over. I've got what Eugene Allred was killed for. Maybe Cavignac was killed for it, too; I don't know."

"Right over to where, Mr. Tipster? You just called me at home." She prayed he didn't know where she lived.

"Oh. Guess I forgot my manners for a minute. What about we meet at the paper?"

"What the hell have you got?"

"Something that's gonna win you a Pulitzer."

She sighed, wishing she smoked. "Look, if this were a movie, you'd get killed on the way over. So just in case, could I have your name, please?"

"Sure. Ray Boudreaux."

He was waiting for her when she got to the paper, a tall, lanky customer who obviously cultivated a rough-hewn

317

cowboy look. She had dated men like him—slept with them anyway. They never planned enough ahead to make dates. Small-scale con men. They could be bothered with the minor con of seducing someone, but hadn't the ambition for major ones. So far she wasn't impressed.

Boudreaux held up a disk. "Here's what's going to get you the Pulitzer." He handed it over along with some audiotapes. "That, and these."

"Let's go look at it."

But he shook his head. "It's just the proof. First, I've got to tell you the story. Where can we go?"

Somehow, Jane thought this was more than a cafeteria kind of story. "I think," she said, "we need a power lunch."

They went to the Pizza Roma on Bienville. It was convenient and it was reasonably noisy—it wouldn't be easy to overhear them.

Ray told his own story first—how he'd built up his own company and lost everything when he was cheated out of his lease by a company that was already making millions out in the Gulf.

They had demolished a vast salad and most of an artichoke pizza by the time he said, "So I told myself, don't get mad, get even. And I hired Gene Allred. Know what we did? We bugged the place. Don't ask me how. Just trust me. Or better yet, listen to the tapes." He gave her a sure-I'll-respect-you-in-the-morning kind of grin. But oddly enough, this was the moment when she did begin to trust him.

He had told the story with so much high emotion and so many doubtless-phony references to his dear wife and soulmate, Cille, that she figured he was probably just shoveling manure.

But when he got to the "get even" part, something in him came alive—and something in her felt it. *That's just what this dude would do,* she thought. He'd be crazy enough to bug an oil company and then tell a reporter.

"We heard 'em talkin' about it," he said. "Actually talkin' about it. The only thing was, we didn't know

318

who it was doing the talking—except Russell Fortier, of course—or who they were talking about: in other words, who their victims were, except me. And then I did a really stupid thing—I started leaning on Fortier."

"Leaning on him for what?"

Boudreaux seemed embarrassed. "Oh, taunting him, I guess. Trying to get him to give up the other names. I shouldn't have messed with him. I just shouldn't have messed with him." He was shaking his head vigorously.

"Why? What did he say?"

"He didn't really say anything. Just disappeared into thin air. Then we did get some evidence, and somebody killed Allred and stole it."

"What evidence?"

"The stuff on this disk. Pretty funny what you said about me getting killed on the way over—that's more or less what happened with Allred."

"You think somebody from United killed Allred? How could they have even known about him?"

"Well, I've thought about it. I've thought quite a bit about it. He must have told them himself."

It didn't make sense. Jane was quiet a minute, and the answer came to her. "Blackmail?"

"Must have been that. I should have gotten a better class of detective."

Jane's mind had kicked into gear. "How many people were involved in this?"

"Four that I know of—Fortier, Beau Cavignac, and two others."

"Was Douglas Seaberry one of them—Fortier's boss?"

"You catch on fast. Seaberry and a guy named Edward Favret."

It was falling into place. "I wonder if they acted with the company's knowledge?"

Ray shook his head. "That I couldn't tell you. But I don't think so—having run a company myself, I just don't see it. What percentage is in it for United Oil to break the law and undergo all kinds of risks for what to them is more or less chump change? On the other hand, if you had a few guys who were pissed off because they weren't out in the high-profile end of things, they'd feel like they had to do something spectacular to get the company's attention."

"So you think it's a sort of cabal of renegades?"

He nodded. "Listen to the tapes. They called themselves the Skinners."

Jane felt a frisson. "Nice name." She sipped her coffee, organizing her thoughts. "Okay, here we go. You taunt Fortier, and he disappears—or maybe, he first kills Allred, then disappears. Is that possible?"

"I'm not sure."

"Okay, you taunt Fortier. Then Allred tries to blackmail all of them—through Fortier, or did he have other names?"

"By then, he had other names."

"Okay, he tries to blackmail one or more of them, and they decide to kill him. Or maybe one of them does it on his own. Maybe Fortier, maybe not. If not Fortier, maybe Allred's killer took *him* out."

"Or maybe they did it as a group."

"Then for some reason Cavignac balks—he threatens to go to the police. And they kill him, too. Is that the way you see it?"

"More or less."

She nodded. "Where'd you get the disk?"

"Does it matter?"

"Probably not. Not if I can confirm the information on it."

"Let's look at it." They went back to the paper, uploaded it into Jane's computer, and looked at it while Ray explained to her what he thought it was. "Try this guy," he said, pointing to Marion Newman's entry. "I found him another way and he told me his story. Beau was his contact the same way Russell was mine."

She would certainly try Marion Newman. But that still wouldn't be enough. She'd have to get at least two more stories, one involving Seaberry and one Favret.

And that was only the beginning. Then she'd have to

run it by her editor, who, in turn, would call in lawyers, though probably not till she had a first draft. She'd also have to call Seaberry and Favret for their sides, and of course, she'd have to ask Bebe and Beau's wife if they knew anything. She didn't at all like the idea of making those last four phone calls—two people were dead for sure, and maybe a third. But by the time she made them it would be too late to bother killing her—the story would be only hours from running.

She felt another frisson. Better call superjerk David Bacardi—her editor and ex—before she did another thing. If she died, at least she wanted someone to know why.

His wife answered. *What fun,* Jane thought. "Hi, Lisa, it's Jane Storey. Sorry to call on Sunday . . ."

"Hi, Jane. I'll get him." A bit abrupt, but that was just Lisa. She was a lawyer—what could you expect?

David himself was damn near nasty. "You better have a story that's gonna keep the lid on this town."

"Bacardi, this is big. Swear to God I've got something here."

"Give it to me in ten words or less."

"Corporate shenanigans leading to the murders of Allred and Cavignac."

"Okay." He spoke in a pleasanter voice. "Start talking."

As she ran it down for him, he peppered her with questions that got more and more excited as she went on. He was buying it completely. Finally, he said, "How fast can you do it?"

"Well, it's a Sunday, so I might be able to get people at home. If I can, first draft by tomorrow. We run it by the lawyers in the morning, while I work on confirming everybody's story, and then I call the honchos at United—at absolutely the last minute. It runs Tuesday morning. That fast enough for you?"

"You're a journalistic dreamboat. I love ya to death, Storey."

She spoke in as sultry a voice as she could muster. "I hate it when you talk like that."

And then she got to work.

The list was a gold mine. Three of the first five people she called were home and eager to talk, and mad as hornets. Seizing the moment, she asked to come over right away.

Five hours later she had the story in her pocket. *Some days,* she thought, *it pays to get up in the morning.*

It was late when she got back to the paper, and hardly anyone was in the newsroom. She was going over her notes when a phone rang somewhere in the distance. And then Jane's phone rang. "This is Angie in the library. The *Miami Herald* called for clips on Russell Fortier—you want to take the call?"

Jane's heart thudded. "Bet your bootie." She picked up the phone. "This is Jane Storey in the newsroom. The library transferred you to me."

"Hey, there. John McGonagil at the *Herald*. We've got a story working about a Coast Guard rescue involving a guy named Russell Fortier and some New Orleans cop. I called 'cause I thought y'all might have some clips on Fortier—seems like I was right."

"You're kidding. Russell Fortier's alive?"

"Who is he, anyway?"

"Who's the cop?"

It went on that way until they both managed to calm down enough to exchange information, and when it was done, each had a mouthful of canary feathers.

Jane looked at her watch—only ten o'clock. They could easily get the story in if they wanted to—and she was sure they were going to want to. She sauntered over to the night city editor. "I'm about to make your day," she said, and proceeded to do so.

Then she went back to her desk and started placing calls to Fort Lauderdale. First she confirmed the story with the Coast Guard, then she mentioned casually that she was a friend of Detective Langdon's, and asked if anyone there knew where she was.

Her source yelled at someone, "Hey. You know where Langdon went?"

Jane heard the yelled-back answer: "Fort Lauderdale PD."

To her surprise, Skip actually took the call. "Jane. Don't run this. I'm begging you."

"Why not?"

"Can't it wait a day or two?"

"There's absolutely no way to stop it—the wires have got it. It's probably coming over now."

"Damn."

Jane couldn't imagine what the big deal was. But one thing she knew—Skip was going to be furious when she saw Tuesday's story. However, there was nothing to be done about it. Cops did their job, reporters did theirs.

Still, it didn't seem right. Something nagged at her. Not a sense of professional courtesy, exactly—more like an unwillingness to blindside a friend.

"Skip," she said. "Are you coming back tomorrow?"

"I don't know. Why?"

"On Tuesday, we're running a story you're going to be interested in. I might want to call you and tell you about it." *After the first edition's all put together.*

"What's up, Janie?" Skip spoke sharply.

"I can't talk about it yet."

"Is it something to do with Russell?"

"Don't make it hard for me, okay? I'll tell you what I can, when I can. Just give me a phone number and I'll do my best." Skip gave her the name of a hotel.

But Jane had a brainstorm. "Tell you what. I'll fax you the whole story."

Twenty-seven

IT WAS MONDAY night by the time Skip and Steve got home.

Russell and Dina were fine, getting better by the minute, but they hadn't come around right away. Because they were so obviously drunk—and because of the evidence of so many glasses and bottles—they had been admitted to a hospital, where they had their stomachs pumped and didn't even seem to notice.

The doctors said they'd probably keep sleeping heavily, at least through the night.

Skip had been the one to call Bebe, a good news/bad news proposition. Oh, well, she thought, surely Bebe could handle news of a girlfriend. It wasn't like she was a model of fidelity herself.

As it happened, she kept saying, "Thank God," and crying, and then saying it again.

After Bebe, Skip called Kelly McGuire and ran the whole thing down.

"Let me get this straight," said McGuire, and there was menace in her voice. "You went to Florida on your own hook and did police business?"

"My friend and I went for the weekend, and I thought while I was here, I'd just . . . you know . . . make a cursory search."

McGuire laughed so hard, Skip had to hold the phone away from her ear. "You're a sketch, Langdon, you know that? What the hell am I going to do with you?"

"Well, Lieutenant, I've been thinking about that."

"I'll just bet you have. Look, you've got to question Fortier—he's not accused of any crime, is he?"

"We couldn't think of one."

"So the Fort Lauderdale police have no reason to hold him. He could just take off the minute he wakes up."

"My thought exactly."

"So just work your regular shift in Florida. You can pay for the plane ticket yourself."

She hung up before Skip could either thank her or protest.

By the time she and Steve got back to the hotel it was well after midnight, but she was up early, and over at the hospital by nine o'clock.

Russell was being discharged. He seemed groggy, in fact had no idea who she was. The woman, Dina Wolf, came in with Rudolfo. She looked pretty shaky as well.

"I'm taking them to Ms. Wolf's apartment," Rudolfo said, and gave Skip the address. "We're putting a guard on them till we find out what this is all about. Let me give you a number."

It was a perfect day in Florida, and Skip could do nothing but chew her nails. Every hour she called the guard's cell phone and each time she was told both Fortier and Wolf were sleeping. At two o'clock, she was told Russell had awakened and eaten some soup. He was sleeping again. Ms. Wolf hadn't stirred.

At three he was also sleeping.

At three forty-five, the guard called her.

She and Rudolfo arrived almost at the same time, to find him pale, shaking, and rubbing his head, dressed in a T-shirt that must have been Wolf's, and the same rumpled khakis he'd had on the night before.

"How's Ms. Wolf?"

"She says a truck hit her, call her in a month." He grinned. "A train hit me, I think."

Rudolfo said, "I've got a friend who swears big, greasy burgers are the best thing for a hangover. Maybe we could go get one."

"I don't know. I don't think . . ."

"Tell you what. Mick needs a break—let's see if he'll do it."

While Mick was gone, Russell rubbed his head almost nonstop and told the story of the night before . . . haltingly, and with lots of pauses, as if he'd forgotten things. Having been at Holser's, Skip knew most of it, but there was one piece she didn't—Russell had no idea who the two thugs were.

"They sound like pros," she said.

He nodded. "Yeah. That's what I thought."

"Any idea who hired them?"

"Yeah. Oh, yeah. Goddammit, I was stupid! Dina could have been killed."

Mick came back with a hamburger and a sack of greasy fries, and Russell began to change almost with the first bite. "Hey, this is good." He started to attack the thing with so much enthusiasm, further conversation was momentarily impossible. Skip could have sworn she saw color come back to his face even as he chowed down.

When he had polished off the burger, he touched a napkin to his mouth and looked the officers in the eye, suddenly a man who'd been an executive at an oil company and still had a few of his marbles.

"I'm a new man," he said, and Skip believed it. "Did anyone call my wife?"

"I did, but I didn't have a number to give her. I told her you were fine."

He nodded, that out of the way. "Okay, you were wondering who wanted to kill me."

Skip and Rudolfo nodded in unison. "Two guys I used to work with—or one of them, maybe. Seaberry and Favret. I talked to Beau about this whole thing the other night. The short version is this—the four of us did some things we shouldn't have. Beau wanted to come clean about it. He didn't exactly say it, but it was obvious he thought one of the other guys killed some PI who'd found out about it."

Skip nodded, not about to give away Allred's name.

"He said they were about to have a meeting about it."

Fortier paused, donning an appropriately sober face for what he said next. "And then I read about Beau in the paper. Guess they got him, too."

Rudolfo said, "I think we need to Mirandize you."

"Yeah, I guess maybe you do."

Skip thought she had never seen a person so completely at peace with the mess he'd made of his life. Rudolfo delivered the warning, and then said, "Do you want to waive any of these rights?"

He thought about it. "I'm going to have to call a lawyer at some point, but let's finish up the easy stuff. I want to give you enough information to move on these guys."

Rudolfo seized the moment. "I still don't get why they were trying to kill you."

"Because if I tell what I know, their lives fall apart. And that's not including the two murders—those kind of up the ante."

"How'd these guys know where you are?"

"Beau could have told them, I guess." He looked at Skip. "How'd you find me?"

She shrugged. "Few lucky guesses."

"Yeah, well. Everybody knew I'd spent time here. Everybody knows I sail. I guess they just looked in the obvious places."

Skip let Rudolfo ask the biggie. "What exactly are these big secrets that people would kill to conceal?"

"We defrauded people out of oil leases. Lots of them." He stood. "And now, I guess I really do have to call a lawyer."

In the end, they all wound up back at the Fort Lauderdale police station—Skip and Rudolfo and Fortier and the lawyer. And late that night, Steve and Skip flew home. As they checked out of the hotel, the clerk handed Skip a fax, which she tucked into her purse to read on the plane.

And Jane's story blew her out of the water. There wasn't a second to waste. She called Abasolo from the plane. "Look, I'm on my way back, and something's come up. Can you meet me at the airport? We might get ourselves a murderer tonight."

"How could something have come up? You just called me before you got on the plane."

"I read something Jane Storey faxed me—the story that's running on Page One tomorrow. Trust me—we've got to get to this dude tonight, before he goes behind a wall of lawyers."

"Could you just tell me one thing? Who is it?"

"I'm getting it narrowed down."

She kissed Steve good-bye at the other end, and got in the car with Abasolo. On the drive back to town, she filled him in.

"So which one is it?" he said. "Favret or Seaberry?"

"Let's flip a coin." She produced a quarter. "Heads, it's Seaberry; tails, Favret."

It came up tails.

The Favret house was dark, but a light came on after about ten minutes of leaning on the bell. A woman's voice spoke through the intercom: "Who is it?"

"Police."

"Oh." And then silence.

In a moment, a woman tying a robe answered the door. "We're looking for Edward Favret."

She looked at her watch. "He, uh, went out about half an hour ago. Is everything all right, officers? I mean—he hasn't been in an accident or anything?"

Skip said, "Nothing like that. Can you tell us where he went?"

She shrugged, clearly not knowing what to make of all this. "He went to see a business associate. Douglas Seaberry."

"Thank you, ma'am. Sorry to disturb you." As they turned away, Skip and Abasolo rolled their eyes at each other, acknowledging their sympathy with the woman.

Abasolo said, "Guess we're getting both of them at once. How do you want to play it?"

"By ear," she answered, and he gave her a thumbs-up. That was what they both liked.

328

Unlike the Favret residence, the Seaberry house was well lit; almost festive-looking. The two officers marched up the front walk and mounted the steps before they heard the yelling.

"Goddammit, you can't do that," was the first thing they heard. "I'm your goddamn boss, goddammit."

The two men were evidently standing in the foyer having an argument.

"I don't have any choice." The second man spoke in a lower voice.

"*Goddamn* you!"

And then a child said, "Daddy? What's wrong?"

"Get the hell out of here! Megan, get that kid the fuck out of here."

Abasolo raised an eyebrow. Skip shrugged and rang the doorbell. Within, all went silent.

Skip rang the bell again, and almost as quickly as the silence came, the door opened a crack, and then closed quickly. Seaberry shouted, "You little idiot. You little *idiot*!"

The woman spoke in a calm, authoritative voice. "Douglas. Douglas! Step back now. You *may* not touch that child."

And then there was the sound of one human being hitting another, followed by a loud, female moan. Skip gave the police knock.

"Mr. Seaberry! Open up."

The boy opened the door again, eyes like shiny brown quarters, face reflecting the end of the world. Favret was holding the woman, trying to lower her to the floor, or perhaps keep her from falling, and Seaberry was halfway up the stairs.

Skip said, "I've got him," and followed. "Better call for backup." Let Abasolo deal with the three below—she'd come too far to let anyone else do this.

Seaberry reached the second floor and kept going. He had a big head start, and he was in good shape. He reached a third floor and sprinted to the end of a long hallway, where there was a room set up as an office. She heard steps pounding behind her.

Seaberry said, "I've got a gun."

He didn't, yet, not that Skip could see. But he picked up something from the top of a desk, and she had no choice but to dive for him. She had him on the floor, but she still couldn't tell whether he really had a gun. She was wrestling him, grabbing for his arm, when someone entered the room. *Adam. Thank you,* she thought, and Seaberry fired. A body crashed to the floor.

Shocked, furious, she tried to knock the gun out of his hand, but he rolled her over, getting her on the bottom. He stood up in one graceful movement and she heard him say, "Omigod, what have I done?"

"Adam?" she said, terrified, unwilling to take her eyes off Seaberry. And Abasolo answered, "It's okay. Take it easy now. Just give me the gun."

Seaberry was pointing it at him. Favret was on the floor, gut-shot.

Seaberry backed away from Abasolo. "Stand back. Just stand back away from me." He was backing toward the far wall of the house, where Skip saw an open window. Abasolo took a step toward him, and he fired again. Glass shattered—he'd hit a picture on the wall—and the moment of confusion was enough for him to swing himself up on the ledge.

Abasolo leaped toward him, but he didn't fire again. Skip scrambled up and ran, arms open, to the window, grabbing at whatever she could catch.

The man's weight dropped, but her grip held, and so did Adam's. They had him, but he was dangling. Skip's arm felt as if it were coming out of the socket.

Oh, shit, she thought, *I don't know if I can do this.*

She heard a sound behind them, and Seaberry's wife screamed, "Douglas. Oh, Douglas, hold on."

You're telling the wrong guy, Skip thought. *Oh, God, I can't handle this.*

Abasolo said, "Breathe, Skip. Keep breathing. Mrs.

Seaberry, go back downstairs and take care of your child."

"Edward . . . ?"

"Call 911 again. Ask for an ambulance. Tell them the situation."

Skip thought she was going to pass out. "Adam. My hand's slipping."

"Breathe, baby. Just breathe. Don't think about holding on. Think about breathing."

When the car came, sometime in another millennium, she thought: *It's too late. I can't make it till they climb two flights of stairs. No way in hell.*

But she kept breathing. She breathed till two guys got there, and among the four of them, they hauled Seaberry in the window.

When they brought him down, the kid was clinging to his mom like panty hose. "Daddy?" he said. "Did you kill Uncle Beau?"

Douglas tried to lunge at him. "You little shit! You goddamned ungrateful little shit!"

Twenty-eight

"DO YOU SUPPOSE," Skip said to Steve later, "he actually thought he was doing it for the kid?"

"Naaah. He's just got to justify it to himself now that it's over. What I think, he's just an arrogant asshole who's always had things his own way."

"Amen. All the Skinners were, even Beau. But it doesn't really explain murder."

"Ah, who cares? Leave it to the DA to figure out."

Instead, she ran it by Cindy Lou. "As it happens," her friend said, "I had occasion to do a psychological evaluation of the gentleman, and one thing is abundantly obvious. He thinks he's right. He's just one of those guys who has to be right all the time. People like that scare me to death. Something else, too—he's very image-conscious. If he hadn't been the big exec, he would have had no identity."

"Uh-huh. Like Steve said."

"What did Steve say?"

"Arrogant asshole who feels entitled."

"Sounds right."

Skip went through all these machinations because she was never going to get a chance to hear it from Seaberry. He had most assuredly not waived his rights, had had a lawyer on the scene within minutes, and had clammed up and stayed clammed.

Favret had survived, but he wasn't up to talking for a while.

And Russell, who turned himself in for fraud, had his own opinion. "He had no soul. None of us did."

"What does that mean? Everybody's got a soul."

"Douglas became the job, the socialite, the high-achiever. There was no Douglas, only words that described him."

"And you?" she said.

"I was the same."

It didn't matter much that Seaberry wasn't talking: the gun he shot Favret with was the same one he'd used on Allred.

As well as she could piece it together, Jane's story had precipitated the confrontation between Seaberry and Favret. Jane called them both for reaction, thereby sounding the alarm. Favret went over to Seaberry's to discuss strategy, and they got into it. Favret wanted to come clean; Seaberry, by this time having a lot more to lose, wanted to stop him.

Coming out of his near-coma, Russell had felt more like Rip Van Winkle than a man who'd been gone less than twenty-four hours. It was like being upside down on the damn boat again. His whole life had once again shifted. Or maybe it had just settled; maybe this was an aftershock of an aftershock—the original quake being the one caused by the boat accident, and the next upheaval the crazy, cowardly flight to Fort Lauderdale.

The man who woke up that Monday and was brought back to life by two cops with a burger and fries was as different from the one who'd fled New Orleans as from the original man who'd been a Skinner.

When he went to sleep that night, after long and arduous talks with cops and calls to lawyers, he couldn't imagine not going home; not being Bebe's husband; not living in Lake Vista; not turning himself in for his crimes and serving his time. Simply couldn't imagine it. Couldn't think what had come over him.

Dina had kept sleeping, waking briefly now and again

to go to the bathroom or murmur or even nibble something, and then going right back to sleep. He watched her and he thought about her, and he felt warm, bittersweet surges of love for her, but he knew she wasn't his mate. In some kind of cosmic, preordained thing, Bebe was. Or maybe he was just so used to her, he'd miss her forever if they weren't together.

"Russell Fortier," she had said when he phoned, "you get your butt home before you get in any more trouble." And a lovely thing like an electric current, except nice and soft and cozy, started at the top of his head and spread through his body.

He wanted to leave it at that. But he had to say what had to be said. "Bebe, there's a whole lot of stuff you don't know. I'm probably going to jail."

"You didn't kill anyone, did you?"

"Not yet."

"Well, then, maybe I can handle it."

"What about your career?"

"This is Lousiana, baby. If it's bad enough, I might end up governor."

Something had happened. "Uh, Bebe, what's going on? You're taking this way too lightly."

"Oh, don't worry, I'll beat you up later. I'm saving my best shots for face-to-face. I just sound calm because I already know about the Skinners. I had a courtesy call from Jane Storey—you know, the reporter. Somehow she found out about you, baby; the story's running tomorrow."

"Oh, shit."

"That's what I said."

"I love you, Bebe."

"I missed you," she said. "I really did miss you."

He wondered if she really could handle what was going to come down.

Later, Dina woke up and squeezed his hand. "You alive?"

"Uh-huh. You?"

"I must be," she said. "I'm hungry."

He did the burger trick with her, and found it worked a

second time. After she'd eaten, she smiled and said, "Well, I can't say it hasn't been fun."

"You sound like you're going somewhere."

"Not me. But you were, even before there were cops in your life. Now you *really* are."

His throat felt all tight and scratchy. Just to prolong the connection, he said something he didn't mean. "I'll write you from the Big House."

She touched his face on the pretext of brushing hair out of his eyes. "I don't think so. I think this is the end of the line for Dean and Dina."

"I'm going to miss you."

"True. True. Who'll go skinny-dipping with you?"

And he had the strangest notion. Maybe Bebe would. Maybe she was different, too. Or maybe she would be after everything that was about to happen. But maybe not. He'd made it this far with a wife who didn't skinny-dip; one who'd stand by him while he went to jail was a lot better than he deserved.

"What do you think of this?" Talba had on fuchsia harem pants with a magenta leotard. She had draped a purple and gold sari over her head, and the thing was so long it dragged on the floor.

Her mama said, "You think Miz Clara goin' out in public with somebody dress like that, you got another think comin'. I didn't send my only daughter to college so she can dress like Whoopi Goldberg."

Darryl Boucree, who happened to be waiting for both of them, asked, "What on earth's wrong with Whoopi Goldberg?"

"That does it," Talba countered, and changed into a long black dress.

"Even better," said Darryl.

"Needs somethin', though." Talba draped the sari again and waited for the expected tirade from Miz Clara.

But her mother said, "Now *that's* nice."

"Well, I can't wear it if you like it."

335

She might have changed again, but Darryl hustled her butt out the door. "Come on, we got to get over there."

On the heels of Jane Storey's much-solicited article about her, which had finally materialized, Talba was presenting the program at Le Petit Theatre's Sunday Salon. This was a fund-raiser held once a month and attended mostly by those in the neighborhood, which was the French Quarter. It wasn't a paying gig—in fact, she well knew she was doing them a favor—but, still, it was her biggest, best-publicized, and by far most mainstream reading ever.

She'd gotten a couple of warm-up acts—an African dance troupe and a kid from NOCCA who played trumpet like Kermit Ruffin—but The Baroness was the main event, and she wondered if anyone would come.

When she walked in, the place was packed. Skip the cop was there, with three guys and the same two kids from last time, one of whom had a shaved head, and the other of whom had a boyfriend who'd look better with one. Cindy Lou the shrink was there, and Talba's client, Ray, and his wife. Aha—even Bebe and Russell Fortier. The famous and the infamous, all in one family.

She started to get stage fright.

And then she was reading. She read her perennial crowd-pleaser, "I Am Like a Cat," aware of Miz Clara's discomfort, and Darryl's pride, and the shock she always evoked from the white people, and quite a few guilty expressions as well.

When she had finished, she said, "Something happened to me since the last time I read that poem. My whole life changed, but I don't quite know what it all means. So you know what I do when that happens? I write a poem about it. I did that this week and I'm about to read y'all my new poem. Listen now, y'all. I'm like more things than a cat."

I am like an athlete.
One of those brilliant child gymnasts, twelve-year-old prodigy swimmers,

Gold medal already and no sign of breasts.
Nothing else to do now.
I lived my life for one thing only.
Get that man was so mean to my mama.
Kill him maybe. Maybe just torture him a couple of
decades.
Tell all his friends and all his family.
Put it in the paper and cry it from the rooftops.
Humiliate *that namedropper, namestopper,*
namekiller,
namethug, nameperv, nameperp, nameHOOLIGAN
Just the way he did my mama.

And I wrote y'all a poem said how mad I was.
And I learned a whoooole new profession, just so
I could
find me that Pill Man name me Exit for Excreta.

I was a private dick.

And when you think about where that old Urethra is,
And how The Baroness Myself is a poet of some
renown,
Doesn't that just make you want to elbow fate right
in the ribs?
Private dickhead's more like it, but you knew I was
gon' say that.
So I won't.
I was gon' use my educated, middle-class,
cuttin'-edge
electronic skills to catch me that elusive Pill Man.
To catch me that namedropper, namestopper,
namekiller,
namethug, nameperv, nameperp, nameHOOLIGAN.

And I was gon' use plain old-fashioned deception
right
along with all that high technology.

337

I was gon' bust my butt right into Charity, that
misnamed old hole.
I was gon' deceive my way in.
I was gon' pretend to be a simple blue-skirted
worker, and private-dick my way to justice.

But then the fates
Or God
Or that funny-boy Legba—
Or maybe The Baroness Myself—

Pasted my aristocratic ass right square on the wrong
damn page.
The Baroness Pontalba,
She of the dependable high drama and the desperate
hand-wringin' foot-stompin', somehow *became a*
mere supporting
player in some upstart parallel drama.
Just like white folks to steal the spotlight.

(Here Talba paused and was rewarded with light
tittering.)

Oh, DESPAIR.
Oh, MISERY.
Oh, suffering, oh pain.
Ancient secrets slimed to the sun
And none of 'em mine or my mama's.

Marriages died.
And so did a couple of men.

For more or less no reason except some crime-boy's
made-up, silly-ass idea about himself.
And guess what?
A Jane named Storey wrote one about little old me.
That's right—
Me Me Me Me.

(Talba sang the "me's" to make sure no one was sleeping.)

Finally.
At last.
Me Me Me Me.

(Once again, she made music of the "me's.")

I finally got to strut and fret my hour.

And then the fates
Or God
Or that funny-boy Legba
Or maybe The Baroness Myself
Elicited thirteen separate confessions from
Thirteen separate Pill Men
Who all named some little girl Exit for Excreta.
(Or said they did.)
And twenty-seven wives, nurses, girlfriends, boyfriends,
assorted orderlies, and liars
Tattled on another twenty-seven Pill Men who also
committed that unspeakable sin. (It is alleged.)
And eight other little Urethras called to express
solidarity in piss.
And did The Baroness Myself get satisfaction?
Well, no, y'all.
Does anybody?
Ever?
In case y'all haven't heard, there ain't no justice.

Don't miss any
of the Skip Langdon series by

Edgar Award–winning
author

JULIE SMITH

Published by Ivy Books.
Available at your local bookstore.

"No one writes about New Orleans, its steamy charms and its seamy sins, as well as Ms. Smith. She catches the tricky nuances of Louisiana speech as well as the sights, smells, and sounds of the Delta City."
—*Dallas Morning News*

Julie Smith's

SKIP LANGDON NOVELS

NEW ORLEANS MOURNING
THE AXEMAN'S JAZZ
JAZZ FUNERAL
NEW ORLEANS BEAT
HOUSE OF BLUES
THE KINDNESS OF STRANGERS
CRESCENT CITY KILL
82 DESIRE

Published by Ivy Books.
Available at your local bookstore.